P9-CQZ-379

mika Riddick

HELL
OR
HIGH WATER

Also by Joy Castro

The Truth Book: A Memoir

HELL

OR

HIGH WATER

Joy Castro

Thomas Dunne Books
St. Martin's Press
New York

This is a work of fiction. All of the characters, organizations, and events portrayed in this novel are either products of the author's imagination or are used fictitiously.

THOMAS DUNNE BOOKS.
An imprint of St. Martin's Press.

HELL OR HIGH WATER. Copyright © 2012 by Joy Castro. All rights reserved. Printed in the United States of America. For information, address St. Martin's Press, 175 Fifth Avenue, New York, N.Y. 10010.

www.thomasdunnebooks.com
www.stmartins.com

Library of Congress Cataloging-in-Publication Data

Castro, Joy.
    Hell or high water : a novel / Joy Castro.—1st ed.
        p. cm.
    ISBN 978-1-250-00457-4 (hardcover)
    ISBN 978-1-250-01511-2 (e-book)
        1. Women journalists—Fiction.   2. Self-realization in women—Fiction.
    3. New Orleans (La.)—Fiction.   I. Title.
    PS3603.A888H45 2012
    813'.6—dc23

                                                        2012009377

First Edition: July 2012

10   9   8   7   6   5   4   3   2   1

For James, who took me there

The devil here has a very large empire, but this does not
discourage us from the hope of destroying him.
—Marie Madeleine Hachard, New Orleans Ursuline nun, 1728

Excuse my French, everybody in America, but I am *pissed*.
—Ray Nagin, New Orleans mayor, 2005

HELL

OR

HIGH WATER

Cecily could find her way to the bathroom perfectly well by herself, thank you very much. She might have been only seven, but she could tie shoes, climb trees like a boy, and ride bikes through the leafy streets of their neighborhood back home in Lawrence. She didn't need any big sister escorting her to the ladies' room. She scowled at her father, who relented, shrugging.

"So go, then," said Sophie, the superfluous big sister, who was eleven.

Quivering with insult, Cecily pushed down from the table and strode off across the restaurant. Sophie watched her go. Cecily's soft brown hair was cut in a bob with bangs, something simple their father could manage, but Sophie could take care of herself. She could braid her own hair or put it up in a swinging ponytail or twist it into a neat low bun like their mother used to wear when the girls were small. "Good-bye to vanity!" their mother would laugh on the phone to her friends. But she stayed vain, even at the end, in the hospital, carefully penciling a fresh pink mouth over her own before they arrived, holding hands and standing hushed beside the bed, their cardigans buttoned all lopsided, their barrettes crooked, while their father stroked her hand and spoke in a low, strained voice.

Once she had forgotten to put it on, and Sophie had worked hard not to stare at her pale, cracked lips, but not hard enough, because their mother had put her hand up to her mouth and said, "Oh."

Now they had visitors from time to time, nice women who appeared at breakfast and were introduced by their father as "my promising student." One of them, Amber Waybridge, had come along to New Orleans with them—"as an au pair," their father said. Amber was twenty-five and an MFA student, which her father usually called "a dime a dozen," but he didn't say that about Amber.

It wasn't just a vacation for fun. Their father was there for inspiration, because his work was suffering. He couldn't seem to produce the kind of sculptures that had made his reputation—the kind that kept Sophie, disgusted, away from his studio: single masculine legs standing on the floor with their big things jutting out or hanging down, all painted in swirling bright reds and greens and blues and blacks, with splashes of silver and gold, so that you could hardly tell what they were. But Sophie knew, and thought they were gross. Since their mother's death, all his pieces were just the color of plaster, a color like sawdust or putty.

Sophie thought the new sculptures were even more gross, but Cecily didn't mind. She was quick and happy in general—she'd "adjusted well," their father would murmur confidentially to adults—and ran around his studio laughing. Sophie thought she laughed an awful lot. Sometimes it seemed like she didn't even remember their mother.

"Don't brood," their mother would have said. "Daddy won't like it."

His next show, "Surrealism(s) of the Body," was already scheduled for the university gallery's fall calendar, and Sophie knew he was counting on New Orleans to recharge him. He was on spring break, as was Amber Waybridge, and he'd taken the girls out of school for the week. They had been to numerous galleries as well as out in a flat-bottomed boat for an alligator tour in the bayous, where tall white waterbirds flapped into flight at their approach. When the guide cut the motor and tossed marshmallows onto the slick, shining brown skin of the water, they all sat silently on the metal benches, squeezed among the other tourists, as the rampant green foliage and the insects' whine seemed to close in upon them. "Hands inside the boat," the guide had barked suddenly into his microphone, and long, muscled bodies had slithered along beside them and risen up. The scaly pale flesh, the lizardy eye. Vast jaws had opened and snapped. "Daddy!" Cecily had screamed, but it was Sophie's arm she'd grabbed.

That had been Saturday. Now it was Monday, and they were getting a fresh start with breakfast at the Copper Pot, a cheerful restaurant with waitresses who joked and grinned when they took your order. The walls were a bright, warm yellow, and the fronds of potted palm trees nodded in the ceiling fans' breeze. It felt tropical, so different from the long, gray Kansas winter. At the table, her father sifted through maps and tourist guidebooks while Amber leafed through the *Times-Picayune*—SECOND BODY FOUND, blared a headline so large Sophie could read it upside down. Their father had explained that New Orleans was one of the murder capitals of America and given them lengthy instructions about safety and the buddy system and always staying close to him or Amber Waybridge— though Sophie would never willingly get close to Amber Waybridge, who kept pausing to lift her tanned wrist, tilting it in the light to admire the new bracelet their father had bought her, a slender gold chain studded with tiny diamonds, "for watching the girls," he'd said loudly. As if Sophie were stupid.

Sophie ran her fingertip across the elaborate castle, all purple turrets and red spires, that Cecily had been crayoning into a sketchpad. "No electronica on vacation," their father had said firmly, but

Sophie had heard, under his dictatorial tone, the plea, almost a whine, and she knew that with a little pressure he could be overcome—that he secretly longed to continue the quiet, familiar isolation of all of them absorbed in their Game Boys and iPods and iPhones and laptops, their bodies moving along together but their minds in separate worlds, the way they had been ever since "the pancreatic" began. Sophie knew she would have to complain only a little for their father to give in, to collapse and let them retreat into their unsharable distractions. So she said nothing. She wanted more. She wanted a real vacation, the kind they'd had with Mommy at Yosemite, when the girls wore matching head scarves and Daddy carried their supplies in a backpack. Their mother never would have let the girls wear the kinds of shirts Amber Waybridge wore, black T-shirts cropped short to show her smooth belly. *When would the food come?*

Sophie sipped her grapefruit juice, pressing her lips close together to keep the pulpy bits out. With her fingernail, she picked at the corner of the laminated map Daddy was studying, peeling the plastic back from its edge.

"Stop that," Daddy said, writing in his tiny notebook. He was plotting their day. The French Quarter had plenty of galleries they hadn't looked at yet, and the Cabildo was full of historical things, including things from slavery days that he'd said he wasn't sure the children were old enough to see. They'd already groped through the dark historical dioramas of the Musée Conti Wax Museum and hurried down Bourbon Street, their father muttering, "Well, this was a mistake," and ignoring their questions about why anyone would want to wrestle in mud, while Amber Waybridge laughed into her hands. Sophie pushed the tiny black ball of the compass that was built right into the map, pushing the N all the way round, then letting it spring back. North could be south if you just kept pushing.

"Where's your sister?" Daddy said.

She looked up. It had been a while. Maybe Cecily was making number two. She always picked the most awkward times to do it, instead of just waiting until they got back to the hotel.

"Go check on her," he said. Sophie rolled her eyes, sighing loudly.

"I'll go," said Amber Waybridge quickly, smiling, laying her hand on his arm. She pushed back from the table and set off.

Sophie knew the word for her. *Ingratiating.* And it seemed to be working on their father, who smiled briefly, watching Amber Waybridge walk away. He liked to talk about how new and bold her work was. On the strength of his recommendation, she had won a summer artist's residency in Vermont. Sophie couldn't wait for her to leave.

Just as the eggs and toast and bacon arrived, Cecily trotted back to the table and climbed into her chair, her small purple tennis shoes swinging.

"Where have you been?" Sophie said in annoyance, not expecting an answer, and not receiving one. Bright wedges of orange rimmed the plates. Good. She was hungry.

But when she picked up her fork, her father frowned. "Wait for Amber."

"Where is old Amber, anyway?" asked Cecily, already biting into an orange.

Their father looked at her. "She was with you."

Cecily shook her head and spoke with her mouth full. "Nuh-uh."

"She went to the ladies' room to find you."

"I didn't see her."

Their father sighed heavily. "Soph, would you go see what's keeping her?"

Sophie sighed in return, sliding slowly from her chair, her every exaggerated motion a protest. It felt good to skid her rubber toes across the tile.

She rounded the corner into a long corridor paneled with dark wood and lit by a single dim sconce. The floor was dark cement, and doors flanked her on both sides, closed doors with faded gold-painted letters that said PRIVATE and EMPLOYEES ONLY and EXIT, and doorways branching into other hallways, narrow and dark. "A veritable warren," her mother would have called it. No wonder it had taken Cecily so long. Near the end of the corridor, Sophie pushed open the glossy black door to the ladies' room. "Amber?" Sophie bent and peered under the doors, but saw no tanned ankles, no strappy sandals, no toe ring. "The food's there already," she said, pushing open one metal door after another, but her voice echoed, and all the stalls were empty, and she knew she was alone. In the wide cupboard under the sinks, there were only big white wheels of toilet paper.

Annoyed, Sophie headed back down the dark corridor, trailing her fingers along the paneled wood. When the kitchen door flashed open and a waiter hurried out, a swath of fluorescence lit the hallway for an instant, and the whole corridor flashed into brilliant relief. In the sudden illumination, Sophie could see a curl of lemon rind on the dark cement and the sticky spots a mop had missed.

And there, on the floor near the door marked EXIT, lay a small and broken gold chain, its tiny diamonds glinting.

Then things got very loud and frantic, with Daddy shouting for the waiter, then the manager, and running with the employees to push doors open with a loud, fast slam, not just the ladies' room but the men's room, the storage rooms, the walk-in, the kitchen, where all the cooks peered curiously, their knives stilled in midchop. All the other diners were on their feet, looking, saying what they'd seen, who'd left the restaurant, a woman with blond hair, a man with a big duffel bag, three loud college boys who looked hungover, but no pretty twenty-five-year-old with dark hair and a cropped black T-shirt. When the police came, Daddy was out on the sidewalk, yelling, and the people said it all again, and Sophie told her story to a big officer who nodded and blinked. Their father yelled, "Stay there! Right there!" at Sophie, and so she stood next to the restaurant manager, gripping Cecily's hand, while her father and the police searched everywhere again, the whole building and the street outside, the alleys and the shops next door, but Amber Waybridge wasn't there, she wasn't anywhere.

1

"You wanted a story, Nola." A thin folder drops on my desk, and Theo Bailey, editor in chief of the New Orleans *Times-Picayune*, props his gangly length against a pillar. "Here's a story."

"For real?" It's April first, after all. April Fools' Day. "Seriously?"

"A feature. Yours if you want it." For a guy who spends his days making tough calls, Bailey has surprisingly gentle crow's-feet around his eyes. He's hoping I'll be pleased.

Here in the Living and Lagniappe pit, the most serious things we report on are Jazz Fest, the zoo's new Komodo dragon, and the latest chichi boutique on Magazine Street. Here, our editor in chief Bailey—a walking emblem of the hard, painful news that's been winning awards for the *Picayune* since Katrina—is a rare sight. All my fellow entertainment reporters have quit talking or typing. Claire, the section editor who's sick of me, is slowly raking a hand through her long blond hair and pretending not to listen. The others are all openly staring. For months, I've been haranguing the chief to put me on a feature story—"real news," as I'd tactlessly put it, within earshot of my colleagues—and now they're waiting to see what will happen.

Slowly, I open the folder.

"It's an evergreen," says Bailey, "so no big rush. I know you'll still be working on your other stories, so just take your time."

"Word count?"

"A thousand." He's smiling like Christmas, like I should be happy with my new fluffy puppy. "Do good work. And then we'll see."

Scanning the prelim research compiled by whatever senior writer decided it wasn't worth his time, I immediately see the story's potential. It almost takes my breath away. But it's not the story I wanted. Not by a long shot.

In 2005, when Hurricane Katrina downed power and Mayor Ray Nagin mandated the evacuation, more than thirteen hundred registered sexual offenders went off the grid. Now, three years later, eight hundred are still free-range—and we all know how New Orleanians love to come back home. That's a whole lot of potential perverts on the streets.

Some reporter over at the city desk had decided to take the city's pulse on the issue. Is rehabilitation effective? Does the registry law work? How can sex criminals settle back into a civilian lifestyle once their neighbors have been alerted? How do the neighbors feel about the whole thing?

This piece could be huge, a career maker, exactly the kind of break I've been begging for. But interviewing sex offenders—rapists, perverts, creeps? Frankly, the thought scares me shitless. Couldn't Bailey have come up with some nice, safe political corruption?

I let the folder fall shut. "Bailey, what the fuck?"

The room goes utterly silent. There's a strong possibility that I'm committing career suicide, and no one wants to miss my screams as I barrel down in flames.

Now, if you're a man, if you're a senior writer at the City Desk, if you're Chris Rose or one of the other guys who helped the paper win a Pulitzer, you can maybe get away with talking trash to the chief. But not me. Not a twenty-seven-year-old who's been stuck in entertainment reporting for the past two years.

And I know they think I'm loud—literally loud, blabbing out over the desks with the leftover lilt of my childhood Spanish, and loud in my clothing, my blouses too snug, too red. The crisply groomed women let their gaze linger disapprovingly on the thick black strokes of liner that wing up at the edges of my eyes, the maroon glisten of my lips, the gold hoop earrings I can slide a wrist through.

For me to say "What the fuck?" to the boss maybe isn't the smartest idea.

Bailey's smile has flattened to a tight, thin line. "Is there a problem?"

I try to talk my way out of it. "Bailey, come on. Seriously. The sex offender registry? This isn't news. This is pure human interest."

"What are you talking about? Over a thousand sex offenders in the city. Storm hits, they go off the radar. And nearly half stay off. That's a story."

"A story, maybe. News? No." I run a hand through my hair, frustrated. "Come on, Bailey. Don't tell me our readers care about the fate of a few perverts."

"Bullshit," he says. "Those guys could be living next door. For people with kids, or women alone at night? That's urgent." We stare at each other.

What kind of editor tasks a young woman with this kind of story anyway? Is this some kind of sick test, to see if I'm tough enough to hang with the newsroom boys? My jaw sets, and I hear Auntie Helene's voice in my head: *Don't you take nobody's leftovers.* I rise to my feet.

Hand on hip, I pass his proffered folder back. He doesn't take it. His voice lowers to a gravel growl.

"What the hell's wrong with you?" he says. "You wanted news."

"All due respect, sir, this is women's interest. Parents and kids. Strictly lifestyles." Everyone's staring. "When I said news, I meant Katrina progress. Crime. The courthouse. City hall."

"This *is* crime."

"No, it's fear of crime that hasn't happened yet. I thought we weren't supposed to fan those flames."

"I'm not going to ask you twice. I'll find someone else."

"Looks like someone else already dropped it," I say. "Sir." I can hear the swing of belligerence in my voice. The air around us goes dead quiet.

But Bailey's eyes look suddenly tired.

"This was Jim Larkin's story," he says. *Shit, Nola. Way to step in it.* Caleb Larkin is eight years old and bald. We've all seen his photo on the coffee can on the reception desk; we've all put in dollars to help with the medical bills. Dollars, it was turning out, weren't enough. "He wanted time with his son," Bailey says.

"I'm sorry," I say. "I didn't know."

"Look, Nola, I don't have all day," he says. His voice has that crisp edge it gets when he's sick of somebody's bullshit. "Is there any reason you can't do an objective job on this story? Because if there isn't, then I'm tasking you." He looks at me. Everyone's watching. "Well? Any reason?"

And that settles it.

"No, sir," I say. "Absolutely not."

And so the story becomes mine.

In the vast, windowless, gray newsroom, where the hard news happens, the lights are kept dim to ease eyestrain, so it's always dark and cool and hushed, serious: the city desk, Money, the photo desk, the copy desk. The art department and editorial offices run along one wall. To offer me this assignment, Bailey made quite a trek.

The Living and Lagniappe pit, where I work, is a different country. Natural light pours in through two walls of glass. My colleagues prop family photos on their desks, and bright stuffed animals perch on top of their computer monitors. Our stories are equally sunny and frothy, the stuff people read to decide how to frolic. Though we share the same worn, green carpet, the same peachy-pink walls with the newsroom, the resemblance ends there. Over in the newsroom, where reporters talk in low tones about crime and corruption, looking *todo* serious with their loosened neckties and rolled-up sleeves, there are no cozy ornaments. Desks and floors are piled high with teetering stacks of folders, books, and lab results. Data, facts. Not the detritus of cute.

Undesirable as it is, this sex offender story could be my break.

I spend most of the afternoon online at my desk, scouring the Louisiana State Police's sex offender registry, which is user-friendly, graphic, and alarming. Little blue squares, which indicate the residences of sex offenders, overlap like roof tiles all over the map of New Orleans. Hundreds of them. When I click on the individual listings, many have red checkmarks, which means those offenders are in violation: missing, loose.

My first goal is to interview some who remain, and as long as I'm stuck with this story, I'm going to make the biggest splash with it that I can. If it gets enough attention, maybe it'll make my name and get me moved onto the city desk permanently. So I choose the kinds of sex offenders who'll push the public's buttons. Carefully, I select twenty men whose whereabouts are still known.

To pull the case files of twenty ex-cons in a functional, scrupulous, squeaky-clean town would take days, maybe weeks. There would be forms to fill out, signatures to get, tangles of red tape to gnaw through. But in a city known for big corruption, little corruptions can slide on through, unnoticed.

"No problem," says Calinda, my friend at the DA's, when I call. "One of the file clerks owes me a major solid. Buy me a drink and they're yours."

I laugh. "Sold."

"You sniffing up a story?"

"Maybe. When can I get them?"

"Tonight? If you email me the names, I can get the clerk to start on it now."

"Excellent." It's as easy as buying drugs in this city. "How long can I keep the files?"

"At least a week or two."

I offer to come buy her that drink at a bar near the courthouse.

"God, no. Get me off this sleazy street."

"How about the Vic?" The Victorian Lounge is the plush pub where my roommate Uri works. It's tucked inside the Columns, a big old historic hotel on St. Charles in the Garden District, where you can sit on the big front porch, hear jazz played live, and watch the streetcars trundle past under the oaks. It's the other end of the world from Tulane Avenue and the tough little bars near the courthouse, where bail bondsmen, wardens, cops, DAs, and freshly released criminals all sit down for a cold one.

"Uptown. Now that's what I'm talking about," says Calinda. "What time?"

"Eight?"

"Eight will be marvelous, darling," she says, practicing her uptown talk already.

At 7:55 P.M., I pull my battered black Pontiac Sunfire, its finish baked gray by the Louisiana sun, into a space between a silver Mercedes and a gleaming Jaguar the dark green of virgin forests.

Angling the rearview mirror toward me, I fluff my hair and slick on a little plum lip gloss. My ride may not be all that, but no one in the Columns has to know. I slam the door and pull my shoulders back. My heels click across the parking lot and up the walk.

To enter the Vic is to step inside a chocolate truffle—a very, very expensive chocolate truffle. Mahogany walls and ceilings glow warm brown. Gold light cascades from the stained-glass chandelier, and dark leather armchairs whisper like clustered succubi, inviting you to sink down and never leave.

The bar's signature scent, magnolia and tobacco, floats over, curling under your nose like aromas in old-time cartoons. Uri told me that his job includes shaking out a measure of fine Cuban tobacco and burning it in a little incense dish. Now that smoking's not allowed, that's the only way they can keep the fragrance fresh and authentic. Out in the front gallery, the brass band plays blues and old jazz at a discreet volume: loud enough to make you certain that the world is indeed wonderful but not so loud that a gentleman need ever raise his voice to be heard by a companion. That's in the handbook. Uri showed me.

He's behind the bar tonight in his black tie and white shirt, the sleeves rolled up, his smile wide and warm.

"Hey, baby." I seat myself on a stool at the bar.

He seems pleased. "What are you doing here?"

"Besides ogling you, gorgeous? Nothing."

"Seriously."

"I've got a meeting. For work." He's never met Calinda. A wise man, he always clears out on girls' nights—and I like to keep the parts of my life in separate little boxes. Clean.

"That's different," he says, but he doesn't press it. "So what are you having?"

"Whatcha got good?"

He looks at me speculatively, pursing his full lips. "You know what you might like?" He gets out a snifter and brings a bottle over from the premium section, turning the label my way. "You ever tried this?"

There's a picture of a ship on the bottle, and it's from Martinique. *Rhum Agricole*, it says. *Réserve Spéciale.* "What is it?"

"It's rum." He pours two fingers in the glass and slides it over to me.

"Just plain like that?"

"You sip it neat. Like cognac." Dubious, I pick it up and swirl the glass. The brown liquid glints and swivels. "Most rums are made from molasses, but *rhum agricole* is made from pure cane juice. Just try it."

I take a sip and my tongue melts. My throat heats.

He smiles a bartender's satisfied smile. "See? I knew you'd like it."

Middle-class people aren't like the sitcoms say they are. As a child in Desire, I used to study TV shows to learn about people, to see what middle-class life would be like. But Uri is my gay roommate, and he's not comic relief—he's not even funny. And he never gives me fashion advice or talks to me about which guys we think are cute. He's kind and serious, and he works on his novel every morning and then tends bar at the Vic every afternoon and night. He's muscled and good-looking but shy, and he wears normal guy clothes and wire-rimmed spectacles that aren't a fashion statement; if he took them off right now, he couldn't see the beer taps. He's the nicest white guy I've ever known.

Uri moves off to his other customers, and I flick my nails on the rolled wood, waiting for Calinda. I'm always on time or ahead of schedule, which, in New Orleans, where time runs easy, means I usually end up waiting. But I can't shake the habit. Being prompt is a skill that got scalded into me in college.

When I first arrived at Tulane University, I was perpetually late. Where I'd come from, in the Upper Ninth Ward, it didn't matter. Time was relative. People showed up when they got there. If you missed the bus, you caught the next one. If you lost your job—well, hell, that job sucked anyway, and you'd find another minimum-wage gig soon enough.

But at Tulane, things ran by a different code. The clock and calendar reigned supreme, and professors got thin-lipped and irritable when you failed to obey. One day freshman year, when we were all crowding out of class, Dr. Taffner snapped, "Miss Céspedes!"

I turned back.

"Young lady," she said, folding her arms across her crisp linen blouse. "Let me give you a word of advice."

"Yeah?"

"In the world you apparently wish to enter, things occur on time. Classes begin and end at the appointed hour. Meetings commence when previously agreed." She raised her finely groomed brows. "Make it your business, Miss Céspedes, to be prompt. Or you will be left behind. That's a promise. And that's my advice, if you wish to ascend the social ladder." Her gaze flicked up and down. "And you're a shrewd girl, if I'm not mistaken."

She nodded, dismissing me, and though I chafed with humiliation, I was never late again. It's the painful lessons that stick.

"Nola, baby!"

I swivel and there's Calinda, smiling in her yellow silk suit, her arms flung wide. I jump down into her hug, her scent of tangerines and musk. "Girl, it feels like a year," she says. "Tell you what, this place is snazzy. I haven't been here in forever."

Calinda grew up in Baton Rouge and went north to study law at Cornell, which was, as she describes it, "freeze-your-ass-off cold, with me stumbling around in the snow, wondering where I could get some decent food." After she got her law degree, she moved down here. Calinda's love of New Orleans cooking keeps her ample, but she still has more dates than she can count. Men can spot her sensual exuberance and genuine kindness. Her skin radiates, and her copper bangles slide up and down her sleek arms as she talks. There's a sort of gold aura around her that makes you just want to sidle up next to her and soak in it for a while. She's looking for better home training than she's found—"Plenty to choose from, none worth keeping," as she says—but for now, it's all just for fun.

We find an empty corner and settle into the leather chairs to chat, crossing our bare legs, letting our sandals dangle and bounce from the balls of our feet, smiling at the fancy lawyers and stockbrokers who give us the eye. Calinda tries the *rhum* and I have another while we chat about work. Finally she heaves her briefcase onto the low table between us.

"Am I glad to unload these." She lifts out a thick batch of manila folders. "This thing's going to be a whole lot lighter on the way home." She stacks the files on the table, snaps the briefcase shut. "I need them back in one piece, though," she warns.

"Of course." I want to reach over and grab them at once, start fingering through them to see what I've got, but this is social, after all. As we sit and chat, I force my eyes to stay on Calinda's face, but the pile of manila glows in my peripheral vision. I clasp my hands together to keep them from reaching out.

"The clerk says you pulled some real uglies."

"You could say that."

"Doesn't sound like typical Lagniappe material."

I sip my rum.

"Yeah, well," she continues, "we've got a case right now that might interest you, if these nasty fellas are up your alley." She taps the stack of files. "An abduction in the Quarter, yesterday morning. Broad daylight. A tourist from Kansas, twenty-five years old. An au pair. She's having breakfast with the family in a restaurant, and then, poof! Gone."

"A white woman?"

"Yeah, the NOPD's up in arms. They've got fliers with her picture up all over the Quarter, and the father of the family's been on TV with a statement."

"The father?" Women are more sympathetic to viewers, less threatening.

"The mother's dead. Survey says the au pair was taking care of more than the kids."

"Are y'all thinking this is connected to the other two?" The second of two women's bodies had recently washed up on the banks of the Mississippi. Rape, then strangulation.

Calinda sits silently for a moment. "I really shouldn't say."

"Hmm. Broad daylight, the Quarter . . . your perp's bold."

"Yeah, that's what's got me worried." She glances at her watch. "It's been almost thirty-six hours now, so truth be told, I'm not hopeful."

"Jaded much?"

"Just being real. The thing is, if he's this fearless, and we don't find him now, he's going to be at it again soon."

"If the PD gets him, would you want the case?"

"Hoo, girl," she bursts out loudly. "On the prosecution? Hell, yes. Take that motherfucker *down*."

Three businessmen at a nearby table glance our way, and we both smile sweetly at them. They lift their glasses.

Calinda leans forward, lifts an eyebrow, and lowers her voice. "Nail that shithead to the wall."

Our talk turns to the upcoming Jazz Fest and which acts will be worth seeing. Then our glasses sit drained and glistening in the amber light.

Calinda finally slaps her thigh and says, "Well, baby, I got to go." I rise, hug, and do the good-bye thing like I've got all the time in the world, but before the clatter of her heels on wood has faded, I'm sinking back down into the soft leather, my hands on the files.

Each folder I open is a horror story, a log of depravity. Perps leer or stare dully up at me, some defiant, some crazy, some tired and defeated. Some files include photos of the victims, too, and transcripts of their testimonies. Their eyes are holes of desperate hurt, or flat, glazed pools of ice.

When I read the details of each crime—the ruses, the rope, a glass Coke bottle—my belly sickens. I can't imagine calling any of these men, politely requesting an interview, much less knocking at their doors.

I shake myself. It's all right. This will be good. Jump straight in, do a killer job, and I'll never have to cover a nightclub or boutique opening again. Maybe, if it's good enough, the story will even be my ticket out of this city.

But that's the rum talking. I laugh and shake my head. Down to work.

I move slowly through the stack, selecting the best men to interview. It's not like covering an art opening, where the gallery owner is dying for free publicity. These guys, even if they're reachable, are likely to say no.

My stack of prospects starts to grow. I weed out the ones who seem certifiably crazy—no sense poking a wolf. I want guys who are lucid, who represent a variety of social classes, to get readers to see the complexity of the situation. I settle on a handful of prospects. Mike Veltri, a working-class white guy in Metairie who liked it when the women fought back. Micah Harris, an elderly black pastor in Tremé who used his position in the church to gain the trust of victims—thirty-two of them over the years, as it turns out. George Anderson, the rich guy in Audubon Place who, unable to confine his urges to biannual southeast Asian sex tours, got busted for feeling up the help. And Javante Hopkins, a young guy from the Ninth who'd finally gone to prison for his third rape. He liked to cut his victims a little, down there.

I shudder. The graphic details make me shaky. I think of the tourist Calinda mentioned—eating breakfast one moment, and then gone. In all likelihood, this is the kind of company she's keeping now. If she's still alive to keep it.

I page slowly through the files that are left, eliminate a couple, then add a couple more to my pile. When I open the last one, my breath rushes out in a quick gust, and I lean back in my chair. *Score.* In the Quarter, a middle-aged white man, Blake Lanusse, a vice principal of a public elementary school and a good ol' Cajun boy, was convicted for molesting three female students in a single year. Their faces, permanently bewildered, stare out from the file. What could be more perfect for my story, more ironic, than an authority figure entrusted by everyone with the care of children? My arm flies up, flagging Uri down.

"Another one of those things, please."

"Are you sure? You've got to drive."

"Oh, I'm sure."

I look at the perp's beige face, read each corrosive detail of his story. With a feeling of satisfaction, I add him to my stack.

Uri takes his time coming back with my drink. When he sets it down, he puts a glass of water next to it. "What is all that stuff, anyway?"

"Nothing. Just work." I close the files and get out my wallet.

"Nope. On the house," he says, waving my credit card aside. "It's nice to see a friendly face."

"Are you crazy?" I may not know a lot, but I know *Réserve Spéciale* can't come cheap.

"Just make some more flan sometime, and we'll call it even."

"You're a saint."

"Yeah, well, you take it easy. Slow down, and drink that water, okay?"

I sit there sipping my rum, looking over at my stack of files: a church guy, a rich guy, a vice principal. White guys, black guys, young guys, old—like some kind of perverted Dr. Seuss book.

I lean back and soak up the warm, brown ease of the Vic, reveling already in the sweet, sordid stench of my success.

When I enter the dark apartment alone, it's midnight. Uri's dog Roux pads over, and I scratch his bony brown skull. The weird aftersag of the day's tension hits me like gravity: the argument with Bailey, my new awareness of how many sex offenders saturate the city—even my neighborhood, even this street—and the disturbing litany of their crimes. I'm tired, and the weight of what I'm undertaking makes me feel, suddenly, like I'm breathing underwater.

So I do what I always do when I'm alone and weary. I kneel on the couch's plump red pillows like I'm praying, reach up to the map of Cuba, which hangs framed on the wall, and touch the homeland I've never seen. Slowly, like a ritual, I slide my fingertips along the island's curves, and the glassy feel of Havana, Cayo Coco, and Santiago under my skin comforts me. The dipping bays, crooked coasts, the pulse of Varadero beach.

And poor Guantánamo. Proof that the powerful can fence off a part of you and claim it for their own.

Crescent City is what they call New Orleans, home of my birth and twenty-seven years, but my mother was straight Cuban, *una Marielita,* and an orphan, fresh from the boat in 1980, who loved Miami but loved a man more. Drawn by his promises of Mardi Gras, of feathered masks and dancing down the streets, she rattled along the Gulf with him in his old Corolla until they slid into New Orleans.

But come Lent, he slid west into history: other women, other names he went by, other children he'd tossed giggling into the air before I was born.

So in 1981, a fatherless girl in a Creole city, I was named Nola after the acronym that so enchanted my mother—"It even sounds Spanish, *querida*." Nola Soledad Céspedes. Mamá spooned her sweet and sticky *plátanos* between my lips by the time I was four months old, because she had things to do, houses to clean, and that baby needed to be on solid food. When you're hungry, you feed on what's there.

Growing up in the Desire Projects—which were finally torn down in 2003, the year I graduated college—there's not a lot you don't see. Like any hustler looking to flip some questionable shit, I put all the gory details (drug deals, stabbings, men beating their women, women selling themselves, your head bent to homework while gunshots pock the dusk outside) into my admissions essay, massaged it into a nice American Dream story of struggle and triumph, and cadged a scholarship to Tulane, just a couple of bus rides but a world away. On its plush green lawns and in its creamy stone buildings, I kept my eyes wide for niggling injustices and eventually nabbed my own late-night radio show on WTUL, 91.5 FM, where I vented with my big, loud mouth about race and class. It was just a way to let off the steam and outrage that built up during my days, but, *milagro* of *milagros,* the timing was right. The school newspaper, *The Hullabaloo*—called "complacent" in a letter signed by twelve alumni and seeking an edgier outlook—liked my wee-hour squawking so much that they asked me for transcripts. From there, it was just one smiling conversation with the *Hullabaloo*'s editor to writing my own column. A double major in history and communications later, I was interning at the *Gambit* and then at the *Times-Picayune,* where the copyeditors spelled worse than I did. *Oye, chica, muy mal.*

And then a real paying job at the *Picayune,* starting in 2006, post-Katrina, when a couple of entertainment writers cashed it in and moved north. Twenty-five thousand dollars a year in one of the country's poorest, most murdering cities lets me rent half a little apartment on the top floor of an old house in Mid-City. Nothing in it worth anything—what's the point? Getting ripped off is a given. Twice I've been robbed, have come home late to furniture overturned, drawers pulled out and left dripping with stirred clothes. It's a violation you get used to. I got a male roommate and say my prayers.

There was no Cuban community to speak of in New Orleans, so I made up my own out of Mamá's memories and recipes and the books I checked out of the library. My *altár,* with its little saucers of Diet Coke and rum, shelters a photo of my mother, a picture of the Virgen de la Caridad del Cobre, and my little statue of Ochún— all lit by a candle emblazoned with Guadalupe, the only kind of Virgin Mary the *botánicas* sell here. I hauled banana trees in bright pots up the stairs and onto the balcony, their green leaves fanned and flopping like the docile ears of dogs in the Louisiana steam heat. From the hook where my rosary hangs, I strung purple, green, and gold Mardi Gras beads, their plastic mingling with its cherrywood and tin. On Thursday nights, I go out with my girls or have them over for *guanabana* mojitos and cold *jamon* soup with little curls of honeydew. I memorize the quirky bits of local lore I learn when I do my reporting, so when my skill at small talk lapses, I can whip out historical anecdotes to fill the conversation. To work, I wear high-heeled white sandals, red blouses, and snug white pants like a Cuban Charlie's Angel.

It's a cultural synthesis of sorts. It's what I have. I make it work.

Around the newsroom, I talk a tough spiel, turn in tight copy, and always beat my deadlines, so people leave me alone and let me climb a ladder of my own design.

2

On Wednesday morning, I'm at the office early, and a wash of April sunlight fills the Living and Lagniappe pit. Entertainment writers cruise back and forth, stopping to chat and sip their coffee and pretend they're real journalists. Everything around me is bright, banal, and benign, as usual, but the file of former vice principal Blake Lanusse is opened flat on my desk, his mug shot staring up at me. My hand, gripping the receiver of my desk phone, is paralyzed. *Just make the call, Nola.* From atop someone's cubicle divider, a fuzzy red and green parrot blankly returns my gaze.

I push the keys of Lanusse's home number, hoping that he won't be there, that I can just leave my message and move on down the list.

He picks up on the second ring. "Yeah?"

"May I speak with Mr. Blake Lanusse, please?"

"You got him. Whatcha want him for?" His voice is jovial and warm, with a pleasing rasp. He's got that easy, casual good-ol'-boy intonation and manner of speaking that plays so well here in the city, even among the upper classes.

"Mr. Lanusse, I'm with the *Times-Picayune*. We're doing a feature story on the reintegration of former sex offenders back into the

New Orleans community. I'd like to set up an interview to get your perspective."

There's a moment or two of dead silence.

"My perspective." The warmth is gone.

"Yes, sir."

"Where'd you get my name?"

"The DA, sir. They recommended you as being particularly smart and articulate." It's an utter lie, but if entertainment reporting has taught me anything, it's the effectiveness of flattery. "I just want to get your perspective on how you've been treated since your rehabilitation and release."

"How I've been treated, huh?" His chuckle is so hollow that my neck prickles. "You really think the good folks of New Orleans want to hear what I've got to say?"

"Yes, sir. Absolutely. Your views are crucial to the story. You represent a significant demographic." Flatter them, then hit them with ten-dollar words.

"I don't know."

"Mr. Lanusse, most offenders never get the chance to state their case in a public forum. There's so much prejudice and fear around these issues. With this story, I aim to change that. By bringing your valuable perspective to bear, you could be a voice of reason. You could really shine a light—"

"Well, I got a lot to say, that's for sure." He pauses. "Where would this interview be at?"

"Anywhere you like." A clean, well-lighted place, preferably, with lots of people around. Luckily, New Orleans has plenty of spots like that.

"How about my place?"

"Your home?"

"I've got a place in the Quarter. We can talk private-like." Although the room around me still bustles brightly, a shiver spirals across my shoulders and up the back of my skull. My vision narrows until all I can see is his photo staring up at me from the open file: his dark, bowl-cut hair, his handsome face gone sullen for the police photographer, his strange, pale eyes like shells pressed into sand.

"I don't know. I was thinking maybe a coffee shop—"

"I know what you were thinking," he says. "Come on. Do you really expect me to talk about this kind of thing with a bunch of people sitting two feet away?"

"I just thought it might be more comfortable."

"Comfortable for who?"

I take a deep breath. "Sir, I would be very happy to meet you at a coffee shop, restaurant, or other public place that's convenient for you."

There's a moment of silence.

"You want this interview or not?"

"Oh, yes, sir. Absolutely."

"Well, I'm not going to discuss my private life in a public place. Period."

Observing him in his natural habitat might be a better idea for a feature story anyway—capture the atmosphere and all that. I should probably suggest it to the other men, too. "Yes, all right," I agree. "Your home will be fine."

Blake Lanusse gives me his address, which matches the one in his file, and says he'll be free a week from Thursday at noon.

"You sound young," he says suddenly. "How old are you?"

How is that relevant? I want to ask. But I don't want to alienate him this early in the game. "Twenty-seven."

"What do you look like?" A long pause grows on the line. "So's I'll know you when you get here," he says.

"I'm five foot five," I say slowly. "Dark hair—"

"Long or short?" His tone is soft.

I pause. "Long."

"I like long." The voices of my colleagues blur to a buzz of background noise, and all I can hear is Blake Lanusse in my ear and my own breath pulsing rapid and shallow between my lips. The plastic eyes of the parrot wink and shine.

"I've got brown eyes," I say. I'm gripping the receiver so hard my wrist is trembling.

"I'll be looking forward to it."

"Okay, then," I say. "I guess that's about it."

I say good-bye, press the receiver down, and gulp water from the bottle on my desk. I rub my hands together for warmth.

Now that Blake Lanusse has broken me in, the other calls are easier. Some don't answer; some say no. Some numbers have been changed or disconnected. The black churchman from Tremé says he thinks the Lord would disapprove. But three men say yes. Mike Veltri can meet this Friday at his house in Metairie; Javante Hopkins, the cutter, sounding edgy and hyped up on something, rattles off his address and says the following Monday will be great, great, great, no problem, yeah. The rich guy, George Anderson, is suave but wary. He needs a lot of massaging and assurances of anonymity, and he still hangs up to call his lawyer. Finally, he calls back and agrees, saying I can come to his home on Audubon Place a week from Friday.

After lunch at my desk, I drive uptown to Tulane University to do library research on sex offenders. The local radio news announces that Amber Waybridge, the abducted tourist, has not yet been found, and I wonder what Calinda's heard about the case.

Tulane University, my alma mater: huge stone buildings, boys with their floppy forelocks and ubiquitous khaki shorts, and sorority girls sleek like seals, EΔT emblazoned on the butts of their short shorts, their manes a glinting sea of blond highlights—which can now be conveniently obtained in the new Aveda salon right in the student union. It's a rich, beautiful university that caters to rich, beautiful people.

I park my battered Sunfire on St. Charles behind Audubon Place, a block of mansions protected by huge iron gates and an armed guard in a booth. When Katrina knocked out the city's power, private generators in Audubon Place kept the mansions lit and cool. While other helicopters were rescuing folks off rooftops, the owners of the mansions in Audubon Place choppered in armed mercenaries to keep looters out.

With spiked black bars as thick as my wrist, the gates mean business. The one at this end of the block is framed by huge stone pillars twice my height. A discreet metal sign reads, FOR YOUR PRO-TECTION, PLEASE CLOSE GATE—which makes no sense, since the sign faces outward, toward us hoi polloi on the street.

Someone has written back in green Magic Marker, FUCK YOU RICH PEEPS! and has drawn cartoon dicks of varying sizes and detail. I grope through my purse, pushing past the soft wad of the cotton gloves I keep there in case I ever get lucky enough to handle evidence. I pull out my black Sharpie, glance around, and mark a curving comma on the sign. FUCK YOU, RICH PEEPS! There.

Through the bars, royal palms sway on the broad green lawns, and a black Mercedes purrs in the nearest driveway, waiting. When I was a new Tulane student, I used to come linger by the gate and wonder what all those lives were like—that house, that car, those clothes—until one day it occurred to me that no rich peeps ever came up to Desire to wonder about us.

Now here I am, staring again, wondering which of the magazine-beautiful houses conceals George Anderson, molester of maids.

But this afternoon is for research. On foot, I cross Freret toward Tulane's Howard-Tilton Memorial Library. Outside on the wide pebbled landing, under the giant old live oaks, it's shady, and the breeze on my skin is cool. Birds sing as they flit from branch to branch.

I'm looking for basic books-and-articles stuff to build context before starting my interviews in the field. Not everything's online. Then I'll interview the offenders, along with neighbors, psychologists, prison guards, and so on. Worried parents. First get all the angles, then write it up. My plan is to start with a good human-interest anecdote and then shift into facts and statistics, remaining sympathetic toward all sides but ultimately neutral, the way they write those front-page features in *The New York Times*.

I pull open the heavy glass door and walk into Howard-Tilton's familiar smell of air-conditioning and a million books. I slide my alumni ID card across the desk, and the student worker with a shining ponytail and a tiny blue star tattooed high on her cheekbone waves me in. I feel instantly at home, as though no years have passed since I last settled into a carrel with my backpack and Diet Cokes for the long haul of writing term papers—a process I actually liked. I was always a little weird that way.

Maybe it's the old saw about school providing an orderly refuge from the chaos of poverty. Or maybe it's the case that my mother gave me the only gift she'd brought with her from Castro's Cuba: literacy. From the time I was born, she sang and recited poetry in Spanish, and she taught me early how to read it. Then we learned to read English together, watching *Sesame Street,* reading Dr. Seuss aloud, and doing the workbooks she brought home.

They say being read to at a young age is a predictor of academic success. They say growing up bilingual increases the number of neuronal connections in the brain. Whatever factors made me an early bloomer, when the friendly white guy with curly hair and glasses made me answer questions and play with weird block puzzles, it turned out that I didn't have to go back to my old kindergarten anymore. It turned out that despite the poverty, single mother, Spanish language, etc., my IQ was 156.

My mother didn't know the statistics when the school's interpreter explained that I'd be traveling alone across town to a different school. She didn't know that living in public housing lowered the odds of my graduating from high school by 26 percent, or that receiving welfare cut my chances by an additional 54 percent. She only knew it sounded like a chance for her girl to move up, and she signed the papers.

The two-bus ride to P.S. McDonogh 15, the pretty red stucco school in the French Quarter where kids wore uniforms, became my daily passport to another world, a world where a coffee shop (not a drainage ditch, pawnshop, and Dumpsters) sat across the street from the school, where big magnolias with glossy dark leaves and creamy blossoms shaded the thick grass where we played, and we had red trikes to ride on and sand to dig, instead of pocked cement and chain-link fence. Each morning I passed wealth, ease, debauchery, and the occasional puddle of vomit on my short walk from the bus stop to my school.

Even as a child, I sensed that P.S. McDonogh 15 was my ticket out of the projects. But being smart's not always a benefit. Back in the Upper Ninth, my little blue pleated skirt, Peter Pan–collared blouse, and big words got me beaten up, no matter how tough I tried to talk. Libraries became a refuge then and again at Tulane, where I didn't have the right clothes or the right assumptions to fit in. I escaped into books, research, and history. The Howard-Tilton library feels almost as cozy as my mother's kitchen.

I spend the whole afternoon doing research in the stacks, where I find several recent books on rape, pedophilia, rehabilitation, incarceration, and recidivism. I learn that rape, due to the stigma, is one of the most underreported crimes in the world, so the number of victims is hard to gauge. In the United States, it's estimated that between 13 and 25 percent of women will be raped at some point in their lifetimes. Since women are particularly unlikely to report rape if the rapist is someone they know, the numbers are fuzzy at best—which also applies to the finding that only about 3 percent of men are raped. But regardless of the sex of the victim, the perpetrator is almost always male. I skim, taking notes on my laptop.

During little stretch breaks, I go outside to the landing and call criminal psychiatrists until I score an interview with Dr. Omar Letley, M.D., Ph.D., who specializes in rehabilitating serious sex offenders. Tomorrow, two o'clock, in the Central Business District, the CBD. If I'm lucky, Dr. Letley will give me crisp sound bites that will crystallize all this scholarly data.

At 3:20 P.M. on a weekday, La Madeleine café at the corner of Carrollton and St. Charles is the perfect argument for affirmative action. Behind the counter, black folks cook and serve, while white mommies bring in their kids for after-school treats. It's a living example of the racially divided nature of the service economy, or what folks in the projects call "the servant economy."

I'm sitting at a table, waiting for my friend Soline, who wants my help shopping. She was supposed to be here at three. New Orleans time. Everyone runs slow around here.

Outside in the parking lot, a priest sits in his gold Camry, eyes closed, straw-sipping a frozen pink drink piled high with whipped cream. A convertible Porsche pulls up, and out gets a smiling father with two daughters, tawny adolescents with identical brown ponytails, pleated gray skirts, and monogrammed white blouses. When they choose a table near mine for their Cokes and éclairs, I try not to stare, wondering how it must feel to be those children, your father there and attentive in the middle of the day, dropping twenty bucks just for a snack. The girls have a casual air, their blue eyes cool and used to all this.

"Hey, girl!" Soline's voice is loud and happy. With her Prada bag and Jimmy Choos, her pristine sky blue halter dress, dark skin, cloud of spiraling coppery hair, and the fluffy white bichon frise under her arm, she looks like a glamorous argument *against* affirmative action—though she'd be quick to tell you that she's here solely by the virtue of her parents' and grandparents' hard work and the grace of Executive Order 11246, which made affirmative action into federal law. "Let me just get an iced coffee," she says, bending to kiss my cheek. "You ready to go?"

"I've been ready."

"Oh, just hush." She spins away on long, coltish legs to order and pay. Five feet nine and narrow as a green bean, she's the perfect model for the linen frocks she carries in her chic shop on Magazine Street, a six-mile boutique row that runs from the French Quarter to Audubon Zoo. When shopaholics come to New Orleans—whether they want hand-stitched French lingerie, gourmet dog biscuits, or the hair sugared off their nether regions—they go to Magazine.

Sinegal, Soline's shop, features the gifts and skills brought to New Orleans by the stolen Senegambians in the seventeenth century: silverwork, goldwork, and cloth dyed with indigo. Soline's ancestors, who came on those first ships, bought their way free under French manumission laws, and have lived in Tremé for almost three centuries. Sinegal honors Soline's people, her history.

The bichon frise is a sweet, cheerful dog named Puppy. "I love him to death," Soline says. "But it's nice to know that if I ever felt like slapping something white, I could." Sweetly, she adds, "Not that I ever would."

Sinegal also carries indestructible little dresses that refuse to wilt in the city's humidity and heat. They look like simple shifts, and if you're willing to fork over four hundred dollars, then you, too, can enjoy simplicity. Soline offers her friends a discount—"at cost!"—but they're still out of my reach. I stick to Target. If you stay in shape and wear a push-up bra, anything looks good.

"Come on," says Soline, grabbing my arm. "Let's go." We're heading to French Fountains, an outdoor shop on St. Charles. Her wedding is three weeks away, and she's taming the nuptial jitters by buying stuff for their new place, which is a few blocks from the nightclub her fiancé owns and runs in the Faubourg Marigny.

She and Rob are movers in New Orleans' black society, their history-conscious, black-positive agendas meshing neatly: hers with Sinegal, and his with his club, Code Noir, its name an ironic reference to the French slave code from the 1600s. After Harvard, Rob spent six years on Wall Street, and on the weekends, he DJed at exclusive private parties in Manhattan. He came back with capital, investors, and a killer strategy. Here in New Orleans, Rob Conti might fool people into thinking he's just a suave dancer and handsome lounge lizard, but he's a businessman first. When I covered Code Noir's opening for the *Times-Picayune,* I saw him in meetings in his crisp white shirt and polished wingtips, his gold tie dangling between his spread knees, one hand turned backward on his thigh, the other roving absently over his shaved head, staring into the screen of his laptop while computing every word uttered around him. He's used to being the only black man in the room; Wall Street taught him that.

It may be possible to do without dancing entirely, as Jane Austen once wrote, but she clearly never came to New Orleans. Down in the Faubourg Marigny, where Rob's people have lived for generations, Code Noir has the best sound system in the city, and it sits on Frenchmen Street, along with the venerable jazz club Snug

Harbor and hipper places like the Blue Nile and the Spotted Cat. Edgier, rougher, and less touristy than the Quarter, the Faubourg Marigny is where the cool kids go.

Rob offers unadvertised corn bread and dollar-a-bowl gumbo—African-style, with okra—before the cover charge kicks in at ten o'clock, when fifteen dollars lets you catch the best funk and brass in the world. Rob's affirmative-gumbo strategy scores Code Noir a huge crowd that's more down-home than a lot of clubs, which can get packed with frat boys and tourists. That kind of success builds on itself: word gets out that it's a cooler crowd, more people clamor to get in, and more bands want to play there. A lot of black bands like that it's a black-owned place, too. Keep the money at home.

So Rob's wedding to Soline is like the union of young royalty, 2008-style.

Soline and I stroll arm in arm past the mansions of the seven thousand block of St. Charles, our heels clicking on the sidewalk. I keep the conversation light; my brain might be crunching sex-offender statistics, but we chat about art openings, fashion—typical Lagniappe stuff.

"So what I'm thinking is, I'm going to plant for scent," she says as we approach French Fountains. "You know? Gardenia, ligustrum, Confederate jasmine." Soline's own single-girl condo sits farther down St. Charles in a beautiful gray-green building surrounded by tall magnolias and guarded by a monitored steel gate. Selling her perfect little nest has provoked a world of angst, but she's coping by focusing on the new place, which she and Rob bought together and which has one of those secret, interior gardens, all bricks and ivy, for which New Orleans is known. "So we can sit out there and just breathe." Soline herself smells, as she always does, of tuberose. Pretty. Light. Sweet.

Arriving at French Fountains, we duck under the arch into a

strange walled world. When Soline said *fountain,* I thought she meant some hundred-dollar thing you buy so you can have the sound of trickling water, but this is for real. The courtyard is full of old fountains taller than I am—bronze fountains, stone fountains, black fountains bubbling, cool water splashing into basins the size of Jacuzzis. Weathered statuaries, curling metalwork tables, birdbaths, reclining stone nymphs, once-white metal columns gone orange with rust, all salvaged from estates and plantations in the region—anything you could possibly desire for your courtyard or stately lawn. In among the merchandise, palms and magnolia trees grow, and the magnolias' ivory blossoms splay their sweet, lemony scent into the sunlit air.

It's disorienting, like a very expensive fun house. Stone women loom at us, beckoning from odd angles. Water splashes from copper spouts. Soft pink blossoms wave on oleander spikes, and ligustrum bushes smell too sweet, like an impending headache. Stone fleur-de-lis plaques lean everywhere.

Our heels wobbling and crunching on the white gravel, Soline starts to point out things she likes, and I check the sun-faded ink on the price tags. Eight hundred dollars. A thousand dollars. Four thousand. I feel weak and a little sick. The sun is too bright, the perfume of the magnolias too strong, and it's weird to be surrounded by all these relics, wrenched up from their original gardens and now for sale. I lean against a three-tiered fountain, its cool water falling into vast bowls of hammered copper.

"You okay?" Soline asks.

"I'm fine." Falling silent, I follow her around. I don't want to envy my friend. I don't. But I'm still struggling to repay student loans, not to mention my maxed-out credit card bills from the Katrina evacuation, and she has this much money to blow on an ornament? She sells pretty dresses, and I'm stuck researching perverts?

She finally settles on a beautiful bronze pyramid of fish spouting streams into shells. It's the size of my entire kitchen. I laugh weakly.

We enter the pink stucco building to pay, and I stand with Soline at the counter. Fifty-six hundred dollars. When the credit card slip is placed before her, she signs without looking.

Out on the street, we hug and kiss and smile good-bye, and she says, "See you tomorrow!" and I act excited. Tomorrow's our weekly girls' night with Calinda and Fabi, and I'm cooking dinner for everyone at my apartment. It should be fun.

Should be. But when I walk back to my car alone, I feel a little blue.

Standing in La Madeleine's parking lot, my keys in my hand and the afternoon sun slanting down between the oaks, I wonder what to do next. I have no more research planned for the day, and I feel mildly aimless. But then I remember Blake Lanusse and the disturbing prospect of interviewing him alone in his own home. It unnerves me. After all, my usual beat is galleries, clubs, and boutiques, not the personal lairs of ex-cons. Since I'm not far from the Quarter, I could go check out the address, walk the job, and make sure the area seems safe.

Pleased with my plan, I leave my Pontiac where it sits, cross St. Charles to the grassy median, and sit down on the bench at the streetcar stop. The Quarter is only a short hop away.

When the streetcar rumbles up, I pick a seat next to an open window, and we head off toward the French Quarter, passing all the fancy houses, the breeze in my hair.

Coming up in the Desire Projects, where everything was derelict, all I longed for was a bright, modern place to live. Everything new, everything clean, everything in working order. I believed in the fresh start: furniture straight from the store, appliances right out of the box. At Tulane I majored in history, but not because I fetishized it. The past was something I wanted to master, escape, transcend. I wanted to keep history safely in books, where it belonged.

So it took me a while to grasp the New Orleans code of decor as practiced by the upper middle class.

For the uninitiated: you must have chandeliers, and fleur-de-lis are simply essential. If you have a courtyard garden—and you really, truly should—it must be paved with red brick. Preferably old, mossy, crumbling brick. You must have mottled walls, their paint peeling down to reveal fascinating glimpses of French and Spanish and Creole history beneath. You must have silk-upholstered Louis XIV chairs next to your marble fireplace.

If anything in your home or garden is tattered, decaying, cluttered, cramped, or decrepit, don't touch it. Don't clean it up, and for God's sake don't have it removed by professionals in hazmat suits. You must prize it, cherish it, enshrine it. It's not a falling-down mess; it's the New Orleans aesthetic.

And if you want your own little two-bedroom Creole cottage on Esplanade, you must have $450,000, even though the market's glutted and FOR SALE signs speckle every block.

All this rich history, mess, and charm belong to someone else.

When the streetcar stops at Canal, I jump off and walk the long blocks down Royal. I can't hear the Mississippi River, but an occasional seagull glides overhead. Taped on all the black iron lampposts are flyers for Amber Waybridge, the missing tourist. I pause at one flyer, staring: dark hair, dark eyes. A wide, sexy smile. She looks a little like me. Slowly, I peel the tape away and fold Amber Waybridge in half and in half again. Sliding her into my handbag, I walk on.

When I get to the address Blake Lanusse gave me, it turns out to be a two-story historic house with thick walls of dark red stucco and glossy black shutters. A brass plaque tells me that it was once the city home of a plantation owner, a place to stay when the family came to town for the opera—*or to sell and purchase slaves*, I mentally add, my fingers itching for my Sharpie. Now it's been split into four condos. Lanusse's is C, on the second floor.

Right across Chartres Street is the Ursuline Convent, a girls' school inside an old compound that fascinated me when we had to learn local history at P.S. McDonogh 15. We even got to tour it one Saturday, when only the nuns were there.

The streets at this corner are clean, the sidewalks freshly swept. Window boxes burst with flowers. It's a well-kept residential block with plenty of tourists drifting by.

Safe as houses. Nothing to worry about.

I check my cell phone: no messages. The sunlight is fading, and the air is growing cool against my bare arms.

I cross Chartres so I can more clearly see Lanusse's windows that directly face the convent. They're hung with some kind of thick red drape. I can't see inside at all.

Suddenly, the curtain twitches. A pale shape appears, a shadowed face above a hidden body. I freeze. My heart pounds hard. Standing alone on the sidewalk, staring up at his windows, I'm excruciatingly visible, a dark target. I slowly swing my gaze around with false nonchalance, pretending to be just one more tourist in the Quarter, but with each moment that ticks past, I feel more conspicuous, like Alice in Wonderland swelling up to a monumental size.

Finally, I lurch into motion, walking away, swinging my arms, trying hard to look casual, jaunty, like just another gawker, but my breath is rushing out in short little gasps, and as I hurry toward the streetcar stop, I feel the gaze of Blake Lanusse like a beam of heat on my back.

3

On Thursday morning, I rise at six. Just to be polite, I say a couple of Hail Marys in front of my little *altár* and ask the blessing of my ancestors, whoever the hell they were. I say my Hail, Holy Queens like any dutiful daughter of the Church, but honestly? Praying to Mary feels useless. Passive, sweet, and accepting as Leda or Europa, how's Mary supposed to protect me? I pray, but *verdad,* I'm just phoning it in.

After my morning run through the streets of Mid-City, I shower and dress, gather up my notes and my laptop, yell good-bye to Uri, and head outside down the green wooden stairs to Fair Grinds—its name a pun, since we're just blocks from the famous Fair Grounds. To prepare for my 2:00 P.M. interview with Dr. Omar Letley, the criminal psychiatrist, I need to digest all my research from yesterday.

There's nothing so convenient as living right above a good coffee shop. Behind the counter, a girl with black nail polish and Mardi Gras beads bunched around her wrists takes my order. I ignore the creamy pastries in the glass case and set an apple on the counter. Overhead, the copper chandelier snakes out its arms like tentacles.

I carry my coffee outside, the ice rattling, the soy milk swirling down. The day feels soft, and the smell of Confederate jasmine sweetens the air. A high wooden fence encloses the patio, where potted palms shade the tables and plump sparrows jump from crumb to crumb. I set down my things, sit, and close my eyes in the sunshine.

As much as I want to get out of New Orleans, I have to confess that I live in a great spot, far from the insanity of the Quarter. Down the block, the Market on Esplanade still carries basically the same crunchy stuff as the Whole Foods it used to be. For French food, Café Degas is across the street from my building, and there's a sushi place, Asian Pacific, next door.

Across Esplanade is Terranova's, an old family-owned grocery with exhausted produce, which my mother prefers since it's cheaper. Next door is the Spanish restaurant Lola's, which serves great paella but puts whipped cream on their flan—and it's not even real whipped cream, but Reddi Whip from the red and white can. I've seen them squirt it. *Abomination.* On the restaurant's walls, hand-painted signs read, GEAUX, TIGERS! and, UNRULY CHILDREN WILL BE COOKED AND EATEN. Outside, strings of lights swing from trees and balconies, and where Esplanade meets Mystery Street, there's a lush, shady little park.

The Splish Splash Washateria on the corner, where I do my laundry, is only a few blocks from Liuzza's by the Track, if you're craving old-school Louisiana grub while your clothes tumble. Their buttery, peppery barbecued shrimp po' boys and thick brown gumbo can raise your bad cholesterol twenty points and still make you say amen. A bumper sticker on the wall proclaims, NEW ORLEANS: WE PUT THE FUN IN FUNERAL.

To work it all off, you can jog up Esplanade, cross the flat, placid waters of Bayou St. John, and head up the long drive into City Park. Once you circle the Museum of Art and cross the stone bridge built in 1938 by the WPA, you're in an immense green swathe of park land: the soft fields, the oaks with their branches dipping to the grass, the Spanish moss, the slow-waddling ducks, the pickup soccer games. Endless, endless soccer games full of young, muscled men.

All told, if someone's going to live in New Orleans and wants to avoid the tourist madness of the Quarter, my corner of Esplanade is a pretty good place to sign a lease. When I found apartments for my mother and me within blocks of each other, I knew we'd gotten lucky.

But until Katrina came, I didn't realize how lucky. Even the land was on our side.

Most people know that New Orleans is a city below sea level. When French explorers arrived, only "the sliver by the river," which later became the French Quarter and Uptown, was dry ground. That's where the Mississippi dumped its deposits of sediment, mud so pure it lacked stones. Early settlers had to drive pilings fifty feet down to keep buildings steady and upright.

Aside from that muddy high ground, almost everything else—all of the present-day New Orleans metro area—lay under water, waiting for the nineteenth century and the miracle of engineering to pump it dry. Except for Esplanade Ridge.

Modern New Orleans is sometimes described as a bowl, its interior protected—or not—by the levees. But more accurately, the city's topography is actually like two bowls, linked by a ridge of high land: Esplanade Ridge. Long before the French began settling here in 1699, this ridge was used by native folks—Washa and Chawasha, Okelousa and Opelousa, Quinapisa, Tangipahoa, Yazoo—as an overland portage route from Lake Pontchartrain to the Mississippi. Those folks knew the land and how to live here. Long before the French arrived, they'd been worshiping the sun, giving their dead sacred burials, and building houses and temples. When gators approached their cooking fires, children laughed, unafraid, and chased them away with sticks.

efore their world was extinguished, they were kind enough to show the settlers that backbone of high land. Over the years, as the wetlands were drained and the city grew, Esplanade Avenue came to look like just another street, so when my mother and I moved into our apartments, we had no idea we'd chosen higher ground. But after Katrina, our dry, undisturbed homes welcomed us back.

If only I liked New Orleans, my little apartment above Fair Grinds would be a sweet, safe place to settle. But I don't. I can't stand the hyped charm of the place, the manufactured decadence of Mardi Gras, the hokey mystique of Spanish moss. I'm sick of sequined masks and voodoo dolls, of the lap dances, the pole dances, and the endless dance of corruption at city hall. Fleur-de-lis flags flutter from porches on any given block, and flower beds are planted with purple pansies and yellow marigolds to show LSU pride. *Go, Tigers.* Even up in the Ninth Ward, where we didn't have the cash to fritter away on flags and flowers, poverty and neglect don't dim local enthusiasm. Crawfish boils, jazz funerals, and hot, unswerving pride belong to everyone. "I was born here," people like to say, "and here is where I'll die."

Not me. Born here I might have been, but I've got no intention of sticking around. The plan is to write a few knockout features, get noticed, pack my bags, and then take my clips to some real newspaper in some real city.

For now, though, the iced coffee tastes of hazelnut, the apple in my teeth crunches cold and sweet, and my laptop opens with that angelic chime that always makes me unreasonably happy.

I spread my notes from yesterday's Tulane research, together with half a dozen photocopied articles, and page slowly through them.

A lot of registered sex offenders are completely irrelevant to my story, because they're not predators. They're streakers, prostitutes, guys caught urinating in public, kids who had consensual teenage

sex when one of them was over eighteen—that's what "carnal knowledge of a minor" means—and sad, tired, obliging wives whose husbands brought home underage girls, claiming they were legal, for
threesomes. In some states, more than a hundred different offenses, including soliciting a prostitute, can get you labeled as a sex
offender. In Louisiana, this includes "crimes against nature," which
range from mere oral sex all the way to bestiality and necrophilia.
Few sex "criminals," as it turns out, actually threaten society, but
under the registry laws, they're all lumped together.

And 2008 is a bad time to be a registered sex offender, anywhere
in the country. Some cities ban sex offenders from public parks.
Chesapeake, Virginia, passed a bill that bars them from playgrounds,
athletic fields, and gyms. Albuquerque's looking to pass a law that
would bar all sex offenders from public libraries, and just yesterday,
an AP story came in about an Indiana man who can't watch his son
play Little League. Convicted of sexual battery twelve years ago
and arrest-free since then, he's still banned from the park where his
kid plays ball. The case is pending.

MySpace has barred sex offenders from their site, since ex-cons
use it to trawl for underage hookups, and New Jersey has pulled
Internet rights from thousands of offenders. Around the country
now, new housing developments forbid the sale of homes to known
sex offenders. It's written right into the deed. Nervous families
are snapping the houses up by the tens of thousands.

So though some of these offenders will never actually be a
threat, they're permanently marked, their freedoms curtailed. Talk
about a human rights issue.

But my story will focus on the hard-core sex offenders, the convicted rapists and molesters of children, the ones who inspired
registry laws in the first place. The facts are ugly. Forcible rape.
Oral copulation with force and violence. Aggravated sexual assault
of a child. Indecency with a child by exposure. Molestation of a

juvenile. Aggravated incest. The typical prison sentence for serious sex offenders is seven years, but they serve an average of only three years before they get out.

Lovely.

Almost all rapists are men, and most pedophiles are men, hands down. Women molest children, too, but the rate is miniscule, and it's the male perp who lurks in that scary crevice of the public imagination.

Most rapists and child molesters have lousy social skills with adult women and rate themselves as shy, introverted, and nervous— like, tell me something I didn't know from *Law & Order*. Most rapists of adult women are guys under thirty—I cross myself swiftly; that's the age I hook up with—but the range for child molesters is much broader, including senior citizens. I almost choke on my iced coffee when I read that one guy convicted of molesting a seven-year-old child was eighty-three.

According to the U.S. Department of Justice, about 70 percent of male sex criminals choose children as their targets. About half molest their own kids, and half choose other people's children. Molesters of girls prefer their prey in the eight-to-ten-year-old range, while the ones who go after boys prefer them a touch older.

My stomach's growling, so I go back to the counter and get another iced coffee, my head buzzing with statistics.

The first thing I want to know is whether these guys can be rehabilitated. Is sexual assault a habit that can be broken, an illness that can be cured?

The odds aren't great. About a quarter of rapists eventually reoffend, and the stats for pedophiles are even worse: more than half. During the twenty-five years after release from prison, the number of child molesters who get rearrested is 52 percent.

On the plus side, that means 48 percent don't molest again.

Or at least, they don't get caught.

I finish my iced coffee and rub my temples. Typing everything into a Word file, I move the facts around until they fall into a logical order. For now, it will have to do.

It's past one o'clock, the sun is blazing overhead, and I'm ready to go interview psychiatrist Dr. Omar Letley, who works with these guys up close and personal. When I put my pen into my handbag, my hand grazes the cool, smooth side of my gun.

After Katrina, when I left my anxious, weeping mother in a motel in Lafayette and drove back to New Orleans in my black Pontiac, I found a strange world. There was the obvious shock and horror of seeing my town underwater, and there was the weird, eerie silence. No birds were left, and no power made the air conditioners hum. Little traffic dared the streets. There was a confusing randomness to the devastation: one building had collapsed in shambles, while one right next door stood pristine, seemingly untouched. There was no rhyme or reason, no justice or pattern to the damage. An unearthly quiet blanketed the hot city.

Among the few people who remained, an odd, cheerful sort of Wild West lawlessness reigned. It was also an instant guy culture, and the men who came back took pride in roughing it, in living out of coolers and doing without. Trying to write a story that would get the *Times-Picayune* to hire me full-time, I interviewed anyone who would talk.

"It's awful, right? We all know that," said a contractor, a white guy in his thirties who now had more construction work than he could ever handle. "It sucks. It's shit. It breaks your heart. But I've got to say it: it's kind of cool, too." He laughed and took a swig from his bottle of Jack Daniel's. "No phone, no fax, no boss, no cops. Driving around, smoking a joint, with a pistol on the seat next to you . . . It's paradise!" Once I drove past a guy mowing his lawn, bare-chested in the ninety-five-degree heat, a handgun tucked into the waistband of his shorts.

When is it okay to take the law into your own hands? When everyone deserts you? When all authorities have failed? Guns were everywhere. After a few days, I headed back to Lafayette—where my mother, as I'd figured, was hysterical with worry. I didn't leave her alone again. A few weeks after the storm, we finally came back together, and one of the first things I did when I got back—aside from sending my story and my résumé to the *Picayune*—was buy a gun.

I remember the day. At the gun shop, the man behind the counter was lanky and tan with a long face and a sandy crew cut. He looked me up and down.

"For your house or to carry?"

"To carry." I got out my application and spread it on the glass counter for him. Approval to carry a concealed weapon takes thirty days in Louisiana, and I wanted to get started.

"Yep, okay. Applications gone up, you know."

"Really?"

"Yep." He said it with satisfaction. "Almost doubled. Katrina's been good to us. Revenue's up forty percent."

"Because of the storm?"

"Yep. Katrina reenergized the market." The phrase sounded unnatural from his lips, like it was something he'd heard at a seminar for gun shop staff. "I get 'em all in here now: grandmas, school-teachers, women that do hair. Black, white, everyone. You gotta do something, crime the way it is."

I wanted to get my notebook out and start asking him questions, but I was there for a weapon, not a story. "I need a semiautomatic, something I can put in my handbag." He took a long look at the red leather shoulder bag I was carrying, nodded, and stooped to reach under the counter. Straightening, he laid a softly gleaming handful of black steel on the glass. My fingers twitched.

"This here's a Beretta M92FS," he said. "What the military uses. Civilian issue, though, of course. Nine-millimeter." I gazed at it. "Go ahead. It won't bite."

I hefted it, held it in both hands. It was solid, comfortable, a little heavy. It felt good. I was too embarrassed to try to grip and aim it, like in the movies. Despite all the guns I'd seen and heard in Desire, it would be obvious that I'd never shot a gun before.

"Aim at that there," he said, pointing to a souvenir silhouette tacked to the wall, pocked with little rips. I did. And it felt right. In fact, it felt perfect. Reluctantly, I lowered my arms. I turned back to him.

"How much?"

"Six hundred and thirty, plus your ammo." Shit. So much for paying down my credit cards.

I left with the address of an indoor range in Metairie and enough ammo to take out Mid-City.

A week later at the Shooter's Club, a guy named Bob rented me a lane and set me up with shooting glasses and earmuffs. Bob seemed like one of those wholesome polo-shirt guys who read *The Purpose Driven Life,* golf, grill out, and own DVDs of *Gladiator* and *Lord of the Rings.* He chatted amiably while I waited for my concealed-weapons instructor, whose name I'd picked from the long list of men (and two women) certified to teach gun safety in New Orleans. I'd tried to pick a name that sounded young and hot—no one named Marshall or Elgin or something else antique, no one with the last name of Domingue or Pellerin or Boudreaux. Middle-aged Cajun guys weren't my thing.

Alonso Sanchez's voice on the phone was promisingly deep, so I wore a little rose-colored silk dress with a fluttery hem and high-heeled sandals for my first lesson.

When he walked up—alas! my dreams died young. He was short and maybe fifty, and he waddled behind the weight of his substantial paunch. Like, *panzóna*. With his little spectacles and bald head, he looked like a Latino George Costanza. My concealed-weapons instructor was officially the antisexy.

"Are you Nola?" I was the only woman there, duh. But I smiled sweetly. *Let's get this over with. Fast.*

He turned out to be surprisingly skilled. He was a good teacher, patient and clear. He showed me how to grip the Beretta, how to sight it, how to brace my arms, how to squeeze the trigger without shifting my aim. His hands on mine were sure and quick, and I found myself liking him, sort of the way I like my editor Bailey. *Respeto,* I guess. He knew his stuff.

Then I put on the glasses, and he clipped a fresh paper target to the rack and flipped the switch that sent it sliding smoothly away from us. The target had the black silhouette of a human figure. We loaded the gun.

"You ready, *mi'ja*?" Something in my chest ripped a little at his words. *My daughter.*

But I cleared my throat and nodded.

"Then let him have it." We both put on our earmuffs.

I squeezed off my first round, and it was beautiful. The crack was a heavenly sound, and the slight kick was pure pleasure in my hands. I squeezed again, and something like power rushed through me. I squeezed again and again. I emptied the magazine, the reports snapping loud and satisfying even through the muffs. When squeezing the trigger finally brought nothing, my arms dropped to my sides. I felt exhilarated, spent. Alonso flipped the switch and the target slid close again.

His whistle was low. "A natural." The little rips were all clustered in the center of the head.

He sent it back out, and I snapped a new clip into the Beretta.

We did it five more times, and I kept nailing the target in the head. Each time, Alonso's look became more wondering, and I was surprised, too. Who knew?

When we called it a day, Alonso unclipped the last target, rolled it up, and handed it to me, a souvenir of my first time.

I felt drained and yet strangely happy. I asked Alonso if he wanted to go for a beer, but he said no, he had to get home to his family, so I paid him his fifty bucks in cash, and he filled out and signed the form that said I'd passed the safety training.

"Gracias," I said, shaking his hand, exuberance still flooding through me, a confused, giddy excitement. I hadn't known shooting a gun would be such a rush. *"Mil gracias."*

"Nada. You take care now." He looked at me curiously, then turned away.

When I arrive on the fourth floor of the steel-and-glass office building a couple of blocks from the LSU med school campus, an entirely forgettable businessman—forties, thinning hair—is just leaving the office of Dr. Omar Letley, the psychiatric expert I'm here to interview. The man walks past me fast, his eyes lowered. A patient? I glance after him. Is this what a sex offender looks like? But he's just a blue suit walking down a corridor.

I push open the glass door etched DR. OMAR LETLEY, M.D., PH.D. and give the receptionist my name. Moments later, a door opens and Omar Letley walks toward me with his hand outstretched. He turns out to be a tall, extremely good-looking man with a dry handshake, a cool-eyed smile, and an air of effortless ease. The fabric of his bespoke suit swishes quietly as he moves. His dark eyes flick up and down me, and he registers (though he's too well mannered to let his eyes linger) the décolletage I've so neatly arranged. With a light touch at my elbow, he ushers me inside his office, where everything is smooth, luxurious, subdued, in shades of taupe and ivory. The framed sepia photographs on his walls feature fountains, Spanish moss, and stone cemetery angels, their edges softened like clouds—the whole nine yards of New Orleans visual propaganda. The place reeks of money, money, and more where that came from. I guess treating pervs is good business.

The AC is pumping, thank God, because the small of my back is damp. He takes his seat behind a wide granite desk, and I drop into a cool leather chair.

"All right, Ms. Céspedes," he says, leaning back with a sigh and steepling his fingers, just like in the movies. "How can I help you?" The faintest smirk wings across his face.

Reminding him of what I explained on the phone, I describe my story's focus while I get out my little silver Olympus and set it down on his desk. I press it on, and its little light begins its steady red wink.

"Tell me about rapists," I say. "Why do they do it?"

"Sure. Well, let's see." He swivels his chair and addresses the window, lifting his chin a little as if going into toastmasters mode. "We cannot, with precision, explain why a rapist rapes, but we can describe the characteristics of rapists and the situational factors that seem to contribute to the development of specific behavioral patterns. Like criminals in general, most rapists and child molesters are diagnosed with antisocial personality disorder, which means, among other things, that they don't feel empathy. They can't connect to the suffering of others."

I nod, scribbling notes as backup.

"Rapists usually have experienced insecure attachments to their caregivers during childhood, and the most violent rapists often have grown up with violent, dominant fathers. Rapists who, as children, witnessed their mothers being abused have the highest likelihood of reoffending."

"That's surprising."

"Not really, if you consider the function of rage in the rapist's psychology." He clears his throat, the smooth, shaven skin of which I can't help noticing. "At least for the two most dangerous types of rapist."

"There are categories?"

"Oh, yes. We typically classify rapists into three groups, and they fall on a spectrum of increasing severity. An opportunistic rapist, the least dangerous kind, is someone who lacks empathy and is motivated only by the desire for sex; he wants sex and wants it now. He'll often drink heavily or use drugs to lower his social inhibitions, and he'll seek environments where women are also using intoxicants."

"Sounds like college."

"Ah. Yes." He studies me for a moment, then continues. "The opportunistic rapist will use force if necessary, but violence isn't his goal. However, for the other two types of rapists, violence is key, because they're motivated by the desire to dominate, hurt, and control. Angry rapists, as we call them, report feeling intense levels of rage toward women during the hours preceding the attack and are often motivated by revenge. They don't target particular kinds of women; anyone will do. They strike in a rage-motivated blitz attack, and they try to hurt the women emotionally and physically, often beating them."

"Are they likely to kill their victims?"

"It's not typical, though it can happen. Some angry rapists have stabbed women. On the other hand, the most dangerous rapist, the sadistic rapist, may well kill his victim. He craves complete control. Sadistic rapists plan every aspect carefully, from the type of victim, to the site of abduction, to the physical environment where they sequester, rape, and often torture her." He looks studiously away from me. "They particularly like to mutilate sexual body areas. Those rapes are likely to end in murder."

I'm nodding and writing. "Go on."

"One final thing to note is that serial sex offenders tend to exhibit strong spatial consistency in offense site selection."

I look up. "In English, *por favor*?"

"They like to take their victims from familiar places, perhaps a specific street, building, or park. They then take victims to a particular site—often the perpetrator's home, or some other site that he owns or can access freely. A site where he has maximum power, safety, and control."

"Where he feels secure enough to do whatever he wants."

"Exactly. Inside a rapist's home is the last place a victim ever wants to be."

I stop scribbling. *Inside a rapist's home.* I can't help wondering where Amber Waybridge is at this exact moment. I keep thinking about her abduction—maybe because she looks disturbingly like me. "Dr. Letley, let me focus on a specific case. Are you familiar with the recent kidnapping of a tourist in the French Quarter?"

I guess experts are obliged to claim they know everything, because although his eyes are vague, he nods.

To jog his memory, I pull out the flyer and spread it open on his desk. While Dr. Letley leans over for a good look, I wonder why I'm bothering. The Amber Waybridge case is not my story, not my business, and not my job. Bailey's already got a couple of guys from city desk working all the angles. And why should I care? What's a white tourist from Kansas got to do with me?

"Oh, yes," he nods. "This was on the news. Quite current, I believe."

"Yes. She hasn't been found yet. She was taken from a restaurant in the Quarter on Monday morning."

"Yes. Yes, I remember the details." He shakes his head. "Very unfortunate."

"What would your professional opinion be? I mean, about the kind of person who'd be likely to abduct a woman in that way?"

His voice turns stern. "I'm not a profiler, Miss Céspedes, and this is not TV. I work with actual, specific people. I can speak about patterns, but—"

"Yeah, okay. But if you were just going to speculate, off the record . . ."

His words come slowly. "*If* I were to speculate—which I wouldn't; it's not my area of expertise—"

"Of course."

"—then I'd probably say not only that the manner of this crime would require a great deal of physical strength, which is obvious, with the abduction of an able-bodied adult from a public place, but that it also shows a lot of confidence. I'd say he occupies a position of social authority of some kind, perhaps in an industry where strength is required."

"What about his intelligence?"

"I'd peg him as more street smart or charming than intellectual—again, because of the manner of his crime," Dr. Letley continues. "He took the victim from a public place with people all around. He likes risk. People don't intimidate him. He's no introvert."

"What do you mean about not being intellectual?"

"Well, a cleverer person might have been more careful, more cautious. This suspect relied on his strength and bravado. However, that might help the investigators on the case."

"How so?"

"He might be more inclined to take risks. He feels confident that his strength and charm will carry him through."

"What kinds of risks?"

"Well, for example, he might commit the rape—and the murder, if it turns out that way"—he raps his knuckles lightly on the wooden desk—"in his own home, rather than using some other, unrelated location as the kill site. Trace evidence in his home would make it much easier to link the crime to him." He frowns. "And this happened when? Monday morning?"

I nod.

"And the victim hasn't yet been found?"

"No."

"I'd posit that he's a sadistic rapist, a careful planner who chose the victim for specific aspects of her appearance—her coloring or body type. Those things matter to his fantasies. If she's still alive, he has her sequestered somewhere in an environment that he controls completely—and, as I said, he's bold enough to do it at home." He clears his throat and says delicately, "I would not predict a positive outcome."

Something occurs to me. "You're talking about rapists as if they're a different species from child molesters. Is that true?"

"Oh, excuse me. Mea culpa. That's a long-standing misconception in the field, based on outworn research. New studies reveal a high degree of sexual polymorphism among sex offenders."

"Sexual poly—?"

"Polymorphism. Switching patterns in any one or more of several dimensions, including the victim's age. Moving from adults to children, or vice versa."

"So hypothetically, a child molester could graduate to adult women as his targets?"

"Certainly. The latest research suggests that up to seventy percent of offenders move among different ages, genders—even different types of sex acts they prefer. Child molesters do trend slightly older than rapists, but that's only because many molesters have been abusing children for several years before they're caught and convicted."

"How many years, typically?"

"Oh, it varies. One study found an average of sixteen years."

"*Sixteen*? Before they're caught?"

"Unfortunately, yes. That's why it's so important to report and prosecute immediately. If they're not caught, they won't stop themselves."

I whistle softly. "Sixteen years is a long time."

"And a lot of children. In 2000, a polygraph study with men who'd been convicted on one or two counts of molestation showed that they had actually committed an average of three hundred and eighteen offenses, on an average of a hundred and ten victims."

"That was their *average*?" The beads of sweat around my hairline have evaporated, and I'm feeling cooler. Chilled, even. "Over a hundred kids?"

"Well, according to polygraph testing. There's some dispute—"

"Is there anything else my readers should know about child molesters?"

He explains that, contrary to the popular notion of molesters as loners, a surprising 50 percent of them are married or in a permanent heterosexual relationship. When it comes to recidivism, more of the married predators tend to reoffend. He meets my eyes and smiles. "Odd, isn't it?"

"So being married is actually a bad sign."

"It is. Another bad sign would be the level of violence in the sex crime, and this is true for rapists of adult women, too. The more force was used, the more likely it is that the perpetrator will offend again."

"Are there any good signs?"

"Yes, there are. Men who hold steady jobs, stay single, and continue to get regular therapeutic counseling after release are the ones least likely to rape or molest again."

I'm scribbling in my notebook: *steady employment, single, counseling*.

"The most dangerous stereotype," Letley continues, "is the whole stranger-danger myth. The fact is that around eighty percent of all child molesters—depending on which study you read—are people that the children know well. Molesters are usually family members, friends of the family, or authority figures from church or school."

"So the places we think are safe—"

"Really aren't. Right." He swivels back and forth a little in his chair.

"Okay, let me shift gears. My story deals with registered sex offenders, released guys who've supposedly been rehabilitated. Can you tell me what kind of rehabilitation treatment an offender is likely to get?"

"Sure." He nods. "Recidivism rates are high, so the core of my treatment philosophy is that the client has to be motivated to change. For offenders who *want* to repeat their behaviors—well, I'll be honest. Not much works."

Dr. Letley explains the standard treatment: cognitive behavioral therapy relapse prevention, or CBT, which focuses on changing thinking and behavior patterns. "But frankly, I'm sorry to say that it doesn't work all that well." He describes penile plesthysmography, or PPG, which is used to test child molesters for true rehabilitation. "Sensors are placed on the convicts' penises, and they're shown pictures of children in underwear. The devices record—well, they record—"

"Whatever comes up?"

"So to speak." His smile is faint. "Yes."

"Hard-on tests for perverts? Glad I don't work in that lab."

He clears his throat. "Yes. Well. A stronger approach is called learned empathy. It requires offenders to empathize with their victims, to recognize the damage that they've caused, and to take responsibility."

"Does it work?"

"Well, if we can get them to do it in a genuine way, it works well. When sex offenders are able to empathize with their victims' pain, see them as innocent, and feel remorse, then they are truly rehabilitated. They won't rape or molest again."

"So why don't all offenders do that?"

"It's difficult. Painful. Empathy for others requires the ability to feel one's own pain, and many offenders have blocked that off. Most grew up in violent or neglectful homes. Some—about forty-three percent of child molesters, for example—were sexually abused themselves. But most don't divulge this until mandatory counseling in prison. Keeping it a secret compounds the damage."

"It's not something people like to admit."

"No, or deal with. But if they can bear to relive and process their own past pain, they're usually able to recognize their responsibility in injuring others, to empathize. But that's traumatic material, and a lot of offenders resist exploring it."

"So, okay." I scan my notes. "CB, PPG, learned empathy—anything else?"

"We sometimes use pharmacological treatment."

"Meds?"

"Yes. In conjunction with other forms of therapy, we use specific drugs to decrease arousal, so that the offender can begin to reprogram himself. To change his arousal wiring, if you will."

"Like some kind of anti-Viagra?"

"If you like. Yes. In combination with other forms of treatment, it seems to help some offenders."

"Huh." I'm scribbling away. "Anything else? Castration?"

He frowns and moves on as though I haven't spoken. "One other therapy that's showing good results is EMDR."

"Which would be?"

"Eye movement desensitization and reprocessing. In its simplest terms—"

"Yeah, if you don't mind."

"In its simplest terms, the therapist helps a patient deliberately recall scenes of past trauma while moving the eyes back and forth. This allows patients to process old traumas that have been disrupting their current lives."

"Moving your eyes back and forth? Why does that work?"

"Some think it's effective because evolving humans looked around to scan for danger. Another possibility is that—well, you know how trauma shuts down language?"

"No," I say slowly. "What do you mean?"

"Our brain's system for storing memories is physiological, just like our digestive system and our circulatory system. When life goes well and we feel in control, our memories get stored in images and language. Later, we can easily access them with language; we can describe what happened. For example, I can tell you what I had for breakfast this morning, and how I got to the office. But during episodes of trauma, Broca's area—"

I shoot him a look.

"The area in the left side of the brain that turns experiences into language," he explains. "During trauma, Broca's area turns off. By moving the eyes to both sides, we tap both hemispheres of the brain, turning Broca's area back on, so the victim can begin to frame the trauma in language."

"So when someone can use language to tell the story of what happened—"

"Then they're on their way to psychological recovery. Yes. When patients recall specific episodes of past trauma while doing these eye movements in a safe situation, they experience increased bilateral activity of the anterior cingulate."

I must be looking pretty blank.

He smiles. "The patient calms down."

"Ah, okay. But how can you be sure that rehabilitation—whatever method you use—has been effective?"

His laugh is wry. "In this line of work, you learn pretty quickly that there's no such thing as sure. As I've said, the recidivism rate is high. But one thing I've noticed, just from working with the men, is that if you ask a genuinely rehabilitated offender to describe the therapy process, he's likely to give a very halting, qualified response—something like, 'I'm thinking about some things I never thought about before.' Real rehabilitation is slow and fairly painful, and it causes real cognitive shifts. Offenders need time to process these changes, and they do so with difficulty."

"What about guys who are trying to fake it?"

"Just the reverse. They're quite positive and enthusiastic, claiming that their rehabilitation was 'fantastic' or that they've learned their lesson. Their statements are simplistic and glib. They can't give specific details or describe an actual process of change."

"Just the candy coating."

"Yes, to convince a parole board, for example. But an experienced therapist won't be persuaded. It's just an act."

The interview winds down, and we rise to say good-bye. When I thank him, his strong, smooth hand in mine, the warmth in his eyes make me wish I could linger.

Dr. Letley's voice is lovely, dark and deep, but I have promises to keep. I thank him again, collect my things, and leave.

4

Thursday night! *¡Híjole!* I'm flying around the apartment, whipping it into decent hygienic shape before the girls get here. Uri's out for the evening, and he took his dog with him. The black beans and yellow rice are simmering in their separate pots, the garlic pork has been slow-cooking in the Crock-Pot all day, and the *plátanos* are good and black on the counter, waiting to be peeled, sliced, and seared in a skillet full of sizzling butter for dessert.

On the table sit a fresh bottle of Havana Club white rum, four glass tumblers, a bucket of ice, a paper towel laid with washed mint sprigs and leaves, a little dish of powdered sugar, and fat green limes already cut in half and waiting to be squeezed. There's a can of *guanábana* juice, too, if anyone wants to splash a little something different into her mojito.

I'm in cutoffs and a pink Saints hoodie, running barefoot through the rooms, grabbing up this and that discarded garment to toss in the hamper, doing a few swipes around the bathroom with lemon disinfectant wipes. ("For the lazy," my mother would say. She believes in a good sponge and the power of Bon Ami. "For this lazy right here," I tell her.)

The doorbell rings, and I open the door to Calinda, who hugs me, drops a handful of daisies on the counter, and collapses onto the couch.

"Do not even ask me how my day went," she says. "The New Orleans justice system is an oxymoron." She launches into an account of the day's legal mishaps, only to be interrupted by the arrival of Soline and Fabi, whose laughter bubbles up the stairs. Fabi is our resident Chicana princess, with her long fall of black hair, dark eyes, and the neat grace of a ballet dancer. They enter, giggling, and hugs go around, mojitos get muddled, and soon we're all drinking and laughing and sampling the black beans.

"This dinner is ready!" I finally announce, and we all carry our warm food, cold drinks, and conversation into the living room, where we settle down to talk about work, work, and more work; men; Iraq; movies; the presidential campaign primaries, and how we're torn between Hillary and Barack. All of us are die-hard lipstick feminists, but we're all antiwar, too, and we all have a racial or ethnic stake in change. And we're all in *loooove* with Obama. "Those *hands*," Calinda keeps murmuring, shaking her head. Being good guests, they also utter those little effusions so dear to the heart of a hostess: "Your cooking is amazing, Nola," "Oh my God, this pork melts in your mouth," and so on.

"Hey," says Fabi suddenly, "what are all these?"

She's spotted the perp files in a stack under the coffee table. Shit, shit, shit—I forgot to put them away. She stretches out a golden manicured hand.

I drop my fork with a clatter and scramble to my feet, snatching them up out of her reach. "Nothing."

"Oh, wait," says Calinda. "Aren't those the—"

"Nothing." I raise a meaningful brow at her. "They're nothing. They're just some stuff for work."

Fabi widens her eyes and rolls them at the other two women. "Well, excuse—"

"It's no big deal. Just let me put them away." I lug them down the hall to my room.

When I return, they're all still looking at each other, their eyebrows high. A little smirk of amusement plays on Fabi's pearl pink lips.

I force a laugh. "Okay, quit it, y'all. It's just boring work stuff. Come on, now. Help me clean up." I reach down to gather up their plates. "Seriously. *Ándale.*" I carry a stack of dishes to the kitchen and let them think what they want.

The fact that Fabi found the files irritates me more than if Calinda or Soline had noticed them. Her smirk irks me. An outsider might glance at Fabi and me and assume we've got a lot in common: both late twenties, both Latina, both *qué* cute—but the differences are vast, from little things, like the blow-out black glass of her hair where mine is a tangle of curls, to more significant stuff like a father at home, loads of money, and the legal right to travel back to her homeland to see *familia* every summer.

She can talk a fiery spiel about anti-Latino prejudice in New Orleans, but honestly, her parents' money has cocooned her from most of it. It's not like the Torres family was denied membership at the Beau Chêne Country Club, where Fabi spent summers perfecting her serve, or like they pile in the car all sweaty every summer and brave rural Louisiana and Texas to make it to the Mexico line. No, they fly straight from Louis Armstrong International Airport to the D.F. and catch a chartered jet down to their family's walled compound in San Cristóbal. And believe me, they may hail from Chiapas, but Fabi's relations sure weren't wearing black ski masks in '94.

The last time she was there, she brought us back key chains with little ski-masked Zapatista dolls from the *mercado*.

"Solidarity, *mujeres!*" she said, handing them out over drinks one evening.

But I know the depth of her solidarity. Her real key chain, the one she uses, is a bar of sterling silver, stamped TIFFANY.

Don't get me wrong. Fabi's a sweet girl—with all her money, she became a teacher, *verdad*—but her idealism is the kind that never breaks a nail. She has that rich girl sheen about her: real diamonds in her ears and a kind of delicacy that wrinkles its nose at the facts of most folks' daily lives. She acts as though we're more alike than we are, as though I've had all the same advantages, but what I've had to work hard for was her starting block.

When we first started hanging out, back when she showed me Cute Shirtless Guy, I tried to mention some of the things that separate us—oh, nothing crazy, not the projects or my mom passed out drunk on the couch—but just little things, like I have to watch my budget or I don't know my dad. And she would give me this look of confusion, then mild pity, and then change the subject to something I guess she figured was more upbeat or socially appropriate. Whatever. I guess if you want to move up in the world and be friends with upper-class people, that's the price you pay. You silence the parts of yourself that point out how privileged they are, or else they make you feel sordid, small, ashamed. To let Fabi know I'm working on something as real-world dirty as child molesters? Ain't happening.

I do like Fabi; we do have reasons to be solid. But a small, mean piece of me hates her, too: her privilege, her obliviousness, how easily she can avert her eyes from what life has rubbed my nose in. Even when I rush to hug her, part of me growls inside. But I keep it on a leash.

In the kitchen, Soline rinses dishes while I fry up the plantains. "Everything okay?" she murmurs, her hands under the warm stream.

"Yeah. Great."

"You good?"

There's no right answer that's true. "I'm good," I say, waving away her concern.

When the *plátanos* are crisp and hot on the outside, all melting sweetness within, I spatula them out into four little bowls and top them with curls of vanilla bean sorbet. It's dark out now, and cooler, so we take our desserts onto the balcony and sit cross-legged on the gray-painted wood. Relaxing again, I prolong the flavor, taking tiny bites, letting the sweetness dissolve on my tongue. Eating *plátanos* always takes me back to childhood and the feel of my mother's lap, the powdery smell of her neck.

Conversation turns, as it has for the past year, to Soline's upcoming wedding, in which we'll stand as bridesmaids. Knowing better than to humiliate her best friends, she's got us in very tolerable indigo sheaths. Her own dress, a white strapless French tulle billow—knee-length, to be modern—will glow on her lean dark frame. She refused to buy Edith Roché because Roché doesn't use African American models, but Soline cadged all her favorite elements from Roché's Luxe collection and sketched her own design. Then she gave the business to a seamstress friend of her mother's in Tremé and kept the money in the black community.

In New Orleans, if you want to mark your social status with a wedding, you say your vows in the St. Louis Cathedral in the French Quarter, dine at the classy old Omni hotel down the street, and dance on the rooftop until sunrise. That was exactly Soline's plan, and she'd had the details in place since seventh grade.

A Saturday in April, a beautiful bride and groom, and a honeymoon trip through Thailand by luxury train.

I always feel strangely naive when I hear my friends talk about weddings and romance. I listen like a kid. Sex I know, but the rest of it, the relationship part, I just don't tangle with, so it's all mysterious to me. How I treat men, how men treat me—it's all irrelevant, because things never get that far. Even if the sex is very good, I don't go back. It keeps things cleaner that way. I don't know. No feelings, no fondness, no games, no lies. Just come and go. The big easy.

"Hey, what's up, Nola?"

I look up from my empty bowl, startled.

"You just looked sad," says Calinda.

"No, I'm good." I scramble to my feet. "Just let me get these dishes in the sink."

Sometimes I'm no good at hanging out with my friends; I feel alien around them. I don't long for a wedding; I don't know what it's like to travel or have money, or even how it feels to have real family: grandparents, or a sister who calls every week just to talk. All I've got's my mom, and she's out of it half the time, lost in *Catholic Digest* or her whiskey. Sometimes around Fabi and them, I feel like I'm from another planet. When it comes to friendship, as with so many things, I'm only passing, passing for normal, watching how my friends play and then doing my best to keep up. In college, I studied DVDs of *Sex and the City* like I studied for exams.

How does Calinda do it? She glides from her gritty days at the DA's to girly chitchat about jewelry and dating without missing a beat. Maybe for her, coming from a good family and plenty of support—her parents are both pediatricians in Baton Rouge— it's not personal.

But for me, it's harder, and it wears me out sometimes. Some days, I don't want to go out to lunch someplace so expensive all I can do is get water and a cup of soup and say I'm dieting so they don't ask questions. Some days, I don't want to go shopping and act like nothing fits right while they pile their arms with packages. I don't want to smile and ask questions when talk drifts to what they did as girls: recitals, horses and sailboats, family vacations. Some days, I just don't feel up for the whole thing.

But I know what normal looks like. So I make the effort.

I make decaf lattes for everyone, and they come back inside and sit at the kitchen table, chatting about how train travel in Europe is nothing like Amtrak. Talk slides to where we'd each like to go most in the world if we could. Exotic place-names ricochet around the table: Tahiti, Paris, Nairobi, London. It's my turn.

"New York," I say. "Just New York. For good." I grin. "With a byline at the *Times,* of course."

Soline smiles softly, shakes her head, crosses her beautiful long legs. "New Orleans is your blood, girl. You know it is."

"*Chale.* It's New York all the way for me."

"Hmm. We'll just see about that." She looks down at her shimmering nails and smiles to herself.

We talk about the city's cane-syrup-slow rate of recovery, the plans that came out a year ago and have resulted in nothing more than a single brick walkway past a warehouse. What about the planners who envisioned New Orleans as the next Amsterdam, with dikes and locks and canals everywhere, a safe system, controllable, secure? Where has that plan gone? FEMA trailers still stand on lots, houses sag toward oblivion, and whole neighborhoods howl with abandon.

It's impossible to have a social occasion here without discussing it. No matter what else you try to talk about, all conversational roads lead back to Katrina and our abandonment by the government. The crime, the hope, and then the long, slow defeat. Now, almost three years after it happened, you can walk through the Quarter without seeing any evidence that a hurricane blew through here. There are whole sections of the city that look just fine, all back to normal, like Katrina never even happened. But our shared awareness never fades. Our lives as New Orleanians were split into before and after, and that doesn't go away. Even if no one mentions it by name, Katrina is always on the table.

When my friends finally rise to leave, it's on a subdued note, despite the food and drink and lively talk. I send them home with tight hugs and plastic containers full of leftover pork, black beans, and rice. When they're gone, the apartment swells with a sudden emptiness that I don't know how to fill.

You'd think I'd feel exhausted.

But I don't. I feel restless.

Bartenders will do in a pinch, but then you can't go back to that bar anymore. Construction workers will surprise you: for all their hooting and hollering, a lot of them turn out to be family men at heart—and if they're not married yet, they'll try to marry *you*. Plus, they've got that gritty dust on them, and when I have to spit and sputter during foreplay, it kind of breaks the mood.

For a surefire good fuck with no strings attached, I hang around the soccer fields and pick up *hondureños* and *guatemaltecos* for quick and dirty assignations. No strings, no romance, no meeting anybody's family. And definitely no waking up together at my apartment for lengths of buttered toast dunked in strong coffee, sitting on the sunny balcony with our feet up, besotted by pheromones and dreaming up some bullshit future together. No, always at their place, or sometimes right on the metal bleachers if I'm in a hurry for it. No conversation, their English as busted up as my Spanish. Since Katrina, New Orleans attracts a steady tide of Mexican and Central American men. They're always moving on, fanning out, so you get good turnover.

At Audubon Park, City Park, or the levee, there are dozens of teams full of lovely brown men, muscled and glistening, with terrible English. After a game, they're happy and high on themselves (I always choose one from the winning team), and if you don't mind sweat, you can accomplish a lot under the bleachers or in a parked car. Sometimes *los machos* get angsty about rubbers, but all you have to do is get up, dust yourself off, and make like you're leaving, and then, damn, don't that latex roll on fast. That plus spermicide plus the Pill keep me about as safe as a Catholic girl can be. When the pope can get pregnant, he can talk to me about contraception.

It's the best way. When the sex is lame, you never have to see the guy again, much less sponge-bathe his ego. And when it's good, it can be wicked.

Restless after my girls take off, I head to the levee, still in my cutoffs and pink hoodie. I sit on the sidelines and watch for a while, picking at my toenail polish.

There's a guy who looks a little older, working defense. He's built like a swimmer: long torso, huge shoulders, legs a little too short for his body. Someone should have told him soccer ain't his game. But he's doing well despite himself, quick and deft, darting in and out. He passes, not hogging the ball, not jonesing for limelight. I feel myself warming to him. He runs like a bull, head down; all the power's in his hips and driving shoulders. I know how he'll fuck: hungry, direct, competent but not showy. Unabashed, at home in his body.

When he shoots out a foot and takes down a young jerk, the guys on the other team call him out. He raises his hands, shrugging wildly in false innocence. *¿Qué? ¡Qué!*

Hmm—not afraid to be a bastard when necessary. I find myself grinning.

His team wins, the crowd thins, and after a little mild flirting, me working my weak Spanish, we go to my car.

He proves me right. He's expert, unhesitating. He's so good I start to laugh—he knows exactly where to put his hands and mouth, and how firmly, and for how long. When I laugh, he looks up but doesn't break his rhythm. This, I could actually get used to. He just *does* the thing, no questions. No talk.

When we're done, I'm sweatier than he is, and I flop back into the driver's seat, switch the car on, and crank the AC. My version of afterglow. I sit there panting and blissed out, already starting to forget him.

He's tugging his nylon shirt and shorts back into place. "May I have your telephone number?" he asks.

"I don't think that's a good idea." I don't give my number out to men. Not even men like this one.

The car hums.

"What's your name?" he asks.

What the hell. "Nola."

"Nola," he says, like it's the word for something delicious. We sit in the cool dark together, staring straight ahead out the windshield. "Well, Nola, I'd like to give you my phone number."

"I won't call." The dark, empty fields stretch in front of us.

"I would like anyway for you to have it."

This is getting annoying. Now I just want him out of my car. "Yeah, okay." Whatever. When I reach across to open the glove box for a pen, his body heat ripples across my shoulder and arm. He finds a receipt between the seats and writes for a minute.

When he's finished, he hands me the slip of paper solemnly, like it's a Japanese business card or something. He turns toward me and holds out his hand as if to shake. Jesus. Okay, fine. I give him my hand. He shakes it like he's being presented to the queen.

"Nola, I am Bento, and this has been a lovely evening. Thank you."

I laugh. But it's true.

"Yes, it has," I finally say. My tongue struggles, but I push the words out: "Thank you."

Letting my hand go, he smiles with delight, like I'm a child raised by wolves who's just used a fork for the first time. Like he'll be returning to report good news to the other researchers back at the lab.

"Good night," he says, and my passenger door shuts, and he's gone. My hand feels strangely cool without his warmth around it.

After a soccer pickup, I love to slip into my apartment slick with sweat and the funk of sex and move to the bathroom without turning on a single light and run the shower in the dark, to stand in the fall of cool water, its soft rain gentling my flesh as I stand, mouth open, eyes closed, replaying each good moment—just the highlights. I edit out anything tedious.

Tonight I stand in the shower for a long, long time.

Alone in bed with my little lamp on, I finger the receipt, the carefully printed numerals and his name in a formal script. *Bento.* An odd name.

An odd guy, all told. *A lovely evening.* Weirdly old-world. But hot. Every inch the bull he'd looked on the field. I crumple the receipt and toss it across the room. It lands on the dresser.

It's true, what people call soccer: the beautiful game.

5

At nine o'clock on Friday morning, I'm driving through the leafy streets of the city, heading to Orleans Parish Prison to interview the inmates and guards about their views on sex offenders.

Whatever T. S. Eliot might say, April is not the cruelest month—not in New Orleans. It's full of sweetness. Jasmine blossoms blow their soft scent everywhere, and each tiny yard has a profusion of gardenias, sweet peas, purple spiced petunias.

Black and orange love bugs fly through the air copulating, their butts nailed together by lust. The heavy pink heads of cabbage roses nod out their drinkable perfume, making you stop in your tracks just to breathe. The air is lazy, sunny, soft, and cool. Days are in the eighties, and nights are in the sixties. The humidity is light, not the hot swamp air for which summer's notorious.

The substance-induced mass psychosis of Mardi Gras is over, but bright strings of metallic beads still hang festively from balcony railings, utility wires, and the street-spanning branches of oaks. The thick, cloying heat of summer, with its threat of hurricanes, has not yet begun.

Everyone's happy: the construction crews out adding more evacuation lanes to I-10, the golfers at Audubon Park. Even the waiters and waitresses at Café du Monde, sworn to surliness, let a breezy smile lift their lips.

April is the cruelest month, Eliot wrote, because spring reawakens yearning, mixing memory and desire.

Perhaps that was true in Eliot's Englands, old and new, where soil freezes and people wrap themselves in wool.

But here in New Orleans, the land never hardens. It seethes and surges, alive with heat and moisture. Green leaves grow lush all year, and vines spiral out, clinging to whatever they can grab.

Here, memory and desire are always mixed, and desire stays awake.

When I turn off Tulane Avenue onto South Broad, there's not a parking spot to be seen. I circle the block a couple of times, cruising slowly past the big Art Deco courthouse where carved stone proclaims, THE IMPARTIAL ADMINISTRATION OF JUSTICE IS THE FOUNDATION OF LIBERTY. As if anything impartial happens inside those walls.

The prison looms a pale peach putty color, its high walls topped by looping razor wire. High up in the guard tower, a couple of ferns hang, yellow with thirst.

On South White, I pass the DA's office, where Calinda works. Circling the blocks of little shotgun shacks that now function as the detritus of the law, I finally find a parking spot in front of Dionne's Anytime Bail Bonds: DON'T POUT, WE'LL GET YOU OUT.

When I planned my interviews with the guards and inmates at Orleans Parish Prison to learn their views on convicted sex offenders, I decided against my usual outfit: white, butt-cupping pants, heeled sandals, and a red blouse cut just a shade too snug for church. On the streets of the French Quarter, it wouldn't turn a single head; New Orleans, after all, is the city of exposed flesh, of tits flashed for Mardi Gras beads, of tube tops tight as Saran Wrap. Even chunky chicks wear their skirts so clingy you can scope out the degree of cellulite beneath. It's a way of life.

But in Orleans Parish Prison, *matronly* would be the most advisable dress code for a female of any species. I dressed in a plain gray pullover and loose khakis, but the reception I get is still loud, crude, and ongoing.

It doesn't really scare me. I just laugh and wave. They're behind bars—at least, the inmates are—and anything but leering is more than the guards' jobs are worth.

Once we all get over my appearance, they settle down pretty quick. I sit with the guards in orange plastic chairs in a bleak office, and my little silver Olympus recorder starts filling up with their remarks. What I learn about rapists—anger problems, loss of control—is unsurprising, but I'm particularly interested in what they tell me about child molesters.

"They're usually quiet guys. Keep to themselves," says one guard. "No trouble or anything. But you know. They look weak. And their crime—well, it pisses people off. They're easy marks."

Talking to the inmates through a scratched Plexiglas wall, my Olympus held close to the receiver's earpiece, I learn that pedophiles—not all sex offenders, but child molesters in particular—are despised even here, among society's other rejects.

"Fuckin' kid fuckers? I fuck 'em up," one guy growls, smacking his fist into his palm, a cliché. Even among criminals, there's a hierarchy, and pedophiles are the lowest of the low.

Rumor even has it that child molesters die mysterious deaths in prison at a higher rate than other kinds of criminals. Cops don't always feel the need to get real thorough, it seems, when they investigate the death of a child molester. A smirking guard assures me, sans statistics, that such deaths never happen in Orleans Parish, and the men around him laugh.

When I finally turn off my Olympus, I have more than two hours of raw stuff from which to cull quotations. I thank the guard who's led me deep into the shadowed heart of the prison, and he volunteers to see me back out. I walk down the long cement corridor beside him, my thin heels clicking past whistles and catcalls, guys licking their lips, guys with blackened fingernails wrapped around the bars of their cells, muscled guys who could snap my neck like a chicken's.

I could stare straight ahead like a scared person acting tough, but I don't. Fact is, a lot of them are in here for nothing worse than possession, and we all know how that goes down for black and brown. *Judge not, lest ye be judged.* I wave and call good-bye and smile big and beautiful like I'm Marilyn Monroe performing for the USO.

Because ultimately, I'm the one who gets to go back out into the warmth and jasmine and daylight, and they're stuck here in the grimy darkness, breathing piss and bleach. They didn't have to talk to me, but they did.

So I give them something pretty to remember, a dollop of something sweet. A little lagniappe, you might say.

After the interviews at Orleans Parish Prison, I take I-10 north toward Metairie to interview Mike Veltri, my first rapist. My belly's growling, so I head up Causeway to Morning Call for lunch and a final quick flip through Veltri's file.

Inside, the large space is cool and echoey with talk. MORNING CALL COFFEE STAND, read the gold letters on the wooden arch. I pull up a stool and set my handbag down on the wide gray marble slab of the counter. One tall waitress is working the whole room. I pull a napkin from the grimy TidyNap metal dispenser. *For over 100 years New Orleans' most famous coffee drinking place, established*

1870, says the napkin in red letters. To anyone looking closely, the grout between the marble slabs is a topography of filth. I check my cell for messages: nothing.

The menu is simple. For six dollars, you can get any entrée: craw-fish étouffée, jambalaya, red beans and rice, gumbo, or corn and shrimp. You can get beignets with your café au lait or hot choco-late. On the counter sits a tin shaker full of powdered sugar, since Morning Call serves their beignets bare.

The waitress's greeting comes with minimal fuss.

"Take your order?" She's looking at the parking lot outside. Only by proximity can I be sure she's talking to me.

"Red beans."

She walks away, and my mind drifts back to one of the rapists in the prison, Jakey Alvaretto, a friendly guy, young, whose hands on the table between us had seemed almost gentle.

"I can't really explain it," he said. "I like women. I like you." In-stead of feeling creeped out, I felt strangely touched. His eyes were kind and bright. "But something just comes over me. I get so angry. And then . . ."

I kept my voice soft. "And then?"

"I get violent. I just do. It's like I hate them. It's like I don't even see them; I keep seeing my dad. But then when I'm done, and they're crying, I don't. I don't hate them anymore. I just feel all crazy and fucked up and scared."

"Your dad?"

"He used to beat my mom. We could hear it at night. He put her in the hospital."

"Where was this?"

"Just over in Algiers."

"And nobody called the police? Child services?"

"Oh, they called. Cops came out to the house I don't know how many times." His smile was wry. "You think that does anything?"

He talked about the prison's job training program and how he hoped to get work as a cook after his release.

But violence witnessed during childhood makes rapists much more likely to reoffend. I kept my stats to myself and wished Jakey luck.

None of the child molesters in the prison would talk with me. They didn't want to draw attention to themselves, a guard said.

Who knows what makes them target kids? Their desires get wired wrong at an early age, and they get punished for it, punishment without end. We condemn them so glibly: they're sick, or evil, or perverts. Animals. Monsters. But labels don't prevent more of the same.

I open Mike Veltri's file, but for some reason I can't concentrate. My eyes jitter and skip across the facts, the dates, the ages and names of the women he raped. I sigh and close the file, and the waitress plunks down a child-sized glass of water and a fat bowl of food. The red beans are hot in their thick, tasty sauce, and the rice beneath is soft and swollen. It's a good, cheap meal. I fortify myself.

Maybe this story will work. Maybe it'll end up like one of those multipart investigative features that run on the front page of *The New York Times*, and Bailey will nominate me for awards and move me straight to the city desk, and I'll be liberated from Beanie Baby Land forever. And then I'll write something amazing, and *The New York Times* will call, and I will be so out of here.

Mike Veltri's one-story ranch in Metairie was not damaged by the storm. Gray siding, a flat green parcel of grass, a straight white sidewalk. Flat-topped shrubs under the windows. Nondescript. Forgettable.

Exactly like Mike Veltri, as I learn when he opens the door. White, average height, medium build, middle-aged, with a black crew cut. In jeans and a white T-shirt, he has a jaw like a semi and a friendly smile. Unless you happen to catch the flicker of belligerence in his eyes, he isn't the kind of guy you'd look at twice. Until Megan's Law passed, Mike Veltri's forgettability had been his ally.

I shake his hand and go inside.

"You want something to drink, darling?" The typical New Orleans welcome. When we come in from outdoors, we're always sweating, always thirsting.

"Yes, thanks. That would be great." The house is modest, boring, with overstuffed blue couches and a flat-screen TV. I know from his file that he's been here for two years. No art hangs on the walls.

"I got water, tea, or Diet Dr Pepper. Or beer, if you want it."

"Tea, thanks." I turn on my Olympus and set it on the coffee table. Six women, all in their late teens or twenties. I hear the rattle of ice cubes in a glass, and then the hiss of his soda can opening.

Settled across from each other with our drinks, we begin.

"Okay, Mr. Veltri. Why don't you start by telling me how things are for you now."

"Yeah, sure." He wipes his mouth with the back of his hand. "I'm just happy to be out, you know? I hate prison. My term was longer this time. Three years. I had time to think. I decided I didn't want to live like that anymore. You know?" I nod. "Always afraid of getting caught. Knowing people hate you. Hiding it from everyone. Even yourself." I didn't need to ask what *it* was. "All of it. I was just sick of it."

"So what did you do?"

"In court, everyone kept talking about the victims, the victims— which felt crazy to me! Because *I* was the victim, you know? I was the one in cuffs and everything. It drove me nuts. So then later, in my cell, with all this time to think, I tried to figure it out." He leans forward, and his hands squeeze his knees. "I kept trying to imagine that the women were the victims. And little details started coming back to me. You know?" He sighs and looks at the wall over my head. "When I was doing it to them, I didn't care. I know that sounds bad, but there it is. I'm just being real with you. Their faces weren't important. But in my cell, I made myself remember their eyes. How they would cry, or just look dead. Then I remembered this one woman that peed herself. When I was doing it to her, I told myself she was just excited. Like a woman gets wet, you know?"

I keep my face very still and pleasant, a mask of agreement.

"But in my cell, I thought about her face, how scared she looked. And then I knew the truth. I knew I was lying to myself." He looks at his hands, turns them over.

He talks easily for an hour, explaining the slow process by which he came to see his victims as innocent, as people he had hurt. When he came up for parole, his remorse was considered sincere, and with help from the psychologist—"who knew big words for stuff"—he convinced the parole board that he'd been rehabilitated.

"This is all wonderful material, Mr. Veltri. I think the readers of the *Times-Picayune* are going to be very helped by your story."

"Sure." He shrugs. "Happy to get the word out."

"So tell me how being a registered sex offender affects you today."

"Well, you know"—he rubs his stubble, staring thoughtfully at the blank TV—"that law was part of what made me try to change. I knew there'd be no more hiding. You know? No starting fresh, like before. I knew people would be on to me, watching me." He shrugs again. "Oh, I know guys who've jumped it. I could have done it. Move to another state, don't register, try to slip between the cracks. It's not so hard. But I don't know. I was tired, I guess. I didn't want to have to run, always looking over my shoulder. I was born in this city, and I aim to die here. Maybe if I had more energy, was younger. But I'm forty. These are my roots. So anyway, I guess the law motivated me to try and change." He brightens. "Worked, too."

"You don't feel those desires anymore?"

"Nope. Not generally. I practiced in prison. If I felt the urge, I'd make myself think about their faces. Their eyes. And I'd feel so bad!" His voice is suddenly loud, a strange mix of anger and pain. "So damn bad. It would just kill it for me. You know." He looks away. "The urge."

"Some people are said to be excited by the victim's fear."

He snorts. "Yeah, well, that ain't me. It makes me feel sick. It made me see how sick I was. In the past."

"And now?"

"I get the urge maybe once a month or so, and I push it away. I just picture their faces, it goes pretty quick. I check in with my parole officer. I go to counseling."

"How often is that?"

"Counseling? Once a week, every Thursday."

"How is that for you?"

"It's all right. I'm not much for the whole talking about your feelings thing, but it sort of helps. It's a good place to talk about it. You know? It's not the kind of thing you can tell to just anyone."

"And how have your neighbors treated you?"

"It hasn't been bad. No flyers up or anything, like some guys get. I keep my yard nice, wash my car, keep to myself. I got friends down in Algiers I go see; I go down there to hang out. Here, I just keep to myself."

"Are your neighbors friendly?"

"Well, they don't invite me to cookouts. Know what I mean?" His laugh is harsh. "But they're all right. I steer clear."

"What do you mean, steer clear?"

"I steer way clear of women and kids. You know? I don't try to say hi or nothing like that. Just keep my distance. Don't do anything that could freak people out. Like, I used to walk up to Deanie's every afternoon, get a catfish po'boy and a beer after my shift ended at two o'clock." Deanie's is a classic Bucktown joint a couple of blocks south of Lake Pontchartrain, a warehouse where you sit at wooden tables and the seafood comes wrapped in paper. "Or I'd go over to Melius, sit and have a beer, talk to the guys. I don't do that anymore."

"And why is that?"

"You kidding me? There's two schools between here and there." He's right: the parish public school Riviere Elementary and St. Louis King of France, a Catholic school. "Two o'clock in the afternoon, I don't want people to think I'm cruising the kids."

"So you just don't go to Deanie's anymore."

"I go later in the evening. Or I drive up. Better safe than sorry, you know? I don't want to get sent to Angola because some mama gets scared and reports me. And plus, this here's Louisiana. People got guns." I think of my own gun, snug in its handbag holster. "I don't want some guy blowing me away 'cause I looked at his wife funny."

"Good point." I nod. "Could I send a photographer out? I'd like to shoot you walking. Like, walking in the evening, up toward the lake."

"Huh?"

"It would be a distance shot, from behind. Your face wouldn't show. I think it would make a great visual for the article."

"Yeah, I guess. Sure."

"Thank you. Someone will call you about it." I sip my iced tea, and something occurs to me. Even though it's a diversion, I can't help myself. "Mr. Veltri, I'm assuming you know about the Amber Waybridge case that's been in the news recently. The young woman who was abducted from the Quarter?" I start to pull out the flyer, but he's already nodding.

"Oh, yeah. That's just crazy."

"Crazy?"

"Man's got no fear, that's one thing for sure. Taking the girl in broad daylight like that, right out from under her family's nose. Or he's desperate. Can't control himself. Can't be smart."

"Be smart?"

"Ordinarily, you'd want to get to know the girl a little, build trust, get her alone, get her used to you, maybe get her drunk. Then do it in a way that won't cause a lot of attention. Not him. He just walked in and grabbed her."

"What else can you tell me?"

"About this guy? Well, ten to one he's got a place near that restaurant, a place he could take her. Somewhere close. He wouldn't want to carry her too far on foot. She could get away, cause a commotion. So either he's got a place with some privacy right there in the Quarter, or a car parked real close that he could throw her into."

"Which would you guess?"

"Well, if he's smart, it'd be a car. Get out of there pronto, go somewhere out of town where people ain't looking."

"And if he's not so smart?"

"Hard to say. If he's got a place in the Quarter and he took her there, that's kind of crazy. He'd have to be a cocky bastard. Like I say, no fear."

"You wouldn't do that."

"No way. You don't shit where you eat. Excuse my French. Not with something splashy like that, a kidnapping. You're going to draw cops right to you. You should take her far away, someplace remote that's got nothing to do with you."

"To play it safe."

"To play it safe, yeah." He looks suddenly suspicious, as though I'm asking him to implicate himself, so I switch focus.

"Mr. Veltri, let's talk about you some more, what it's been like for you here since your release." My glass is almost empty. "It must get lonely."

"It ain't so bad," he says. "I got friends. I see women, time to time."

"You're dating?"

"You could say." He grins.

"What would *you* say?"

"I'd say I got women I see, time to time."

"I see." Prostitutes. I clear my throat and smile brightly. "Okay, let's change gears. Overall, Mr. Veltri, how would you rate the quality of your life?"

"Rate the quality? I never thought about it." He rubs his jaw. "On a scale of one to ten, I'd give it about a six. Six or seven."

"And why is that?"

"Well, you know, compared to prison. What all happens in there. Anything's pretty good, compared to being inside."

"What happens in prison?"

He eyeballs me. "Come on, honey. You know what happens in prison."

"Beatings?"

He nods. "Yeah. Beatings."

"Rapes?"

He shifts on the sofa. "Yeah, all that."

"I know from your file that you were first incarcerated at twelve, in juvenile detention, as an accessory to auto theft."

"Yeah. So?"

"What was juvenile detention like for you?"

He snorts. "What do you mean? Juvie's juvie. It sucks, you do your time, you get out."

"Do the same kinds of things that happen in prison—rapes, beatings—happen in juvie?"

He scowls into his can of Diet Dr Pepper. "What do you care?"

"I'm just trying to get at the quality of your experiences when you were in juvenile detention. At twelve."

He turns the soda in his hands, squeezes its metal. "What do we got to be talking about that for?"

"Research suggests that many sex offenders were themselves molested at an early age. Juvenile detention sometimes includes sexual violence. So I'm just wondering if maybe—"

"Jesus Christ," he says, his voice quiet with venom. "I didn't know you were coming here to dig up that shit."

"I'm sorry, Mr. Veltri." My voice is low and smooth. "We don't have to talk about this if it makes you uncomfortable." I glance deliberately down at the Olympus, its flashing red light. He glances, too.

"It's all right," he says slowly. "I'm just—we're just starting to talk about that in counseling. I'm not real okay with it yet."

"I understand."

But it's the wrong thing to say. His eyes snap hard.

"Bullshit," he says. "If you been through it, you understand. Otherwise, you don't know shit. Period. Ain't the kind of thing you understand with your head."

I keep my voice calm. "Why is that?"

"I don't know." His voice quiets. "It's—outside thinking, somehow. It works on you. . . ." He stares down at the worn, tan backs of his hands. "I don't know. It just works on you."

"I see."

"It's hard to put into words."

"Well, I certainly appreciate—"

"Yeah." He looks up. "We done here?"

Ah. I slide the strap of my handbag onto my shoulder. I've worn out my welcome. "Unless there's anything else you'd like to add."

He shakes his head, and his smile comes back. "Naw. You talked me right out! You're a good little reporter." I hate being called a little anything, but I smile and stand up.

"Thank you so much, Mr. Veltri." When I lean over to shake his hand, his eyes dart to the front of my blouse. They don't come back up.

"No problem." His voice has thickened.

"I'll just see myself out," I say, and I grab my Olympus and go.

As I gun my Pontiac down I-10, I dial Calinda's number.

"Hey, girl," she says. "What're you doing?"

I blow past a semi. "Listen, do you think you could go over to the Copper Pot with me and walk the job?"

"The restaurant where that girl went missing?"

"One and the same. Thought we could check it out."

There's a thoughtful pause. "If you give me half an hour to get some information together, I could do it. And I'm dying to get out of this office anyway."

"See you there."

When I arrive, there's no yellow crime scene tape, just Calinda waiting out front, looking excited. "I've got the lowdown on the whole thing," she says. Inside the restaurant, it's business as usual: a few late-afternoon diners sprinkled around the room, and wait staff sauntering through with their trays.

Consulting a hastily scrawled floor plan someone's faxed her, Calinda walks me through what happened, showing me the table where the young woman sat, the hallway she went down. In the dark corridor, she scuffs the toe of her bone-colored pump against the floor near a wall. "It looks like about here's where they found the bracelet."

I squat and press my fingertips to the cool cement. Grit and dust. During questioning, it had come out that the father wasn't just her employer—that they'd been lovers, and that the bracelet had been a gift, the promise of more, of a possible future together. Real diamonds, real gold. She wouldn't have let that go without a fight. Still crouching, I close my eyes and breathe in, trying like a crime-show psychic to sense the struggle that took place here, but the corridor is cool and dark and just smells of food.

I sigh and push to my feet.

"He could have hidden in one of these," says Calinda, pushing open a pantry full of industrial-sized canned goods and janitorial supplies.

"Or he could have been in the kitchen."

"An employee? No. All the staff were questioned, and everyone's story checks out."

"He could have been a customer in the restaurant."

Calinda looks at me thoughtfully. "Just sitting there?"

"Watching. Waiting."

"And then when someone he likes heads down the hall . . ."

We look out at the diners, all so innocuous in the sunlight.

"Maybe so." She nods. "Maybe so. And gets her out how?"

I gaze at the bright dining room. "No matter how strong he is, he couldn't have muscled her out past everyone. Someone would have noticed."

"And he couldn't have taken her through the kitchen."

We walk down the hallway to the door marked EXIT and push it open. Outside, the alley is lined with Dumpsters, softly reeking with the faint winelike smell of garbage on a warm day. The alleyway's so narrow that the rooftops nearly touch overhead.

"If you had a car parked right here," says Calinda, gesturing, "you could push her into the front seat with you, especially if you had some kind of weapon to threaten her with."

"Trunk," I say. "Trunk's safer. Think how slow traffic is around here. If she were in front, she could jump out at a corner."

She nods slowly, as if seeing it unfold in front of us.

"Then you can drive her to wherever your crime site is." We look down the alley. It's only a few yards to the corner, and then the car would have melted into traffic. "He could have gotten her out in a couple of minutes, tops."

She nods again. "Less, if he'd had practice."

"And then if his kill site's nearby—"

"Jesus, Nola. Don't call it that. She might still be alive."

I give her a long, steady look.

She sighs. "Yeah, all right. Probably so, probably so. But you don't have to jinx the poor girl."

"Is the abduction MO similar to the previous two murders?" I ask. We head back into the dark corridor of the restaurant.

"It is. Those women were both taken from the Quarter, and both in the morning hours. Both local, though, and both prostitutes, so the media wasn't as—"

But I'm not listening anymore. "What does that tell you, the fact that he takes them in the morning?"

Her brow wrinkles. "He works the night shift?"

"Or he doesn't work at all." Our heels tap on the tiles of the bright dining room. "Which means what? He's retired? Rich?"

"Or on disability."

"Yeah. He's strong, though, so not too old or too disabled."

She pushes the front door open and we step out onto the bright sidewalk. "Forensics thinks both of the bodies were dumped between three and four A.M.," she says.

"Smart. Quietest time of night." I'm still thinking out loud. "So he takes them in the morning, and then he has all day to play with them before night gives him cover. Which means he has a secure location somewhere."

She nods.

"And they both washed up?"

"Yeah." She pulls her keys from her purse as we walk toward her silver Prius.

"So if there's a correlation—prostitutes, river—will he dump this body somewhere else, since she's a nice middle-class girl?"

"Nola, she's *not dead yet*."

"Right, right. But think of it from his perspective. If he's in the restaurant, watching her eat, then he can see she's obviously no working girl. As far as he knows, she's a pretty young wife out with her husband and kids."

Calinda chews her lip. "Maybe he's getting more confident as he goes."

"Or more desperate."

"Hey." She frowns at me with sudden concern. "What's your big interest in all this, anyway?"

I shrug. "Just a hobby."

"No, seriously, Nola. What's got you so interested in this case? And all those files you wanted. What kind of story does Lagniappe have you working on?" She pauses. "Or is this something personal?" She squints at me.

"No, look," I say, "don't be silly. It's just something extra I'm helping out with at the paper. No big deal. Anyway, before you take off—how do you know all this stuff, anyway? Where the bracelet was found? All the details?"

The corner of her mouth twirls upward in a sweet, sly grin. "Nothing on the record, now," she says, "but it could be I'm seeing someone on the force."

"Seriously?"

"Hell, no, not seriously." She laughs. "We're just fooling around."

"No. I mean, you're really dating a cop?" Call me an old-school projects girl, but dating the police feels like sleeping with the enemy.

Calinda looks at me, puzzled. "Sure. He's cute." She waves a hand back toward the restaurant. "And useful, obviously." We hug, and she slides into her car.

I watch her drive away. In the Quarter with no pressing plans, I amble over toward Blake Lanusse's. I want to check out the convent again. I once did a Lagniappe story on the architecture of the Quarter, and the convent's history gave me a fascinating glimpse into class and sex in early New Orleans.

In the 1700s, the fledgling colony of Louisiana needed a perpetual influx of warm bodies—which France, sick of its criminals, was only too happy to provide. Prostitutes, thieves, and the merely homeless were rounded up on the streets of Paris, their shoulders seared with the French branding iron, a fleur-de-lis, which signified their life sentences as criminals, and herded against their will on ships to the New World. When they rioted in protest, as 150 French girls did in 1719, police shot them.

In the New Orleans colony, with no other French women available, even these corrections girls, as the women were called, were desirable mates for soldiers and settlers. The men forgave the girls their pasts of prostitution and poverty, married them, and let them begin again. Crossing the Atlantic had sponged their slates clean.

In 1727, the convent was founded by twelve Ursuline nuns. The following year, the first shipment of good, clean virgins from Paris arrived, well bred and well raised by bourgeois families who couldn't find them suitable husbands at home in France. Eager to be wives, the girls hoped for sudden wealth in the New World.

Each girl had been given a box—a casket, it was called—in which to carry her belongings across the ocean. When the young ladies arrived at the Ursuline Convent to be educated in music, languages, religion, and the exacting French standards of homemaking, they were known as *filles à la cassette*. Casket girls.

When the shipments of casket girls arrived, pure as dolls still unopened in their boxes—and far more desirable than street whores—a caste system sprang up. As New Orleans society grew and solidified, it became a matter of status to claim descent from a nice, clean casket girl rather than from a corrections girl.

Casket girls were valuable commodities, and the Ursuline Convent, though just two blocks from the debaucheries of Bourbon Street, provided an elegant, pious, and well-chaperoned warehouse until they married. In the 1750s, the current structure was built. Inside the high white walls, nuns taught the girls to play Italian Baroque compositions on the pianoforte and to embroider with silver needles thin as a thread.

Two and a half centuries later, the Ursuline Convent still stands, a damp dove gray—still walled, still vast, still fronted by a formal French garden. Now the daughters of the wealthiest New Orleanians, girls from five years old to eighteen, are tutored within its walls. Pretty and privileged, they file into the school every morning and out each afternoon, wearing their pleated skirts and monogrammed blouses, their knee socks and barrettes.

Three o'clock finds me sitting on a bench across from Blake Lanusse's condo—looking, I hope, just like any tourist. Dark sunglasses hide my eyes.

A bell tolls, and the gate of the convent school swings open. Girls of every description stream out onto Chartres, flooding the sidewalk in both directions, pulling out hair ribbons, whipping out cell phones, jumping into the BMWs and Jaguars that wait idling, and talking, talking, talking. The second-story curtains twitch apart, and the pale shape of a face appears. I can see a hand curled around the red fabric. For several minutes, I watch his still figure. The swarm of girls thins to a trickle.

Eventually, the last two stragglers head southwest on Chartres, both of them still fussing with their backpack zippers, chattering blithely in their matching uniforms. They look about ten years old.

The face disappears, and the curtains fall closed. I stretch my legs and watch the convent school settle into quietude.

But then the door of Blake Lanusse's building opens, and a man shuts it softly behind him and begins to walk southwest.

Panicked excitement shoots through me. I pull the digital camera from my handbag, hit the zoom, and suddenly the face is crystal-clear: pale eyes, heavy features, a handsome face now corrupt with too much drink. If it's Lanusse, prison aged him. His dark hair is thinner than it was in the mug shot.

I don't want to see him this closely, this clearly—the intimacy of it makes my stomach heave—but I snap three shots in quick succession so I can compare them later to the photos in his file. I tuck the camera in my purse slowly and let him get some distance. In his khakis and loose T-shirt, he could be anyone.

It's weird how people never look behind them. It makes tailing someone easier than you'd think. All the way down Chartres, Blake Lanusse walks half a block ahead of me, unaware of my presence, while the two girls scamper half a block ahead of him, oblivious to his. The girls laugh and elbow each other, showing each other things on their cell phones. We pass the Hotel Provincial and the Hotel Chateau; we cross St. Philip, Dumaine, and St. Ann. His build is tall, his shoulders broad and muscled. Even though he's loaded down with a few extra pounds now, he knows how to carry himself. His gait is easy, confident. As he moves through the streets, I find myself wondering if he's strong enough— late forties, post-prison—to force a woman down a corridor and into the trunk of a waiting car.

One thing for sure. Amber Waybridge, as described on the nightly news, was a bold and joyful young woman. She wouldn't have curled silently in the darkness, waiting for rescue. She would have fought.

We're on the pedestrians-only segment of Chartres between

St. Louis Cathedral and the landscaped green park of Jackson Square. Tourists are everywhere, and I have to hustle to keep the girls in sight. Blake Lanusse is closing the distance between himself and them. Just as I'm wondering what kind of parents let their ten-year-old daughters roam the Quarter alone, the girls skip, arms linked, into the grand entryway of the historic Pontalba Apartments, and my question is answered: very rich parents. With a third-floor view over Jackson Square from iron lacework balconies dripping with blossoms, New Orleans real estate doesn't get any more prime.

Lanusse pauses, then collects himself and moves on. I keep following him down Chartres another two blocks. On the right, in all its subtle gray-green luxury, is the Omni Royal Orleans, the hotel where Soline will hold her wedding reception. Was he ever really following those girls? Or was it a random afternoon stroll? My overheated suspicion could be manufacturing things. Lanusse turns left, ducking out of the bright afternoon sun into the shade of the Napoleon House—ruining, in one stroke, what has always been one of my favorite watering holes.

The old tiled roof of the Napoleon House looks like something out of *The Hunchback of Notre Dame*. A little mosaic on the ground spells out the bar's name, which it got in the 1800s when a former New Orleans mayor offered it as a refuge to Napoleon during his exile. Napoleon declined, but the name stuck, and people have been seeking refuge at the bar ever since.

It's beckoning me inside, and after watching Lanusse trail ten-year-olds, I could use a nice cold highball for sure, but the thought of pressing my lips to a glass in his company makes me feel suddenly queasy.

In the Quarter, it's legal to drink openly, so I don't have to be surreptitious when I draw the flask from my purse. I head back up Chartres toward my car, my pulse rapid. Friday night starts early here, and there are tourists everywhere, dressed up and ready to party, hungry for whatever debauchery the Quarter can purvey. New Orleans is a city of glittering masks, of roles and disguises. Exquisite crypts. Deception is part of our allure.

During the War of 1812, when British troops headed for the Battle of New Orleans, the city's glamorous women were the only women in the United States, except whores, who wore makeup, and they had already earned an international reputation for elegance. The British forces looked forward, wrote one soldier, to "beauties and booty"—the same reason, with a different lexical spin, that people flock here today.

We make ourselves up to seduce, to hide the truth. We make ourselves up as we go along. When death comes, we dance in the streets.

As I walk, I pass lamppost after lamppost. Amid neon posters for bands and mud wrestling, the simple white flyers for the missing woman flutter like prayer flags. Far too little, and surely too late. Each time I pass a flyer, her dark, sweet eyes haunt me.

Our city is built on shallow ground, the water table lurking just below our feet. When those same British troops lost the Battle of New Orleans, they tried to bury their dead, but the corpses rose back up from the mud, dripping and rotting like a bad zombie dream.

We slick on our makeup and carve angels in stone. We drink absinthe and double-knot the ribbons of our masks. We pretty up what we can. Here in New Orleans, nothing that's buried can stay buried long.

Sipping bourbon as I walk, I review the day's research. An inside look at the Orleans Parish Prison. The Veltri interview. The restaurant where Amber Waybridge disappeared. Three clear head shots of a man who's probably Lanusse, and a sense of his pattern: gaze, then stalk, and then drink off the edge.

For now, at least. For now, he was just drinking it off.

Back in the *Times-Picayune* office, I type up the interview and arrange for a staff photographer to go out and shoot Mike Veltri.

And then it's Friday night in New Orleans, and I'm a single girl and fine. I've got no plans, so I drive to Tipitina's and dance and flirt and toss back mai tais until I can't see straight. Amen.

6

On Saturday morning, I wake in the dark to the sound of howling. Groggy, groping for the green-lit numbers of the alarm clock, I hear the echoes still sounding. It feels like I've been hearing howling for a long time in my sleep: prolonged, eerie wails from too close by. Four fifty-three A.M. I sigh.

Wild dogs hunt the streets at night now in packs of three or four, though not usually here in Mid-City. There's not much to find since Katrina wiped out so much of the city's wildlife—even birds. The dogs rely on unsealed trash cans, overfilled Dumpsters spilling garbage onto the pavement, and the occasional stray cat too foolish to hide herself away.

It's dark and silent now, and my room feels suddenly small and ghostly, as if there were someone else inside. I lie quietly, one hand on my cell phone, the other easing open my nightstand drawer and feeling for a reassuring handful of Beretta. For long minutes I lie there, safety off, my finger locked in the firing position, my eyes wide open as the clock's green numbers change. My head pounds, and nausea makes me dizzy. But nothing happens.

I sit up and click on the lamp. I'm just being paranoid. Crazy fears.

To calm myself, I think back to the comforts of childhood. When I was a little girl and my mother had to work, she sometimes left me with our neighbor, Auntie Helene. Helene Robinson was elderly and thin and, because of the bend in her shoulders, not much taller than I was. But her cheeks were soft, like little pillows of smoothness between the wrinkles, and her apartment was clean and smelled of baking. She let me sit on her lap and rest my face against her shoulder while she rocked and stroked my hair and told me stories from what she called the old days, the bayou times. She crooned in a voice as sweet and thick as Steen's cane syrup, and I'd sink into her arms, hypnotized by the sing-song music of the tale.

Her favorite was the story of the *rougarou,* and she always started it the same way.

"This old-time story come from not so far away now, child, you hear? And a long time ago. Older than me, older than you, older than my mama and her own mama, too. This here be the story of the *rougarou.*"

I'd mouth it softly, silently: *rougarou.*

"Now the *rougarou* ain't no pure man, and he ain't no pure beast, but a evil mixture most unholy."

The words "most unholy"—the way she said them, in a voice gone suddenly chill and grave, so ominous and different from her usual tone—made my neck shiver, as though she'd blown cool air right on it.

"Now the *rougarou,* he be cursed, a cursed werewolf. And he eat"—here she paused for a long moment— "human flesh. He drink on human blood."

This horrified and thrilled me. "What do the *rougarous* look like?" I whispered.

"Oh, daytime, they plain regular. Just folks. They walk around like you or me. A little sickly, maybe, they look. They know they be cursed, but they don't tell nobody. No, they go around acting regular, looking regular. But at the nighttime, you go down in them there swamps, you see good. Body of a man, head of a wolf. Big teeth. Yellow eyes see right through you. Eat your flesh right up."

"They kill you dead?"

"Sometime they do, yes. Suck your bones clean white. Other time just suck your blood. Leave you 'live. Then you got the curse, too. You be a *rougarou*."

"You have to eat people?"

"Oh, yes, child. Hunger like a sickness. Like infection. You go on doing destruction everywhere you touch. Forever. Never get old, never die. Nothing hurt you. Human blood keep you strong, fresh, make you young again."

"Like a vampire?"

"Like a vampire, child, yes." She pushed me suddenly away from her, frowned at me, stopped rocking. "Now wait just a minute here. How you be knowing 'bout vampires?"

"TV."

"Hmph. Well." The chair tilted back again into her rhythm. "The *rougarou* stay forever young, sure, but none of that silver stake, crucifix business. No caskets and suchlike. *Rougarou* just regular in the day." She sighed and rocked back and forth. "But ain't all wonderful for the *rougarou*. Part of the curse: he can't know his own self."

"What's that mean?"

"*Rougarou* lost to his self. Can't read his own heart no more. Lonesome all the time, night and day."

Wrapped in her arms, sure of my place on Auntie Helene's lap and in my mother's heart, I felt sad for such a lonely creature, even an unholy one.

"Is there a way to break the spell?" I asked.

"No spell about it, honey." She snorted. "This ain't no fairy tale. This here's a curse. Old-time."

"But can the curse ever get broke?"

"Oh, yes, baby, the curse can get broke, but it take a mighty man to do it. A brave and mighty man."

"How do you do it?"

"Mm, mm. Let me see. Three things you need to do to break the curse of the *rougarou*. You got to call him by his human name. That's the first thing. Call him by his name. Then you got to look into his eyes—his yellow wolf eyes if it's night, his regular eyes in the day. That's the next. Then you got to spill his blood. That's the third and last and final."

The third and last and final. "And then the curse is broke?"

"Yes, *bébé*. If he die, he dead for good. If he survive, the curse is broke. He a regular man again. Someone brave enough to do all those, go up against the *rougarou* and win, the curse will break."

Lying in her arms, rocking comfortably back and forth in the ruts her chair had worn in the thin carpet, I tried to imagine myself tall and fierce, like a superhero in a cartoon, shouting out the werewolf's name at him, but I still felt chilled and alone. In my mind I could see the black swamp, the slick glimmer of moonlight on water, the glint of the beast's yellow eyes. *Spill his blood.* With a knife, a gun? What if you missed? I imagined the inhuman hands grasping my shoulders, the shaggy head descending toward my throat. Shuddering, I pushed my face into her warmth.

Her hand patting my back was firm. "But you a good girl, go to school, go to church. You obey your mama, you never have trouble from no *rougarou*. You hear?"

"Yes, ma'am."

"People get in trouble, they bring it on theyselves. Go to church, say your confession. Stay to your mama's side. Don't break Lent."

"Lent?"

"Some say, people break Lent seven years running, they turn into *rougarous* right automatic. Then they stuck."

My mother always took care of all the fussing about Lent; I was hardly aware of it. She made me give up something I liked but could easily live without—bananas, maybe, or Oreos; never some broad category like candy or TV—so I wouldn't be driving her crazy, she said, for the whole month.

"You keep Lent, obey your mama, be a good girl. Don't be wandering off, and you be fine. The *rougarou,* he leave you alone."

I loved the story, the peril of it but also, ultimately, the sense of safety. By following simple, known rules, one stayed out of harm's way. In childhood, dangers were deliciously far off, with terrible, impossible creatures doing their orderly damage. With orderly magic, one broke the spell, and the neat set of three pleased me. How tidy were all the rules of it, and they meshed with the pleasure of Auntie Helene's lilting voice, her thrilling pauses, the gory details, the warmth of her body rocking steadily beneath mine.

And then the story would be done, and she'd clap and shoo me from her lap, and we'd fold laundry or drink cold lemonade from the plastic pitcher and crunch her small, round lemon thins dusted white with powdered sugar. How neat and pleasing, the story's delicate terror, definite end point, controllable charm. *The third and last and final.* How different from the random, real, adult world.

A howl coils out across the night again, faint and far away this time. What if it comes from humans, people out causing trouble and howling in the dark? Human beings are as dangerous as any *rougarou.* I rub my bare arms under the sheet.

There's no point in trying to get back to sleep, despite the good it might do my pounding head and queasy gut, the cotton misery in my mouth.

Five-fifteen. I climb out of bed and pick up the empty vodka bottle from my nightstand. No harm in getting an early start. A hot shower and some coffee will do me good, wash all the *rougarous* away.

7

On Saturday afternoon, I'm nervous and driving north toward Metairie for my first visit with Marisol, my new Little Sister.

Why I felt abruptly compelled, around last Christmas, to take care of a child, I cannot say. I'm only twenty-seven; it can't be my biological clock. Maybe the desire germinated because I was spending more time around my mother, who hints incessantly about marriage and babies. Or maybe it was all that extra time in church spent staring at Mary and the Christ child. I didn't want an infant, for sure, and Jesus's little wiener always freaks me out—it feels unseemly to stare at the schlong of the Lord—but something about the tenderness in Mary's eyes lured me. A gentleness absent from my own life. I thought, *Maybe if I take care of a child, I can feel some of that.* Or something. I don't know. I can't even explain it to myself.

Young, single, and barely breaking even, I knew I'd make a lousy mother, foster or otherwise, and who had the time? No, I wanted something minimal, no strings, some volunteer thing organized by other people. Nothing too personal. Plus, folks at work always yammered on about giving something back to the community, and it made me feel a little guilty. Maybe by mentoring, I could kill both birds at once.

Big Brothers, Big Sisters seemed just right. All you had to do was hang out with the kid for a minimum of two hours once a week. You had to act like a sensible adult—no drinking in the kid's presence—and you could write off any expenses the kid incurred. I did the online app and waited, and I guess my paperwork turned out okay, because I got a call for an interview in February.

It was a chilly, drizzly day when I met Guidry Danserne, the match specialist from BBBS, in the Quarter at the high-ceilinged CC's coffee shop at the corner of Royal and St. Philip, just across the street from my own old P.S. McDonogh 15.

She took my Social, my driver's license, three references. I swear, she did everything but swab my mouth for DNA. I guess it's a good thing; I guess they have to screen for weirdos, for pervs like the ones I'm researching. Still, Guidry Danserne was working my last nerve.

When she asked why I specifically wanted to mentor a Latina, when there were so many more black and white girls available, I gave her my little speech about giving back to my community. I told her about my own isolation coming up as a brown girl in a black-and-white city, and how developmentally important it is for children to have role models from their own racial and ethnic group.

I guess she bought it, and I guess the background check cleared, because I got a call last week. As soon as I heard those lilting tones telling me good afternoon, I knew it was Guidry Danserne.

"GD!" I said. "Hey!"

"Well, hello," she said, sounding flustered, but she got back on script quick enough. "We have a very nice little girl who might interest you."

"How little?" I was driving on I-10.

"She's eight years old, and her name—"

"Too young," I broke in. "Way too young. I'm not looking to babysit. I want a girl at least twelve."

"Yes, we know, but this little girl—"

"Nope. No way. Too young." A semi cut me off, and I blared the horn at him.

I heard Guidry Danserne clearing her pretty throat and moving some papers around. Her desk probably had a monogrammed blotter and one of those leather cups for pens and pencils.

"We do have one other Hispanic girl," she said doubtfully.

"Bring it on."

"Marisol is twelve. Um, let's see. She moved here from Houston in 2006 and is in the eighth grade. Her father works in construction." I wondered if he was one of the crowds of Latino guys who suddenly materialized after Katrina. Dozens of them hung out, waiting for work, at the Shell station on Veterans Highway—the Taco Shell, as people soon started calling it. Men kept coming, and New Orleans got its first taste of Hispanic panic. "Her mother has five younger children, so she's unable to spend as much time with Marisol as she'd like." The note of disapproval in Guidry Danserne's voice was mild but unmistakable.

"Sounds good. I'll take her."

"She has a B average in school and has no behavioral or developmental—"

"I said she's fine. Sign me up."

"Are you sure? I can share more of her file."

"Nope, she's good. When do I meet her?"

"Well, we have to set up a time that works for the family. Then you'll all come here to our office so that everyone can get to know one another."

I laughed. "You mean so the parents can see if they approve of me."

There was a short pause.

"Well, frankly, yes."

"No problem. Call me when you've got a day and time." I dropped my cell into the passenger seat and swerved around an SUV to catch my exit.

The meeting went smoothly. Over my backless red top, I wore a white granny cardigan; I knotted my hair in a ladylike bun and didn't swear once. I mentioned my degree from Tulane, my job at the *Times-Picayune.* I played the pristine Catholic good girl, a text-book Latina role model. The parents seemed tired, grateful, and eager to get home for the evening.

They agreed that Marisol would go with me every Saturday from one o'clock until three in the afternoon, which we could extend later on, if Marisol and I decided we wanted more time together. In my book, that was a big *if,* but we'd see. I would pick her up and drop her off at their place near the Causeway in Metairie.

I knew the neighborhood—cheap little apartment complexes, failing strip malls, exterminators, and self-storage companies. North of the city proper, Metairie is contiguous with New Orleans but not of it. Folks who live there claim affection for it, but Metairie is all subdivision, all boring brick ranch houses with small suburban yards. Sports are everything there; purple and yellow LSU flags wave from front porches. There are cement statues of poodles and pelicans stuck in the lawns.

If a person who grew up in Metairie moves away, she never claims it. When you ask where she's from, she always says New Orleans, even though shotgun houses, absinthe, and avenues lined with live oaks are as far from her experience as from a Wisconsin farmgirl's. Metairie could be any bland subdivision in any city in the South. And it's seriously white—David Duke territory. Black men working construction are the only black men there.

With their post-Katrina insurance payoffs, folks have been fancying up their houses big-time, so some streets in Metairie are starting to take on the sheen of modest wealth. But not all of them, and definitely not the industrial area where Marisol's family rents.

"And you'll both be thinking about what you might like to do this first Saturday?" chirped Guidry Danserne, nodding encouragingly at Marisol and me. Yeah, sure, okay, whatever.

A thin girl with a bush of dark hair, Marisol herself stood opaque, a watcher, a mask that nodded but never smiled.

No problema. A girl after my own heart.

When I arrive at her family's tan, nondescript apartment building surrounded by asphalt, Marisol's waiting outside on the steps. She gets in the car and buckles up without a word. As I say hello, it occurs to me that it's touching and a little disconcerting, the way her parents just let their adolescent daughter go off with me. Their trust. I could be anyone. Sure, I've been vetted by BBBS and the likes of Guidry Danserne, but people fool parole boards every day. I think of my own mother, sending me across the city alone on buses for a shot at a real education. But what are the options, if you want your kid to have a chance at something better? You let her go. You hold your breath and depend on the kindness of strangers.

"Can I change this?" Marisol asks, gesturing toward the radio, which is intoning NPR.

"Yeah, sure." I veer back onto I-10, heading toward New Orleans proper, simply because I don't know where else to go.

She taps the search button until she finds a hip-hop station, then leans back in the seat and stares out the window. She answers my predictable questions about school.

"Boring."

What else has she been doing?

"Nothing."

"So you've been living here for how long now? Two years?"

"Yeah."

"So you've already seen all the tourist stuff? The zoo? The aquarium? The French Quarter?" I glance across.

She frowns, shakes her head.

"No? None of that?"

She looks wary. "I don't think so."

I believe her. Most people assume that if you live in an interesting place, you automatically reap the juicy benefits. But that would require your parents to have the energy and the money—not to mention the desire—to take you to all the cool cultural stuff. Growing up poor in the Upper Ninth, I did go to the Audubon Zoo once, but only because my fifth-grade class from P.S. McDonogh 15 went there on a school trip. My mother didn't hang out in the Quarter, that's for sure. The architecture familiar to my eyes was not the wrought-iron lacework of the Pontalba Apartments but the endless brick boxes of the 262 buildings of the Desire Projects and the little sagging shotgun houses that filled the streets to their south. We stayed in the Ninth, orbiting out on the fringe of the city with thousands of other people who never saw the river. Why leave? You could get almost anything you needed at the Family Farm Market or Quicky Discount, and why go somewhere you're only going to feel awkward and wrong?

Marisol's father labored full-time, and her mother had five younger kids to deal with. Naturally, they weren't going to head out for too many culturally enriching jaunts on the weekend, even if they'd been able to afford the entrance fees.

"No problem," I say. "Let's hit some of those places." I think for a second. It's a hot, bright day. "How about the aquarium? Dolphins and stuff."

She nods. The barest hint of a grin lifts the corner of her mouth.

When we get downtown, I park in the lot near the Westin hotel, and we walk back up the ramp toward the broad plaza that runs along the edge of the Mississippi. The sun is fierce, the crowds of people moving steadily. That area by the river—the aquarium, Harrah's Casino with its neon lights and fountains, the streetcar stop, the steamboats blaring their eerie calliope music—is sort of a weird, cute, Disneyfied zone, all its details picked out in cheerful, clean colors for tourists and children. As we near the entrance, black-skulled seagulls whirl and cry around us.

Inside, the aquarium is dark and cool and blue, a relief from the hot glare outside. We stand near the tall metal waterfall to examine the map, and then begin to wander.

We begin at the vast blue tank where sharks and stingrays swirl in giant, prowling loops. Gar and tarpon swivel through. Sea turtles bigger than Marisol paddle past, and we watch, hypnotized, as an eel oozes over a rock.

"I wish they'd feed the sharks," she whispers. Blood and action—I like this girl. So we stand around for a while, but nothing happens except the perpetual loops of the predators' caged hunt.

When Marisol says she has to go to the bathroom, I join her, hanging around by the sinks, washing my hands forever. Somewhere nearby, there's a guy who operates just that fast, and in broad daylight. If someone had accompanied Amber Waybridge to the bathroom, she might be sleeping in her own bed tonight.

We drift upstairs to the second floor, where the otters' somersaults make us giggle, and she touches my arm to point out the goofy flips a penguin keeps doing. I take her photo as she strikes a pose within the broad jawbones of an eighty-foot prehistoric shark, its teeth around her like a jagged white frame. Then we switch places, and she takes a photo of me.

We enter the humid rain forest room, which enchants Marisol. With its tanks full of anacondas and gators, its suspended bamboo walkways, and its giant tropical trees, it does seem like another land.

"This is so cool! I wish I could live in here," she says. "I wish our apartment was just like this."

"Yeah." But she has wandered ahead. I don't know how to talk to twelve-year-olds. I'm suddenly not sure why I'm doing this. I'm not exactly mentor material.

"Hey, check this," she says, tapping the tank of piranhas, big iron-colored fish with eyes that look confused. "I thought they chewed people up."

I read the placard, too, and learn that piranhas have gotten a bad rap from B movies. Only when they get trapped in shrinking pools, unable to access their food sources, and only when they're threatened, do they attack people. Not otherwise.

"Poor piranhas," she says, stroking the glass wall with one finger. "Nobody likes you, but no one even knows you."

"Come on. Let's go see the Gulf stuff." We head back downstairs, where the jellyfish fascinate me. There's something mesmerizing about their slow thrusts across the black water. Lit pink or gold or unearthly blue by bulbs in the tanks or by their own shifting bioluminescence, they look ghostly, like hot air balloons made of lace, collapsing and filling. They're parasols opening and closing their way across black space, the long threads of their tentacles blowing like streamers behind them.

But Marisol thinks they're boring and wants to get moving.

"Hang on," I say.

She sighs.

I don't know why I'm lingering, why I can't stop staring at the strange, delicate little bubbles of sting. They're sexy. They tap something in me. I want to say they remind me of a woman's sex pulsing in orgasm. I want to say I admire the way they suck in their environment, whatever it might be, and then shove it out of themselves in order to move forward. But BBBS probably wouldn't approve of my saying any of that to a twelve-year-old, so I just stand there, mute and watching.

"Come *on*," she says, sighing heavily, shifting her weight, rolling her eyes.

"Okay, okay. All right, already." Suddenly I remember, for just a brief flash, what it's like to be twelve and impatient with grown-ups. I laugh. "Are you hungry?"

She nods, her smile lighting up her face in the dim hall, and we head for the exit. Bursting back out into the light, we walk, sweating, up Decatur through Jackson Square. There's the smell of fried shrimp, fried oysters, fried chicken, the sweet smell of fried dough. Tourists mill past. Marisol's head swivels constantly, taking it all in.

We get to Central Grocery, one of the oldest delis in the United States. The Lupo and then the Tusa families have owned and run it for more than a hundred years, since the big waves of Italian immigration to New Orleans. Up above the shelves of groceries, faded color posters of Italy ring the room, and an Italian flag hangs next to a U.S. one. Three ceiling fans push the air-conditioned coolness around.

At the counter, I order half a muffuletta for $6.95 and send Marisol with dollar bills to get us cold sodas from the Coke machine humming at the back. The guy hands me the sandwich wrapped in white paper. *I love N.O.,* says the wrapper. The propaganda's everywhere.

The dining area at the back of the store is bare bones: cement floor, tables made of white countertops with metal pipes for legs. I pull up a stool and unwrap the half sandwich on the counter. I pull the sections apart and put a wedge of it down on a napkin for her.

"Wow, I'm glad you didn't get a whole one," she says, plunking down our drinks. Even half a muffuletta looks like more than we can eat—it's the size of half a pizza. I pick up my piece. You can see where the oil has soaked into the bread. She looks dubious. "What's in it?"

"Well, let's see." I open up my sandwich and show her. "You got salami, you got ham"—with big white globules of fat—"you got some kind of white cheese here, and then you got your olive salad."

"Gross. What's olive salad?"

I push at the mix with my finger. "Looks like black and green olives."

"Duh," she says softly. "But what's that other stuff?"

"Looks to be—let's see. Red peppers. Garlic. I don't know what these orange things are."

She picks a fragment out of her own sandwich and inspects it. "Carrots?"

I taste a piece. "Yeah! I think you're right. Carrots." I smile at her. "Good job, taste tester." I take a big bite of the sandwich. Salt, oil. "I think the cheese is provolone." Convinced it's safe, she begins to nibble, and we chew happily, swigging our cold drinks and looking around us. Draped with a black lace scarf, a poster of Pope John Paul II gazes down.

"So do you speak Spanish or what?" she asks around a mouthful of muffuletta.

I swallow. I have to explain that my mom quit speaking Spanish to me as soon as she could get by in English. It's what all the educational experts used to recommend. "And there wasn't much of a Latino community here, back when I was coming up," I say. "So my baby Spanish got rusty pretty fast."

"*Que lástima,*" she says, lifting her chin and eyebrows in a superior, knowing way. *What a pity.* I suppress a smile. "And you're mispronouncing the sandwich," she adds, pointing to the little menu above the counter.

"Ah, no way, baby." Now it's my turn to gloat. "Muffa-LOTTa

is how the locals say it. Go around saying muffa-letta, folks know you're from out of town." I grin. "A *turista*."

Chagrined, she mouths the word *muffuletta* silently while I pretend not to notice. She must know already the sting of not belonging, how language can be a way in.

"*Mira,*" I say, pointing to a sign over the kitchen area. It's a sign that says no cameras are allowed.

"Why would they care?"

"Because the muffuletta is a secret recipe. Highly secret."

She looks at me skeptically. "Whatever," she says, but her eyes are intrigued.

Finished and full, we throw our trash in the big plastic can and poke around the grocery store, marveling together at the dozens of different hot sauces, including Tabasco, of course, but also Mexican Cholula and Nurse Nan's. There's a red cooler full of cheeses, a shelf with a dozen kinds of mustard, and onions jarred in vermouth. Gallon-sized metal cans of olive oil line the walls, and we investigate the jars of capers, garlic puree, and anchovies.

"Hey, I can read this!" she says. Some items are from Spain. I have her translate for me, which she does, proudly.

How did it get to be almost three o'clock already?

We catch the riverfront streetcar from Jackson Square back to the parking lot. The streetcar's almost empty, and she jumps from one varnished wooden seat to the other, earning us a tired look from the conductor. Then the open windows are too tempting, and I have to tell her ten times to keep her hands inside.

I know the distance is short. We could have walked. But I was born and raised here, and I never rode a streetcar, the icon of New Orleans, until I was eighteen. On my watch, things will be different for Marisol.

———

Well after midnight, I arrive home sweaty from dancing and drinking at the Rock 'n' Bowl. Fair Grinds is closed, the street quiet. Only a security light shines yellow in the darkness. I veer onto a side street and park the Pontiac. Weary and a little wasted, I walk the block alone and head up the flight of wooden steps outside my second-floor apartment.

"Hey, there." From underneath the staircase steps a ghost, his hand reaching out toward me. He's thin and pale, about fifty, in a black wife beater and jeans. His mouth is an open O, his eyes dark pits in his face, his cheeks gritted with stubble.

Junk, or crack, or meth. It's not unusual.

"Yeah, I got nothing for you, buddy." I take another step up.

"You Nola?" His voice is a low mumble I have to strain to hear, and when I glance back, he's staring at me like the undead. "You work for the paper?"

Nodding, I try to calm a sudden surge of nerves.

"I been waiting," he mutters. "My friend says I should talk to you."

"And why's that?"

"He said you was talking about guys that went off the grid during Katrina. That's me." The sneer on his face is proud. "I'm off the grid."

As if by its own volition, my hand starts foraging through my purse for the Olympus. *Score.*

"Who's your friend?"

"Nobody. A guy inside."

Inside. An inmate in Orleans Parish Prison must have contacted him after my visit there. Fast work.

I pull out the recorder and press it on. "What's your name?"

"No names," he says. "Call me an unidentified source."

"Where do you live?"

"Here in the city. No details, doll. I don't want you siccing the cops on me."

"Right. Okay." I hold the recorder out toward him. "So why did you come back after the storm?"

"How about we go up to your place, sit down comfortable-like, and I'll tell you all about it?"

I glance up. My windows are dark. Uri must be out working late at the Vic. Only Roux is home.

I look back down. "Do I look stupid to you?" Fair Grinds is shut down for the night, and I'm not getting in my car with him to go anywhere else. "We can talk right here." I lower myself to the warm, painted surface of the wooden step and wave a hand toward the ones below me. "Have a seat."

Instead, he steps up beside me, his movements oddly feline, delicate, and sits down on the same stair. Though his hip is too close for comfort, his body radiates no heat. Inching away, I hold the Olympus between us with one hand, its red light pulsing.

"So how'd you know where to find me, anyway?"

He grins. "White pages ain't classified."

Great. Now the brotherhood of sex offenders knows where I live.

"Okay, so talk to me. Why'd you come back?"

He tells me about evacuating to a cousin's in Texarkana—"After a month in that shithole, I'd have *walked* back"—and how landlords in poor neighborhoods don't bother with a background check if you're just renting a room, and how between odd jobs and a little dealing on the side, a man can get by.

"I was a locksmith," he says. "Used to be. Licensed and everything. Now I can't get a job with a company, 'cause they need you to get bonded, and nobody'll bond an ex-con. Still got my tools, though. I can get into cars, houses, whatever. Word gets around that I'm cheap, and people call."

"So what's it like, being off the grid?"

"I'm a free man, doll. I got a normal life again. Don't have to be registering, checking in all the time, like those other morons. Bunch of sheep, doing what they're told. Katrina gave me my life back. I don't have folks looking at me funny, don't have the cops breathing down my neck asking questions every time there's a sex crime round the way."

"Which reminds me." I pull out the flyer of Amber Waybridge and smooth it open on my knees. Her dark eyes and wide, sweet smile make my throat catch. She'd looked into that camera with love and confidence, unafraid. "Do you know anything about this disappearance?"

He gazes at the picture speculatively for a moment. For maybe a little too long. "Think I seen her on TV," he finally says, his tone supremely, unnaturally casual, his choice of words careful. "She's a tourist, ain't she?"

I nod. Why is he here, anyway, risking all his newfound precious freedom to tell me his story? Is he moved by a compulsion to confess, a telltale heart? I wonder if, with his lanky build, he's strong enough to muscle a woman down a dark hall.

I choose my own words with care. "What can you tell me about her?"

"Me? Oh, me, darling—shit, I don't know nothing."

"Then just speaking hypothetically."

"Well, one thing I can say." A glimmer of pride darts through his eyes like a small glistening fish. "Whoever did it's got to be plenty smart. Least if he plans to get away with it."

"Meaning?"

"It's obvious." He leans against the railing. "Take a local girl, cops'll be after you, sure. It'll be in the paper. If a body turns up, it's a tragedy and so on, but it blows over." He rubs the stubble on his jaw with a corded hand. "But take a tourist—in this city? Now, when everyone's all wired up about the economy? They'll nail your ass to the wall, darling. Make an example."

"You said, 'if a body turns up.' What makes you think she's dead?"

His laugh is hollow. "Oh, she's dead, all right. Or will be."

"What makes you so sure?"

"Who's going to let a piece of walking, talking evidence go free?" He shakes his head. "No way. He's gonna kill her. Probably killed her already."

The night is dark and still around us. "Is that what you would do? Hypothetically?"

He shifts on the stair, then reaches out and strokes Amber's cheek with a single finger. Through the sheet of paper, I feel the soft pressure on my thigh.

"She's a pretty little thing," he says. "I might keep her around awhile. Soften 'em up, and they'll do about anything you want."

My throat is dry. "Will they?"

"Oh, yeah." He flicks the flyer with a dirty nail. My thigh flesh stings.

Anger seeps into my voice. "Why are you here? Why are you really here?"

His chuckle rasps, as if my frustration pleases him. "I'm here as a public service, darling. I'm here as the horse's mouth. I'm here to let the good people of New Orleans know what it's like to live under sex offender laws."

"But you're living outside them."

There's a glimmer again in his grin. "That's right, doll. That's exactly right. I'm an outlaw, gonna stay an outlaw. Cops think they're so smart. Lawyers, judges. Bunch of suits with their college degrees—"

He mutters on, and suddenly I know. He's not here to help me grasp the psychosocial ramifications of Megan's Law, or to enlighten the reading public. He doesn't know anything about Amber Waybridge, either. He's here to brag, to preen, to show off. For him, it's not enough to evade the courts and police, to live off the grid like an urban survivalist. He wants the world to know he's outsmarted the system.

I may be a rookie reporter, but I remember hearing about his type in J school: narcissists who want an audience. He wants all of New Orleans to sit up and listen to his vast and clever accomplishments—which consist of fooling and hurting vulnerable women. He wants to show off his handiwork and watch fear ripple through people's faces, like an arsonist standing in the crowd with his hard-on while the building burns.

I'm nobody's vehicle.

"Well, thank you so much for your time." I cut him off midstream and stand up, and it's his turn to be taken aback. I make a production of turning off the Olympus and putting it away. "Is there some way I can get in touch with you again? I mean, if I should want to follow up, Mr.—?"

I take out my cell phone and make as if to type in a number, looking over at him expectantly.

He's frowning. "Mr. Nothing. And no, there's no way for you to get ahold of me." As he levers himself up to his feet, I snap a quick, silent photograph of his face.

"Then let's set up another meet," I say, "in case I have more questions later." I step down onto the sidewalk. "Next week, maybe."

He laughs. "What, and have the cops waiting for me?"

"Well, then," I say, gesturing toward the dark street, "I think we're done here."

Standing on my staircase, he makes no move to leave.

"You know," he says offhandedly, "I wasn't even in for rape. Those charges got dropped." He stares into the darkness as if reading his own rap sheet. "Technicalities."

A chill sweeps over me. "So why did you do time?"

"Aggravated sexual assault of a minor. Three counts." His bony face swings toward me, and something new flickers across the gray skin. "I got an unusual profile, the psych guy said. I like 'em all ages." His eyes rest on my cleavage, which I know, without looking, still gleams from hours of sweat and dancing. Meeting my eyes, he snaps his teeth together twice with a clack.

But it lacks the menacing effect he's after. In the glare of the security light, his teeth are small and gray with shadowed gaps between them—the teeth of creeping age and no dental plan—and the thought of them sinking into my flesh makes me think only of infection and disease.

I sigh. "Look, buddy, you need to get going."

"I don't think so." Instead of descending, he moves up toward my deck, toward my home, and his footsteps make no sound. "I got more I could explain to you. Up close and personal-like." Skinny and spectral, he stands above me. Old needle scars speckle the gray flesh of his wiry forearms. "I could tell you all about it. With my tools, doll, I can get into just about any house I want, day or night."

"I'm not your doll, motherfucker," I say, "and I don't need a demo." My free hand slips into my shoulder bag and closes around the Beretta. I glance around. All the normal foot traffic is gone, all the restaurants and shops closed down for the night. A rapist stands between me and my front door. "You need to go now, or I'm calling the police."

"Call them." His chuckle rasps. "I've had women dial nine-one-one when I get in, and I'm done and gone before the cops get there." Not far away, a car door slams.

"Oh, impressive," I say, jeering. "Fast work."

His eyes narrow, and he takes a step down toward me, his hands flexing by his thighs. Inside the purse, my finger slips into the trigger, into position.

Footsteps grow loud, and Uri appears from the darkness, the concern plain on his face. "Hey, Nola," he nods, but his eyes never leave the man on our stairs. "Who's this?"

The perp looks uneasy. Wiry he may be, but Uri's got at least thirty pounds on him, as well as health and youth.

"This guy was just leaving," I say. Reluctantly, Mr. Nothing descends to the sidewalk. His upper lip quivers with rage as he brushes past me.

"Good," Uri says, mounting the steps. He stands close to my side. "It's late."

The perp chuckles, his face twisted in a leer. "I notice you got no security system." One pale eyelid slides down over a dark eye. "You should be careful."

And then he turns, and the dark street swallows him.

"It's on my list," I yell into the shadows. "I've got a guy coming next week."

No reply. I stare into the air where he disappeared. My finger eases off the trigger. I can still feel the energy of fear, the tension thrumming in my shoulders. I climb the steps with Uri.

"What guy next week?" he says. "Who was that?"

We reach the top. "No one. Just some bum giving me a hard time."

"Don't bullshit me, Nola." Uri lays a hand on my arm. "Seriously, what's going—"

"Look, it's fucking no one, all right?" I shake him off. My own hands are trembling. "Leave it alone."

"Whoa." Uri steps away, lifting his hands.

"Look, I'm sorry," I say. I give his arm a quick squeeze and try to smile. "Really, it's okay. Just let it go."

His eyes search my face, but he says nothing, for which I'm grateful. I pull out my keys and let us inside.

8

On a bright Sunday morning in New Orleans, you can do any number of things. You can dunk beignets in your coffee at Café du Monde, tee off on the green at Audubon Park, or tiptoe away from last night's Bourbon Street indiscretion.

But if you're a Latina daughter like me—no matter if you're single and fly, or partied late at the Rock 'n' Bowl—then there's only one place for you to be on a Sunday morning: hungover, sitting next to your mother in church.

So here I am, clad in my trusty Catholic-girl outfit: a modest gray skirt that actually grazes my kneecaps, a pretty white blouse, and white espadrilles. Plain and saintly, I've even pulled my hair back into a tidy knot. On the wooden pew next to my hip nestles a gray purse just big enough for my lipstick, Beretta, and keys, and on my other side sits Mamá, hands clasped, eyes closed in concentration—which is a good thing, because she can't see me yawn and rub my temples. *Ay, mi cabeza.*

The Church of the Holy Rosary is an old tan brick church on Esplanade, just a short walk from our apartments. Its interior has simple cream walls, a painted dome, and a wash of pale, pretty light. The congregation is full of Italian families who've been coming here for generations. We sign petitions against the death penalty, the Ladies' Sodality has bake sales, and everyone's nice to my mother. Unfortunately, from our pew at the rear of the nave, my view is a straight shot at the portrait of Saint Augustine, the wickedest saint in the pantheon.

At Tulane in this course called Human Quest, required of all the freshmen, we had to read Augustine, along with Homer, Thucydides, Plato, Shakespeare, and some guys from the Bible. We read a grand total of one book by a woman, and that was Jane Austen. I was like, Are you fucking kidding me? All her characters do is pour tea, dance, and scheme about which heir to marry.

When we read Augustine's *Confessions,* our professor—a short, paunchy guy who wore actual bow ties—was almost delirious with the great wisdom and honesty of Western culture's first memoir, but I, on the very other hand, was going out of my mind with Augustine's hand-wringing, his journey to God, his so-called remorse, when he couldn't even bother to mention the name of the working-class North African girl who was his lover, the one he kicked to the curb when his mother told him that this common-law wife, the mother of his son, wasn't appropriate given his aspirations to the Church. Augustine shipped his true sweetheart, flesh of his flesh, back to Africa, but kept their little boy, because his unnamed lover had no rights, no income, and now was ruined, cast off.

Confessions, my sweet ass. More like those memoirs that politicians write for public consumption, or that ministers and mob bosses write from prison. *I was lost, but now I'm found.* Augustine was positioning himself as a founder of the Church for all time.

His mother snapped up a suitable wife from a wealthy family: young, pure, rich, European, stoned on her own scrupulous virginity and utterly willing to be the dumb lamb led to the altar. A genuine fourth-century chickenhead—or so I thought at first, until I found out the wife-child was only eleven years old. *Pobrecita.* Younger than Marisol, and traded to a grown man. Today, Augustine would be just another perp.

But he's still up in the dome being worshiped, and I'm down here with a gun in my purse.

When we file up for communion, my mother's face is rapturous. I take the wafer in my hand—none of this obedient opening-my-mouth-for-the-priest weirdness—and put it on my tongue, where it dissolves in a tasteless mush I force myself to swallow.

Confession is always easy for me. When I think back over a typical week, it's like a vice buffet: anger, sloth, greed, gluttony. Impure thoughts by the dozen. The dark, fogged face assigns my penance, and I slip out to do my duty.

But I never confess my soccer field adventures. My lust and how I slake it—that's none of the Church's business.

There are things you can tell old men sworn to celibacy, and some things you just can't.

After the service, arm in arm, Mamá and I stroll down quiet streets under trees heavy with white blossoms. My mother's dark eyes are full of peace and joy. All I want is some aspirin.

Back at my mother's apartment, I perform my most disgusting weekly ritual: cleaning out her refrigerator. Even after years without me, she still can't get used to cooking for one, so each evening, she pushes a plastic container of fresh leftovers into the fridge. She tries to use them up, but some get nudged to the back. My job is to open and sniff each one, inspect the macaroni or *picadillo* for white fuzz.

Mamá sits at the kitchen table with a fresh cup of *café con leche* while I squat, grimacing, in front of the refrigerator's open door.

"Ay, Nola, pull your skirt down."

"Ain't nobody in the vegetable drawer gonna see nothing."

She laughs. I'd laugh, too, but I just got a whiff of ancient cauliflower. Yuck. I put it on the counter next to some decrepit celery stalks and a container of moldy black beans.

"*Mi'ja,* you're too good to me."

"Not good enough, Mamá. Not good enough." It's our usual exchange, the call and response of our lives now.

While she's in the bathroom, I rummage through the cupboards for her whiskey bottle, thinking a little hair of the dog might help. But I can't find it. It must be next to her bed.

"What are you looking for, *mi'ja?*" she says, padding in her pink house shoes, and I close the cupboard doors too quickly.

"Nothing, Mamá." She worries about my drinking like she worries about my love life. "Just straightening up."

In my mother's apartment, me and the Holy Virgin are the principal sources of decor. Dozens of photos of me, taken over the years and framed like icons, rest on every available shelf and windowsill, and prints of the Virgin Mary grace the walls of every room. I remember asking my mother once, back in the Desire Projects, why we didn't have one over the toilet: Our Lady of Regularity. "Ay, the mouth on you," she said. But not long afterward, a small laminated card with the Virgen de Guadalupe appeared over the bathroom light switch.

When you grow up surrounded by images of yourself and the most famous virgin in history, it sends a certain kind of message about your mother's expectations. I've never told my mother about my soccer field liaisons. The sin of premarital sex aside, the Catholic Church prohibits contraception. If I told Mamá about the men, she'd worry I was going to get pregnant or diseased, and if I told her I use protection, she'd worry I was going to hell. She's completely observant; she'd sooner slit an artery than break with Catholic dogma. ("Doctrine," she always corrects me. "Not dogma.") So I keep my little exploits to myself. I do tell her about my few fizzled dates with Latino professionals, but I'm telling the truth when I say they don't go anywhere. She thinks I'm a career girl, too busy with my job for a relationship, and I let her think it. She frets about my lack of romantic prospects, and I let her. It's simpler than the alternative.

Every week after church, I clean out the fridge, dust the ceiling fans with her mop (it makes her dizzy to lean backward like that), nail up anything that's coming loose, and do any other little odd jobs or cleaning she needs. If she needs to have the landlord fix something, I write the problem down and call him on Monday. Talking to him on the phone makes her nervous. Sometimes she can't think of the right word to say in English, and he gets impatient. I also comb through her bank statements to make sure everything's square. Money makes her nervous; banks make her nervous; anyone or anything with power makes her nervous.

She's fifty-nine years old and has been powerless all her life, first in Cuba under communism, working in the fields, and then in the U.S. under capitalism, cleaning houses. Now that the Spanish language is finally seen as an educational asset, she works at a day care for minimum wage, changing diapers and feeding strangers' children. Always manual labor, always at someone else's beck and call.

Now we're hoping she can afford to keep her apartment when she retires. No wonder the masses crave opiates. My mother's are the weekly shot of pomp and glamour the Catholic Church provides, and the Wild Turkey she sips whenever she's uneasy—and even now that we've left the Desire Projects and she has a snug little place of her own, just blocks from me, she's uneasy a lot. I get that and I don't judge. A lifetime of ravaged nerves doesn't just go away. Damage lasts. Poured into a coffee cup, Wild Turkey looks perfectly respectable, and it helps her sleep.

Though her apartment is only two rooms and a bath, it feels like luxury, she says, because it's larger and nicer than the apartment where we lived together for the first eighteen years of my life. The apartment in Desire, too, was only two rooms and a bath: a living room, with kitchen counters and appliances along one wall, and her small bedroom. Beyond her bedroom lay the tiny, windowless bathroom the cockroaches loved. I had to squeeze past her bed to go pee.

The floor was covered in flat indoor-outdoor carpet, dark blue, and there were only two windows, small, high up, and barred, and the one in the bedroom held the air conditioner, so the place was dark. Dark and cool and full of my mother's gentle attentions, it was a refuge from the world outside.

My own bed, a twin mattress on the floor, lay wedged in the corner of the living room. She made sure it always wore pretty, fresh-smelling sheets. Around me hung my paintings from school and, later, my awards. My clothes lay folded neatly in stacked plastic milk crates. When I was little, she tacked a peach-colored bedsheet to the two walls, stretching it like a canopy or tent over where I slept. There was a little lamp. At night, she crawled under and told me stories of Mary, Cuba's own virgin queen, la Virgen del Caridad del Cobre, who calmed the Caribbean waves and saved the three men from the sea. She'd recite poems by José Martí and stroke my forehead until I drifted to sleep. It felt safe and good in there.

An old wooden desk jutted lengthwise from the opposite wall. When I got home from school, its surface would be clean, with only a glass of milk and two Oreos on a plate. Homework time. Mamá would ask how my day was and then cook quietly while I labored over spelling and math.

When I was finished, I'd clear all my books and papers into my backpack and take the green cotton tablecloth from the drawer, shake it over the desk, and smooth away the wrinkles. Then I'd set out our yellow cotton napkins, big blue plastic bowls, cups for water, and silverware. I was in college before I fully understood that some people—real people, not just on TV—had full-time dining tables, that everyone didn't sit down to dinner on metal folding chairs.

In my childhood, with my *mamá,* dinner was a sweet, easy time. With a cassette tape of Arsenio Rodríguez, Celia Cruz, Benny Moré, or Machito and his Afro-Cubans playing in the background, we would talk about our day and butterflies or swimming pools or Cuba or whatever came to our minds, and it would feel so pleasant and effortless, as though an unbroken stream of love circulated between me and her, weaving a net, a hammock that held us up and gently swung us, and everything was beautiful, once we had shut and locked and chained and dead-bolted the door against the outside world. I grew up in the faith and promise of my mother's perfect love, a love unadulterated by her need to please some man. All her light sweetness went to me. All I knew was that at home I was happy. I knew I was completely loved. My mother's affection was a rising tide that lifted my little boat until I could sail away.

When the Desire Projects were razed in 2003 to make New Orleans a safer, cleaner place, we all proclaimed our official gladness. Yes, they were a blight. People referred in print to the "infestation of crime" the projects had housed, as if we were cockroaches and the wrecking balls were a big can of Raid. Yes, it was a good thing for the city to have them removed.

But my mother and I were not the only ones who held hands and cried when the walls came down that day. Dangerous as the projects were, she'd made a haven there. It was our home, our history. Strangers marched in and blew their horns, and everything we knew crumbled to dust.

Now the old desk stands in her new bedroom, which has two big windows draped with white lace, and the living room holds the little wicker settee she dreamed of. She still has only a kitchenette, instead of the kind of kitchen she gazes at in magazines, but there's a kitchen table just for eating, and the window over the sink has a view of trees. This, she says, makes all the difference. Her apartment is one-sixth of a big old house on Crete, and she can walk to the bus stop. Of course, she still makes sure to be inside and locked up tight by dusk every night. Old habits die hard. But she's happy. It's safe and pretty, the kind of place she always deserved.

Her salary from the day care covers almost all of her expenses, and I chip in for her utilities and phone, and then give her a little extra for clothes, going out, whatever. When I used to tuck the money into her hands, she was so grateful and apologetic. "A mother should not be taking money from her children." I always felt uncomfortable. Now I just slide folded cash under the edge of the Folgers can.

I'm almost ready to leave. Is everything safe, snug, secure, and functional? Have I hugged her a dozen times, told her she's the sweetest *mamá* ever? Has she called me her *cielo,* her *querida,* her *tesoro,* her precious pet?

"Nola," she says hesitantly, "there's a friend of mine I want you to meet sometime."

"Okay, sure."

"I met her at the center." My mother does literacy volunteering, teaching ESL and reading. "She's very nice. She has a son about your age."

Oh, no. A dreaded fix-up coming on. "Mamá, I don't want to meet anybody's son, okay? I'm just not in the—"

"No, no, *mi'ja.* She's just a nice lady, and I want you to meet her."

"Sure. Okay." I bet. Meet the mom, and here comes the son to drop off the car or something. *Oh, hello, this is Antonio.* And so it goes.

"Maybe she could have dinner with us one Sunday." She rubs the gold cross at her throat.

"Sure, I don't care. Look, Mamá, I'm happy to meet your friends.

I'm glad you *have* friends." Her life, to tell the truth, revolves around me a little too much. If I do get the chance to go to New York, I want her to have a support system in place. "Just tell me ahead of time, okay?"

"Thank you, *mi'ja.*"

"No problema. Whatever you want." I lean and kiss her cheek.

Near the door, I pause in front of the big, framed mirror to smooth my hair. Tucked into the frame, there's a wallet-sized photo, and I ease it out to get a closer look. It's me as a little kid, smiling wildly, my curly hair pulled back in a ribbon, the crisp white shirt of my school uniform unmussed. Picture day. My eyes are big and brown. Radiant, sweet, open. When did I stop smiling like that? Mamá always bought a photo package, even if we could only afford the cheapest set.

I turn to her. "Mamá, can I borrow this?"

"Ay, no, *mi'ja.* I can't let you take that. It's my only copy. *Mira,*" she says, turning it over. Look. *Mi querida Nola,* loops her careful cursive. My darling Nola. *8 yrs old. 3rd grade. 1989.* "Ay, qué linda," she murmurs, her voice full of fondness.

I kiss her.

"Just to borrow," I promise her. "I'll bring it back, I swear. I'll get a copy made and bring you this one back."

She's shaking her head, but she lets me take it. I tuck the picture into my wallet.

"I love you, Mamá." I hug her tightly, and her face presses into my shoulder. I know she wants me not to go, but she pulls away, kisses both my cheeks hard, and pushes me out the door. My last glimpse is of her soft and lonely eyes.

That afternoon in my apartment, working on my laptop, I remind myself that she's only blocks away, that I spend every Sunday with her, that I love her, for God's sake, but I'm twenty-seven, and if she's built her existence around me, it's not my fault. When I get a job in New York, she'll have a big decision to make. I remind myself about boundaries, independence, and the way the other kids at Tulane felt so effortlessly free of their parents.

But it doesn't work.

What works is shot after shot of Grey Goose, straight from the freezer, until the image of her sad eyes fades.

Flopped on the sofa, I flip on WWL-TV for the six o'clock news.

The screen fills with Amber Waybridge's photograph while the newscaster says there have been no new breaks in the case.

Jolted into recollection, I pull out my cell phone and text Calinda the photo of last night's visitor. Mr. Nothing. The shot, taken as he was getting to his feet, is dark and not crisp. While the newscaster drones on about the latest financial scandal at city hall, I type with my thumbs that he's a perp and ask Calinda to run it for matches in the system.

I switch over to CNN, where there's a breaking story from Texas about a raid on a polygamous compound. Now the bleach-white buildings are on national TV, and we're all watching the electronically blurred-out faces of children as they climb aboard buses.

There'd been a bed in the temple, claims the blandly pretty newscaster, safe in her CNN studio: a bed where the polygamous marriages of these children to men in their thirties, forties, and fifties were consummated, while male elders of the church "witnessed the ceremony." Listening to her, I can feel my blood start to pound. *Consummated?*

I chose journalism because I love language's potential for precision: all the possibility for nuance, the promise of exactitude. So it drives me nuts that she's using the abusers' language. She keeps calling it the bed where "marriages" were "consummated"—vague, passive, abstract—instead of *where men raped children* while the porno elders stood around, cupping their holy hard-ons.

Obviously, I'd never make it in broadcasting.

Reporters are trained to stay at a distance. We learn to wait, to speak carefully, neutrally, until the power structure—whether it's porno uncles or a government—has actually been convicted of a crime. Until then, we're cautious, pruning our tongues against possible libel, because we know too damn well it could be us next, us taken off the air or extradited to a camp somewhere. It could be our strand of hair on that pillow in that bed.

Restless and angry, I slip on my sandals and drive down to the levee, where late soccer games are breaking up. It's getting dark. Men scatter to their cars. After a little negotiation, a rather nicely hung Salvadoran accompanies me to one of the little concrete gazebos that jut out over the Mississippi River and obligingly fucks me from behind, both of us standing.

Half-drowned willows sway around us, screening us from the road. I grip the blue metal railing and stare out at the water. On the river's brown, roiling surface, huge cargo ships slide by like dinosaurs of red steel.

I keep my eyes open, even when I come.

9

When I get to the *Times-Picayune* office on Monday morning, my plan is to review the file on Javante Hopkins, my second sex offender, for our interview this afternoon. But there's a note on my desk from Claire, the section editor of Lagniappe. She had to take Marci off a plantation story that's due to run this week, so could I please, please, please do it? She knows I'm good at turning work around fast.

Oh, for fuck's sake, Claire. Plantations? How many plantation stories does the paper have to run? Nothing changes about the plantations except the entrance fees. They're historical, frozen in time. Where's the news in that? I could just pull an old story out of the archives, slap today's date on it, and no one would know the difference.

I stand up and look around the pit, but Claire's long blond hair, perpetual white flowy tunic, and semiprecious pendant—totally Soft Surroundings—are nowhere to be seen.

"Have you seen Claire?" I ask Floyd the Droid, who's typing dutifully in his cubicle.

He doesn't look up. "Out for the day."

Guess there's no talking my way out of this one. I sit back down.

I'm so pissed. Why is Claire saddling me with this crap when I have actual work to do? Grabbing a scratch pad, I scrawl my own note in reply: *Can't see why we need to run yet another puff piece on the charms of slave labor. And I am working on a feature story for Bailey, in case you didn't know, so I'm not exactly drowning in free time.* I stop and take a deep breath. My merit reviews keep mentioning diplomacy, tact, and the appropriate way to address one's superiors. *But if you need it, sure, okay. I'll have it to you Wednesday morning.* I walk over to her desk and drop the scrap of paper onto the stack in her in-box.

At my desk, I spend a little time online, skimming old plantation pieces we've run, and then fact-checking addresses, fees, and hours of operation for five of the closest plantations out on River Road. I randomly pick one, Moss Manors, and call their office to request a personal tour.

Oh, yes, says the high, quavering voice of the historic-preservation lady, they'd be delighted to *include* me in one of their *regularly scheduled* hourly tours tomorrow morning. She sidesteps my request without ever saying the word no. It's a skill. Cultured folk, they turn you down so sweetly you feel grateful.

You want clarity, talk to poor folks. They give it to you straight.

Before I leave the office, I hook my camera to my computer and download the photographs of Blake Lanusse. I watch the printer smoothly spit his face three times from the flat slit of its mechanical mouth. I stand there, staring down, the photos fanned in my hand. I slip them into my handbag and grab my keys.

Javante Hopkins, who liked to cut the women he raped in the Ninth Ward, now lives alone in the back half of a little white shotgun house in a sketchy section of Faubourg Bouligny. Released from prison six months ago, he's already been ticketed for suspicion of animal cruelty when a pit bull in his care couldn't be saved by the emergency vet clinic. Her head had been almost severed by a machete. They had to put her to sleep. Hopkins claimed he acted in self-defense when the dog attacked him, but the pattern of blows indicated that she'd been lying on her side.

It might have been wiser to meet him in some public place.

But house arrest was part of his parole. It's his home or nowhere.

Banana trees shade the sidewalk that runs alongside the house, so I feel like I'm walking down a long green tunnel to his door. Even before I knock, it's opened by a tall, muscled young man in a white wife beater and long blue gym shorts, a cigarette in his mouth and a monitor on his ankle. He must have been waiting and watching for me.

We sit down on his sagging sofa and launch quickly into the interview. His eyes dart around, and his hands twitch from time to time, like he's on something, but he's affable enough, and he doesn't mind being recorded. There's no coffee table, so the Olympus perches on the sofa cushion between us.

People have mostly ignored him, he says, since he was released. He hasn't been harassed by anyone.

"Be a black man on the streets of this city in the first place," Hopkins says. "White folks keep they distance. You don't have to be no rapist to get that."

"And black folks?"

"I moved out the neighborhood. Folks around here don't know. Least, they don't act like they know." He shifts restlessly in the cushions. "A hundred years ago," he says, "it wouldn't have been no big deal."

"How do you mean?"

"Frontier times. Didn't have the same kind of laws we got today. Men was men, all that."

"Talk to me about rehabilitation. How do you know you're re-habilitated?"

"Oh, I am most definitely rehabilitated. I learned my lesson good on that one."

"But how do you know?"

"I ask girls now. I don't just start up. I ask. I got over all that in prison."

"So you're sexually active?"

He laughs, waving his cigarette through the air as if waving off paparazzi. "Pleading the Fifth on that one."

"What about the cutting, Mr. Hopkins?"

"What about it?"

"Is that also something you got over in prison?"

He laughs shortly. "Prison ain't nothing but cutting. Inside, you learn how to make a knife with anything. Like look here," he says, rising abruptly and crossing the room in three strides. The room is hot, close. There's no air-conditioning. By June, it'll be hell. He opens a kitchen drawer and brings something over to me.

It's a nail that's been wrapped a hundred times with shiny black electrical tape, the pointed end scraped sharp.

"Check it," he says, dropping it into my open palm. I squeeze the tape handle. "Nice grip, right?"

I nod.

"Feel the tip." I lower a finger to the metal and quickly pull back. "That's what I'm telling you! Sharp, right?"

"Very."

"I can make a shank out of anything now, man. Give me a dirty diaper, I make you a shank out of shit."

"That's quite a skill." I hand the makeshift weapon back, and he pockets it.

"Yeah, sometimes I just be sitting around bored, and I make

me one of these. I got a whole drawer full. Different ones. Like a hobby."

"And how does this hobby relate to the women you go out with now?"

His eyes narrow. "Ain't no relation. Just something I do, all right? I don't be cutting nobody."

"Why did you before? Why did you like to cut them?"

He shrugs. His gaze flits from one corner of the room to the other.

"Mr. Hopkins?"

"Can't tell you. Don't know. Just liked to, I guess."

"But can you explain why you liked to? Please. For my readers."

"I don't know." He shrugs again. "Why anybody do anything? Example, why you doing this?" He frowns at me.

Good goddamn question. "Well, it's my—"

"Hey," he breaks in.

"Yes?"

"I like the way you call me Mr. Hopkins. Don't nobody call me that."

"Thank you."

"How old are you?" His hands jitterbug on his knees.

"Excuse me?"

"How old you be?"

I stare at him, try out a grin. "Old enough to know better."

He grins back. Whew. Rapport maintained. That could have gone either way.

"You know what?" he says, like he's going to tell me a secret, like I've earned my way into his trust.

"What?"

"Ancient Mexicans used to bleed they dicks."

"Excuse me?"

"Kings down in Mexico. Mayans and shit. For they religion.

They get high and cut they dicks. Dance around, bleed on stuff. Women, too. Cut they pussies. Just the kings and queens, high-up folks, with priests and shit. Dance around, get blood on everything. Make the rain come, fertility, all that shit."

"Huh," I say, that useful, all-purpose sound. "That's very interesting."

He leans back and looks at me expectantly, one eyebrow raised, smoke streaming from his nostrils, waiting.

I smile and correct myself. "That's very interesting, Mr. Hopkins."

"Damn straight it be interesting. If I lived back then, I wouldn't be sitting in no jail. I'd be a fucking king, man!" He laughs and leans back against the sofa, one hand behind his head, and takes a quick, hard drag off his smoke. "People worshiping me and shit."

"How did you learn about Mayan rituals?"

"They got books in prison, man. There ain't nothing to do with your free time but lift or read."

I smile again. "Or make shanks."

He laughs. "Ain't that the whole truth."

"And the dog, Mr. Hopkins? Your pit bull?" I flip through my notes. "Sadie? Was it necessary to cut her?"

"Aw, shit." He pulls his hands down to his lap, turns them over, looks at them as if looking for a clue. "We got to talk about that?"

"If you don't mind."

"She a good dog," he says softly. "Sadie. I don't know. I just get these feelings."

"Can you say more about the feelings?"

"I just get these feelings like I got to cut something, fuck something, fuck something up. Fucking dog kept whining, wouldn't shut up."

I scan the report. "The vet said she hadn't eaten in forty-eight hours."

"Fucking whiny bitch," he continues, as if I haven't spoken, staring down like I'm not there, like the dog is on the floor between us. His eyes are wide and glassy. "I slap her, she don't shut up. I slap her again. Then I remember that knife my cousin got."

"The machete."

"I think, that'll shut the bitch up good." He rubs his eyes as if waking. "And then I'm on the floor crying and the cops is here." He looks over at me, his gaze still vague. "A terrible thing," he says, his tone rote and insincere. "A terrible sad thing."

I feel a weird frisson, a shiver at his words.

His gaze snaps back into focus, and he looks into my eyes, then at the Olympus. "I didn't mean to kill her," he says loudly.

"She was just hungry."

"We all be hungry time to time," he snaps, his face cruel. "Ain't no cause to be whining." My heart sags suddenly.

"Mr. Hopkins, did you receive therapy in prison?"

"Therapy? You mean like psych ward stuff?"

"Counseling."

"Yeah, I had to go talk to some guy." He stabs the cigarette out in a blue bowl full of butts.

"How often? Weekly, monthly?"

"Don't know. Three, four times, maybe." In a five-year stint. If he's remembering accurately.

"And was that useful for you?"

He reaches up to his skull, palpates its dome with his fingertips. His eyes fog again.

"I guess. I don't remember. Some white guy ask me questions, I play along. Tell him whatever shit he want to hear."

So much for rehabilitation.

"Do you think you might ever rape someone again?"

"Oh, no. No way. I'ma be staying away from all that. Never." He leans toward the Olympus. "Ne-ver," he says loudly.

"Thank you so much, Mr. Hopkins. I think we're done." I reach down and turn the recorder off, slip it into my handbag, and stand up. I reach out to shake his hand.

"Already?" he says, not letting my hand go. "I ain't gave you the tour yet."

"That's all right. Really."

"No, come on. You got to see the crib." His grip tightens, and he pulls me across the room toward the mouth of the narrow hallway.

"I'm sorry, Mr. Hopkins, but I have another appointment."

Suddenly the tape-wrapped nail materializes in his other hand. We stop, staring at each other. He grins. "You scared?"

Fuck, yes, I'm scared, you psycho son of a bitch.

"Of course not," I say firmly. "I'm just on a tight schedule today."

His eyes appraise me, flicking up and down. "You tight all right." He takes backward steps down the hall, pulling me toward what can only be a bedroom. "Don't you want to see what I got back here?"

My ears buzz, and my legs feel heavy and numb as we take one step and then another. The bones of my hand ache in his tightening grasp. The smoke of a thousand cigarettes hangs stale in the air, and my head is light, floating, ringing with fear. It feels like old hallways in Desire I fought my way out of.

"Mr. Hopkins!"

He stops, my hand still in his grip.

"Mr. Hopkins, I am going to write a wonderful story about you, and everyone in New Orleans will read it. You'll be famous. Do you want me to say that you were rude when I had to leave?"

He looks at me for a long moment, then drops my hand.

"Aw, I was just playing," he says, but he shifts his body between me and the front door. The shiv still glints in his hand. "I was just playing with you."

"I know you were. No problem."

"So you going to leave this out of the story?"

"Yes, if I can go now."

"You going to put how I should have been a king?"

"If it's relevant to the story, yes."

"You going to say how I never meant to kill Sadie?"

"Yes, if it's relevant."

"Okay," he says. "Come on, then." He moves aside and walks me to the door, opening it with a flourish and holding it for me. I slide past him down onto the step, the fresh air rushing into my mouth like clean water. I'm safe on the hot cement, the green fronds of banana trees lapping the shade around me.

"Hey, Nola."

"Yes, Mr. Hopkins?"

He grins and leans close, wreathed by the smell of cigarettes.

"I say the shit you want to hear?" he asks. His eyes gleam, and the door slams shut.

I spend the late afternoon and evening at my desk at the *Times-Picayune*, typing up the Javante Hopkins interview. I keep hoping Claire will flow into the office so I can fight her on the plantation piece, but she doesn't. She's probably off at yoga or menopause class or something.

When I write my stories for the *Times-Picayune*, I stick to the journalist's stock-in-trade: who, what, when, where, and how—and if I'm lucky, why, or at least a gesture toward it. Even in my puff pieces, I practice keeping the story lean and mean, with the lead in the first sentence and no padding. Just the facts, ma'am.

But this story feels too big, too slippery, too complex. Even as I'm writing things down, I feel the larger whole eluding me.

Sometimes I wonder what our articles would look like if they mirrored the structure of the Mississippi. Where the river runs through the city, wide and roiling, the color of chocolate or steel,

it's easy enough to see it as a unified thing: obvious, simple, clear—
the way a crime is clear. But south of New Orleans, the Mississippi
fans out like a duck's footprint, branching into a labyrinth of tiny,
slow-running rivers. Once the river starts to unravel, all its eventu-
alities become hard to track. The little rivers are almost impossible
to distinguish from coastal bayous. It took the French explorer Iberville forever to discover the Mississippi's true mouth.

What would a news story look like if we patterned it after our
land? Would it start with a clear, definite originating event and then
explore a hundred possible effects, like the French did when they
mapped the coast?

As reporters, we don't have the time to track down the origins or
outcomes, the aftermath, the damage still playing out years after a
crime occurred.

When I finish, it's seven o'clock, and my head is light and aching with hunger. I call Calinda.

"Hey, you! What's going on?" she asks in a voice like honey
butter.

"I'm starving. You got plans?"

"I'm just heading home. What did you have in mind?"

"Well, it's Monday, so I'm thinking Jacques-Imo's—"

"And then some funk?" Her voice lights up. Every Monday night,
the local band Papa Grows Funk plays at the Maple Leaf Bar, right
next door to the old-style Creole-Cajun eatery Jacques-Imo's, which
serves gumbo you can drown in.

"Exactly. Sound good?"

"Give me twenty minutes."

We make kissy noises and hang up.

Calinda spends her days in the DA's office and at the courthouse
on Tulane Avenue. I've visited her there. The first floor is where you
pass through security, where they take away your cell phones and
cameras and knives. Wide staircases lead you up to the long second

floor, the hall of so-called justice, with its high arched ceilings and pale, peeling paint garnished with fading fleur-de-lis. Gold and glass light fixtures as tall as a woman hang from the ceiling, punctuating the long cool vault. On one side of the broad hall are windows that overlook the street. On the other side are courtrooms.

Calinda's job wears her down: the trials that go wrong, the children sent to Bridge City Correctional, the de facto segregation of the Bench, the bar where the DA folks go to drink, talk, play cards, and smoke—even smoke up evidence, or so rumor has it. The Bench's barred windows are painted black, and to get in, you have to buzz—and be white, as Calinda soon realized. As an official member of the DA's team herself, she was allowed in, but the proprietors' pattern of ignoring the buzzes of black folks soon became clear, and when she complained, she was told to lighten up. No pun intended. And then there's the woman whose calling it is to come to the courthouse each day and sing gospel music, mournful and echoing like a dirge in that high white corridor, as prisoners are led away in their shackles. "It's like something out of a movie," Calinda told me back when we first met. I told her she should write an exposé, a column, a blog.

"Oh, right," she said. "Like my job is worth that. Not to mention my life."

She said she was trying to focus on the humor in all the craziness, like the sheriff who so reliably slept during cases that prisoners regularly made a break for it, or the moment when the guy in his twenties, freshly convicted, had jumped up and pointed his finger at the warden.

"All my problems," he yelled, "all the damn problems in my life, come from *fat women*," and the whole courtroom cracked up.

"That's just fine, honey," she snapped right back. "You just think on that when you're sitting up at Angola."

Any humor that happens in the courthouse is gallows humor,

because everyone knows the realities. The Louisiana State Penitentiary at Angola, the Alcatraz of the South, is bigger than Manhattan. It's named after African Angola, where slaves were once kidnapped, and it's built on land that used to be a plantation, a slave breeding grounds. Tobacco and cotton grew there. Now it warehouses Louisiana's new brand of forced labor, the prisoners who work its huge farm.

"It's like some kind of crazy sitcom in those courtrooms," Calinda had said. "Heartbreaking and hilarious. But nobody would believe it if you put it on TV. You just have to stand there and try to keep your face straight."

I'd lifted my bottle. "To the art of the poker face." We'd clinked the glass necks of our cold beers.

But tonight at our little table at Jacques-Imo's, her eyes are serious as she slides into her seat across from me. "Hey, girl." She doesn't reach for the menu. "They found a body."

"Is it the missing tourist?"

"We think so."

"Think?"

"Nola, get this. Jane Doe had her face sliced off."

I sit silently, my mind rocking.

"And her fingertips," she continues. "He peeled her like peeling a fruit."

"Jesus." I think of Javante Hopkins with his penchant for blood and his drawer full of shanks. "But you'll get dental?"

"Records are on their way from Kansas. But we think it's going to be a match."

"What makes you so sure?"

"Right height, right hair color, skin color. And the timing, too. Her body washing up so soon after the Waybridge girl got taken."

"Washing up?"

"Over at Algiers. He dumped her in the Mississippi."

"Same MO as the two earlier vics," I say.

"Yeah. But that's about all I know right now. Forensics should be in soon. Listen, do you want me to keep you up on the case?"

"Yeah. Definitely."

"Off the record, though."

"Sure. I promise."

"Oh, and I sent that photo over, the one you texted me."

"Yeah?"

"Don't hold your breath. They're swamped over there. It'll take a few days."

I nod. We sit there in silence, each thinking our own thoughts about Amber Waybridge and her gruesome end. Finally Calinda takes a deep breath, puts on a smile, and opens her menu with a flourish.

"All right. Enough of that," she says. "So how are things?"

Things. It's hard to shift gears, but we try. We order and chat and sip our cold beers. I gripe about the plantation story for the Lagniappe. "There's even one Web site that plays the theme song from *Gone with the Wind*."

Her jaw drops. "Oh, tell me you are not for real."

"Swear to God."

"Baby, that wind done gone." We laugh as our food arrives. "I do not envy you that research," she says. "But enough about work. What's going on with you in the love department?"

"Not so much. I've been seeing a couple of guys."

"Anyone special?"

"No, not really." I examine my crawfish étouffée, and Calinda slams her beer down on the table.

"Girl! Is that a blush? I never thought I'd live to see the day. Tell the truth, now. Who is it?"

"No, there's nobody. Really."

"Ooh, girl, you play it close to the vest, don't you? Don't you worry. I'll find out when I get a couple more beers in you."

I smile and look away. "What about you? What else is going on at work?"

Her face drops. "I'm working this one case right now that's no good. Damn, it's breaking my heart." She shakes her head, pushes her spoon through the shrimp in her gumbo. "We're prosecuting this guy for molesting his kids, and it's a bad case—he's got four daughters, and we're thinking he might have done them all. So somebody needs to go talk to these children, right? Get their statements. And the family lives over in the Magnolia Projects."

I nod. My stomach tenses. When people don't know you come from a particular kind of place, they don't always choose their words with tact. As far as Calinda knows, I'm a Tulane grad with a fun job covering clubs and festivals, and that's all I am. When public housing comes up in conversation—any conversation, with anyone—I brace myself.

"So you remember how when I got hired I was the only black woman at the DA's?"

"Yeah." I slide my nail under the corner of the Abita label and start to peel it away from the brown glass.

"Well, two years later, I am *still* the only black woman. So everyone's like, 'Calinda, you do it.' Because you need a woman to do it, if possible, right? I get that. But they're all like, 'If we go down in there, we might not get back out,' and 'You'll blend in.'" She throws her hands in the air. "What? Me in my suit and briefcase, getting out of a Prius? Yeah, right."

I think of the fit I'd pitch if Bailey or Claire did something like that to me. "Did you say no?"

"No, I took it." She shrugs. "You know. One for the team." Calinda's goal is to get a few big wins and lay the groundwork to move to one of the better firms in the city. The DA's office is where you pay your dues, learn the ropes—not where you make a career. Not if you want a sane, ordinary life. "Besides, it did make sense." Her voice softens. "Who are four little black girls going to talk to? Some strange man? A white lady? Or me?" Her brown eyes are warm and kind and sad. "Me, right? It's obvious. If you had a scary secret, wouldn't you pick me to talk to?"

"I guess so." The knot in my stomach twists uncomfortably, and I take another quick pull off my beer. "So what happened?"

"So they told me they could send an investigator with me, for security, but you know those guys we've got down there. What I'm needing is Will Smith, armed to his pretty white teeth, and they're all more like Barney Fife."

She smacks the table, and we both crack up. Or I try, at least.

"Anyway . . ." I prompt.

"Right, so anyway, me and Barney Fife go into the projects. And I'm scared, right? It's just scary up in there. It's a mess."

I keep my gaze even and just nod.

"Four children, from ten years old on down to a little three-year-old baby girl, and they're all scared—scared of me, scared of the law, scared of putting their daddy in jail. So I can tell it's going to be quite a job, getting them to talk." She takes a big bite of gumbo. Whole bay leaves and smooth chunks of duck muscle float among the rice, and an orange-brown line of scum rings the bowl. "Mmm, this is something else." She blots her mouth. "So to warm them up, I offer to take the mother and girls out for pizza, and the girls get all psyched, so okay, I think it's going to work."

I nod, fingering my fork.

"But then, as we're walking out through the projects, all these relatives come out of the woodwork to join us, all these members of the family, or so they say, to get free pizza. Seventeen people, Nola. Food and drinks, on my credit card."

I keep my face as still as a mask to see what she'll say next.

"And when I get back to the DA's and tell everyone about it, they're all laughing and like, 'How many did you have to feed, Calinda?' and calling me the Pied Piper of the Projects. Like it was funny." Her eyes look wounded and pissed. "Nola, those people were *hungry*. They just wanted a good meal. They wanted to go out to eat, have a little fun—something we take for granted," she says, waving her hands at the full tables around us. At our own table. Her eyes flare. "It's not funny. It's *sad*."

I exhale. "Yeah. It is."

"My colleagues are idiots."

"Yeah," I agree. "Well, they just never had it like that themselves, so they don't know."

"Still," she protests, "they could take five minutes and imagine."

I smile at my friend. "Most people don't."

"No, not generally."

My belly relaxes, and I take another bite of my étouffée. It's a thick, fishy brew on my tongue. "So did you get their statements?"

"The little girls? Yeah. Not there at the pizza place—too many grown-ups and cousins around. Know what I mean?"

I nod.

"But then later, back at the apartment, we put Barney Fife out in front of the TV and used one of the bedrooms. They gave plenty of incriminating details." She takes a big bite, a pink shrimp perched in her spoon. "Not that they weren't scared shitless, poor things. They looked shell-shocked."

"And the guy?"

"Oh, he'll go down," she says with satisfaction. "Not for long, maybe. Not long enough. And with the state footing the bill, those children will not get the help they need."

"Right? And who's going to monitor the situation when he gets out in three on good behavior, and that smallest child is still just six years old?"

Her eyebrows lift. "You were paying attention." She takes a long drink of her beer, then forces a smile. Her eyes are weary. "You do what you can, right? Truth and justice."

I nod and smile back. "Truth and justice." We drink to that.

But I hear the deathbed words of Auntie Helene echoing in my head: *In this world, baby girl, there's no such thing as justice. You got to make your own.*

Later, next door at the Maple Leaf Bar, crowded between red walls among a hundred hot and jostling bodies, Calinda and I grin at each other, happy and sweating. The *guero* sax player wears a T-shirt that says, ONWARD, UPWARD, 9TH WARD, and the funk's too loud to talk over. I'm grateful for the way that the music and vodka shots drown the sound of my speeding brain. The drums pound, obliterating thought, and the bass line weaves a spell your hips can follow. We move to it, our arms lifted in the air, the sweet smell of someone's joint floating over us like a blessing. I close my eyes and let it take me. To my surprise, the images that surface in my half-intoxicated mind all feature Bento. His kind eyes, his low voice full of amusement. His large, warm hands that knew what to do.

But I head that off at the pass. Later, out in the alley, braced against a Dumpster, while Calinda thinks I'm in the ladies' room and some frat boy's jerking into me like a mechanical toy, I stare at the security light above us until it blinds me. All I feel is weary. I'm thinking about a young woman, raped, her faced sliced off. I'm tired of it all and wishing for sleep.

But frat boy can't tell.

"You are one hot tamale," he mutters, doing his thing, grunting, getting close. "You know that? One red-hot tamale."

10

I wake early to gray skies, a steady rain, and a headache that pulses and throbs. It's Tuesday, April 8. Plantation day. Ugh.

"Do you want to go check out a plantation with me?" I ask, shuffling through the kitchen. Uri's at the table with coffee and his little black Moleskine notebook. He stops writing and watches me, a speculative look on his face, as I soft-shoe from fridge to counter, counter to stove.

"Are you hungover again?"

Like I need this. "Are you a wanna-be novelist?" That shuts him up.

Hot coffee. Cold tomato juice. Tylenol. A hard-boiled egg. I slump at the table across from him, peeling the eggshell away with my nails. Uri writes in his little notebook.

"So what did you do last night?" I ask.

He doesn't look up. "Just sat around wishing I were a novelist."

"Oh, don't be mad."

"Then don't be a bitch, Nola." His tone is flat. I sputter tomato juice, then grin, wiping my mouth.

"Deal," I say. "I'm sorry." He looks up, sees me grinning, and smiles a little. "Really. I'm sorry," I repeat. Roux pads in, toenails clicking on the hardwood. More New Orleans fetishizing: Uri names his dog after the food, my mom names me after the town. Pretty soon, people will name their baby girls Katrina and brag about what little hellcats they are. "Hey, buddy." I reach out and scratch the warm fur of Roux's neck. "So do you want to come with me? I'm so not looking forward to doing this alone."

"Thanks, no. As much as I'd relish doing something that repels us both, no. Got to work."

"Fine, then. Be that way."

Sometimes I think I could be in love with Uri—his being utterly gay and all making it a total impossibility. He's just *nice,* you know? Decent.

What Uri wants more than anything—except to get his novel done and published—is to meet a nice, equally hot man and settle down, have a commitment ceremony, adopt kids, all that stuff. I initially thought that living above Fair Grinds would make him ecstatic, since after sundown it becomes total Gayville down there, all the young guys in their tight, stripey sailor shirts, the male nurses just off their shifts sprawling on the benches outside. But while it may be a great place to have a heart attack or pick up someone for a night, it's not Uri's scene. He does go out to clubs, but he likes Snug Harbor, where you sit at a table with your drinks and listen to jazz. In other words, he's looking for a fellow grown-up. A soul mate, not a fling.

He's not with anyone right now, and I know that whole thing about making them switch back is just a myth, just one more anxiety Latinas concocted to flagellate ourselves with: *If I were only woman enough, I could save him from his sin. . . .* You should hear my mother. She used to go on all the time about where the true blame lies for homosexuality. I know it doesn't work like that, but if it did, sweet, muscled Uri would tempt me to try.

Not right now, though. I couldn't seduce a billy goat right now.

My head throbs, and I must look like hell. I drink my tomato juice and stare out at the rain.

After the Tylenol kicks in, I make myself hit the treadmill, and once I've showered and dressed, the rain has lifted, and the sun shines.

Driving out of the city offers a mosh pit of glimpsed images, conflicting evidence of hope and dereliction: makeshift signs that offer discount tree cutting, rust-colored waterlines ringing houses, a house party with a sign: OUR LADY OF PERPETUAL CRAWFISH. There's a yard full of hauled-out trash, a doorway flanked by white stone angels, boarded stores strung with banners that promise, WE'RE OPEN, the cool green shade from branches of oaks arching over the street, a thousand shotgun shacks flickering past.

When my phone rings, it's Calinda. "Hey, Nola. You doing okay today?"

"Yeah. Sure. Why wouldn't I be?"

"Nothing. Listen, you wanted to be kept up on the Waybridge case, right?"

"Yeah. What's up?"

"We got dentals for the Waybridge girl. She's definitely our Jane Doe."

"Shit. I'm sorry."

"Yeah. Well, at least the family knows for sure now. And Nola, you want to hear something weird?"

"Peeling her face off isn't weird enough?"

"We got forensics back. They found traces of chemicals in her vagina."

"Semen?"

"No, but there's damage to the soft tissues. He likely used a condom."

"So what chemicals?"

"Let me see here." I hear the rustle of paper. "Sodium citrate, octoxynol, and cetyl pyridinium chloride."

"Which are?"

"Which are all found in Massengill products."

Seconds tick by, maybe ten of them. "He douched her?"

"Yes." Her voice is quiet. "What does that say to you?"

The city flickers past as my mind races. "He knows his DNA's on file. He's been convicted for this. He's taking every precaution." He's exactly the kind of guy I'm researching.

"Right. And Nola?"

"Yeah?"

"He took a nipple." For a moment, the sun goes dark and cold. The Pontiac's motor is loud in my ears. Then I can breathe again.

"A trophy, you mean."

"Yeah. A souvenir."

"While she was still alive?"

"Coroner says no. After death."

"At least—"

"Yeah." She clears her throat. "Hey, all this is still off the record, you hear?"

"See no evil, hear no evil."

"I'm serious. We're not telling the press about the specifics. We're going to say 'mutilated,' but that's it. It'll help us weed out the crazies who call. Okay? So you can't tell anyone this stuff."

I promise. We say good-bye, and I drive on through the city. The wall of one abandoned home cries out a ragged, spray-painted message to corporate America: WHERE ARE THE GOOD HANDS NOW, ALLSTATE?

I think of the douche. A final violation. A piece of plastic shoved up a woman to erase what was done. I wonder if she was alive or dead by that point.

Once I'm out of the city, the rolling green fields come as visual relief. I put the car on cruise control and zone out to Dr. John singing, *"Home sweet home, home sweet home/We're gonna be back twice as strong,"* on WWOZ.

Why the Lagniappe section keeps needing to "cover" plantations is beyond me, but when I pull up and park the Pontiac, I have to admit I'm dazzled. P.S. McDonogh 15 never took us on field trips out here. The rain has rinsed everything to a glimmering sheen, and a flat brick path runs through a lawn of cool green grass bigger than a football field. Giant oaks shade everything. The peach stucco manor house is vast, and huge white columns stretch from the ground to the roof.

I pay my fifteen dollars, glance at the brochure, and stand around, fiddling with the branch of a pretty green bush, shaking the rain off its leaves onto my sandaled toes, waiting for one of the scheduled tours to start.

The tour group gathers. Six old ladies in purple dresses and red hats talk and laugh loudly, as if to make sure everyone can see they're having a hell of a grand time being old.

"Are we all ready to start?" Our guide clasps her hands together and scans the twelve of us with her smile. "I'm Amy, and it's my pleasure to welcome you to Moss Manors Plantation. Come absorb her beauty, and imagine her lush past."

She leads the way, explaining how old the oaks are, and how the manor house is a classic Greek Revival, and how river commerce worked back in the day. Moss Manors's land rolls right up to the banks of the Mississippi, so barges could transport crops and products to the market in New Orleans. All along River Road, plantations produced food, supplies, and cotton that were shipped to the city, and the city shipped back mail and finery.

"Merchant Zadok Cramer wrote in 1801 that New Orleans was 'the grand mart of business, the Alexandria of America.'" Amy pulls open the wide double doors, and we enter the brick-paved foyer. "You'll notice that there's no step up to enter the house." She gestures around the large, airy space with its high ceilings and natural light. "The young gentlemen would gallop up the walk and ride their horses right inside." A delighted murmur ripples through the small crowd.

Not so romantic for the person cleaning up horseshit.

Amy turns and beckons us. "Now let's see the dining room." She bobs in a sort of little curtsey, swinging her eye contact around to everyone.

The long dining table is laid for a formal dinner. The old red-hat ladies coo over the china and silver.

"Observe this ingenious contraption," says Amy, gesturing toward an iron handle. "Invented by one of the owners of the house, it can turn several fans at once. Fans were very important during meals, not only because of Louisiana's intense heat, but also to keep insects away from the food during a period when there were no window screens. This was before electricity, remember, so this invention was a great labor-saving device. A single servant could stand here—" she moves to demonstrate—"and turn all the fans in the room." She winds the crank, and all the wide paddles spin once. The air stirs.

I note her words. *Servant.* Not *slave.*

We wander through the downstairs, the elegant little parlor and the music room, and then into a strangely small and underfurnished kitchen.

"Most of the food was actually prepared in a separate structure, away from the main house, due to the heat and the risk of fire," explains Amy. She herds our little group upstairs, where the women sigh over the canopy beds and the porcelain pitchers and washing bowls. A middle-aged man taps the molding with his pencil. The guide keeps using the words *gracious, genteel, romantic,* and *tradition.*

The warm, still air of the bedrooms feels stuffy and dead. Within these walls, people made love. People were born and died. The rooms should throb with life, but they feel claustrophobic, heavy.

It's a relief when we move out onto the terrace, where the breeze is cool and you can breathe. The terrace wraps around the whole top floor and affords, I'd say if I were a travel writer, a marvelous view of the grounds. The view really is lovely. Green meadows roll, hot pink azalea bushes dot the landscape, trees are in pale bloom, and the grass slopes gently up to the riverbank. Our guide slowly shepherds us around, pointing down with her gemmed hands.

Finally we've circled the house's perimeter, and I'm tired of fetishizing the beauties of wealth.

"Where are the slave quarters?" I ask.

Amy nods, her smile gracious. "Those were removed some years ago."

A breeze stirs my hair. "They were what?"

Everyone else is silent, motionless.

"They're gone," she says. "They were removed."

"Removed? As in torn down?"

Suddenly, Amy's smile is not nearly so wide. "Yes. As in torn down."

"But that's erasure."

"Excuse me?"

"Those cabins matter. Damage doesn't stop when you tear one set of buildings down." I think of the Desire Project and feel my face get hot. Amy the guide lays a hand on my arm, but I shake it off.

She shoulders her way between me and the group. Her voice is bright and stern.

"If you would like to explore the fascinating world of slave cabins," she says, "you should visit Peachtree, one of our neighboring plantations, which has an intact set of cabins in pristine condition."

"*Pristine?*" My mind flickers inexplicably to the French casket girls, pure and protected in their convent. Pristine is just a useful fiction. "I want to see the cabins that should be *here*."

"If you'd like to head down to the office now, they can provide you with a brochure and a map for Peachtree." Turning back to the rest of the group, she clasps her hands again, but more stiffly now. "Yes, the slave cabins at Peachtree will send chills down your spine. If you have time, it's an adventure you shouldn't miss."

"An *adventure*?" I say.

She wheels. "Miss," she says, "I'm going to have to ask you to leave."

"You're throwing me off the tour?" I stare at her for a minute, at all of them, then break into laughter.

"If you don't head for the exit immediately, I'll have to call security. You're being disruptive."

"And very rude," pipes up one woman. The hatted old ladies all nod, their red brims bobbing.

"Okey-doke." I head back indoors and cut through the stuffy rooms, down the broad staircase, and out the brick foyer onto the lawn.

From the terrace, they're all staring down at me, making sure I go. I wave up cheerily.

Frankly, my dear, I don't give a damn.

During the drive back to the city, I dictate a piece into my Olympus and then put plantations out of my mind. My interview focus now is parents, and how they use the sex offender registry—or not—to protect their children. Gwyneth Bigelow, mother of two and a board member of the children's museum, which is how I found her name online, is my first interview subject from the Garden District, the city's wealthiest area.

When I pull up in front of the Bigelows' cream Creole cottage on St. Charles, I cut the ignition, flip down the visor for a quick inspection, and fluff my hair. My cheeks are pale from too much coffee, so I give myself a quick dusting of blush and pop an Altoid. Better.

New Orleans front yards, if they exist at all, are generally tiny—even those of the fanciest houses here in Uptown. It takes me only three strides to cross the brick courtyard, where a black Mercedes SUV sits shining. The staircase flares wide at the bottom, like water flowing graciously out. A lot of houses here are built this way, with the living quarters on the second floor, a preemptive strike against flooding. I ring the doorbell and wait. A blue Obama '08 poster sits in a window. A discreet security sign is spiked into a flowerbed.

Gwyneth Bigelow opens the door. Rail-thin, blond, and smiling, she extends a cool hand.

"Won't you come in?"

Her living room is plush. One of those damn blue dogs hangs on a wall, and of course there's a chandelier, which she tells me is Murano glass, brought back from a trip to Venice.

"Something a little different, you know?"

I nod like I do.

She gets us each a glass of iced tea with a sprig of real mint and a thin disc of lime floating on top. We settle into squishy floral chairs made to look antique, and I set up the Olympus on a glass table between us. Everything smells like just-mown grass, and a profusion of fresh flowers covers the mantel.

"This is a great time for you to come, too," says Gwyneth Bigelow, "since the girls are still at school." She crosses her legs at the knees, moves her arms and wrists in graceful, expansive angles.

"Tell me about the girls."

"Well, Ella is eight, and Lynnie's just six. They both go to Sacred Heart, which is only three blocks from here, but I always drop them off and pick them up. I don't feel safe if they walk."

"Even though this is a nice neighborhood."

"It's a wonderful neighborhood. We love it, and I walk with the girls quite a bit. We go to Audubon Park all the time." Right across from Tulane University, Audubon Park is vast, green, and lovely, full of squirrels, ducks on the lake, Spanish moss hanging from oaks, paths for cyclists and joggers. I used to go running there when I was a student. As long as it was daylight and there were people around, I always felt pretty safe. "But I don't want the girls going off by themselves," Gwyneth Bigelow continues, "for exactly the reason you're here."

"Yes. How much do you know about the sex offender registry?"

"I know enough to check it once a month. Here." She twists to take a piece of paper off an end table. "I got this out to show you."

She hands me a computer printout of a satellite photo. It's a hybrid image of an aerial photo that shows the twenty or so blocks that surround us. Red *X*s are mapped onto several houses.

"The girls and I don't even walk down those blocks," she says. "I don't want any molesters starting to watch them."

"Doesn't that impede your freedom of movement?"

Her laugh is brisk. "Yes, of course. But that's like asking if a rattlesnake impedes your movement. Certainly. You give it a wide berth, and you don't get hurt."

"Do you discuss this with your daughters?"

"We've had the stranger-danger talk, and we've talked about their bodies, how no one has the right to touch them, or even say things to them that make them uncomfortable. They know they should tell us immediately if anything happens, and not to be scared, even if someone threatens them not to tell." She runs her hand through her gold hair and smiles. "We put them both in soccer and karate, too, so they can gain a sense of control and strength in their bodies. They both have a healthy sense of boundaries."

"How about the map? Do you talk about that?"

"No, I just make sure I'm always with them when they're outside, and I steer them away from those streets. I guess when they're old enough to go out alone, then I'll show them. But there's no point in scaring them now. That's what I'm for, as a parent. To protect them. I want them to feel free and happy, not like the city's full of wolves."

"Even though it is?"

She nods and takes a swallow of cold tea. "Even though it is."

"How old is old enough to go out alone?"

"I don't know." Her eyes look sad. "Fifteen? That's terrible, isn't it? Maybe I'm overly protective. I don't know. Thirteen? Twelve? I guess we'll figure that out as we get there."

I take a long drink. "Let's move to something different. How do you feel about the rights of the sex offenders themselves?"

"Their rights?" Her voice stiffens. "What rights?"

"Well, for example, their right to privacy."

"They gave up their rights when they did what they did. They don't deserve privacy anymore. Privacy is what let them molest children in the first place. They're sick, and they need to be watched."

"But not all sex offenders molest children."

"I don't care what they did." Her voice rises in pitch. "If they got sent to jail for it, it couldn't have been good."

"Well, let me just complicate the picture a little for you, Mrs. Bigelow. Some sex offenders are sentenced for statutory rape, when they have consensual sex with a partner only a year or two younger."

"Yes, well, I'm sorry, but society has rules. You follow the rules, you don't go to jail. It's not rocket science." She taps the rim of her glass in agitation. "Look, I don't go around harassing these men. I don't burn crosses on their lawns, or threaten them, or put up fly- ers. I just use the information that I've been given." Her voice has gotten even higher, and the cords in her neck look strained as she leans toward me. "I have the right to know. As parents, we have the right to keep our children safe."

"So you think Megan's Law is a good idea."

"Absolutely. It's the information our own parents should have had. It would have prevented a lot of . . ." She passes her hand over her eyes and takes a quick drink of cold tea.

"Mrs. Bigelow?"

"A lot of unnecessary suffering." When she looks at me again, her smile is bright. "What else would you like to know?"

"Let's see." I check my notebook. "Okay. What do you and your husband do?"

"My husband is a surgeon at the Ochsner Medical Center. Me?" She waves her hand around the living room. "You're looking at it. Full-time mom. I like to be at home. We entertain a lot, too, of course, and that takes time."

"Right. Is there anything else you'd like our readers to know?"

She stares at me for a long moment, her eyes empty. "No, that's all."

"Mrs. Bigelow, are you sure there's nothing else you'd like to tell me?" Her eyes drop, and we sit in silence. I'm about to repeat my question when her lips part.

"They should never be let out," she says softly, staring at the floor. "They're monsters. They should rot in there. What they do, it destroys life, just like murder. It destroys souls. They should never be allowed back out."

11

Every age has its hot technology. In the 1930s, homing pigeons flew rolls of film back to the *Times-Picayune* office for late-breaking stories. This was especially useful for football games, since the pigeon could travel much faster than a reporter stuck in post-game traffic.

Yesterday afternoon, as I risked tickets all the way home to the city, my snazzy silver Olympus allowed me to dictate my neutral little puff piece about Moss Manors Plantation while it was all still fresh in my mind. Back at my apartment last night, wireless let me sit on my bed and type the whole thing up on my laptop. The miracle of email let me attach the story and send it to Claire.

But technology can't protect you from the wrath of a pissed-off boss.

The minute I walk into the pit this morning, Claire thunders like Boadicea toward my desk, her long gold hair flying.

"What the hell is this?" She drops a sheaf of paper on my desk.

I examine it. My byline: Nola Céspedes. My headline: EXPLORE PAST GLORIES AT NEARBY PLANTATIONS.

I snap my gum. "Is this a trick question?"

"It's bland, it's forgettable, it's insufferably dull."

"You're not pleased."

"Damn right, I'm not pleased." Her voice is loud and brassy. "I put you on this story because you can write, because you can turn *good* work around fast. If I wanted crap, I could have asked anyone."

I feel the room grow quiet around us. *Nice one, Claire. Way to build the team.*

"What's wrong with it?"

"Everything." She glances at her watch. "And I don't have all day. I've got to leave for an ed board meeting in two minutes."

"In a nutshell?"

"In a nutshell, it's boring. Nothing happens, nothing matters. And the writing's crap." She turns to page two, pokes at the text in disgust. "Look at all those *be* verbs. Look at those flat descriptors."

She's right. The writing sucks. Because the assignment sucks.

"It has all the life of a fifth-grade book report. This does not"— she jabs it again—"make me want to go see a plantation."

"Oh, so that's my job now?" My shoulders square. "Writing ad copy for Moss Manor?"

"If the Lagniappe helps promote local tourism, then yes, that's a good thing. You know that, Nola. Especially now." She means after Katrina. "That's our job." Her spine straightens. "Our mission."

Spare me the melodrama. "Okay, I'll fix it."

"No, you'll do it over from scratch. There's nothing here worth saving."

"Yeah, okay, whatever—"

"And by tonight."

"Tonight? Claire, I've got interviews lined—"

"I don't care if you've got lupus," she snaps. "It's due to run Friday, so I need it by eight o'clock tonight, or I'm calling Bailey."

"Bailey? Oh, come on—"

"Oh, wait." Her red mouth twists, sarcastic. "He's your new best friend, right?"

There it is. Out in the open. Here's why she's screwing me.

"Well, I don't care," she says. "If I don't have a rewrite by eight, he'll hear from me about how you're *really* doing. And then we'll see if he wants you writing features."

"Yes, ma'am." I keep my tone right on the glimmering edge of mockery, just a shade too faint for her to call me on it. Bitch. Her eyes rove my face.

"Good," she says finally, and she turns and walks toward the newsroom. The fabric of her blouse clings to a ridge of fat spilling over her bra. *Spanx, Claire. It's time.*

Fine. Fuck her. If she wants something memorable, I can do that. I'll give her a story she won't forget.

But first, I need reinforcements. I take the escalator down to the second-floor cafeteria to load up on coffee. Oh, there's solid food there: bagels, apples and bananas in a basket, a lame salad bar, and lasagna or bland étouffée on the hot line. But mostly the first-floors eat that stuff, the heavyset women in payroll, the cashier, the advertising staff, and the blue-overall guys who run the big machines of the press itself. Up on the third floor, we live on Diet Coke and coffee. Headlines and deadlines.

My first interview's at noon, and before then, I need to conjure up something memorable. I head back up the escalator, balancing three large coffees, and settle in at my desk. Okay. Just do what they taught us at Tulane: Cut loose. Go for the jugular. You can always edit later.

The jugular. My fingers start to fly over the keyboard.

For an hour, two hours as the morning ticks by, I see nothing, hear nothing around me as I write and delete and rewrite. The Living and Lagniappe pit fades into a blur in my peripheral vision, my colleagues' chatter an indistinct hum. Only the screen's alive.

Finally, I give the piece a last polish. I love it. It's a story I feel, a story I'm proud of. I feel like I used to, back at WTUL, just me alone in the booth, cutting loose, rapping out my rants in the dark.

It's certainly a story Claire won't forget. And there's not a *be* verb to be found.

I draft a little email to her—*Here's the rewrite, as requested. Hope you like it*—and attach the file, *plantations.doc.*

But I don't hit SEND. Not yet. I save the whole thing to my drafts folder. Eight o'clock? Fine. Claire can wait. I'll send it later, when I'm good and goddamn ready.

I don't know what I was thinking, squeezing in a perp interview before my interviews with other well-to-do parents in the Garden District, but at a quarter till noon, I swing out of the newspaper's parking lot and head for my first official encounter with Blake Lanusse. I'm a little jittery from the coffee, and the memory of my interview with Javante Hopkins doesn't help. Nervous cramps twist my belly.

I need to calm down. Breathe. Focus on the facts of the case. After serving only three years of an eight-year term for molesting schoolgirls, Lanusse got out on good behavior. He's been out of Orleans Parish Prison for two years now, so he's had plenty of time to settle back in, to reflect. He should be able to provide some revealing insights—if I can ask the right questions, instead of envisioning drawers full of shanks and a woman with her face sliced off. If I can forget everything else and just focus on what's happening. If I can get my hands to stop shaking.

When I hit the Quarter, I circle Lanusse's block, hunting for a parking spot, and finally end up walking a ways. Sweating a little, I stand on the bright sidewalk, pressing my hands together, waiting for him to answer the doorbell.

When the door swings open, Blake Lanusse is a good foot taller than I am, and his shoulders are twice as broad. He stands in the shadowed entryway, handsome, blinking, his eyes a little glassy.

Good: he doesn't recognize me. He seems a little dazed. Buzzed, maybe.

"Mr. Lanusse?"

He nods.

"Mr. Blake Michael Lanusse?" I say carefully. Something in his pale eyes flares up suddenly, like the blue broiler flame in the bowels of an oven.

"Yeah, that's me." He looks guarded.

"I'm from the *Times-Picayune*. We spoke on the phone."

"Oh, right!" A broad smile lights his face, and the corners of his eyes crinkle. "Yeah. The interview thing." He scratches his head, shifting his black hair askew. His warmth and casual air are suddenly endearing, inviting. I see how he could gain a child's trust. "Come on in." He turns.

The door swings shut behind me, and I hear the automatic lock click. He climbs the dark steps, which creak under our feet, and I follow him up the narrow staircase, trying not to stare at his hips, which jostle at eye level all the way up. A dusty chandelier dangles overhead, and his body casts long, warped shadows on the walls.

When he opens the door to his apartment, a haze of cigar smoke ushers us into the dim room. Brick walls, a point of pride for any Quarter resident, have been left untouched, and the oak floor is glossy with polish. Three of the tall windows are shuttered, and all four are hung with red velvet curtains, shrouding the room in darkness. Large gold-framed mirrors reflect three red velvet sofas crowded together, fringe dangling. It's like a Storyville bordello in here. A black chandelier with long waving legs crouches over us like an Art Nouveau spider.

Lanusse gestures toward a black dining table, where a cigar smolders in an ashtray next to a half-empty glass of brown liquid. I set my handbag and clipboard on the table, lower myself to a chair, and take my Olympus out.

"You don't mind if I record our conversation, do you?" My voice sounds weirdly small. I clear my throat.

He shakes his head. "Help yourself." He sits down, spreads his strong hands on the table. A red glass bowl sits between us, full of foil-wrapped candies. He lifts the bowl, shakes it at me. "You want one?"

"No, thank you."

He sets it back down and then reaches in, grabs three, and tosses them over to me anyway. They clatter across the table. "Just in case," he says. His smile is warm, comfortable.

Ignoring the candies, I settle my things into place, check the Olympus, and start with a softball. "I like your condo." Your dark, smoky condo, furnished with clichés, as creepy as Mickey Rourke's fingernails.

"Yeah, I couldn't get my old place back," he says. "The guy wouldn't rent to me anymore." He waves his cigar. "But you know, whatever. What are you going to do? I found this place for sale, and I used the money from my buyout package. All that money just sitting in the bank, so why not? And I'm still in the Quarter. Still feels like home. Just a few blocks away from my old place."

"Your buyout package?"

"Yeah, from the school system. When I was charged, they put me on probation. When I got convicted, they bought me out. Twenty-five years I'd worked there, you know? Enough to get my retirement. They didn't want me taking the school down with me, giving it a bad name, all that. Afraid of parents starting lawsuits, maybe. You know how people are."

"Yes. Yes, I do. So you had to sign something?"

"Yeah. I signed some form that said I wouldn't talk to anyone about the school or my time there." He leans back, looks me up and down. Cigar smoke wafts up. This is not a nervous man. "So that's off-limits today. Can't talk about it."

"Yes, I see. All right. I won't ask you about that. So you've got this great place here in the Quarter."

"Love it," he agrees.

"Is parking difficult? I always have trouble finding a space."

"No, the building has a garage. An old carriage house," he explains. "Period and everything. Out behind."

"Oh, how convenient. And what kind of car do you drive?"

He frowns. We both know it's not relevant.

"Nothing special," he says. "Just a sedan."

"Of course, of course." I smile brightly. "You're so lucky to have somewhere to park it!" My laugh sounds forced even to me. A car and a place to conceal it, just blocks from where Amber Waybridge was taken. "So tell me what it's been like for you here, how people treat you."

"Oh, it's pretty good here, really," he says. His easy smile returns. "People in the Quarter don't really notice each other much—don't look at each other, even. A lot of these apartments are short-term for tourists, you know. Mardi Gras, Jazz Fest. Tourists go by every day here. Hundreds, when it's busy. Thousands. You can get lost in the crowd. So it's hard to tell who's a neighbor and who's just passing through. Even the permanent residents don't bother learning your name."

The back of my neck chills. He's about as close to invisible as you can get. "And what's that like for you?"

"It's all right," he says. "I was born in the Quarter, lived and worked here all my life, and I'll die here."

"You know, a woman was abducted in the Quarter recently."

"Is that right?"

"Her body was found. She'd been sexually assaulted."

He swallows the last of his drink, pushes back from the table. "You want something? I'm going to get me some more rum." He moves with the thickened grace of an aging football star.

"No, thank you."

"You got a problem with hospitality?" He laughs, but his tone is shading toward aggression. It's the voice of a former vice principal, the muscle, someone who does the dirty work so the principal can keep his hands clean. Someone who enjoys it.

"I'm not thirsty," I say, but he has already disappeared into the kitchen. Left alone in the room, I do feel a fierce and sudden thirst. My hands jitter on top of the file, and I see little sweat prints on the manila where my fingertips have been. My mouth feels stuffed with a wad of plucked cotton, but I don't want rum to drink, much less a piece of Blake Lanusse's candy to suck. What I want is fresh, cold water in a clean glass, but I can't bring myself to ask.

He's taking forever, and I rise and pace the room, hungry for the natural light from the one unshuttered window. In the kitchen, he's opening the freezer, rattling ice.

When I look through the window, I can see directly across Chartres into the walled garden of Ursuline Convent. The view is perfectly clear, crisp. From here, I can see each brick in the pathways, the closed gray shutters at each window, the green fronds of the palm trees. I can read the gold lettering over the chapel entrance: *VIRGINI DEIPARAE DICATUM.* It's the noon hour, so the girls must be inside, eating their lunch. But at 8:00 A.M. and 3:00 P.M. and anytime there's recess, anyone standing at this window would be able to observe the children quite clearly. Girls in their skirts, running, jumping. Squatting to play jacks, or whatever game rich kids play.

My eyes fall to the wide black sill. An expensive pair of binoculars lies there, out of its case.

From my research, I know that sex offenders rehearse their crimes through fantasy. The more they rehearse, the more their self-control deteriorates.

"Hey, there," says Blake Lanusse, and I jump. When I turn around, he's standing in the kitchen doorway, staring at me, a bottle of rum in one hand, two glasses pinched in the other. "What do you think you're doing?"

Flashing my brightest smile, I clear my throat again. "Admiring your view," I say. "And your lovely decor! It's so unusual." He squints at me as if weighing my words. I try again, channeling all the perkiness of a Tulane sorority girl. "Such atmosphere."

He takes a step toward me. I feel a wave of real fear, realizing how large he is, how alone I am with him, here on his turf. My cell phone is across the room in my purse, useless. Lanusse's muscled bulk blocks my path to the door. His pale eyes blaze.

Desperate, I finger the top button of my blouse. "It's all so inviting," I say, running my other hand along the back of the red velvet sofa. "So suggestive."

The hostility begins to slip from his eyes. "Yeah?"

"Yeah. Why don't you pour me some of that rum?"

He nods, moves toward the table.

A sudden thump comes from the outer hallway, down near the bottom of the stairs. We both freeze, listening to each footstep ascend, followed by a heavy bump, like something banging on each stair. On the landing, keys jingle.

"Aw, fuck," says Lanusse under his breath.

The door opens and a woman enters, dropping her purse and rolling suitcase and surging toward him, arms outstretched. She's a platinum blonde of maybe forty whose clothes strain at her bustline and whose ankles cry out for a diuretic. Apricot lipstick gives her mouth a ripe, neon sheen.

"Lily! Baby!" he booms in his other voice, the jovial one. "You weren't supposed to—"

When Lily sees me, all her delight sours.

"Why, Blake, who's this here?" she asks, her accent pure Yat, her smile forcing more wattage than her eyes.

"This girl just came down from the *Times-Picayune, cher*," he says. I cross the room, pull my press pass from my handbag, and hold it out to her. She eyes it, nodding, still suspicious. "The paper wants to know about what-all I been doing to help the Quarter Association." His eyes flick to me and widen just the slightest fraction. It's a silent plea.

So she has no idea what I'm really here for, then. Which means she has no idea what he's done, who he is, what to watch out for.

And he wants me to keep her that way.

"Oh, yeah?" She grips his wrist with one hand and runs her other hand up and down his arm in a move that's part pride, part possession. "Blake here is a great contributor, a great neighbor. Very involved in keeping up the Quarter."

Lanusse is still watching me, waiting to see if I'll play along.

I want this interview. I want him back alone in this room again.

"Yes, ma'am," I say. I clear my dry throat. "His record is certainly noteworthy."

Lanusse visibly exhales. "Well, I guess we can finish up talking some other—"

"Oh, no," says Lily, waving her hand. "You two go on ahead. You won't even know I'm here. I've got this unpacking to—"

"Are you kidding me, babe? You been gone for weeks. Business can wait." He turns to me. "You got a number I can call?"

"Sure." I'm nodding, fumbling automatically in my handbag for my business cards. "I'm out of the office a lot, so this is the best way to reach me."

"Okay, yeah." He takes it, and for a moment, his shining wood floor seems to buckle and heave beneath me. I've just given a convicted child molester my cell phone number, the one for the phone that's in my purse or on my nightstand or on my body, day or night.

He nods. "Good," he says. " 'Cause I got more to say."

"Don't worry." I gather up my things. "We're not finished."

The door is still open, and I step around Lily's purse and suitcase. My heels clack down the dark chute of the stairs.

Outside in the bright, broiling safety of my parked Pontiac, I grip the top of the steering wheel and lower my head to my hands.

That evening, after interviewing two more well-to-do mothers and a father from the Garden District, I sit on my bed with my laptop, typing it all up, choosing the quotable quotes. At 6:00 P.M., the golden sounds of the bells of Holy Rosary float through the evening air.

When I'm finished, it's seven o'clock. I heat up some frozen *paneer makhani* in the microwave and sit alone on the balcony to eat. Uri's off tending bar at the Vic, and Roux pushes the screen door open with his nose and pads out to keep me company. He curls at my feet, and I rub my bare toes along his back. Every now and then, he heaves a deep, doggy sigh.

The city's hazy with late evening light, and I prop my brown ankles up on the railing, balancing the little dish in my lap, and watch people drift in and out of the restaurants and shops. I sift through the events of the day, and lines start to write themselves in my head.

When I come back inside the apartment, it's 7:58 P.M.—two minutes before Claire's eight o'clock deadline. I lean over my laptop, open my email, and open the draft of my note with the plantation story attached. Somewhere, Claire is seething, her eyes on her in-box, wishing me fired. Seven fifty-nine. I press SEND.

12

On Thursday morning, I drive to work through thunderstorms and heavy rain. Drops big as quarters pelt the windshield, and my Pontiac feels sluggish. The *Times-Picayune* building is quiet, and the ride up the escalators to the third floor seems to last forever.

When I enter the Lagniappe pit, Claire's standing by my desk, waving her hands and conferring with Bailey. I back up slowly, hoping I can slip away before they spot me.

"Nola!" It's Bailey's voice, hard and loud. "Get over here."

The walk between the other desks feels long, endless, all eyes hungrily upon me, like I'm heading for the guillotine.

When I get to my desk, Bailey's holding a printout. Claire's hands are on her hips, and her lifted chin is smug and vindicated. Her face and throat are flushed. *Hey, Claire. Is that a hot flash, or are you just happy to see me?*

Bailey reads the headline out loud: "'Thirty-five Million: At What Cost?'" He clears his throat. "'Offering the public a sanitized, romantic version of slavery pours an estimated thirty-five million dollars a year in tourism revenues into Louisiana's needy post-Katrina coffers. But in catering to white tourists hungry for a little taste of Tara, the plantation industry distorts history, erases the suffering and accomplishments of black workers, and demeans the ethics and intelligence of all Americans. It's not a heritage of which Louisiana can be proud.'" He lowers the pages and sighs. "Nola, what am I supposed to do with this?"

I shrug. "Run it. You can thank me later."

"You knew this wasn't an investigation." He shakes his head. "Claire didn't send you out there to rake the muck."

"But, Bailey—"

"What's wrong with you?" He closes his eyes, pinches the bridge of his nose. "You're bright, a good writer. You got a second chance with this piece, and you deliberately blew it. This is two strikes." He gestures toward Claire as if handing me off to her and turns away, heading for the newsroom.

Claire jumps in eagerly. "I'm giving your first version to Marci as a template," she says. Marci, who wasn't good enough to write it in the first place. "She'll punch it up, do what she wants with it, and we'll run it under her byline."

"Good," I say. "I don't want my name on that shit anyway."

Bailey overhears. He spins, coming at me, his finger raised and pointed. "If you don't get your act together, your name won't be on anything." He's down in my face, loud and angry. Something about his aggressive posture catapults me straight back to Desire. Instantly, I'm tensed, hot all over, muscles clenching.

"Is that a threat?" I'm quivering.

His gaze is level. "Does it feel like one?"

We stare at each other, motionless, rigid. His jaw pulses.

"Two strikes," he says, and finally turns away. "Two strikes."

I'm still shaking, pissed, as I wheel out of the *Times-Picayune* parking lot and onto Howard. Damn the plantations, anyway.

The rain has lifted, and I'm heading over to interview more

parents, but at the other end of the socioeconomic scale, the working poor of the Ninth Ward. I had gotten the names of ten people known as good parents, strivers, from the office secretary at an elementary school in the Upper Ninth. Most hung up or said no. Three moms agreed to see me.

Hurricane Katrina's destruction may have briefly brought the Ninth Ward to national attention, but the Ninth Ward was economically devastated long before Katrina hit. In falling-down shotguns with rusted window units that strained against the heat and dripped an unscrubbable green slime onto the cement, people made their lives. They loved and raised their families. They also drank, used, and beat each other. They died too young from things proper medical care could have cured.

The Lower Ninth—the wasteland you see on TV—is still a hot, sad, barren mess, but the Upper Ninth was far less damaged by the storm. It's holding steady. It's my old stomping grounds, where my mother raised me on Cuban cooking, Popeyes chicken, and Hubig's Pies, ninety-nine cents each, in every flavor a child could crave: coconut, lemon, banana, chocolate. I haven't been back to the neighborhood since 2003, when Desire came down. Five years ago.

The sun beats down, frying the leftover rainwater into the humid air. As I turn up Franklin, I begin to see what middle-class people call urban blight. A boarded-up school. A tiny convenience store with barred windows and hand-painted red signs full of misspellings. On a porch not an arm's length from the busy street, an old man sits smoking, while small children run and tumble and squat around him, some just in diapers. I stop at the light, beginning to feel it all. Closeness, familiarity. Dread.

I look around as the car idles. In a parking lot next to me, a man pisses on a blue Dumpster, making no attempt at privacy. His dick is short, thick, and uncut, and when he sees me watching, he shakes it at me. I want to roll down the window and yell that he could get himself stuck on a sex-offender registry for life. But I don't, and he won't. Any cops who come to the Ninth have got more urgent things to do. I leave my window up, my doors locked, the air conditioner blasting.

Turning off the main drag, I zigzag through little cross streets, swerving to avoid potholes. All over New Orleans, the streets are bumpy because the town's built on a swamp. The streets rise and fall as the city shifts, so they're always a patchwork of asphalt and holes. But here in the neglected Ninth, where there's little money for construction crews, the roads are so torn up I can do twenty miles an hour at best.

The small, low houses, mostly white—white paint is cheapest— are one-story, peeling, leaning, with trash in their little yards. The land is so flat that all you can see from behind the steering wheel are these tiny houses, one after the other, going on forever in all directions, like you're trapped down low in a tunnel. I drive past houses with graffiti scrawled across the plywood where their windows used to be. I pass a burned, blackened car, torched as a warning or for fun.

When the post-Katrina tour vans roll slowly through, I wonder what people think as they stare out the windows at black families on porches, knots of young black men clustered on corners, the high-cheekboned, high-assed girls with head wraps and dead eyes, walking arm in arm, the thin older men sagging on milk crates and ice chests, on steps, on heaved-up chunks of broken sidewalks, talking on cell phones, holding their beer cans, or just staring at their beat-up shoes.

Perhaps the tourists think *tragedy*. Perhaps they think *hordes*. Perhaps they think, *If they were just working instead of tossing dice in the middle of the day* . . . Perhaps they think they're inconspicuous with their digital cameras and pity.

———

As distant as the Upper Ninth may be from the Garden District in material wealth, human kindness and hospitality are the same. When I mount the little porches and knock, I'm welcomed warmly and ushered inside. The living rooms are tiny, shabby, and spotless. I'm handed cool tap water in scratched plastic cups.

Tisha Johnson has gentle, exhausted eyes and smells of gardenias and cigarettes. We sit on two sagging chairs. Her approach is tough love. "I got six," she says. "You can't be watching them twenty-four-seven. You just can't. They got to learn sometime. I tell them, but they got to watch out for they own selves. They got to learn." Two of her daughters have been molested, one by an adult cousin and one by a neighbor who was judged incompetent to stand trial. "It's sad." That's all Tisha Johnson will say. "They got counseling for them up at the school. But my girls ain't the same no more."

I thank her for the water and her time.

On the way to the next house, I come face-to-face with an SUV at an intersection. We both pause at the stop signs, staring at each other. The driver is Asian, maybe Japanese, and he looks lost and scared for the three seconds we make eye contact. Then I push the gas and he shrinks away in my rearview mirror.

At the next little white house, Viola McIntyre, as pragmatic as Ms. Johnson, takes a more interventionist view.

"Coming up ain't no picnic. We all know that. There's always some crazy uncle around, some grandpa putting his hands where they ain't got no business. Trust me, I know. You just got to watch out. Be alert. Kids got to learn." She smoothes a hand over her sleek hair, smiles. "But I tell you what. Any man touch my girls, I cut him. Don't stand for none of that."

Neither of the women has heard of Megan's Law. Neither knows she can access a sex-offender registry online. Neither one owns a computer.

Gnawed by the first twinges of depression, I check the address of my third good parent and push the Pontiac on. Here the road's surface is so pocked by craters that I can't go faster than ten miles an hour. A rusting purple Pinto crawls in front of me. Parked cars line both sides of the streets, so the passageway is narrow. From one house's collapsed roof, grass and saplings sprout.

Six young guys on a porch, shirtless and all holding beer cans, silently watch me pass. I feel small and young and vulnerable here, as I did in childhood in Desire: conspicuously light-skinned, conspicuously female. *Wetback pussy,* as I used to get called. It's not like New York or L.A. Here, a Latina in public housing stands out. Nationwide, fewer than 50 percent of the folks in public housing are black, but in New Orleans, it's 95 percent. I want to say, *Wait, I'm on your side!* I vote with you; I'd march with you. But in the black-and-white world of New Orleans, black people read me as white. Period. There's no escaping your skin.

At least my ride is suitably beat-up. There'd be little point in 'jacking it.

But when the Pinto in front of me stops for no reason in the middle of the block, there's no room to get around. There's nowhere to go but backward. My scalp feels suddenly hot, and I crack my knuckles on the steering wheel.

In my rearview mirror, I see one of the young guys step down off the porch, his beer can dangling from his hand. Another joins him, heading my way. They could want just a friendly chat. They could want anything.

My heart pounding, I ease the Pontiac's gearshift into reverse. My foot hovers over the gas, ready to gun it, to hurtle backward down the street as fast as the potholes will let me.

And then the car in front of me moves off. My hands grip the wheel, sweating, and my breath is high and shallow in my throat. I shift into first and pull forward. The young men stop in the street, watching me pull out of reach.

Just a routine moment in the Ninth. My pulse begins to slow.

When I get to the next house, Evie Wilson opens the door. A gold cross gleams at her throat, and she smells like buttercream icing.

"Nola! Hey!"

I stop, uncertain.

"Ms. Wilson?"

"Shit, girl. You don't know me?" I smile blankly, scanning her face for anything familiar. "Huh," she says, folding her arms. "You don't exactly keep in touch, do you?" She steps aside to let me enter. "I thought you was calling me 'cause we come up together. On the phone, I just assumed . . . Nola Céspedes." She sucks her teeth. "Girl, you wouldna known me in the street."

"I'm sorry. Did we—"

"Six years in the projects together! We lived right upstairs of y'all. My name was Downes then. Evie Downes?" It doesn't ring a bell.

"Ah, yes . . ." No clue.

"Whatever, right?" She looks me up and down. "That's all right. Come on, sit down." She swerves into the kitchen. "You hungry? I got beans here from lunch. Just heat 'em up a little. Got some sweet tea, cold in the fridge."

"No. No, I'm fine. Thank you."

"Glad to get out the projects, right? This here's nicer." We sit, and she investigates the little Olympus, impressed with its sleek silver efficiency. "You gonna quote me in the paper?"

"I hope to. If you say something relevant to the story."

She laughs. "Then let me just get all my relevance together here."

The flashing Olympus records her, her hopes and fears for her three children, her resignation to the fact that perverts exist, a fact of life. Her dedication to keeping her children safe. Like the other mothers, she doesn't know about sex-offender registries.

When we wind it down, she shows me to the door.

"So you still stay tight with anyone?"

"Not so much, I guess. I don't know, Evie. I put a lot of things behind me." She's a nice woman, and apparently she used to like me. We could have remained friends. Maybe there were other people I could have stayed close to. But I made a strict habit of not looking back.

"So you really got out, then, huh?"

Her voice is quiet, a mixture of too many things to read. She stands on the porch, arms folded, watching me drive away.

I steer through the streets with a punched feeling in my gut, and when I get to the intersection with Alvar, something makes me turn left. North. The afternoon sky is filling with gray, low clouds, and I'm heading toward what's left of Desire.

I pass Musicians' Village, the row of pastel houses dreamed up after Katrina and built by Habitat for Humanity—even Bush scampered around with a hammer for a day. Musicians' Village was the brainchild of Harry Connick Jr. and Branford Marsalis, and the goal was to lure back musicians who'd lost their homes in the storm. But anyone can live here. Each house is new, pretty, painted in bright pastels, and each stands at least a foot higher than the flood level. No unwashed babies roam the yards here yet. No tired ladies rock on porches. A rainbow of fresh paint, green lawns, and neat little fences runs along Alvar for blocks.

Of course, whoever ends up living in those sweet, clean, sturdy little houses will have to navigate the Ninth to get home at night.

Heading farther north, I finally arrive. My foot eases off the gas.

Here, no one's on the streets. On my right, the Florida Projects still stand, condemned and deserted, their jaunty pastel hopes now boarded up. The Desire Projects, on my left, were made of brick, like most of the public housing in New Orleans. Now they're nothing.

I park the Pontiac, shoulder my handbag with its comforting gun, and get out. The air is hot, humid, sticky, and I'm the only human being I can see as I walk into the stripped foundations of Desire. The only home I knew for eighteen years is now just a bleak wasteland of cement slabs split by weeds. It's hard to imagine that 262 buildings once stood here. A whole world. Darvis got shot, Mabel lost a leg to diabetes, Angel held his twin grandbabies in his arms at the age of thirty-five. My mother made a tiny Cuba in two rooms, an island of love. Auntie Helene passed away one night in her sleep.

Pushing through the tangled grass, I find the slab of our building and step onto it. It's like stepping onto the moon. At the base of my rib cage, around my solar plexus, a weird, uneasy vibration starts to churn. More than five years have passed since I stood in this spot. Now it's a wilderness. Nothing lives here but birds, wild dogs, and a few small trees that have cracked the concrete and grown as high as my chest. The air is heavy, and I hear thunder.

Across Florida Avenue still stand the high chain link fence, stagnant ditch, and highway overpass that once formed the northern border of my life.

Evie's voice echoes in my ears. *So you really got out, then, huh?*

I feel like vomiting, like sobbing. But nothing comes.

I wonder what she'd say if she could see me now, arms clutched around my waist, sick tears leaking down my face and throat.

It's Thursday, girls' night, and we're due to meet at Asian Pacific Café, the sushi place on Esplanade by my apartment. I haul myself out of the hot bath where I've been wrinkling since I got back from the Ninth, listening to the thunder and downpour. By eight o'clock, it's clear out again. I dress and walk over.

But I'm in no mood to socialize, and I can't help feeling disoriented. My head is too full of Desire and the Ninth, of torched cars and Dumpster dicks, of the sad struggle of the women I saw. The knots in my shoulders are gone, melted away by hot water, but my mind still aches.

Here's my confession.

When Katrina came, I finally felt at home. I know that's blasphemy, but I did. Everyone was devastated; everyone's heart was broken. Suddenly, the whole city was in it together, sharing the shit and the nightmare.

For the first time in adulthood, I felt like the mood of New Orleans matched my own mood, the one I carried and hid: a bleak, dead sort of anxious feeling that I credited to the Desire Projects and my *mamá*'s drinking and long hours away at work. I blamed it on the sorry little Christmases when I'd pretend so hard to be excited over some crap I didn't want. I'd hug my *mamá* and act all surprised, saying how I loved peanut butter tacos so much that I *wanted* them for Christmas dinner, but still hear her crying at night after I'd gone to bed. The shabby little birthdays, the Easters without a new dress, just scraping by, and the chronic wariness of navigating a place where drugs got sold, women sold themselves, and occasionally folks got shot or cut up bad, as a lesson.

Only 2 percent of Americans live in projects, but most of us never get out.

Ever since I left Desire, I've carried this anxious fear, like sooner or later I wouldn't be able to outrun it all. My breath lived high and rapid in my chest; my belly never unwound. The jittery sleep, the caffeine to wake up, the booze at night, the way during meetings at the *Times-Picayune* office I was the only one who jumped when a door slammed, and everyone would glance at me and then look away. Sometimes I even worried that I smelled, that the grime of the Desire Projects emanated from my skin, that it was something rich white people, like Catahoula hounds, could scent and track, no matter how carefully I dressed or hard I scrubbed.

But after Katrina, when bodies lay putrefying on the medians and folks dragged their ruined refrigerators out to the curb, the whole city reeked. We all stank. People's throats clanked shut against the nauseous sweet stench of it.

Finally, me and the rest of the folks in New Orleans—rich folks, white folks, black folks, the solid members of the middle class—we all had something in common. Our lives had been forever sliced into a before and an after. It wasn't just me exiled from my past. All of us were.

And for the first time, I could breathe easy. I felt free and at home, the grief and shit of my inner world writ large.

At Asian Pacific, the clean, ornamented space of the restaurant's brick patio jars me, its wrought-iron tables and chairs, its trickling fountain, its palm trees twinkling with tiny white lights—all safe and enclosed, all furnished for human delight. Back in the land of the middle class where everything's secure and bright, all I feel is unsettled.

More than a hundred years ago, writing on a different continent, Friedrich Engels described the avenues of London, lined only with prosperous shops, on which the carriages of the rich drove into the city. It wasn't coincidental, Engels argued. The squalor and sufferings and hovels festered unseen down side streets the rich could avoid. When I read that chapter for Political Theory, I cried alone in my dorm room. Cities are structured so you can avert your eyes forever.

For nine years, I've tried to carve a foothold for my mother and me in the middle class, and a single afternoon unravels it. I'd thought all my tender spots had thickened with scar tissue, that I'd moved on. But as I sit alone at our table—early, as usual—waiting for my friends, I'm not so sure.

My cone-shaped glass of unfiltered sake, Momokawa Pearl, comes wedged in a highball of blue ice. Weird. I breathe its coconut scent and sip the milky liquid, staring up into the night sky.

"Hey, girl!" calls out Calinda, coming down the wooden steps onto the patio, and I have time to make myself smile. "What's up with you?" I rise and we hug. Her warmth starts to ground me. "Hey, NOPD checked out that photo you sent." She slides into a chair across from mine. "No match."

"The one I texted you?" Mr. Nothing. "But he said he was from here. He said he went AWOL in the storm."

"Yeah, sorry. Nothing. Maybe he was yanking your chain. Or maybe he was from some town nearby, and his records aren't pulling up with the metro area." She shrugs. "Or maybe the picture didn't work with the visual recognition software. Busy as they are, they probably wouldn't put someone on it manually."

"It wasn't a great photo."

Wonderful. Somewhere out there lurks a floater, a ghost, a rapist who knows where I live—and for nothing. He's melted into the scenery now.

Soline and Fabi arrive, laughing and talking, and we drop the subject. They all order drinks, and we pass the sushi list around. At Asian Pacific, in addition to traditional maki, you can get a FEMA roll—which is served only after you've already finished your dinner and aren't hungry anymore. Even the restaurants here have gallows humor now.

For almost an hour, our conversation veers between politics and Soline's preparations for her new place. The fountain's up and running in the courtyard, she says, and I think of Tisha Johnson's thin carpet. Platters of cut maki arrive, and we all mix our various pastes of wasabi, soy, and teriyaki sauce in the little blue dishes. Talk turns to work and our chopsticks sail over the table, snatching up food.

When I tell my story of getting pulled from the plantation piece, they look at me strangely, their laughter uncertain. Soline puts her hand lightly on mine.

"You're not fucking up, are you, baby?"

Oh, it's fine, I assure them, pulling my hand away. I'm working on another story, something big, and I still have my regular club coverage, which I could do in my sleep. No worries, no worries. They seem mollified and ask about the other story. I say it's something different, something good.

Jazz Fest? they guess. A new exhibit at NOMA?

I shake my head, smiling. "You'll see when it comes out."

Calinda lifts an eyebrow. "You sure know how to keep it quiet, girl," she says, and I know she's wondering about the files.

"Nola's always like that," Fabi adds, smoothing her long hair. "So secretive."

Talk turns back, naturally, to Soline's wedding, which is only days away now. Describing the details, Soline seems preternaturally calm. She drones on about floral arrangements and her railway itinerary in Thailand.

My third sake doesn't taste as sweet, and I wave the waitress over. She's a pretty Polynesian woman in short shorts, flip-flops, and a long black ponytail.

"Yes, it's Momokawa Pearl." She looks mildly offended. "You like something else?"

"No, that's fine. Thanks."

She sniffs and walks away.

"Maybe," says Fabi, her mouth prim, "you should slow down."

"Uh, maybe," I say, "you should back the fuck off." Silence falls on the table, and I realize my mistake. I've switched codes. Shit. I *have* had too much to drink. I backpedal. "Hey, I'm just kidding." I smile sweetly, trying to reassure them that I'm one of their kind. "Look, y'all are the ones who need to slow down. I'm not even driving."

Hesitant smiles appear, and they let it drop.

Talk turns to our wedding escorts, or lack thereof. Fabi, of course, will bring Carlo, but Calinda can't decide which of three guys to invite, and we parse the dilemma for so long that I start to get sleepy. Sometimes I can't get it up for girl talk. I like the sound: it's sweet, like doves cooing. But sometimes I just don't have the energy to care.

"How about you, Nola?" asks Calinda. "Who are you bringing?"

"Oh, I don't know." I try to focus. "Somebody. Maybe I'll come by myself."

A chorus of horror greets this, and I have to listen to a dozen reasons why a date is essential. I mentally scan through my options: those stooges from the Hispanic Professionals Association, the name-less soccer fucks?

"I don't know. I'll think of someone."

"Time's a-wasting. You'd better get on it."

"You can't just go without a date," says Fabi. "Listen, I know this really nice—"

"No way. No blind dates. Besides," I turn to Soline, "this is all about you. This is your day. Let's not be worrying about if I can find a boy to take."

"I know, I know," she says. "But y'all are my bridesmaids. My girls. I want to make sure you have good times."

"A man on my arm does not guarantee good times. Believe me."

"I hear that," says Calinda.

"You'd better bring someone," Soline says. "You RSVP'd for two, and if I have to make one more change with the caterers, they're going to have a nervous breakdown." The conversation shifts to food and then to our bridesmaids' dresses, which Soline says we need to swing by her shop to pick up. The evening winds down. The waitress glares at me as she lays down the tab.

On the way out, Soline leans close, touches my arm, and speaks under her breath.

"You doing okay, Nola girl?"

"Yeah, sure. I'm fine." I ease away from her hand.

"You're looking kind of tired. Have you lost weight?"

"It's nothing. I just had a long day."

Out on the sidewalk in the dark, as we all say our good-byes, she rummages in her purse, then holds out her furled fist.

"Here, baby," she says. "This'll cure what ails you." She opens her hand into mine.

Back in my apartment, it's late. Uri's still out. I pour myself a finger of vodka from the bottle I keep in the freezer. Roux wanders in, wanting a scratch.

On TV, the news is full of the death of Amber Waybridge. I stand there staring, the remote in my hand, able to follow the story easily even with the sound off. For a long moment, the screen fills with Amber's photograph, now iconic, in painfully vivid, lifelike color. Then Mayor Nagin, trying to avert a full-scale PR disaster, promises a manhunt like New Orleans has never seen, and the chief of police is nodding and clenching his jaw, all determination. Now Amber Waybridge's outraged and grieving lover, the art professor, is saying something to reporters. He stands with an arm around his dark-haired older daughter, a taller, more solemn version of the little one. Wide and still, the girl's eyes reel with shock, as though something deep inside her has simply, quietly snapped,

like a twig or a thin stalk of glass. Something delicate but necessary. I close my eyes and switch off the set.

In my bedroom, I drop Soline's joint into my top dresser drawer.
One thing for sure, weed from Soline will be good. Rob is nine
kinds of connected.

I lean my elbows on the dresser. In the mirror, my eyes look
strange, hollow.

"Hi," I say to my reflection. "It's Nola." The eyes stare back.
"Remember me?"

I shouldn't do this. It's stupid. It's late, and I'm drunk. But my
cell is in my hand, and I pick up the crumpled receipt from behind
a bottle of perfume. I smooth it open. *Bento.* I think of his eyes,
dark and glowing, as he held my hips and pulsed up into me. His
phone rings.

"Who is this? It's late." I'd forgotten how low and appealing his
voice is, whole octaves below mine, and how beautifully accented.
A man's voice.

"It's Nola." I tap my nail anxiously on the dresser. "The woman
you met in—"

"I know you." I can hear his smile. "Nola."

"I hope I didn't wake you."

"I am awake."

"*Mira,* I've got this wedding to go to. A friend of mine."

"Congratulations to your friend. *Felicidades.*" The pause length-
ens, spins out into the dark universe. He's not going to make this
easy.

"And I need a date."

"And you are calling me."

I sigh. "Evidently."

"To invite me."

"Apparently so."

"This is an honor."

"Yeah, okay. Will you do it?"

"You would like me to come as your date to your friend's wedding?"

"Yep. That's the gist."

"¿Qué?"

"Yes, I would like you to come as my date. Please."

"And when will this happy event take place?"

"Saturday the nineteenth, in the Quarter. The ceremony's at six in the evening, and the reception at the Omni is at eight, so you should be out by midnight at the latest."

It suits his agenda.

"No sex," I specify. There's a pause. "I don't go back for seconds."

"You're an interesting young woman, Nola."

"So I'm told." I describe the menu: crawfish étouffée, lobster, filet mignon. At least he'll get a good meal out of it, along with all the good French wine he can swill. "And there'll be a lot of cute women," I say, hoping to seal the deal. "It's fine if you get people's numbers, but just don't embarrass me while we're there, okay?"

"Embarrass you?"

"You can flirt, but don't ignore me. And do not, for God's sake, leave with someone else." My friends would never stop consoling me, and I'd have to pretend to care.

He laughs. "I have no intention of flirting, Nola." I wish he'd stop saying my name. "At what time should I pick you up?" he asks.

"Pick me up? Oh, no. God, no." It hadn't even occurred to me that he would come to my apartment, knock on my door—that this would in any way resemble a regular date. No one I fuck gets to know where I live. "No, no, no. I'll meet you there."

He clears his throat. "This is somewhat unusual."

"You're telling me." I run a hand through my hair. In the mirror, I look rosy. My eyes are bright. "Look, you know where the St. Louis Cathedral is, don't you?"

"Who does not know where is the beautiful St. Louis Cathedral?" He really talks like this? Jesus. How am I going to get through an evening with the Count?

"Great. So just be there at, like, five-thirty. Okay? And I'll meet you. I'll be in a dark blue dress. Indigo. You remember what I look like?"

"Of course, Nola. And myself, I will wear a gray suit. Do you remember what I look like?"

I haven't stopped thinking about what you look like.

"Gray suit. I'll find you," I say.

13

Q: How many central air-conditioning units—*central* air, the big ones chugging like engines on cement slabs, not scrappy little window units—does it take to cool a mansion in Audubon Place?

A: Four. I'm not kidding.

On Friday morning in the Garden District, I give my name to the armed guard at the gate of Audubon Place. George Anderson, the guy who felt up his family's maids, has put my name on the list of approved visitors. The striped arm of the gate rises, and I drive through.

I circle the loop of the private road. The grassy median, dotted by royal palms, is wide enough to play catch on. Old oaks shade the landscaped lawns, and the sidewalks roll smooth and flat, not broken and buckling from tree roots as they are on most New Orleans streets. Here, a child could roller skate with ease.

But no humans are outside. Audubon Place has the glossy Stepford perfection of a magazine shoot. I pass the Anderson mansion and park on the street two doors down.

Audubon Place, Audubon Park, Audubon Zoo. Naturalist and artist John James Audubon lived only briefly on a Louisiana plantation, giving art lessons and sketching the birds of the South before sailing off to England, but his name is everywhere.

Before Audubon, illustrators killed and stuffed their models, and then drew from the birds' stiff forms, so the portraits were rigid. The birds looked as dead as they were.

Audubon's great innovation was to prop the birds' bodies and limbs into natural positions with wires, as if in motion, and he painted them against foliage and flowers from their actual habitats.

It's wondrous how lifelike a dead thing can look.

In Audubon Place, the mansions' lawns are large and lovely, the kinds of lush yards people call *grounds*. Green vines spill over privacy walls. Walking—and sweating already—I trail my hand along bumpy stucco, reach up to squeeze a green frond. Even though I'm in the thick of New Orleans, Audubon Place has the hush of wealth. There's little noise here except the chirp and squeal of a gray mockingbird.

George Anderson lives in an Italianate villa, all gold stucco, lemon trees, and palms. I press the doorbell and stand for long moments until an old lady opens the door.

She's fragile, with blond hair scraped back in a bun and a little lavender Jackie O suit. Square diamonds glitter at her ears and throat. She puts out a small hand, and I shake it.

"Do come in." She ushers me into the coolness. "We're so pleased to have you." She leads me through palatial rooms floored with wood and marble and Oriental rugs—real ones, not the $199 kind from JCPenney. There are no typical New Orleans smells of heat and rotting garbage, and it doesn't smell like honeysuckle plug-in air freshener, either, or cedarwood incense hastily burned before guests come, or even reeds stuck in a bottle of peony oil. It smells like purified cool air and the expensive objects within it: leather couches, bronze statues, framed lithographs. It has the thick, cool, scrupulously empty smell of real wealth. I feel awkward, like a maid or an intruder.

"I'm George's mother, dear," she says. "I live here with him, and he has asked that I be present for your conversation."

"Sure," I say. "No problem." I'm still following her; the place is huge. Acres. And the walls must be a foot thick: it's completely silent.

We pass stone Buddhas on pedestals, long black wooden African masks on the walls, blurry pastel paintings in gold gilt frames. Finally, we step down into a low sitting room with a wall of glass. Beyond, an interior garden bursts with banana trees and hibiscus. Just looking at it is like drinking iced fruit punch.

The sitting room is cloaked in the warm gray of discretion: gray walls, gray rug, gray suede sofas, and a gray marble fireplace with no fire. In a leopard-skin chair sits a gray man. He's only forty-two, but sitting there, slumped, George Anderson looks sixty. Averting his eyes, he rises, a tall man with stooped shoulders. He's in creased khakis, a yellow polo shirt, and wire-rimmed glasses. With thick sandy hair and pleasant features, he might even be called good-looking. He clasps my hand softly and lets it go.

"Hello," he murmurs, and sits down. His palm had been moist. He's nervous.

I'm suddenly grateful, because his nervousness puts me at ease. I can feel like the gracious hostess responsible for drawing out a shy guest, instead of like a timid maid, afraid to touch or break something in a house so grand. George Anderson's anxiety puts me back in charge. He's a perp, and I'm the reporter, here to make him trust me, to make him comfortable enough to relax, to be honest, to blurt things he'll later regret.

"Mr. Anderson, thank you so much for agreeing to see me." I plaster on my biggest, most winning smile. "It's so generous of you to help me get this important message out to the public."

"Thank you, dear," says his mother. George Anderson says nothing. So I guess she's going to call the shots. "Won't you sit down?" I love it. Even wrinkled up and with a rapist for a son, she's still channeling Grace Kelly.

We all settle into our places. I'm on a gray suede sofa, close enough to George to reach over and touch him, and she's perched on the sofa opposite, watching keenly like a small, bright bird. It's less than ideal.

I take my little silver Olympus recorder out of my handbag.

"You don't mind, do you?" I ask, not making eye contact while arranging it on the glass table between us. He shakes his head, and I press the ON button.

"Would you like something cool to drink, dear?"

"Oh, that would be great. Thanks."

She takes something small from her jacket pocket and pushes it. A moment later, a door opens, and a young black woman materializes. She's wearing an actual black-and-white maid's uniform, like out of a porno.

"We have lemonade," says Mrs. Anderson, "iced tea, sparkling water, and soda pop." Ah, it's the *soda pop* that Grace Kelly would never say, that marks Mrs. Anderson as a daughter of the South.

"Iced tea, please," I say. "Unsweetened."

"And George and I would like lemonade, please, Dahlia."

"Yes, ma'am." Dahlia evaporates.

"You have such a lovely home," I say, shooting my cover-girl smile at both Andersons again, but George, who is staring down at his hands, doesn't notice.

"Thank you, dear. This house has been in the Anderson family for generations."

"What a distinguished legacy," I chirp, all ingratiation. "And Mr. Anderson, did you feel comfortable coming back home here?"

He lifts his eyes. His lips part to speak.

"Of course he felt comfortable," his mother interjects. "Why wouldn't he feel comfortable? This is his home. This is George's birthright." Mrs. Anderson smiles brightly, but her eyes are snapping, and her posture is military straight. Audubon could have stuffed her himself. "George isn't going to be exiled just because he made a mistake."

Her final verb *made*, catches me, and my overheated brain literalizes it. I visualize George Anderson making something, molding it with his hands, like clay, like God made Adam and Eve. I can feel my smile still fixed stiffly on my lips. *Focus, Nola.*

"I'm glad you feel that way," I say, angling my body toward George. "It must be a comfort to have such a supportive mother."

George nods glumly.

"And did you find your neighbors to be understanding?"

"Oh, yes," she warbles in my peripheral vision. "Oh, yes, very understanding. We've known these families for years."

"They didn't exactly throw a parade," says George.

"No, dear. Of course." Her hands smooth her skirt. "You're right, of course, dear, but they have been very supportive. On the whole."

The drinks noiselessly arrive, Dahlia silking so softly across the gray rug that I barely notice her.

I sip the cold tea. "What do you mean, Mr. Anderson—they didn't throw a parade?"

He looks up at me at last. His brown eyes are actually sort of kindly, sort of sad.

"They're more reserved now. As one would expect. They smile, say hello, but they don't engage. There's no chatting. Just a wave on the way to their houses or cars. They don't stop."

"So you could say they're civil."

"Yes, civil. But not warm. Not anymore. As one would expect," he says again.

"Did you have good friends here in the neighborhood before it all happened?" To ex-cons, the phrase *when it all happened* is more palatable than *when you molested that child* or *when you shot your wife* or *when you skimmed sixty thousand dollars from state funds.* Journalism 101. People don't like to look too directly at their crimes.

"Well, yes, a couple of people."

"And how have they received you back into the neighborhood?"

"They've been very—civil." He seems to like the word, to find it apt and useful. "One guy even shook my hand."

"Oh, that's wonderful. And do you still see each other socially?"

His eyes drop again to his lap. "No, not so much."

"Oh, I'm sorry. That must be hard."

He just nods, but Mrs. Anderson says, "It is hard. It's very hard. George gets quite lonely now sometimes."

"Is that true, Mr. Anderson?"

He nods.

"So do you ever think of relocating? Starting fresh?"

He looks up, laughs. It's a bleak sound. "What's the point?" His eyes are hopeless. "Everywhere I might go, I'd have to register within five days, and then I'd be marked, tagged."

"True, true. But it would still be a different environment. Maybe only a few people would really be aware."

"No, you don't understand. I'd never be sure who knew and who didn't, who was talking about me, who was afraid of me. How could I relax? No." He shakes his head vehemently. "There's no starting over with something like this."

"And besides, this is Georgie's home—"

"Not that I blame anyone," he says. "The laws make sense. They're in the best interests of society. I do believe that." He sighs. "And it's not like I'm trying to run from what I've done. I'm not trying to evade anything." He stares out at the greenery.

"But it's lonely," I prompt.

"Yes. To lose your social world, your friends, parties, dinners . . . yes, it's lonely. But I'm not exactly a desirable dinner guest anymore." He laughs the same bleak laugh. "No one's going to pair me with a lovely young doctor or society girl." Again I'm struck by how old he looks, how defeated. "But everyone has been very kind, given what happened."

"Yes, these are our old friends," Mrs. Anderson puts in. "These are fine old families, very cordial, very gracious. And not just our neighbors here in the District but our entire circle. They're some of the best families in Louisiana—in the whole South. They're not going to turn on one of their own."

"But your social invitations have dropped off," I prompt George. He nods.

"And yours, too?"

Now it's Mrs. Anderson's turn to look down. Her nails are immaculately done, like perfect pools of coral lacquer on her wrinkled tan hands.

"I don't get out as much as I used to," she says. "But I prefer being here with Georgie, anyway, keeping him company. We go to the museums together, out to dinner at nice restaurants, to plays. We still have our season tickets everywhere."

"Just not so many social occasions."

"Yes, not so many."

"What do you miss most?" I smile sympathetically at them both.

"Oh, the yachts!" she says immediately. "The yacht parties. Those were just marvelous." She sighs, her hands clasped together.

George looks at her, clears his throat again.

"I guess I miss . . ." He pauses for a long moment. "I miss being viewed with trust. Like an equal. I feel lesser now, all the time. And I *am* lesser. I know that. I lessened myself, you could say." He runs a hand through his hair. "But I *did* bad things, you know? Whereas I feel now like I *am* a bad thing. That's how people treat me, like I'm a bad thing. Like if I live the whole rest of my life without ever doing another bad thing, I'll still *be* a bad thing in people's eyes. There's no redeeming yourself from something like this. You're branded." His eyes look lost—and resigned to staying lost. "For life."

"That's a pretty high price to pay," I say quietly.

"It *is* a high price," says his mother. "Making a man suffer forever—"

"It's not that high," he breaks in. "It's not as high as those girls paid. I know that. What I did to them, they've got to live with that. They're paying the highest—" He breaks off, clasps his hands together. His dampened eyes beseech the recorder. "Can I just say I'm sorry? Can you put that in the story? That I'm so, so sorry."

"Yes, of course, Mr. Anderson," I say softly. "I can include that."

"Jesus," he says. "I really never meant to hurt anyone. Never wanted to hurt people. . . ."

We sit in silence for a moment.

"Mr. Anderson, research shows that many sex offenders were themselves once victims of molestation. With this article, I'm trying to help the public understand how that cycle works. Can you speak to that at all?"

"Oh, no." Mrs. Anderson rises to her feet. "No, you don't." I can't tell if she's talking to him or me.

"Sit down, Mama."

"I told you this interview was a terrible—"

"It's my decision. I want to talk about it. To stop hiding." George looks tired. "And besides, he's dead."

"Our good name isn't dead." Mrs. Anderson bristles where she stands. "Not yet."

"Yes, it is." George Anderson sighs again. "It is, Mama. Sit down."
She sinks slowly back to the gray suede. "Yes, I was molested as a
boy. It was my uncle, Frank Anderson."

"Circuit Judge Anderson?" *Score.* Judge Anderson was a legend-
ary icon of moral rectitude. George's mother crosses herself.

"Yes, my uncle. He used to sit me on his lap, touch me. Then
he'd give me a ten-dollar bill and tell me to go play." He laughs
flatly, runs his hand through his hair again. "I had no idea, you
know? It felt weird, wrong, but it also felt good, you know? And he
was nice, funny. He never hurt me, never made me do anything to
him. He just did it, gave me money, and let me go."

"Did he tell you to keep it a secret?"

"Yes. Yes, he did say that. But I didn't mind. I was a boy; I had
lots of secrets. We all did, as kids. We liked secrets. They made you
feel special."

"And how long did this go on?"

"It started when I was about four, and Uncle Frank died when I
was nine—heart attack—so about five years, I guess."

"And it went on all that time?"

"Yes. I just thought it was normal. And I never did tell anyone.
Not until I told the prison counselor."

"And what was that like, finally talking to someone about it?"

"What was it like?" He runs his hand back and forth through
his hair, which is now standing on end like a spiky tan bush.
"Well, it was the weirdest thing." He sounds genuinely mystified.
"The shrink was a good guy. I liked him, trusted him. When he
said it was okay to cry, I thought, *Cry? Why would I cry?*"

"Why was that?"

"Because like I said, I hadn't really been upset at the time. Uncle
Frank was always nice, told jokes, all that. And like I said, it didn't
hurt. But I kept going to the counselor every week, and he kept
saying, 'It's okay to cry.' And then one day, I did." He stares off.

"And what was that like?"

"It was the craziest thing. At first just a few little leaky tears came, and the shrink said, 'That's right, go deeper, breathe into it,' stuff like that, so I did, and *that's* when I felt the fear. I was *terrified*. That's all I could feel: fear. This overwhelming fear, all over my body. I could barely breathe. And it wasn't like the fear came first, and then I started crying. No, the crying came first—"

"What was it like?" In the corner of my eye, Mrs. Anderson sits stiff with attention. I'm guessing this is a conversation they've never had.

"It was intense. It was like waves. I started sobbing, really crying hard, from here"—he taps his fist against his abdomen—"crying with my whole body. I thought I was going to throw up. The shrink thought so, too. He put the wastepaper basket next to me."

"Did you?"

"Throw up? Not that time. But the third time I cried, I did."

"You kept going back and crying?"

"Yes. Five times altogether. It was very physical, very intense. I only vomited the one time, and the last time I cried, it wasn't as hard as before. I could feel the difference. It was lightening up. I knew I was getting to the end of it."

"The end of what, exactly?"

"That's the weird thing," he says. "I can't tell you. I don't know. I just know it was powerful, and it was stuck inside me all those years, like something buried, and it was finally rising to the surface."

"That must have been something."

"Oh, yes. Letting go of it changed me. Each time I cried, I felt so relieved afterward. I can't tell you the relief. Like I was actually, physically lighter. When I'd start crying, it would be so overwhelming, so terrible, I'd think, *This is never going to end. I'm going to die of this*, but the shrink kept saying, 'It's okay, it's okay, let it go.' Without him there, I could never have done it. I would have been too scared. And I wouldn't have even known to start, wouldn't have known it was there."

"And what happened after you cried that fifth time?"

"I felt like a new man," he says slowly. "Seriously. New. Clean and light. At home in the world, for the first time in my life."

At home in the world. "That must have been——"

"It was unbelievable. Like I said, I hadn't even thought that stuff with Uncle Frank had bothered me." He shakes his head, astonished even now.

"And did that experience change your feeling about the women?"

"Oh, God, I felt so terrible," he says. "It was like——I don't know how to say this——like this blanket had been removed from my nerves, like I could feel things directly for the first time. And I felt terrible. I knew exactly what kind of damage I had done. Because I knew how it felt to me. God, it's awful. The weight of that. Knowing. The guilt."

Mrs. Anderson's eyes are dry but fascinated. She's staring at her son.

I smile encouragingly at him. "And you've felt differently since the crying?"

"Yes, utterly. I even feel like I could have a real relationship now. A healthy relationship, you know, with a woman. Before, I always just went out. Dates, a little kissing. When it got too close to——" He glances at his mother. "Whenever it became serious, I'd find a reason to break it off. I know people wondered. But now I think I could handle it." His smile is shy. "I mean, I'd like to try." His face falls, and he shrugs again. "But who's going to want me? Now, after this?"

"Don't you worry, Georgie," his mother says quickly. "There'll be someone. Just you wait."

My iced tea's drained, and I'm parched. I lift the glass. "May I have some more?"

She looks distractedly at me. "Of course, dear," she says, fumbling for her electronic maid-calling device. "And you need some more lemonade, Georgie." She turns to me. "A mother feels so terrible," she says. "His own uncle, right here in our house. I had no idea. My own husband's brother, rest his soul. How can you know about these things?"

"And your husband is deceased also?"

"Yes." She crosses herself. "These ten years. Also a heart attack. It was a blessing he didn't have to see all this."

George looks up.

"Darling. Not that I meant—"

Dahlia silently enters, and Mrs. Anderson shuts up. Dahlia disappears with our glasses.

It's a good time to change the subject. "Mr. Anderson, I'd appreciate your expertise on something." I take out the flyer, unfold it on my lap, and hold it up briefly. "I assume you're both familiar with the case of Amber Waybridge, the young woman who was abducted from the Quarter last week."

George Anderson nods. His mother says, "Yes, poor girl. We saw it on the news." Her lips tighten. "But what does that have to do with George?"

"As you may know, a body has been found, and damage to the soft tissues indicates sexual assault." The old lady winces, and George Anderson avoids my eyes. "The body was mutilated." I remember my promise to Calinda, so I keep it vague. "Rather brutally, I'm afraid, and in a way that temporarily obscured her identity from police."

Mrs. Anderson makes a small, moist sound in her throat, and George Anderson shifts uncomfortably in his chair. Her eyes grow wary.

"Georgie's mistakes were nothing like that, dear. No brutality."

"Oh, yes, ma'am. I'm familiar with the case files, and Mr. Anderson, I'm not implying that you were involved in any way. However, I would value your speculation. If you could just allow yourself to imagine, for a moment, what might compel a person to do such a thing—"

"This is ridiculous," Mrs. Anderson says. "My George had nothing to do with this, and I see no reason to bring it up. I won't have him associated with some dirty, sordid—"

"No, ma'am, but if I could just—"

"One more word about it, and this interview ends now. Do you understand?" Her lips are pressed sharply together. I glance at George Anderson, but he only shrugs.

"That's fine." I fold Amber Waybridge away into the sheltering confines of my purse. "Then let me shift gears a little."

He nods. "Sure."

"You have a lovely home here, Mr. Anderson. So much lovely art."

"Yes, thank you so much," his mother chimes in. Her face relaxes into a tentative smile. "It's been in the family since 1920. The Andersons have always been collectors and have traveled widely. And we're great supporters of the arts here in New Orleans. We see it as our legacy, a sort of trust." I can hear her thinking how fine that line will look in print.

Dahlia appears, sets our glasses down, and leaves.

"Of course, the Anderson legacy and fortune are much older," adds Mrs. Anderson. "The Andersons have been a first family in New Orleans for two hundred years."

"That's just wonderful." I beam. "That's really something. So the Andersons have been here since back before the Civil War, then?"

"Ye-e-es," she says slowly. A distinction with cachet among her circle might not play so well to the larger public. I turn back to George.

"So it would be fair to describe you as the son of a wealthy old New Orleans family, then? Whose distinction and wealth stretch back for several generations. To the antebellum era."

"Sure," he says. "If you like."

"So I'm wondering if you've made plans to compensate the women and their families."

"Compensate?"

"Make financial restitution. Reparations, if you will."

He shifts in his chair, clears his throat. "There was nothing about that in the court's decision. I was sentenced to two years, and I served it."

"But, as you say, you're *very* sorry. And you know how much therapy those women are going to need, and how much support, and how expensive that—"

"Excuse me, Miss . . ." His mother pauses. I guess my name's hard to remember.

"Céspedes."

She mangles it. "My son has paid his debt to society. And he's reformed, not like some of those animals they let back on the streets."

"Mother—"

"Well, it's true, George. You've done everything the court ordered, and the women haven't brought a civil suit. You've done your duty."

"And yet," I say, "here you sit, surrounded by plenty. There's more you could do."

"Now just wait a minute," says George, sitting up straight for the first time. "I did my time. I obey the law. What else do you want?"

"It's not a matter of what I might want, Mr. Anderson, but there are a number of different organizations that work with victims of sexual assault," I say. "My readers at the *Times-Picayune* might be interested to know if you've been a benefactor of such organizations, helping the victims of other offenders. Therapeutic treatment is very expensive, as I'm sure you know, and not everyone comes from a family that can afford psychological help. That's a pretty big bill out there, just waiting to be paid. Given your fortunate circumstances, my readers might see a contribution as an act of good faith."

As it turns out, Andersons look alike when they're pissed off. Both sets of eyes narrow, and both mouths purse white in irritation. The mother starts to speak, but George cuts her off.

"Listen here. I have served time in a federal prison. I have successfully completed rehabilitation. I'm not responsible for every kid in America who got felt up."

Priceless. Only with the greatest discipline do I prevent my gaze from snapping to the Olympus on the table, checking for its small blinking red light. *I'm not responsible for every kid in America who got felt up.*

"Of course you're not, Mr. Anderson, and I am so, so sorry for any unintended implication." My voice is melted butter. "I definitely did not mean to suggest that you should be doing more. I just thought that, if you *were* making charitable contributions, I would love for our readers to know that about you."

"Well."

"Please accept my apologies."

"Of course. No offense taken."

"Well, then, I think that's just about everything." I move to gather my things, unobtrusively leaving the Olympus on and letting it poke out of the handbag's outer pocket. Who knows what else they might say on the way to the door? "You've both been so lovely and generous with your time, and I so appreciate your perspective on this difficult issue." I can talk like that when I want to.

We all rise, and both George and his mother escort me from the room. I see Dahlia slipping in to collect our glasses and wipe or fluff away any evidence of our presence.

We stroll slowly from room to exquisite room, making our leisurely way to the front entrance.

"This is all so gorgeous," I say, drinking in my last few sips of cool, tasteless air. "You must have been relieved that Katrina didn't make it here."

"Oh, we had damage, dear," corrects Mrs. Anderson. "We certainly had damage. We had a beautiful Asian pear in the back garden that lost several branches."

I just stare at her. Then we all shake hands, and I'm ushered back out into the bright and stifling air.

14

"Nola! Are you okay?"

My room is dark. I'm in bed. Uri stands silhouetted in the doorway, light streaming in around him. There's a baseball bat in his hand.

"Nola, what's wrong?"

"Nothing. I'm sleeping." My voice is thick, muddy.

"You were yelling."

"What? I'm fine." I struggle to sit up. My muscles feel tired, like I've been running in my sleep. "I'm fine," I say more clearly.

"Are you sure you're okay?"

"I'm perfectly fine. Bad dream or something. Go back to bed."

"Jesus," he says. "You scared the shit out of me." He turns slowly away. "I'm going to leave this open, just in case." He turns back. "Are you sure you're going to be all right?"

"Seriously. Swear to God. Nothing's wrong. Go to bed." Even in my disoriented state, Uri looks pretty fine in boxer briefs. And from all angles, too.

He leaves, and I lie in the dark, wondering what the hell just happened, until sleep sucks me back in.

When I wake up late on Saturday morning, I take my laptop, Olympus, and earbuds downstairs to Fair Grinds. It's drizzling, so I set up camp at one of the sturdy wooden tables inside. Bailey set no deadline for the piece, but I want to get it over with. Get this story into print, get on with my life.

Parked with my stuff and a giant cappuccino, I download the most recent interviews, press my earbuds into place, poise my fingers over the keys, and plunge in. As I type, I boldface each quote I might use. When I'm done transcribing the Garden District, Ninth Ward, and George Anderson interviews, there are so many potentially quotable quotes that the pages look dipped in darkness.

With words swirling in my head, I feel a strange hunger, so I go to the counter and order a piece of praline cheesecake. Back at my laptop, scanning what I've typed, I spoon the sweetness into my mouth, its creaminess so soft I hardly need to chew.

When I finish the slice, I still feel restless. I skipped breakfast, so what the hell? I eat the second piece like a ritual, starting at its sharply angled tip and moving toward the wide crust edge. First I scrape the brown praline topping off, sweet and sticky with its faint burned-sugar taste, then dig into the pale fluff beneath. I read and reread what I've typed, moving, deleting, shaping. It's starting to come together. The intimate words of strangers whisper urgently in my head.

The second piece of cheesecake is gone, and my head is spinning with the sugar rush. I gather up my things and head to the counter again.

"A piece of praline cheesecake. To go."

"A third piece?" The chick's eyebrows almost hit her hairline.

"Is that going to be a problem?"

"No. Just checking."

She smirks to herself as she hands me the Styrofoam box.

Upstairs, Uri's gone already, out with Roux somewhere. I close the bathroom door and sink to the floor. I pick up the slice and wolf it down. My eyes feel hot, like crying, but I don't cry. I don't want to do this again. I did it in college. I read what it does to your teeth, to your heart. I know better.

But just one more time. Just once. Just this once.

The apartment's empty, so there's no one to hear.

Afterward, I stand before the mirror, my eyes a little red and teary with the strain. I feel light again, free, released. Empty. I'm trembling, but the pressure's gone.

I brush my teeth. After I rinse, they're big and white and gleaming when I flash my test smile. Perfectly safe. And then, slowly, as if my hands are someone else's, I squeeze out another line of toothpaste onto the bristles and bare my teeth at the mirror. I brush them and brush them and brush them.

By noon, the drizzling has stopped, and the sun is bright and hot when I swing over to Magazine Street. Inside Soline's shop, it's cool and elegant, and ceiling fans stir the smell of citrus around the luxury goods. Soline's not working today, so a pretty young woman with long lashes and shorn hair fetches the bridesmaid dress from the back still swathed in its white paper garment bag. Though the policy is written down nowhere, Soline hires only black girls to work in her shop.

The shopgirl leads me upstairs to the fitting rooms. The floors are pale hardwood, and the curtain she draws aside is a length of plush gray velvet. In the stall, three full-length mirrors are framed with silver gilt, and the low stool is a soft bulb of suede. The shopgirl clicks away in her heels.

I slide the dress over my head and reach back to zip it. It's a dark blue sheath of lined linen, knee-length, with a square neckline and a low-cut back. I twist my hair up and inspect. Simple, stunning. Flanking Soline, we'll look exquisite, and she'll look like a goddess.

I hear the click of the shopgirl's heels approaching.

"Soline says to ask you will it need alterations?" Her voice is high and sweet.

I pinch at the fabric at the sides of the waist. The dress does seem a little large, though I ordered my size. I turn from side to side in the mirrors.

"No, I'm good."

"Soline says, do you want to take it with you or have her bring it to the church?"

"Oh, good idea." Lugging it around in the Pontiac is not likely to improve it. "Yeah, I'll leave it here." I unzip it. "Hey, how much is this going to set me back, anyway?"

"Soline says the dresses are her gift."

"Hang on a minute. No way am I—"

"Soline says it's not a matter for discussion."

Apparently whatever Soline says goes. "Um, okay. Are you positive?"

"Yes, ma'am."

"Well, thanks."

A long pause ensues. She's right outside the curtain, waiting. I hate salesclerks who hover. Do they think you're going to steal something? How many times have I been tailed through department stores?

"I'll be right out," I say with that fake lilt that rich women use to mean *Get back.*

A moment passes, and then her little heels click away.

At one o'clock, Marisol's waiting out on the sidewalk in front of her apartment complex in Metairie. Two guys, maybe seventeen or eighteen years old, are chatting her up, their muscled arms ripe and brown against their white wife beaters, their jeans slung low around their little behinds. Next to them, she looks tiny in her shorts and wedge sandals, her small bust in her pink T-shirt. I roll down my window.

"Hey, Marisol!" I yell. "We going or what?"

We jump back on I-10 and head for the city. The traffic's light, the day sunny. Sprinklers damp down the dust of construction sites.

"So who were those guys?"

"Just guys."

"They live there?"

She shrugs. "I don't know."

"They kind of old for you?"

She rolls her eyes and slumps back against the seat.

Oops. Strike one. I start again. "So what do you want to do to-day?"

"I don't know."

"I had an idea. How about we go down to the Quarter and get beignets? You had beignets yet?"

She shakes her head no.

"Then I could show you the church where I'm going to be in a wedding. It's right near there."

"Ooh," she says flatly. "A church."

"No, come on. This is not just any church. It's a cathedral. You'll see." She says nothing, and we ride in silence for a while. "Hey," I say, "I got you something. Could you get me my purse?"

She reaches behind me and pulls it up to the front. With my free hand, I prop it beside us and rummage. She stares down into it, then gives a sudden gasp.

"*Chingado,*" she says. "You got a gun?"

Shit. "Oh, right. Yeah." I glance over at her. "I've got a license to carry it. It's just for protection." She's looking at me with newfound interest and respect. "But here," I say, shaking the orange disposable camera at her, "this is what I got you." She takes it from my hand. "During the week, you could take pictures of anything you think is cool, and then on Saturday, we'll get them developed at one of those one-hour places, and you can tell me about them."

"Huh." She turns the camera over in her hands. "Cool," she finally says.

"That way, you can show me what kind of stuff you're into."

She stares down at the gun.

We cruise in my Pontiac, seeking the impossible grail of a parking spot in the French Quarter on a sunny Saturday afternoon. Finally I give up and pay ten bucks to park in a lot. *Híjole,* this Big Sister shit adds up. We get out and cross the asphalt, then thread our way down Decatur through crowds of tourists. Calliope music floats over from the riverboats.

"Come on." Under the green-and-white-striped awning of Café du Monde, we make our way through the bustle of tables to one that's free and sit down. The place is loud and crowded, a jumble of voices and bare shoulders in the open air.

Marisol looks around with interest. "How come so many people come here? Is the food so great?"

"I don't know about that. It's good, but I don't think that's why they come."

"Why do they?"

"It's special, unique. This place is famous all over the world. If someone comes to visit New Orleans, this is something they do."

"What's it called again?"

"Café du Monde. It's French. It means the same as *café del mundo.*"

"The café of the world."

"Yeah. So everybody's welcome here."

She looks around, and indeed, we can hear German being spoken by some blond, sun-pinked people, Spanish by a young couple with their fingers entwined, and an African language by a table of six, their hands gesticulating in the crowded air.

"Cool," says Marisol.

The menu is glazed onto the side of the metal napkin holder, and I push it over to her. "We'd better decide what we want."

She reads it. "So what's a beignet?"

"It's a pastry. Like fry bread."

She looks at me blankly.

"Like *sopapillas*."

"Oh." She nods.

"But with powdered sugar. No honey."

She studies the menu, and our waitress arrives looking already fed up with us. "What do y'all want?" The service is no frills, that's for sure, but then I can't imagine how many people she waits on in a day, and how many of us are rude, cheap, or both.

"Marisol?"

"Cocoa, please."

"No beignets?" She shakes her head. "Okay. I'll have café au lait and one order of beignets." The waitress nods and melts away, and I turn to Marisol. "How come you don't want any?"

"I'm counting calories," she says primly. The girl is a stick.

I nod. "Okay. There are three in an order, and they're sugary, but they're pretty small, so they're not that bad. If you want one of mine, you can have one."

"I'm not going to want any."

"Okay." We stare around for a while. There's plenty to see, both inside and out: customers eating and talking, a guy on the curb playing sax, two women setting up with a violin and bass, seagulls whipping by, a white limousine so long it can't make a turn.

"Can I see your gun?"

I'm startled. "Um, that's a no."

"How come?"

"My license is for carrying a concealed weapon. That means hidden."

"I know what *concealed* means, duh."

"Well, if I take it out so people can see it, then it's not concealed anymore. Duh. I can only take it out if I need to use it for self-defense."

Her eyes glimmer. "So like, if right now a bunch of guys came in with Uzis, you could shoot them?"

I snort. "If guys came in with Uzis, I'd be on the floor with everyone else, doing whatever they said. But if I was alone somewhere and someone attacked me, then yeah, I'd use it."

"That's so cool."

"It's not cool. It's not like I'm an exciting gangsta chick or something."

"Chick?" She gives a little grimace of derision.

"Chick, shorty. Whatever word y'all use now. Anyway, to tell you the truth, those girls aren't that exciting, either. And they don't last very long."

Her irises give a little half spin, like they can't be bothered to roll the whole way. "Well," she says, "but you know how to shoot, right?"

"Yeah, sure. You have to learn if you want a license."

"So you could teach me?"

"Huh." I don't know what the legalities are on that—much less how the national Big Brothers, Big Sisters organization would feel about it. "Let me find out. If your parents say it's okay, I guess I could."

She smiles and nods. "Cool." Her eyes shine. "They won't care."

We'll see about that. But enough about guns. "What's your favorite subject in school, anyway?"

Her irises do their little dance of disdain. "Lunch."

"No, for real."

"I don't know." She looks completely bored again. "Math?"

"Oh, cool." A girl who likes math. "Really?"

"No."

I'm rescued by the arrival of our drinks and beignets. They're hot, crisp puffs of fried dough blanketed with white powder, totally nutrition-free. When Marisol takes a sip of her cocoa, her eyes soften. My café au lait is good, too, and I lift and bite into my gold beignet. I love these things, the hot bland sweetness of them, the crunch and the chew, the melt. Dunked in café au lait, they're as good as it gets. Marisol watches me for a while, then succumbs.

When she takes a bite, her eyes widen, and she smiles over at me. "They're good," she manages to say around a mouthful.

I laugh. "I'm telling you."

We drink and chew, looking around, enjoying ourselves.

"So what are you, anyway?" she asks, halfway through her cocoa.

"I'm a reporter. I work for—"

"No, I mean, what *are* you? You're not Mexican."

Oh. "I'm Cuban."

"What's that?"

"Cuba's a country, an island in the Caribbean."

"Like with palm trees and stuff?"

"Yep. Palm trees, beaches, mountains, cities. It's a really old country. You know who Christopher Columbus was?"

"Duh."

"Well, he landed there on his first trip over."

This fails to thrill her. "You been there?"

"No. My mom came over before I was born."

"Don't you want to go see it?"

"Americans aren't allowed to go there."

"For real? How come?"

Wow. How to explain communism, the Cold War, the domino theory, the Cuban missile crisis, and the Bay of Pigs to a child who was born after the Berlin Wall came down? How to explain the ban on one tiny, poor holdout of a country that poses no threat to the United States?

"It's a long story. It's got a lot to do with politics. Cuba has a really different kind of government, for good and for bad, and people in this country disagree with it."

"So nobody can go to Cuba? Just the Cubans who live there?"

"Oh, people from all over the world can go. And they do. There's a lot of tourism, like here in New Orleans. Everyone else can go, but U.S. citizens aren't allowed."

"Huh," she says, tilting backward to get the last slow dregs of chocolate. She swallows and plunks her cup down on the table. "I thought this was supposed to be the land of the free."

We leave money on the table and walk farther up Decatur, our T-shirts speckled white with telltale powdered sugar, a guy playing "Pennies from Heaven" on sax.

"Hey, cool!" She points up, and we stop to admire the statue of Joan of Arc, Maid of Orleans, gleaming gold in the bright sun.

Everywhere else in the city, you can see dark, oxidized statues of men on horses, the conquerors: Bienville, Generals Lee and Beauregard, Jefferson Davis, Bernardo de Galvez.

But here at the corner of St. Philip and Decatur, tucked out of the way, shines a young woman gilded in bright gold. Sword at her side, Saint Joan gleams. Her gold horse prances, and her split standard ripples above her like a forked tongue in the sun.

She's the kind of girl we honor here. She heard voices, and she damn well went to war.

Marisol and I veer into Latrobe Park, a shady little alcove paved with gray slate. We sit on a wide, comfortable bench—no spikes or dividers here to deter sleeping: this is New Orleans, city of slack.

In fact, two old guys nearby are napping, their thin heads drooped forward. An old oak and a huge magnolia tree shade us all, and the fountain plashes prettily. The sweet, heavy scent of tobacco wafts over from the cigar of another old guy, his lean brown ankles bony above his penny loafers, his elbows on his knees. A live band somewhere is kicking up strains of "What a Wonderful World."

"All this is free? We can just sit here?"

"I know, right?" It's nothing like the flat, hot parking lot of her Metairie apartment complex. "Kind of cool."

When she's had her fill, we head back up Decatur to Jackson Square again. Turning right on St. Ann, we amble past all the sidewalk vendors and their wares: the oil paintings of crooked, surreal Quarter scenes, made to look as if the artist were blitzed on absinthe; the caricaturists eager to distort you for thirty bucks; the psychics, tarot card readers, and readers of palms; the folks selling jewelry, feathers, and beads; and one guy specializing in charcoal drawings of Brangelina, the city's new patron saint duo. A couple of guys are break-dancing next to their boom box, and Marisol wants to stop and watch, so we do. A guy painted silver from head to toe like the Tin Man poses motionless, one foot up on a bench.

Just an ordinary day in the Quarter.

I wave at the redbrick building on our right. "Did you know a woman had these built?" The Pontalba Buildings with their lacy Spanish ironwork are famous, even to people who've never been here. "Her name was Micaela, and she was one of the richest girls in New Orleans. Micaela Almonester. Those are her initials." I point up. In the black iron railings, the letters curl into each other again and again down the block.

"Cool," says Marisol, peering up.

"She was also called the Baroness de Pontalba, and she inherited the property from her Spanish father." We stare up at the lush green ferns and pink flowers on the balconies. "When she got married, her father-in-law wanted her fortune, but she wouldn't give it to him."

"What happened?"

"He shot her."

This gets her attention. "No way!"

"Four times in the chest, with his dueling pistols. This was over in France. And her hands got shot, too. Her finger bones were shattered."

"Ew."

"But she survived, and he killed himself—or so it's said—with those same pistols. But other people say that she managed to get the guns and murder him, and then shot her own hands, so no one would suspect her of the crime."

"Ew. What kind of person does that?"

I glance down at her. "A smart one."

"Did she get to keep her money?"

Suddenly, my breath stops. Fifty yards away stands Blake Lanusse, staring intently at us. Or a man who looks exactly like Blake Lanusse. I can't be sure. The sun is bright, and hundreds of people crowd the square. I squint. It's Blake Lanusse's dark hair, his face, his thick, slouching body. Sunglasses cover his pale eyes. A quick clutch of panic hits my gut, and instinctively I move my body between his gaze and Marisol, blocking his view of her.

"Well, did she?"

"Hang on." I put my hand on her shoulder, glancing down for only a second, but when I look back up, he's gone. My eyes sweep the crowds, searching the area where he stood. But if it was Blake Lanusse—if I wasn't just imagining things—he has melted away.

"What's wrong?"

"Nada, mi'ja." I make myself smile. "Where were we?"

"I was asking if the lady got her money."

"Eventually, yeah, she did." I'm sweating profusely, and I wipe my forehead with my hand, trying to concentrate, to remember the rest of the story. Around us, calliope music blares like the sound track from clown nightmares. I try to slow my breathing. The Pontalba Apartments are where those little girls from the Ursulines Convent had gone when I followed Blake Lanusse days ago. These are his hunting grounds.

Marisol is frowning up at me. *"¿Y qué mas?"*

"And so then she left her husband and moved back here." My eyes keep sweeping the crowds like a searchlight. "She wanted to use her wealth to make the city beautiful, so she had the old wooden buildings torn down and had these brick ones put up on both sides of the square." Early gentrification.

There's no sign of Lanusse anywhere. My grip on Marisol's shoulder loosens. "Now the Pontalba Apartments are a landmark." People pay a fortune to live in them or rent retail space on the ground floor. "The baroness went from being a victim to being a civic leader."

"Word," says Marisol in a serious tone. "Respect." I try not to smile.

We turn left on Chartres, and soon we're in front of St. Louis Cathedral, its three creamy spires reaching into the blue sky. Just looking up at them calms me down.

Maybe I just imagined him. Maybe I'm not getting enough sleep.

"Here's the place where my friend's getting married."

"Wow," says Marisol. "It is pretty cool." She squints. "For a church," she adds.

"Yep. That's kind of the idea."

"What's your dress like?"

I describe it, and she seems disappointed by its dark severity. I guess style means something different when you're twelve.

"I'll show it to you after the wedding, okay?" We turn left on St. Peter, heading back toward the parking lot.

"I wish I could come with you," she says suddenly. "I bet it's gonna be pretty."

I look down at her, unaccountably touched. "Oh, honey," I say, putting my arm around her shoulder for a quick squeeze, and I'm surprised when she doesn't shrink away. "I wish you could, too. Next time. I promise."

That night, I'm already in bed with the lights off when my cell phone rings. I grope the nightstand while two bars of my ring tone fill the dark air.

"Céspedes," I answer.

"Nola? This is Bento."

I sit up immediately and snap on the light. "How'd you get my number?"

"You called me. Remember?"

"Oh, right." I exhale. "So, okay, what is it? Do you need to cancel?" The wedding is only seven days away; there's no way I can scrape up another date.

In spite of myself, his low, appealing chuckle makes me smile. "We are going out together on Saturday. I thought it would be conventional to call."

"Why?"

"To talk with you a little. Be—*¿cómo se dice?*—sociable. Get to know you."

"That's conventional, for sure."

"I am old-fashioned."

I snort. "You didn't seem so old-fashioned in the car that night."

"No. You are right." His voice is warm. "That was not conventional courtship."

"Not even a little bit."

"But not every day does a beautiful girl offer herself. What man would say no?"

Offer herself? Christ. "So what did you want to talk about?"

"Whatever you like."

I think for a moment. "How about that name of yours? Bento. You don't hear that every day."

"Yes, my mother gave me that name. It is an old custom."

"Doesn't it mean 'lunch box' or something in Japanese?"

He laughs. "Yes, I have been told this."

"Some custom."

"In my case, it means 'blessing.' "

"Oh, God." Not just your typical entitled macho, but *un macho milagroso.* Great. "Were you one of those late-life babies everyone prayed for, and then when your mom finally got pregnant, it was a miracle?"

He chuckles again. He's quite the chuckler, and my surliness seems only to amuse him, which comes as a surprise. Once I open my mouth, most men find me irritating.

"No, my mother had eight children before me. Six boys, two girls. But I was the seventh son of a seventh son. In my country, that is bad luck. Parents call those children *bento,* blessing, to ward off the curse."

"Ooh, freaky." More superstition. "So have you always felt cursed?"

"No, never. I have always felt—¿cómo se dice?—protected. But that might be only because there were so many older brothers and sisters watching over me. I was the baby."

"And spoiled rotten, no doubt."

"Ah, yes. Most certainly. My father says so."

"Was your family poor? All those kids."

"Not poor, not rich. My great-grandfather had a farm in the mountains, and all his children and grandchildren, like my father, we all have small houses there. We could work on the farm if we did not wish to go to university and make careers. We were secure, *pero* not rich. Close. We took care of each other."

"Do you miss them?"

"*Ay, sí, sí.* Very much. I call home every week. My mother cries," he says. "At the end of the year, I will visit."

"At Christmas?"

"*Sí,* Christmas."

We ramble on aimlessly, asking random questions.

"What's your favorite color?"

"White," he says immediately. Oh, great: internalized racism. Just what I need. "Because it is all the other colors together, united in light." Well, so much for the racism. He's a New Age freak.

"How about your favorite number?"

He thinks. "Eight."

"Why?" My tone is sarcastic. "Because it's infinity, only upright?"

He laughs. "It reminds me of a snowman. I like to make the circles."

"Okay, here's one." I crack my knuckles. "What's your ideal date?"

"Ah, this one is easy. A beautiful woman comes to me when I have just won a soccer game, and we make love."

"Get out of town." I pull the covers up around me.

"What?"

"I mean, shut up."

"Why?"

I take a deep breath. "I mean, thank you. That's very flattering."

"*Very* flattering," he agrees.

"But seriously, if you could go on any kind of date, what would it be?"

His voice lights up. "First, we would drive south together to the wetlands. We would plant marsh grass together and work all day in the sun and water."

All righty, then. Nothing like mud and labor to make the sparks fly.

"Then we would fish together. I would make a fire and cook the fish for you, and we would drink wine. When it is dark, we would climb in the back of the truck onto many blankets and make love. Then I would hold you in my arms and we would watch the stars." He pauses for a long moment, and I can't find anything to say. "Does such a date sound good to you?"

I clear my throat. "Well, I was thinking more like dinner and a movie. But yeah, it sounds good."

"Every hour, two acres of wetlands are lost. Twenty-five square miles a year," he says, his voice earnest. "It is important to restore. I go down on weekends. It is important for the wetlands themselves, for the waterbirds and the plants, but also for New Orleans."

"Why for New Orleans?"

"What makes a hurricane die down? A lack of fuel. What is the hurricane's fuel? Hot water from the ocean or the Gulf. Once the hurricane gets over land, it begins to die."

"So the more wetlands between the coast and the city—"

"The more time the hurricane has to die down. Yes."

"Hey, how come we never learned this in school?"

He ignores my question. "Katrina was very bad. But worse storms can come. We need to make the wetlands grow, to protect the city."

We talk a little more, and then he says it's late, he's kept me too long, and we say good-bye. I wrap my arms around my knees and sit with the light on, smiling in my empty room.

15

On Sunday morning, I walk my mother to church, holding her arm when the broken sidewalk catches her heels. The air is cool and fragrant with jasmine, and we swing umbrellas from our wrists in case the low, dark clouds begin to pour. From inside my handbag, my phone rings.

"*Ay, mi'ja,* turn that thing off before we get there."

"I know, Mamá," I say, fumbling to find it. *Unknown number,* says the screen.

"Hello?" I say. My mother tugs me onward.

"Hey," says a rasping, jovial voice. "You wanted me to call."

Blake Lanusse. A quick, visceral chill runs through me, and I stop short. My mother glances up in surprise. The fact that he's able to reach right into my Sunday morning is unnerving. Why, why did I give him my cell number?

"Mr. Lanusse," I say, trying to get my bearings. "What a surprise."

"Yeah, well, you said to call. I got a couple of free days the week after—"

"Were you in the Quarter yesterday?" I keep my voice light, take my mother's arm, and keep walking.

There's a pause.

"Sure, baby," he says. I can hear his easy smile. "I'm in the Quarter every day. I'm in the Quarter, and the Quarter's in me."

"Were you in Jackson Square?"

"Hmm. Can't say as I was, can't say as I wasn't. Out and about, you know. Things to do. Here, there—"

"Were you following my friend and me?"

My mother's eyebrows shoot up, full of questions, but the guffaw that bursts from Lanusse would be hard to fake. I shake my head at my mother. *Not to worry.*

"Following? That's crazy talk, darling. That's not Blake Lanusse's style." But of course, I know it is. My mother's expression is worried as she looks up at me. I steer her around a tree root. Great, so now I know he's a convincing liar. "What's the matter, *cher*? You getting spooked, talking to all of us big, bad wolves?"

I let the comment pass. "When are you available to meet?"

"I got time in the afternoon on Tuesday the fifteenth."

"But that's over a week from now."

"What can I tell you? I'm a busy man."

Busy with what? Staring out the window with binoculars? Tracking children down the street? He doesn't have a job. But I take a breath. *Evergreen*, Bailey said. *No deadline.* "That would be fine," I say. "What time works for you?"

"How about two o'clock?"

"How about two-thirty?" I want to be there when school lets out, just to see what he does.

"Yeah, all right."

"I'll be there at two-thirty, then, Mr. Lanusse, and I appreciate your cooperation." We've reached the broad swath of cement in front of the church, and my mother has gone to greet the other parishioners who are streaming up the steps toward the wooden doors. She gives me a little frown, which means I should hang up and act like a proper Christian.

Lanusse's tone in my ear is suddenly crafty, soft. "Like 'em young then, do you?"

I freeze. "Excuse me?"

"Your little friend. She's mighty young-looking to be a friend of yours. Looks like maybe we got us a little something in common."

My mother has climbed the stairs and is frowning impatiently from the doorway. Furious, I keep my voice quiet. "That's disgusting. I have nothing in common with you."

"This is New Orleans, sweetheart. We put disgusting in a pot and eat it."

"You stay away from that girl, do you hear? And stay away from me."

His laughter roars in my ear. "I'm not after you, *cher*. You're the one who's after me."

Sunday, the day of rest, a day for contemplation. I'm wedged into the pew next to my mother, and I'm supposed to be thinking about wisdom, peace, and compassion. But I can't seem to concentrate—not after Blake Lanusse's call. The priest's homilies about love and harmony are bouncing right off me.

Instead, I'm thinking about water.

When the priest says something about Jesus calming the waves and walking on water, I start thinking about the way that floods destroy not just people but stories, knowledge, culture. In a ruined city, there's not just the bloat and stench of corpses. There's a terrible silence.

New Orleans has her own story, but she's not the first. I think of green, wealthy Baghdad in the 1250s, and how invading Mongols wrecked the intricate Sumerian system of dikes and canals, flooding the city, drowning the inhabitants, and dumping scrolls into the river until the Tigris ran black with ink. I think about the delicate indigenous culture of the marsh Arabs, who resisted the rule of Saddam Hussein until the 1990s, when his soldiers drained the marshlands and burned the vegetation, killing the people and ruining thousands of square miles. I'm thinking of the destruction of wetlands in south Louisiana, of drilling in the Gulf, of droughts and tsunamis and biblical floods.

Recently I read that some rich oil guy is now buying up water reserves around the planet, waiting for the day when he can make his next billions from the desperation of human thirst. Movie stars urge us to buy bottled water from Starbucks so little kids in other countries can have fresh water to drink. How weird will all this get?

Fixated on my sex-offender story, I consider how messing with natural water systems is kind of like messing with someone's sexuality. Such systems are intricate, delicate. Private and hushed. It's one thing to observe and channel those natural forces carefully, with respect, like the ancient Sumerians and the marsh Arabs did. It's another to loot and demolish them. Attackers—whether they're invading soldiers or common rapists—don't even know what they're ruining, much less respect it, and the damage can be permanent.

It's pouring rain when we leave, and Mamá and I link arms and huddle under our umbrellas on the walk back to her apartment. There's nothing scary in the fridge, and while I'm spraying WD-40 on some squeaky door hinges, she reheats a pan of *picadillo*. We eat together, and then spoon out flan for dessert.

"Next week," she says, "I'm thinking of having Ledia come to Sunday supper."

"Who?"

"Ledia. My friend." Her forehead wrinkles. "I told you."

"From the community center?"

"*Sí, sí.* Don't you listen?"

Oh, the one with the son. "Right. *Lo siento, Mamá.* I forgot. I've just been working hard at the newspaper, you know?"

Instantly, her frustration melts. "*Ay, mi niña,* don't worry about it." She strokes my hand. Her touch feels powdery. "You just concentrate on your job, okay?"

When she asks, as she always does, if I'm seeing anyone, I say no. I don't mention my plan to take Bento to Soline's wedding.

We hug and kiss, and I walk back to my apartment in the rain.

When I arrive, Uri's sprawled on the red sofa watching ESPN, and I kick off my sodden espadrilles and sit down.

"You're soaked," he says. "Come here." He puts his arm around me, and I snuggle into his warmth. Really, Uri's the ideal man for me: sweet-tempered, good to look at, and none of the complications.

He watches the game, and I zone out, staring at the green screen, the little players zipping around. Out the window, rain pours down, and my mind drifts back to water, power, destruction. Resistance.

The rural Cajuns of the bayous, who build their shacks on pilings, are notoriously hard to find—or so my newsroom colleagues complain. Eluding officials of all sorts, they push their silent pirogues through the glassy brown water of the swamps, gliding right up to a heron before it flaps its wings and lifts away. Cajuns fish from their front doors. They cook turtle, raccoon, and gator the way we fry up chicken. A thick, diverse roux made up of Acadians, runaway slaves, free blacks, lingering native tribes, and Cubans and Filipinos from the old Spanish-galleon days, Cajuns have their own music and live by their own code. It's an old culture, polyglot, tough, and strange to us who live with sidewalks and TV.

"Half-time," Uri says, extracting his arm from my drying curls.

I reach over and mute the TV as he heads for the kitchen with his empty glass and chip bowl. "You want anything?" he calls.

"Some water. Thanks." I hear the snap and hiss of a can opening, and the fizz as he pours cold soda into his glass. A cupboard opens and shuts; the tap runs and turns off. "So how's your novel coming?" I call.

He comes back and sets my glass in front of me. "It's coming." His typical answer.

"Is it really just all about you? 'Dear Diary, today I saw this really cute—'"

"Shut up. No."

"So what's it about, then?"

He shakes his head. "No way. It's bad karma to talk about it until it's done."

"Ooh, Mr. Private."

His eyebrows lift. "You're one to talk."

"But why even write a novel? If you've got something to say, why not just stick to the facts? I mean, not to sound like a journalist or anything."

"Some stories are better with a twist." He grins. "Not to sound like a bartender. I'm hungry. You want more chips?"

"No."

"Well, *I* want more chips." He moves off into the kitchen again, and I hear the clatter as chips pour into the bowl. He comes out and sets the mountain of baked and salted corn down on the coffee table. "So," he asks, not meeting my eyes, "what were you dreaming about the other night?"

"The other night?" I stare at him. "Oh, God, right. I almost forgot." I hadn't thought about it since. "Yeah, that was weird."

He sits down and takes a drink. "So what were you dreaming?"

"No idea."

"You don't remember?"

"I never remember my dreams."

"Never?"

"No, never. What's the big deal?"

He frowns. "Really? That seemed like a pretty bad dream you were having."

His concern suddenly feels stifling. "Look, it was just a dream, all right? I sleep, I wake up, I get on with it."

He chews a chip, studying me. The next words out of his mouth are so carefully neutral that they sound rehearsed. "Have you ever considered," he says quietly, looking out the window, "seeing someone?"

The pause grows long between us, filled with the smacking sound of rain against the deck outside.

I unfold my legs and stand up. "Do we have any salsa?"

"I'm taking that as a no, then?"

"Oh, shut up. I'm just hungry."

"Well, good. You could stand to eat a little more."

I find a V8 in the fridge and walk back out to the living room, my bare feet chilled against the wooden floor. Half-time's over. "Don't you have a novel to write?"

"Shh. I just need to see this." He leans forward to de-mute the game.

I settle back, push my shoulder against his arm until he gives in and puts it around me, and nestle into his warm side. Roux wanders over, heaves a long doggy sigh, and collapses at Uri's feet. Out the window, it's still pouring and gray.

See someone? I'm fine. A bad dream, a little anxiety—no big deal.

Roux gives a contented canine groan, and we all settle in for the second half with the hyper drone of the sportscasters and occasional thunder for backdrop. It's cozy like that, just Uri and me on the sofa, and Roux and the rain and the game.

16

On Monday morning when I get to work, there's a yellow Post-it note from Bailey stuck on my desk. *Nola—My office @ 8 a.m. Tuesday re: sex crimes story.*

That's weird—why not just email me? I always check my email compulsively, in or out of the office. Is Bailey testing me to see if I'm coming in regularly?

Well, I'm here now. I shoot him an email that says yes, sure, I'll be there at eight tomorrow. No problem, boss.

Claire flounces by.

I spend the morning working up a series of little featurettes about Jazz Fest: who's playing on the Congo Square Stage, the Ray-Ban Stage, the Fais Do-Do Stage, et cetera. Stuff that's mindlessly routine.

Long about noon, I get a sudden craving for *plátanos*, so I head to Cubaney in the CBD. A block off Canal on Chartres, it's a tiny new place, stark and bare, which means the owners either started on a shoestring or else chose a weirdly Scandinavian aesthetic for a Cuban restaurant.

I like the place. It's quick at lunchtime and reasonably priced. Great aromas of pork and garlic float in from the little kitchen, and all the women who work there have accents like Mamá's. They bring me a *papa rellena,* a hollowed baked potato stuffed with spiced ground meat, olives, and its own scooped-out, mashed-up self, then deep fried. *Delicioso.*

But my appetite's not good. Almost all of my research has focused on the perps—their psychology, their troubles, their rights, their reception back into society—but I've set this afternoon aside for the victims. Gwyneth Bigelow's comment keeps haunting me: *What they do, it destroys life, just like murder. It destroys souls.* So today I'll be researching the long-term aftereffects of sexual assault, which doesn't do much for the appetite. For dessert, I order a little bowl of blackened *plátanos,* sweet and soft, and a mojito, which I see as my cultural duty to taste test.

Back at my desk, I type in my alumni ID number, log on to Tulane's electronic databases, and skim articles. And I learn that Gwyneth Bigelow has a point. The effects of rape can last for years, and the effects of pedophilia can last well into adulthood. I learn that 94 percent of rape victims display signs of post-traumatic stress disorder—shock, intense fear, numbness, confusion—immediately after the rape. Their beliefs about safety, power, trust, and intimacy are damaged. They no longer believe that they're safe in the world or that life has meaning. They experience shame, guilt, worthlessness, and self-blame, and they develop a general distrust of men.

For most women, these symptoms subside after three months, but for a full quarter of survivors, they persist and worsen. These women are plagued by fear and anxiety, including panic attacks; they experience sleep and appetite disturbances, jumpiness and difficulty concentrating, and feelings of alienation and loneliness. Some develop major depression, as well as drug or alcohol dependency. They suffer from various forms of sexual dysfunction and health problems, including chronic pain, digestive disorders, and headaches. One in five attempt suicide.

Pedophilia is no better. People who were molested as children can develop eating disorders, depression, a chronic sense of fear and worthlessness, and substance abuse problems—for all of which they blame themselves.

If no one intervenes with therapeutic help, being raped can become a life sentence. Or a death sentence.

Why have I never heard any of this? Not in college, not on the news. We see rape, the crime itself, on prime time every night. But the long, ugly aftermath . . . no one talks about that.

I type it all up and shape it into clear, bite-sized paragraphs that *Times-Picayune* readers can chew. Wrapping up work for the day, I check local news online, expecting nothing more than humidity and corruption, but there's something relevant to my story: the Kennedy case will soon be debated by the U.S. Supreme Court.

New Orleans resident Patrick Kennedy, convicted of raping his eight-year-old stepdaughter, was sentenced to death by the state of Louisiana, but since the death penalty is now rarely used to punish anything but murder, his case is going all the way to the top.

I've opposed the death penalty since college, when the Tulane chapter of Amnesty International hosted a big panel on race and injustice in the courts. They described cases of black folks getting exonerated by new evidence, years after all-white juries had sent them to the chair. Now more than a hundred death-row prisoners have been cleared by DNA tests and new methods.

That decided it for me. Nobody wrongfully accused should die. Period. Ever. Our system may claim to be just; it may carve fine mottoes on its courthouses and put up endless statues of blindfolded women. But ours is a flawed, broken system. Justice needs to open its eyes.

My mind full of Patrick Kennedy and the disturbing aftereffects of sexual assault, I feel uneasy and jittery, so after shutting everything down, I drive to the Quarter, park, and head for the Napoleon

House. In the middle of the sidewalk, graffiti artists have scrawled, STOP HERE FOR BONG TOKES, big and raw, and close to the edge of buildings. BESOS appears again and again, in subtler, smaller, rust-colored cursive. That's New Orleans: hits and kisses.

Inside the Napoleon House, where Blake Lanusse came the day I tailed him, I quickly scan the room, but Lanusse is nowhere to be seen. The flaking walls are mottled brown, and the floor is a check-erboard of small tiles, rose and cream. Tall double doors are propped open to the tourist trade and the heat. Three ceiling fans spin, stir-ring the warm air. I seat myself at the wooden bar and hook my heels on the brass footrest.

The Napoleon House is old-school. Classical music plays, and the clean-shaven bartenders wear long-sleeved white tuxedo shirts and wilting black bow ties.

One with damp hair pauses in front of me. "What are you having?"

"Vodka, rocks." And then the glass is there in front of me, cold and lovely, and before I can think of any bar chat, he's gone again.

It's a nice place. I come here a lot. You can sit and sweat and stare at the white plaster bust of Napoleon, which stands on top of the old-time cash register, stopped forever now on $400.00. You can gaze at the rows of glass bottles, all arrayed against arched mir-rors so the intoxicating possibilities seem doubled, endless. You can spin around and face the street, stare at the locals and tourists jostling their way to a happier hour. Your eyes can skim the knots of people for a particular heavy body. You can watch a light rain fall and then stop, slicking the streets with shine as the clouds break up and the sun sinks low and golden.

Time flies in the Napoleon House. You can indulge the yahoos who sit down next to you and say they're from Tennessee or New York or Wyoming and damn, it's hot in here, their bottle of Dixie warm before they drink it halfway down. You can talk and let them buy you drinks, and when you get fed up, you can shut them down hard and turn away, looking down into your melting ice and thinking about what you learned on the Internet. Your eyes can flick around the darkening corners of the room, making sure no one familiar has slipped in and silently taken a seat.

The bartender plunks down a meatball sandwich. I look up.

"On me."

"Thanks, but—"

"Have some." He takes my empty glass and replaces it with a tumbler full of water. "Hydrate," he says.

I eat some nuts to pacify him and drink the water.

It's just the edge of dark when I leave.

Outside, my car is nowhere to be found. I walk up and down the blocks, trying to recall where I parked it. Veering down Bourbon Street, where pink neon signs blare out BARELY LEGAL, I see girls who look no older than Marisol standing topless in doorways, shifting from hip to hip on their high heels, their small breasts magnetizing the tourists who gather around, catcalling over the seventies rock that's jacked up loud, beer sloshing from their cups. I walk by.

I find my Pontiac wedged low between two SUVs, and when I get home, dusk is easing over the city. It's the long sigh of evening, and I want to feel calm, like a person who's done a good day's work and can relax now, weary, a little buzzed, in earned peace. But I don't. My nerves itch, I pace the rooms, I can't sit down. I open the fridge and stare into it, scanning, but my eyes don't latch onto anything. It's not that kind of hunger.

In the bedroom, I find myself stripping out of my clothes and rifling through my closet. There: a black cotton skirt, full but short. I slip into it, pull up the zip, unhook my bra, and grab a blue

T-shirt from the drawer. I slide it over my head and step into high wedge sandals with rubber soles, good for walking on grass.

In the bathroom mirror, I pull my handfuls of hair up into a high, off-center ponytail—a *hon*ytail, as Fabi would call it—and coat my mouth with maroon lipstick. It's hard to meet my own eyes. They flicker strangely, and I look away.

When I pull into the parking lot at the levee, the last two soccer teams are still battling it out in the fading twilight. I grab my handbag and walk over to the field. The drenched men are moving slowly, with effort, and when the ball's not near them, they stand still, panting. When they run, they look as though they're running underwater, as though the New Orleans heat and humidity have finally coagulated into a mass around them, a gel, a solid thing that weights the muscles and slows the limbs.

I walk along the sideline, back and forth, up and down the field. The few tired Latina wives are preoccupied with keeping toddlers away from the white line. They talk quietly to one another or stay mute, tending their children, watching their husbands play and eyeing me with suspicion. Still young, they're already heavyset, running to fat.

I stride. It's like fishing, like I've cast my line and can now just wait for a bite. I feel my whole delicious body stretching and pulsing, my legs sliding slippery against each other, brown and still gleaming from this morning's application of cocoa butter, and my bare breasts bob a little under my T-shirt. The high heels of the wedges make me wobble, and the black cotton skirt flips and sways with each step.

One player glances my way, then another. Then it's like a ripple effect on the field: shoulders straighten, they mutter and glance, the speed of someone's dash across the green picks up, a man dives and slides, his leg outstretched in front of him, his foot connecting with the ball at the last possible moment. When the slider gets to his feet, glancing around, I see that he is taller than the rest. I stand still, positioning my body to face him. Clapping, I smile. From then on, he runs even harder.

The game winds down, and the tall one slaps his teammates' hands while they talk in fast Spanish about next time. When the rest of them drift en masse like a cloud to the parking lot, their wives and babies trailing, he picks up his gray gym bag and heads my way. His brown eyes say he's perfect: affable, but not too interesting. Nice, but not too bright. Just right.

"Hola," he says. *"¿Cómo estas?"*

"Bien, bien, gracias." I smile and try to look welcoming. Sometimes *machos* need a lot of encouragement. They've all got their mamas and the Holy Virgin swirling in their psyches.

His answering smile seems shy. *"¿Te gustaría tomar un café conmigo?"* Sweet.

"No. No, thank you, *y no hablo español."* Coffee and conversation aren't what I came for. He looks a little disappointed, and I say brightly, "Good game."

"Gracias, gracias," he nods. He stands there, holding his gym bag, curious, confused, off-kilter, his head tilted like a German shepherd's. I'm going to have to lead this one to water.

I reach for his hand, still smiling. His eyebrows shoot up, and a knowing look fills his eyes. He grins like he's just scratched off a winning number on a Croc-Cash card. Nodding and gesturing toward the dark grassy slope and blackening trees, he takes my arm to usher me along. Fast learner. The park has emptied, and I nod.

We walk silently into the darkness and he begins to grope my waist, my ass, sliding his hand inside my T-shirt, putting his arm around my shoulder and reaching down inside my neckline to cup my breast. No finesse with this guy; he's hungry. But that's cool. Finesse isn't what I came for. My wedge sandals teeter a little on the uneven turf, and I squeeze my handbag to my side. The ground under us is warm and dry; the evening dew hasn't begun to settle.

Subtle he may not be, but when we find a good spot on the grass, dark and far from any lights or people, he shoves me down deliciously, and my thoughts stop. The kissing is bruising, fierce, and I push back against him hard. Something is easing inside me, going limp, like the melting of a terrible tension. I twine my arms around him, my legs around his legs. His hand slides briefly under my shirt, stroking, then squeezing. My mouth dissolves open under his tongue. Then he's pushing up my skirt, cupping my ass, and I'm wet. His fingers push inside me, and he's kissing and biting his way down my jaw, my throat, my collarbone, and my mind goes dark and blank.

This is what I came for. This silence, the voices in my head drowned out. An end to the chronic stream of words in my head, an end to the low-level panic I always feel. Only this silent motion and hunger and twisting bodies on the ground.

With his free hand, he catches my wrists and pushes them above my head, pins them to the dry grass, and I groan and arch against him.

My sound startles him, and he pulls back. Then he smiles in the darkness.

"So you like it rough, huh?" he mutters. "Dirty little *puta*. You like it with a little *susto*, do you?"

Susto. Terror. The gust of wind that steals the breath, the soul.

He chuckles, and the sound makes me sick. His hand lets my wrists go and he rummages in his gym bag. "I got *susto* for you. I got just the thing for fucking *putas* like you."

And then the world funnels into a tiny, tiny point, the size of the blade glinting silver above me, his knife, his grin. And suddenly it all seems inevitable, as though a door has opened and revealed this: the thing I've been hunting. Not sex, but something else. *Pray for us sinners now and at the hour of our death.*

A terrible chilled sinking floods through me, a cold knowledge that freezes my knees and belly and tongue. He lifts my T-shirt up with the blade, sliding it along my breast. I don't look down, but he can't take his eyes off the metal against my skin. The tip prods my nipple. "Give you something to remember," he breathes.

For a long moment, I think, *Why not? Peace. An end to it all. Maybe this is what I'm restless for. A little blood, a little pain, then sleep.*

It washes over me, and I'm shocked. I haven't, until this minute, even realized that I might secretly long for death, that such a desire might lurk within me. And yet there it is. An urge, a drumbeat, a hunger for finality.

But I don't want to die. And I'm not interested in hurting, torture, a little sadism to get off to, like a favorite song to fuck by. He must have thought he'd found his kindred spirit, his lucky night.

Well, sorry, asshole. Ain't gonna happen.

I immobilize my hips, forcing myself not to pull away, not to alarm him, as my hand steals across the warm, crisped grass to my purse. An inch more—

He drops the knife, grasps my wrist, yanks it up above my head again.

"*No mueva.*" Don't move.

I nod and close my eyes.

He takes the blade back in his hand and runs it along my rib cage. I feel a little hiss of pain as he slits flesh. Light and thin, like a paper cut. *Most honored of virgins, pray for us. Virgin most wise, pray for us. Virgin most powerful, pray for us.*

My hand creeps out again toward my purse, inch by inch, while his knife strokes across my abdomen. The metal tip lifts the curls of hair between my legs. He's enthralled by his blade glinting against my skin.

Only when the safety of my Beretta clicks off does he look up, and by then my gun's in his face.

"What the fuck?" His hands and knife rip away, and he's on his feet and backing away fast. I keep the gun trained on his face, sit up, pull my skirt and T-shirt down over myself. He glances at his gym bag.

"Don't even think about it," I say.

"Mis llaves." His eyebrows arch up now, all pitiful, and the knife dangles, useless in his hand. *"Necesito mis llaves."*

With the gun and my eyes still aimed at him, I pick up the gym bag by one end and shake its contents onto the ground. I kick his keys over to him, and then see his wallet under some sweat-pants and kick that over, too. He crouches, grabs them, looks up into my eyes.

"Fucking *puta*," he spits, and then is up and running fast away from me toward the parking lot.

With my toe, I stir the spilled contents of the bag: nothing inter-esting, so I leave his crap there, pick up my handbag, and stumble toward the river. I don't know why. Getting to the sidewalk, I grab the railing. My heartbeat skitters in my throat. I look up and down the length of the Mississippi, its black oily skin glistening and sparked with lights. A slight breeze carries the smells of grilling beef and night-fresh trees. The heat is in my hair. When I reach up, my hand still trembling, my scalp is drenched with sweat.

Across the park, an engine guns to life, and there's the squeal and grind as a car wheels out of the parking lot.

I gulp the thick, warm air like water. My heartbeat doesn't slow. He's gone.

I head carefully toward my Pontiac, and then suddenly I'm jog-ging across the asphalt to my car. I'm imperiling my ankles, but my legs have kicked into high gear, and I can't slow down. I need to get out. I slam the door, mash the gas, and drive home fast through the dark with the windows rolled up and the radio off.

Back in my apartment, I don't bother with lime juice or mint or sugar; I don't even bother with a glass. I sit in the dark at the kitchen table like a defeated person, taking long pulls straight from the bottle of Havana Club white, and the hot swallows burn but don't revive me. I pour a little rum into my hand, lift my T-shirt, and splash it onto the slit along my rib cage. The sting is fierce but far away.

You like it with a little susto, *do you?*

I sit in the dark with the bottle, shaking and swallowing, hearing his words in my head and feeling very, very afraid.

Because maybe I do.

Some things you can't tell a priest.

And some, you can't tell anyone.

17

Groggy, I wake on Tuesday morning to gusts of hot, damp breath in my face.

"Get lost, Roux." I must have forgotten to close my bedroom door last night—as well as the blinds, apparently. The room is weirdly bright. When I run my hands down my sides, it turns out I also forgot to get undressed.

When I sit up, my skull begins to pound a quiet, miserable throb. My stomach roils. Slowly, slowly, I shift into action, slipping off yesterday's skirt and T-shirt, shrugging on my bathrobe, gathering clothes to wear for the day, heading for the shower.

The hot water and steam embrace me like a *milagro*. I stand there, staring at the clear pooling swirls on the floor of the tub, letting the stream hit the back of my head like anointing oil, heating and easing my aches. The cut on my ribs burns as the water hits it, but the flesh around it isn't puffy or red. Good.

As I stand there, images of the previous day come flashing back in fragments: drinking alone in the dark kitchen, the hookup in the park that went bad, drinking at Napoleon, all the research about the aftermath of rape. Ugh. I squeeze a white worm of shampoo into my palm and begin to soap my hair, working my fingers against my scalp. Suds foam up and slide down my neck. Lunch at Cubaney, those nice ladies and the mojito. Writing up the Jazz Fest featurettes, the note from Bailey—*¡Ay, caramba!*

I jump out, feet slippery, hair full of shampoo, and run sliding down the hall to my room. The clock reads 9:37. *Oh, fuck. Oh, sweet Jesus fucking Christ.* I was supposed to be in Bailey's office at 8:00 A.M.

I sink my nude, wet, completely busted ass onto my bed's rumpled sheets and drop my aching head in my hands. *Oh, holy fucking shit.*

Now what? *Think, Nola, think.* But all my brain's gears are clogged with thick white fuzz.

Okay, first things first. Damage control. Call the office. Which means finding my cell, which means finding my purse . . . I start wandering around the apartment, looking. My handbag's in the kitchen, hanging on the back of the chair where I sat and drank. I rummage inside.

"Shit, Nola!" I spin, and it's Uri, aghast at my nakedness. "Put something on, would you?"

"I'm sorry, I'm sorry. I'm a mess—"

"Yeah, well, you can be a mess with your clothes on." He looks at my hair, which must be a sodden, suds-ridden pelt, then lifts his head to listen. "Is the shower running?"

"Oh, Jesus, yes. Sorry." I go turn the faucets off, put on my robe, wrap my hair in a towel. Maybe Uri can help.

When I go back to the kitchen, I explain everything, even the near date rape with the knife—though I don't mention that it happened on the ground at the park, much less confess that that's where most of my dates transpire. Uri listens thoughtfully.

"Okay," he says. "Here's what you do. Call your boss. Say you had a personal crisis. If he acts skeptical, explain about the date rape, but don't get too lurid. It'll shut him up; it's like talking about diarrhea or something. Say that when you get home, you were too shaken up to sleep, so you took a tranquilizer." He frowns. "Just don't mention that the tranquilizer that you took was booze. Tell him it was stronger than you realized, and you just woke up but you'll be there in forty minutes. Sound good?"

It sounds like genius. "You're amazing, Uri." I hug him.

"I make stuff up. It's what I do."

I take the phone to my room and dial Bailey's office number. He's not at his desk, and plebes like me aren't privy to his cell number, so I leave a calm, detailed, totally professional-sounding message on his office voice mail, explaining it all just like Uri said. I hang up and exhale. I've just bought myself forty minutes.

In the shower, I'm scrubbing away at warp speed when Uri knocks.

"Yeah, come in."

A discreet hand appears behind the shower curtain and unfolds to reveal two aspirin. I take them, swallowing them down with shower water, and the hand reappears holding a mug of hot coffee, the handle turned toward me.

"Oh, bless you, Uri. Thank you. You're an angel."

"You don't deserve me." The door closes.

I rush through the rest of my routine, gather my handbag, laptop, and notes, give Uri a quick squeeze, and head out.

When I get to the *Times-Picayune* building, the first-floor receptionist, Mary, says, "Good morning, Ms. Céspedes. Mr. Bailey's looking for you."

"Thanks," I call, already walking fast up the escalator's moving steps. Shit, shit, shit. If Mary all the way down on first knows I blew my appointment, who doesn't? I catch the next escalator up, trying to calm myself. If Bailey had been on a rampage earlier, okay, fine. That was this morning, before I called.

When I enter the newsroom, I head straight down the long glass wall to his office. It feels like the walk of doom, but I slap a smile on my face and pull my shoulders back.

"Is Bailey in?"

His secretary, Margie, frowns tightly at me. "*Mr.* Bailey," she corrects, "is right over there." She points a single ruby nail.

I see him, leaning against a desk in Sports, his back to me, talking to two of the reporters. Okay, moment of truth. I wend my way through rows of gray steel desks. When I get close, the two reporters fall silent, watching me approach. In slow motion, Bailey turns.

"Excuse me," he says to the men. He catches my arm and spins me ninety degrees in midstride. "Walk with me."

"Good morning, sir. I'm extremely—"

"Just walk."

Silently and fast, he steers me out of the newsroom, through the back exit, and onto the observation deck, which, except when school tours come through, is always deserted. Along one wall, photographs and memorabilia hang, a collage of the paper's long history. The opposite wall is thick glass, through which you can watch the giant machines, three stories tall and an entire city block long, churn out the 200,000 newspapers New Orleanians read each day.

As soon as the door shuts behind us, Bailey explodes. "Céspedes, what the fuck is wrong with you?" He pinches his fingers close together in the air. "You are this close to getting canned. Where the hell were you this morning?"

"Did you not get—"

"I tell you eight o'clock, I mean eight o'clock. And now here it is—what?" He glances at his watch. "Ten-fucking-thirty, and you come waltzing in?"

"Sir, let me—"

"Just a fucking minute. Are you . . ." He gets in my face, peers closely at me, sniffs. "Are you hungover?" He says it like priests say *Satan*. "Are you two and a half hours late and hungover?"

"Sir, did you not get my message?"

"Message? No, I didn't get any message."

"On your voice mail. I explained—"

"I don't care what you explained. I don't care if your dog died, your grandma died, or you saw the second coming of Katrina in a dream. You hear?"

"Yes, sir. But—"

"I'm not finished. You know what? I'm glad this happened. You give Claire more trouble than you're worth. That great CV you came in with, those clips—all of it's not worth a damn if you can't work with people. All you've done is piss people off." He paces the room. "We can't afford deadweight—you know circulation's down thirty percent since the storm. I've been wanting to let you go for a while now." I gasp. "Oh, yeah," he nods, smiling bitterly. "So this is perfect. I should thank you, really. Two and a half hours late to a meeting, and hungover to boot."

"Sir, please—"

"But you know what?" He stares at the gallery of photographs behind me, as if seeking counsel from the past. "I'm going to be generous. I'm going to be a fucking prince. I want that Megan's Law story on my desk Monday morning."

"Monday?" I say in a panicky voice. My draft is still in chaos, and my interview with Blake Lanusse isn't until Tuesday.

"Monday morning, and I want it brilliant. I want it to be the best damn feature since Katrina. And when I say morning, I mean eight A.M., polished and ready to print, or you're fired. And why don't we shake hands and say good-bye now, because I know you've just been dicking around."

He grabs my hand roughly and pumps it in the air between us while my fingers try to squirm their way loose. Before, I was contrite. Now I'm getting pissed.

"Bailey, I can do it. I know I can. It's almost there now."

"Yeah. Sure, it is." He lets my hand drop, and I flex my sore fingers. "You know what's sad, Céspedes? I've seen a lot of mediocre writers come through here in the past twenty years, a lot of people who really don't have it. But you know what? They want it. And they work their asses off. They do a decent job, and they make a career out of what they've got. They aren't brilliant, they don't win any awards or change the world, but they do their time."

I nod, confused.

"But you know what's sadder? Someone with passion. With talent. A lot of talent. Who pisses it away." He shakes his head, looks at me with disgust. "I thought you had something, Nola."

"If you'd just let me—"

"Get out of here. Take the rest of the week off—I'm docking your pay. If you don't show up Monday, nobody here will lose sleep. Get out."

"But, boss—"

"I don't want to hear it. Go get your mind right. Go on." He opens the door and nods. "Go." And there's nothing to do but leave. My face is hot with rage and shame as I storm past him and out the blue steel door. I rush down the two flights of stairs and through the huge room with the presses, my heels skittering on the cement. I shove past people with their blue overalls and orange earplugs, who look at me like I'm a ghost.

Fuck you, Bailey, is all I can think. My brain won't formulate a plan.

And that's how I find myself speeding west on I-10, so furious I can barely see to drive, my only goal to put as much distance as possible between me and this damn city.

When I pass the airport and turn south onto 310, my gas pedal mashed to the floor, the raised white highway lifts me up over the swamp. It looks unearthly, like something out of *Star Wars*—the sterile white curves of high-tech transit, the lush green wetlands below. Tall pines dangle their Spanish moss at eye level as I zip by.

But once I cross the Mississippi, the fantastical landscape doesn't last. The road settles back down to drained pastureland, and I catch 90 West with my Pontiac's windows down and the Radiators cranked loud. "Papaya," they croon in the rushing wind, making the simple fruit sound like an invitation—which makes me grin, given what *papaya* means in Cuban slang.

I catch Highway LA-1 and blow past mundane little towns— Mathews, Lockport, Larose—with nothing but branch banks and gas stations. Eventually the highway swings east, hugging the intracoastal waterway, which is one of the canals engineers dug to drain the marsh and create a path for commercial boats. Now shrimp boats sit stagnant as I pass, their FOR SALE signs whimpering out the financial ruin Katrina brought here, too.

Folks are still eking out a living. Hand-painted plywood signs promise sno-balls, frog legs, turtle meat, hog cracklins. WE GOT SHRIMP. The drive gets easy and boring; there's not much to see except big tugboats in the channel to my left, banana trees, and the rows of corn and tomatoes planted by the roadside. Shacks with sheet-metal roofs brushed with rust.

As I drive farther south, my anger ebbing, the land becomes strange again. Flat wetlands stretch on both sides of the road: high green reeds, the glint of water, gray herons, and those ubiquitous white waterbirds with their snaky necks. An occasional dead tree juts up out of the grass, its trunk bleached a satiny silver, an eerie testimony to the way things used to be. The engineers destroyed the trees: by connecting all the bayous to the saltwater of the Gulf, they killed the roots of cypresses and mangroves, which need freshwater to thrive. Without the root systems, more soil erodes. More wetlands disappear.

A fish jumps from the water on my right, flashing, and I pass a sign for Grand Isle.

In college, we read a book about Grand Isle that made me curious, but the three-hour drive had always been a good reason to put it off. Who had the time, the money, a car that wouldn't break down? Now I'm nearly there. Commercial boat cranes loom huge and strange over the flat wet earth.

High arching bridges lift me up to soar over the vast glittering water, gulls and pelicans swooping at eye level, and link me down to the last scraps of land. Careening through space, I feel small, with just the wide watery horizon ahead.

Finally, I arrive on Grand Isle, where a wooden sign assures me that Jesus reigns as king. I have to stretch and pee, so I pull into the gravel parking lot of Bridge Side Marina. The store is raised high on pilings, so I climb the wooden ramps with their switchbacks, which look and smell newly built—post-Katrina reconstruction, I guess. On the deck at the top, I stretch my legs and breathe the salt air. It's hot and sunny, and seagulls whirl and bitch over the boats docked at the marina below. Fuck Bailey, anyhow.

Inside, I buy a big orange beach towel, a map, a T-shirt, shorts, flip-flops, sunscreen, a couple of bottles of drinking water, and a cold Diet Coke.

All I can see are houses on stilts and fishing camps as I drive slowly down the main drag—the only drag, really—reading the corny signs people have nailed to their beach houses: SIX-PACK, LAST RESORT, THE MONA LISA, MY BLUE HEAVEN.

It all feels deserted. I've heard people refer to Grand Isle as the Redneck Riviera, and now I see what they mean. The place has a scrappy feel. For the rich of New Orleans, it's now as fast to fly to Miami or the Caribbean as to make the drive down here. There's nothing grand about Grand Isle.

At last, I arrive at the entrance to the state park, a small yellow booth. The fee is exactly one dollar, which might explain why the park looks so bleak.

From the booth window, a plump young woman in a brown ranger's uniform leans out to hand me a map full of warnings. While she writes something down and the car idles, I read about strong currents and undertow.

Finally, she hands me the little sticker for my windshield.

Ranger-girl blows thoughtfully on a strand of her brown hair. "You by yourself?"

I look at her, at the empty seat next to me, shrug. *Does it look like there's anyone else?*

"Well, just be careful," she says.

I head to the beach and park in the empty lot. There are no palms, no cypresses, no huge old live oaks draped with beards of moss. A yellow shower house straddles the high dunes, so I grab my new purchases and climb the stairs toward the ladies' room.

I come out, comfortable in my garish new clothes, and head down the wooden ramp toward the blue waters of the Gulf stretched wide, past the sign: NO LIFEGUARD ON DUTY. STRONG CURRENTS. SWIM AT YOUR OWN RISK.

I turn right and head up the beach, which is brown and strewn with sea junk, tiny wood chips, seaweed. A waterlogged onion? This is nothing like the white sugar of my imagination. Tiny shells crunch underfoot, and crabs skitter fast across the sand ahead of me, plipping into little holes as I approach. A pontoon plane glides overhead. I pass a sign that reads, CAUTION—PETROLEUM PIPELINE—DO NOT DREDGE OR ANCHOR. Far out on the horizon, oil rigs squat like black Legos.

The novel we had to read at Tulane, *The Awakening*, featured a wife back in Victorian times. To escape steamy New Orleans, her rich husband would take her down to the beautiful resort at Grand Isle. But lying around on the sand, Edna Pontellier got restless. She had time to think, and the conclusion she drew was that her proper, conventional, upper-class life was dull as death. She wanted something juicier. She wanted more.

So Edna P. experimented. When she got back to town, she moved out, took a lover, and started having unrepentant hot sex—which the book only implies very subtly, it being Victorian times and all—and then she took up some kind of art: painting, or the cello, or something.

While New Orleans high society convulsed with the scandal of it all, Edna P. charged ahead like the happy, sexually satisfied, budding artist she was—until her husband cracked down with the law and told her she couldn't see her kids anymore.

She couldn't figure out a way forward. She couldn't reconcile the dictates of society with her desires. In the book's last scene, Edna is back down in Grand Isle again—but alone, swimming out into the Gulf, farther and farther.

And that's it. She drowns out there. The end.

In class, we were pretty bummed about it, because some of us had really gotten attached to old Edna P. and her pioneering, foxy ways. We wanted her to live. But the professor made a long, windy speech about how her suicide was actually a feminist act of protest within the closed patriarchal system of the period that forbade her authentic desires. Et cetera. Moreover, she said, the act of writing the story—which pushed readers to get outraged by Edna P.'s plight and feel moved to change that system—was even more of a feminist protest, so we should all be thankful to Kate Chopin, the author, for making us think. We should be grateful for her inspiration.

But what I found out, researching my final paper, was that Kate Chopin, when the book came out in 1899, was totally ostracized.

People called her book immoral. She never got back her reputation as a writer. She lost her respectable position in society and died disgraced—and she was even a rich white lady. *The Awakening* fell out of print until scholars resurrected it in the 1970s.

Not so much an inspiration, I concluded in my term paper, as a cautionary tale. Professors might get excited up in their ivory towers, but down in the real world, some stories are dangerous to tell. As I'm now learning all too clearly myself.

I got a B on the paper. Still pisses me off.

I walk for a long way with my stuff under my arm, and then jog some, until my muscles are loose and *Fuck you, Bailey* has faded to a mellow backbeat in my brain.

Choppers spin over, heading out to the rigs, and big commercial fishing boats dot the horizon, but on the beach, there's nobody in either direction, as far as my eyes can see. I spread out my new towel.

Lying on my stomach with my chin propped in my hands, I stare out into the dark blue water. Gulls prowl the air, hunting. All I hear are the soft waves breaking and the *peep-peep-peep* of the little black-and-white terns hobbling in their hunched rush up and down the beach.

And finally, in the peace and solitude, with nothing to occupy or distract me, despair sweeps in like a flood. I've run as far as I can go.

Bailey's had it with me, and as pissed as I still am, I can kind of see his point. He's got his job to do, his paper to put out. He believes in it. All he wants is for me to do my job.

Why can't I, then? I put my face down onto my hands and shut my eyes. Everything goes dark. What's wrong with me? Why can't I get it together? Why can't I do what I'm supposed to do, want what I'm supposed to want? I see my mother's anxious smile as she asks if I'm seeing anyone nice. Random strangers fucking me under bleachers. Nightclubs spinning when I've drunk too much, my room spinning, the poor, wincing hole of the toilet spinning as I throw up yet another night of food and booze. Even Uri, who's practically a saint, thinks I need professional help.

Why can't I shut up and fit in? Why can't I just adore New Orleans, like everyone else, and gorge myself on gumbo and meet a nice man and write stupid little Lagniappe stories and be happy? For God's sake, I'm one of the lucky ones. I'm not in Haiti eating dirt cakes or exiled from Tibet or in Iraq getting killed. I got out of Desire, and I've been told a thousand times I'm talented, bright. So why can't I make this *work*?

Hideous, self-pitying tears are starting to leak onto the towel, so I stand up quickly and walk down to the water's edge, wiping my eyes. *Shake it off, Nola.*

At first, the water is chilly around my ankles, but as I stand in it for a while, it warms up. It feels comfortable, silky, welcoming, and the wet sand under my toes is like drenched velvet. I walk out into the waves.

The mild cool shock of each deepening inch takes my mind off my angst. I keep wading farther out: knees, hips, waist. As my breasts go under, the wet T-shirt starts to drag uncomfortably with each wave, and I suddenly recall how our Tulane professor marched all of us over to the theater department, to wardrobe, where we took turns putting on the accoutrements of a nineteenth-century upper-class Victorian matron: the corset, the hoops, the petticoats, the draping gown. She wanted us to understand how it felt to be Edna P.—to understand with our bodies, not just our minds.

"Now walk," our professor commanded, and it was horrible. It felt like at least thirty pounds of *stuff* hanging off my body, heavy and torpid, as if I were trapped inside a machine. "Now imagine yourself walking into the waves," she said, "with all those garments on." I imagined it. "Now take it all off," she said, and each of us did, piece by piece, as Edna P. had, while she walked and then swam farther out, replaying the hope and mess of her life, letting it all go, until she was perfectly naked, perfectly free, swimming out away from the shore and everything that bound her.

"Sometimes even death," our teacher said, "can be a kind of freedom."

I take off the T-shirt and grip it, wadded in my hand. The waves lap and lift me. It does feel easier, more free, like I can move. I open my hand and let the T-shirt drift away, and then slip out of my shorts. I didn't like them anyway.

And then it occurs to me: there's no one around for miles. No one can see. So I strip completely, and strike out into the water, cutting through the waves until I can't touch bottom, swimming away from Bailey's frustration and my disappointed mother and all the nameless men. My arms stroke out fast.

When I get well past the circling gulls, I hang, breathless, treading water easily, bobbing. The shore is a thin, tan, forgettable line in the distance behind me, and the afternoon sun is fierce. Up to my neck in cool dark water, all I hear is the dim crash of waves and cries of gulls. A pelican skims past just above the water's surface, its prehistoric body, so ungainly on land, now gliding and graceful in flight. Everything is beautiful, peaceful, cool.

I could hang here forever, weightless and free, insignificant, just a small dot in a vast seascape. I could just disappear. I could wait here in the waves for night and thirst and exhaustion to come, and then I could relax, give up, and let the water swallow me down.

Twenty feet away, something breaks the surface. Large, gray, triangular. A fin.

Oh, sweet Jesus.

It sinks back below. Oh, Mother of God. *Holy shit Jesus Mother of Christ.*

I try to remember what to do. Swim back to shore as fast as possible, or hold still and float so my moving legs don't attract attention? I can't think. I'm not on my period, so that's good—no blood scent. I can't breathe. Oh, God. What do I do? I look frantically around. There's no one in sight, no one. No one on the sand. No boats nearby. Oh, sweet Jesus.

The fin breaks again. A little closer. *Holy fucking Christ Jesus Mother of God.*

And then there's another one with it, another fin cresting, and I see the gray curves of their bodies.

They're dolphins. Sharks swim alone.

A shudder of relief runs through my whole body, and my breath comes in little gulping gasps.

Suddenly all I want to do is get back to dry land, and I turn and start swimming hard toward shore, fueled by adrenaline. The Gulf tides pull blindly at me, and the thin strip of shoreline won't grow bigger, and as my arms tire, I begin to worry. But I just keep stroking and kicking and saying the Hail Mary in my head, pushing on, patient, thankful for the miles I run.

Eventually my right foot clips sand. And then I'm dragging myself the rest of the way, beginning to cry and still shaking with relief. When the water is only knee deep, I turn and collapse in the shallows, staring back out toward the horizon.

To my surprise, the two dolphins cruise nearby in shallow water, playing, splashing water with their silver tails, no farther from me than when I first saw them. Almost as if they followed me, as if my safety mattered.

Maybe—just maybe—the world isn't as predatory as I fear. Maybe I don't have to be so tough, hold myself so tightly in. Maybe the fin's not always a shark.

Sitting there in the warm waves, rocking gently back and forth, I feel soft, empty, like water pouring into water.

And then I'm laughing and crying at once, and my heart feels full and strange.

18

When I tumble out of bed Wednesday morning, still coated with Gulf salt and the residue of Bailey's threat, Professor Guillory is the first person I call.

At Tulane, Professor Guillory had been teaching journalism in Newcomb Hall since before I was born. A tall, thin man aging fast toward retirement, he looked, with his bony angles, four-pocket guayaberas, and creamy straw Panama hat, as if he were channeling the entire Buena Vista Social Club. Before I took his Journalism 220, I laughed and called him the Colonel like everyone else. But his courses educated me in more ways than one. I stopped laughing and started taking notes.

When Fidel Castro came to power in 1959, Tómas Guillory was just twenty-one and living in Havana, the only son of a white British father and an Afro-Cuban mother. A cub reporter for *El Mundo,* he had socialist leanings himself, but he could see which way the wind was blowing. His highest value, which he'd inherited from his journalist father—who'd left the London *Times* in disgust over the suppression of a royal scandal—was the freedom of the press. Unfortunately, the communists didn't share his priorities.

His parents bundled onto a plane to London, where his mother shriveled on the cold Tube among tall, cold people, and Tómas flew to New York, where he lived in the East Village, wrote for the *Village Voice,* and began his lifelong love affair with *The New York Times,* which never would hire him but continues to arrive daily on the front porch of his Creole cottage in the Faubourg Marigny. He moved here in 1980, when Tulane's offer of a teaching post and the Caribbean heat finally outweighed his youthful need to dwell in the center of the known universe.

Professor Guillory educated me out of my stereotypes. He might have emanated worldly knowledge and a crisp authority, might have written for the *Village Voice* in the sixties and seventies, reporting on events we'd seen only in PBS documentaries, but Professor Guillory was attentive, thoughtful, and respectful—to everyone, not just to his bosses at the university, and not just to students who dripped their daddies' money. To Professor Guillory, everyone mattered. Everyone was interesting; everyone had a story worth hearing, if you could just listen closely enough to find it.

He taught us to strive for a clean, neutral stance in our work. He was a stickler for syntax, too; he had practically memorized Strunk and White, and in class he would put up articles from *The New York Times* and the *Times-Picayune* on the overhead projector and dissect their structures. It's from Professor Guillory that I learned my love for the Grey Lady and my disdain for the *Times-Picayune.* He was always terribly civilized about it, of course. "I would hesitate," he'd say, "ever to disparage the work of our fine local journalists." Then he'd shred the piece to quivering fragments.

Most winningly, he railed with passion against racist and sexist assumptions, and he took an interest in his students as individuals. He cared about our work and who we were. Not long into that first semester, he called to me after class.

"*¿Eres de Cuba?*"

I turned. It took a few seconds for the words to translate themselves inside my head, and then I nodded slowly. I felt shy joy break over my face. It was the first time in my life a stranger had identified me correctly, and I'd never known how good it would feel.

"My mother is. How did you know?"

He shrugged, smiled. "Just a guess." He waved me on my way.

In other classes, professors were sometimes taken with my outspokenness, but they treated me like a rare breed of butterfly, or a microbe newly isolated under a microscope. I remember one professor's excited smile as he pulled me aside after a particularly vigorous class debate. "You have an authentic oppositional consciousness!" he said.

If he could have clapped a glass bell jar over me, I believe he would have.

Professor Guillory was different. He encouraged my angry way of talking back to texts and history. He asked where I grew up; he knew about Desire. He told me about Antonio Gramsci, the Italian journalist and leftist intellectual who spoke for the working class, even at his own peril, and he urged me to become an advocate for people from the Ninth, people like my mother. It was all a bit weighty—I was only nineteen—and I sure didn't want to die in prison, like Gramsci did, but it all made me feel important, purposeful. I grew to trust Professor Guillory, and I did my best work in his classes, where I felt taken seriously—where I felt, for the first time at Tulane, seen.

He's a professor emeritus now, which means he no longer teaches, and Tulane has moved him into a tiny, windowless office no bigger than a janitor's closet. It's their subtle way of encouraging retired professors to leave for real. Some professors unwittingly collude in the process by speaking to emeriti in loud, slow voices or offering to show them how the photocopier works.

When I call Professor Guillory to ask if he'd be willing to

read and critique a draft of my article, he remembers me immediately.

"I'd be delighted," he says. "Tell me more."

So I do. I leave out the threat of unemployment that hangs over me if the piece turns out to suck. "I have kind of a tight turnaround," I say apologetically. "How long do you think it will take you?"

"Is it finished?"

Dear God, no. It's a hot, sloppy wreck. "Almost," I say. "I could have it to you by tomorrow morning."

He pauses. "Well, my dear Nola, if you send it to me first thing, we can discuss it over dinner tomorrow."

"Are you serious?"

"As a heart attack. Which I hope not to have before then," he adds dryly. He's seventy. I guess he thinks about stuff like that.

"Thank you so, so, so much. This is awesome of you."

"My pleasure. I'm happy to have the chance to be useful." There's no trace of self-pity in his voice. It's just a statement of fact.

"Would Ignatius be all right for dinner? My treat," I say.

"A fine choice. And thank you. How pleasant to be treated to dinner by a young person. What time shall we meet?"

I try to remember what I know about the dining habits of the elderly.

"Five?" I hazard. "Six?" There's a pause. "Is that too late?"

"Oh, *querida,* let's eat at a civilized hour. Eight o'clock?"

"Ideal." I thank him a dozen times, and he urbanely parries away my gratitude. We hang up.

After I shower, make a fresh pot of coffee, and reread the sections I've already drafted, the task of writing the article seems less daunting—which comes as a relief, since the five days before my Monday deadline include a visit with Marisol, the wedding, and church and lunch with my mother. I've already culled the best quotations from each interview, written vivid descriptions of Mike Veltri, Javante Hopkins, and George Anderson, and compiled the statistical data on offenders and victims. It's all in separate files, though, and it needs to be woven together into a coherent story—a flawless one, if I want to keep my job.

But first, preparations. I slice three apples and drop a thick, sticky scoop of peanut butter in the middle of a plate, pour myself a tall glass of milk, and set them next to my laptop on the kitchen table. And I'll take a genuine break—walk somewhere, clear my head, get a hot meal—around dinnertime, so the draft can cool and I can come back to it with a fresh, critical eye. Then I can work into the night until the article's done. My job at the Lagniappe has been such a cruise that, unlike most real reporters, I haven't pulled an all-nighter since college. But I want this story, and I want my job.

I open the untouched multivitamins that have been sitting in the cupboard for months. As I'm gulping one down with a swallow of milk, Uri comes padding out of his room in his pajama bottoms.

He looks at the milk, at the open bottle of vitamins on the counter. "Who are you?" he says. "And what have you done with our Nola?"

"Go ahead. Mock all you want. I've got to write this story today, and I need whatever help I can get."

He peers at the chaos of overlapping files on my screen. "Might I suggest prayer?"

"Might I suggest you get the fuck out of here, so I can get some work done?"

"Ah, it *is* you."

Later, I hear him call, *"Au revoir!* I'm taking Roux." The door closes, and then I'm alone with a swirling mass of opinion and fact, trying to herd the words into something Bailey will deem genius.

———

In the beginning was the Word, and the Word was with God, and the Word was God—or so we're told in church. But words are faulty. As journalists, we're pulled up short by the sad knowledge that our wordy creations are incomplete, imperfect despite our best efforts. We know readers might misinterpret what we write.

It's always been that way, especially when writers chart new territory. French explorer Antoine-Simon Le Page du Pratz, a sort of foreign correspondent here in Louisiana during the early 1700s, recorded everything he saw: the flora, the fauna, the customs of the Natchez. He knew he was making history, so he strove to be precise. But when his European illustrator read the manuscript years later and began to draw, things got lost. When the *Histoire de la Louisiane* appeared in 1758, it was littered with visual errors.

The sketch of the skunk, for example—a creature never before seen in Europe—does sport stripes, but they circle around its body like those of a tiger. Its tail is a flat paddle, not the bushy C curve of Pepé Le Pew, and its face, *pobrecito,* looks strangely like that of A. A. Milne's Piglet. It is a skunk of the blind imagination.

But Le Page distorted nothing deliberately. He was an engineer, an architect, a man given to facts and precision. His were the sins, as we Catholics say, of omission. So perfectly clear was each detail to Le Page—there on the ground, seeing the real, furry, malodorous, black and white skunk—that it never occurred to him to state something so obvious as which way the stripes ran.

Some experiences don't translate. Some things must be lived to be believed. Therein lies the problem, for which teller of tales can you trust?

Gradually, as the apples and a pot of coffee disappear and sunshine sweeps slowly across the floor, a coherent shape begins to emerge from all the sentences, like a human figure gradually emerging from shadows. Eureka. At last.

I pass through it once again, making sure it's solid, and push back from the table, my heart skittering with excitement and caffeine. It's good. It's really good. The material may be disturbing and bleak as hell, but the story's coming together.

I pace the kitchen. It's five o'clock, a good time to take that break and get some food and distance. Exhilarated, exhausted, and restless all at once, I throw on jeans and tennis shoes and grab a box of ammo from my closet shelf.

I'll drive up to the Shooter's Club, then pick up some dinner.

No soccer fields, no booze.

19

After shooting dozens of rounds at the Shooter's Club, I spend a long, dark night at the kitchen table, startled by faint howls in the distance and rising only to make more coffee. When fatigue finally blurs my vision and my motivation flags, I gaze down at the three photographs of Blake Lanusse that lie flat on the table. *For you, motherfucker, and for everyone like you.* Dawn is only a promise when I give the text one final polish. I'm so tired that the screen glows and throbs like a hallucination. Early birdsong is the only sound.

At 6:02 A.M., I press SEND, and my story wings its way to Professor Guillory's in-box, along with a note begging him to find sections that can be cut, since it's still a little long.

My whole body feels heavy with exhaustion. All I want is the peace of sleep. But I need to call the girls and cancel our regular Thursday night dinner, since I'll be with Professor Guillory at Ignatius.

Who's awake at this hour? Fabi's probably on her way to her classroom already, so I press her number.

When I explain, she's disappointed. "I can't believe you're wimping out. I'm making coq au vin." That's right. She's hosting tonight. I'd forgotten.

"I'm sorry. I can't help it. It's a work thing."

I can practically hear her pouting. "Well," she says finally, "can I come over then? Just for a minute? Calinda and I picked out the gift for Soline, and you need to sign the card."

"Yeah, okay. What did you get?"

"You'll see. It's beautiful." She sounds excited. "So when can I come over?"

I glance around the apartment. It's a mess, with dishes and dirty clothes everywhere, and I've taped up my dark tattered shooting targets all over my bedroom walls. I'm not sure I want Fabi to see.

"How about you come over to Fair Grinds when you get off work? Give me a call when you get there, and I'll come down."

"Okay. It'll probably be around three-thirty, okay?"

I promise her it is, and we make obligatory kissy noises and hang up. I beeline for the bed, topple onto sheets still gritty with sand and salt, and sleep like the dead for nine straight hours.

When my cell phone blares, I startle awake.

"Yeah?" My voice sounds thick and scratchy. I clear my throat.

"I'm here!"

"Who is this?"

"It's Fabi, you idiot. I'm here at the coffee shop." Her voice frowns. "Are you high or something?"

"No, I'm good, I'm good. I was just sleeping." She gives an exasperated little sigh. "Give me ten minutes."

She clicks off.

Fabi got lucky; she doesn't share the values of her parents or her social class, but it's easy enough for her to slip by without causing offense. She took the pure, Christly, idealistic dreams inculcated by her expensive Catholic school and shaped them into a practical desire to teach. She pays her respects to social convention by getting her hair and nails done and wearing nice clothes, but she just does it and forgets about it; she doesn't obsess about fashion. "It's just a different kind of habit," she says, alluding to her abandoned early dreams of becoming a nun.

Her parents don't quite know what to do with her. I've visited their large white plantation-style house in Old Mandeville on the opposite shore of Lake Pontchartrain. I've spent the weekend there with Fabi and used the pretty shell soaps that weren't just for show. I've walked up and down the serene miles of grassy lakefront park, past the live oaks and the gazebo, and contemplated what it must have meant to grow up amid such peace and plenty. I've sat on their wide veranda, sipping Arnold Palmers and gazing out at the blue horizon. The Causeway bridge is only twenty-four miles long, but New Orleans is invisible. You can forget the jumbled hustle, the clutter, the crowding, the murder rate, the dampening heat at the small of your back, the stench of spilled liquor and fermenting trash. Fabi's parents don't understand why she wants to live there, in the hot thick of it—on a teacher's salary, no less—and they sure wish she'd stop talking about the Peace Corps.

Fabi's mother is a tall, beautiful, quiet woman who golfs and waits for Fabi to get married. She doesn't know where she went wrong. All those crosses and those years of Catholic schooling were supposed to prepare Fabi, like her brothers, for marriage, children, travel, and the country club. Mrs. Torres's Catholicism is all about the red velvet and gold gilt of papal splendor, not liberation theology and the renunciation of worldly goods. She doesn't know what to do with Fabi's emails, which all close by citing Matthew 19:21, about selling all your belongings and giving your money to the poor, and quoting Brazilian archbishop Hélder Câmara: "When you give food to the poor, they call you a saint. When you ask why the poor have no food, they call you a communist." Fabi says

Mrs. Torres hopes it's all just a phase. She lives for the day when Fabi announces her engagement.

Which could be soon. Carlo has asked her once already, and I've seen the ring. A fat three-carat pear, it would tempt a more material girl. And Carlo himself is plenty fine.

An Italian stockbroker, Carlo came to New Orleans on business six years ago, fell in love with the city, and stayed. To feel productive, he opened a restaurant in the Quarter—one of those tiny, dead-chic, impossible-to-get-into places. Located on the second floor of an old Spanish-style building and marked at street level by only a small, discreet placard, Carlo's serves fresh, organic Italian pasta dishes with seafood that can make you forget sex.

When Katrina hit, he didn't run for Rome. Instead—like a lot of folks with the money to do it—he just dug in deeper. Seeing an investment opportunity, he bought up the buildings on both sides of the restaurant, which are now occupied downstairs by chichi shops, upstairs by rich tenants. So Carlo's doing all right. His insurance is through the roof, of course, but so is everyone's now.

Carlo's wealth, success, cosmopolitan sheen, and good looks offer only partial compensation, though, to an idealist like Fabi. Since he's not out building houses for Jesus, she still considers herself an injured party—which is probably a good thing for the longevity of her marriage, if she ever accepts him. Alpha-dog Italian males, according to what I've gleaned, don't sit still long for a grateful, humble woman. But if Fabi treats him like a minimally acceptable substitute for what she'd rather have—which is to say, a saint—maybe she'll keep his pride and libido in check and have a better chance of hanging on to him for the long haul. But honestly, I don't think her heart is in it. I think she'd like to meet a man more like herself.

Part of Fabi's well-groomed outrage, I think, comes from the fact that her father is an investment banker, so she grew up hearing that the financial bottom line was the only measure of worth. But she also grew up reading accounts of the life of Jesus and the saints. The resulting contradictions wouldn't let her slide into the groove her parents had sanded smooth for her. It goes without saying that 100 percent of her 401K is sunk in social equity funds, and that she spends her vacations building houses for Make It Right. Her missionary zeal gets a daily workout at Cabrini High School, where she teaches world religions and postcolonial literature.

That's how we met, actually. Cabrini High, right across Esplanade Avenue and the exquisite crypts of the St. Louis Cemetery, is also just blocks from where I live in Mid-City. Though Fabi lives Uptown, it's convenient for her to shop after work at the Market, where I shop, and she grabs coffee at Fair Grinds, below my apartment. It was inevitable that we'd bump into each other sooner or later, and eventually we chatted in line at the Market, and it turned out that she'd been a college student at Loyola during the same years I was right next door at Tulane.

"Listen," she said, grabbing my arm. It was the abruptness of a reserved person who finally reaches out. "Would you like to have coffee sometime?" Sure, I said, and she told me to meet her on the front steps of Cabrini High the next day at three.

I got there a little early and took a good look at the place, a heavily ornamented white building three stories high, with a vast marble entrance arch. Despite spikes placed next to the white stone cross, pigeons nest there anyway, adapting themselves, making a home where they're not wanted. A sign says Cabrini High was founded in 1957, but if you look way up near a statue of Christ stretching his hands out, you can see SACRED HEART ORPHAN ASYLUM carved into the white stone, so its history is even older. I waited on the gray marble steps, leaning against the metal handrail, its black paint worn off by a thousand hands. The long branches of oaks swagged lushly to the ground, green parades of baby ferns growing from their bark. In a hand-built grotto of dark rocks, a white stone Mary, hands pressed together, turns her blind eyes heavenward.

The bell rang, and soon Fabi was by my side, weighed down by a messenger bag.

"Oh, you have to see this," she said. Students jostled past us. "It's the weirdest thing." And as all the high school girls came pouring down the steps, giggling with their backpacks and books, the most glorious-looking man in the universe rode past. On his bike. Shirtless.

A hush rippled over the girls like it was doing the wave, and then he rounded the corner and was gone.

"Every day," Fabi whispered. "Every day at exactly this time, he goes by like that."

"Like a vision," I said in awe. Black hair, dark eyes, thick plummy lips, and bronze skin stretched like satin over boxer's shoulders and flat abs. I wanted to toss myself on his handlebars and be pedaled away.

"Gorgeous he may be," she agreed. "But what on earth's wrong with him?"

"Not a thing," I murmured. "Not one single thing."

She frowned and smacked my arm. "He's a grown man. What kind of adult gets his kicks from displaying himself to high school girls?"

I grinned, a thought striking me. "Maybe he's not doing it for the girls. Maybe he's doing it for you."

"Oh, shut up," she said, but a faint blush tinged her cheeks and ears. "Don't be ridiculous." She gazed at the corner where he'd disappeared.

"So do you want to go get some coffee or what?" I asked, and our unlikely friendship began.

When I finally stumble down the stairs and onto the patio of Fair Grinds, Fabi has managed to fold her slim legs into a full lotus on the metal chair. Her elegant hands are arranged in a latte mudra around her cup, and her linen capris and little Ferragamo flats look effortless.

"What's this?" She waves a pitying hand at me. "An homage to college?"

"Shut up." I've twisted my hair up with a Bic pen, and I'm in cutoffs, flip-flops, and a faded T-shirt from a Galactic show so good I can't remember it. "Let me get some coffee."

When I return, she says, "That guy is back."

I glance around. "What guy?"

"Handsome shirtless guy. He's been gone for months now. I thought maybe he moved or something. But he was back riding his bike this afternoon."

"Still sexy?"

"Sexy's not the word. He looks better than before, if that's humanly possible."

"Maybe the warm weather brought him back out," I say.

"A sign of spring?"

"The first robin," I agree.

She giggles and reaches into her handbag, slides a gray velvet box across the table.

"Open it," she says.

Nestled on the satin lies a slender chain strung with a pendant, a cut stone of pale blue. I hold it to the light. "What's the gem?"

"Aquamarine." Her voice is anxious. "Do you like it?"

I turn it from side to side. "I love it." She exhales and breaks into a smile as I tuck it back into its satin. "Fabi, she's going to love this. You know this is her favorite color."

"Exactly. That's why we picked it."

"And it's going to look great against her skin."

"I know, right? That's what we thought."

I shake my head in gratitude. "Y'all did a great job. This is perfect."

"Oh, good. I'm so relieved. We were hoping you'd approve." The pale stone glitters in its nest.

I reach back and pull my checkbook out of my back pocket. "So what do I owe you?"

She takes a deep breath. "Two hundred and fifty."

"Two hundred and—what the fuck?"

"I know, I know."

"We agreed on no more than a hundred each."

"I know, but this was just so completely right for her. We had to get it."

"This is fucked up. We agreed—"

"Oh, Nola, please don't be mad. We just loved it so much. This is her wedding. And you said yourself it was perfect."

"Perfect and affordable are two different things. Way different." I have trouble making rent, and I'm supposed to pony up for this fairy-princess shit?

"Look, I'm sorry. If you can't pay it all right now, I can cover your share for a month." Her eyes flick over me. "Or two."

That stings. No way am I getting on the layaway plan to Fabi. I take a breath. "I can pay it. That's not the issue." Which is not entirely true. "I'm going to have to scramble hard to cover this. "You got a pen?" She fishes one out from her purse. "But it's the principle." I think of Evie Wilson in the Ninth and what $750 would mean to her. Instead, we're giving a gift to someone whose jewelry box already overflows.

"I know," says Fabi. "I'm sorry. We were worried you'd be upset."

Then why the fuck did you do it? I force a smile and write the check. "Where's the card?"

She draws it from her handbag and out of its translucent rice-paper envelope. The card has white silk ribbon hand-stitched on the front and back.

"It was twelve dollars," she says. I look up at her, letting the seconds tick in the air between us. "But don't worry about it," she says hurriedly. I scrawl *Love, Nola* under Fabi's and Calinda's signatures and stand up. I want to go punch something. "Seriously, Nola," she says, becoming a little indignant. "I didn't think it would be that big a deal."

"Thanks," I say. "I've got to get back to work."

"But you just got here," she says. I keep my gaze even until she drops hers. "Well, we're sorry we won't see you tonight."

"Yeah, well, I'll see you at the rehearsal tomorrow."

"Six o'clock at the church, dinner at Carlo's at seven," she chirps. Her cheer is fake. She knows I'm still pissed.

"Right. See you."

Upstairs, I print out the article and go through it again. In the light of day, I find a few paragraphs that need to be reorganized. I sit cross-legged on my bed, reading aloud, marking up the pages with my pen, polishing each sentence until the whole story gleams like glass.

Finished, I sigh and flop backward, stretch my legs. My brain is officially mush.

The light that falls across the bed is the pregnant gold light of late afternoon. In a minute, I'll have to get up and shower and dress for dinner with Professor Guillory, print out my fresh revision, and make myself look like a promising young star reporter instead of a bedraggled heap of laundry.

But for now, for just this moment, I bask in the ceiling fan's breeze and the glow of a job well done.

The soft blue ink of dusk is descending over the city when I arrive at Ignatius. With my crisp white blouse tucked into a navy skirt, I look like an eager young professional. When I enter, Professor Guillory rises from the table, sweetly old world, and holds out his hand. But I see shock in his eyes.

"Nola, are you all right?"

"Of course." I smile brightly and shake his hand, which feels like bones wrapped in paper. "I'm just fine."

"You're just so—you've lost weight."

You're none too plump yourself, pal, I don't say, *and you're looking about ready for the home.* "I'm good, I'm good," I reassure him.

We sit, and he hands me the wine list, still watching me with concern. "I'd advise the pinot," he says. "It's very good, and you look like you could use some iron."

Way to get personal, Professor G. So I order the pinot, and he asks for a plate of boudin with mustard. I love boudin—as the Cajuns say, it's got stuff in it that you can't get in society. At Ignatius, it comes with sour cabbage on the side and a brown paper bag full of warm baguette rounds, and we use our hands and knives to make our own little hors d'oeuvres, the mustard spicy on top of the meat.

I'm dying to know what he thought of the piece, and my impulse is to plunge in and ask directly, but I've learned the rich-people ritual of not cutting to the chase. Food, drink, chitchat—and then, if you're lucky, a brief stroll, a few cryptic exchanges, and the deal is done. It's a weird way to keep business looking like pleasure. Too much directness is déclassé.

He's right about the pinot, and we eat, drink, catch up on the last five years. My chair faces Magazine Street, and the restaurant has huge floor-to-ceiling plateglass windows, so I watch the parade of street traffic as the dusk deepens into night.

Ignatius has only nine tables, and we were lucky to get one at this hour on a Thursday. The spicy Cajun Creole food pulls in crowds, and if dinner's not enough, you can take home bottles of wine, loaves of fresh bread, and Louisiana condiments like Tabasco sauce from New Iberia and cans of Steen's cane syrup from Abbeville. Ignatius ships their boudin in from real Cajun country, so it's that spicy, ricey mush you can't get in stores. *If it ain't New Orleans, we ain't got it,* a chalkboard proudly proclaims.

Professor Guillory, as it turns out, has been occupying himself with traveling and travel writing. He's been rereading all of the works of Polish travel journalist Ryszard Kapuściński, and we chat with pleasure about a piece we both admired in the *Times* by Tom Bissell about climbing Mount Kilimanjaro. Professor Guillory himself has been haunting Buenos Aires and trekking Patagonia. I guess he's hardier than he looks.

"And Havana, of course. Oh, my dear, Havana. Have you been?"

The thought comes as a surprise. "Isn't it illegal?" Besides which, duh, I've never traveled. Anywhere. I can barely pay for parking. But part of hanging with folks who have capital is never mentioning your lack of it. If you confess that vacations, therapy, and other accoutrements of wealth are things you can't afford, they look at you like you're vulgar, and you don't get invited back. Even Professor Guillory, who knows where I come from, must be swaddled so thickly in his comfortable assumptions that he can forget.

"There are ways around the legal issue," he says, building a delicate stack of bread, sausage, and cabbage with his long fingers. "And why bend to Cold War ideology? It's outworn, irrelevant. Some laws deserve to be broken."

Some people can afford to break them. "I'm really just not that interested."

I don't mention the map that hangs above my sofa or the time I've spent gazing at it.

"But wouldn't you like to see where you came from?"

"Where my mother came from," I correct him. "She was an only child, and her parents died before she left in eighty, so I don't have any family there. And they were just poor people, farm laborers. They didn't leave a mansion or anything, like all those rich Miami Cubans. So it's not like I have anything to go back to."

"Except a culture. A land. The music, the way the air smells and feels. You might be surprised."

All right, already. "Like I said, there's nothing for me there."

"Except perhaps a home."

"I don't need a home."

He watches me thoughtfully, chewing his bread and boudin, and then takes a swallow of wine. "That will change," he says. "You're young."

I hate it when old people lord it over you, like you'll definitely end up just like them one day. When my mother does it, sweet as she is, I just nod and tune her out.

Our food arrives, my bowl of creamy crawfish étouffeé, his dark jambalaya. We dig in, and he tells me about Patagonia, the estancias and deep blue glacial lakes. Only after we polish our plates clean with still more of the fragrant French bread, only after we share a piece of hot, melting, sweet bread pudding, its raisins swollen with brandy sauce, only when I'm sinking into a stuffed, pleasant wined-and-dined stupor, does Professor Guillory lay my manuscript on the white tablecloth.

Instantly, I snap awake.

He pauses for a long moment.

"This," he finally says, tapping the pages, "is not only good. It's important. What you've got here, Nola—what you've accomplished— is the kind of story that can change people's lives. It can change how we choose to live together in society." He gazes at me, deeply pleased. "And you've done a strong job of it. A very strong job. This is—superior. Some might even say superb."

A long, soft sigh of pleasure and relief escapes me. "Thank you, sir." In the plateglass windows, reflections of the restaurant's four Tiffany ceiling lamps seem to hover out over the dark street, magical, like bright ghosts. "Thank you for everything. I'm so glad you think it's good."

"No need, no need." He flicks a quick wrist, and our waiter materializes. "Two more glasses of the pinot," he says. "We're celebrating." He turns to me. "It's well beyond good, and you didn't need me to get it there. And you know, Nola, I've quite revised my opinion of the *Picayune*."

I almost choke on my last swallow. "How come?"

"Well, I was always hard on them in class. And they were, to my mind, something of a journalistic joke. But when Katrina hit, they rose to the occasion. Nobly, even. Crisis brought out the best in them. And the level of reporting has remained high. Honestly, they've become the kind of paper where any reporter could be proud to work."

"You really think so?"

"Oh, yes. And having this piece of yours published there—well, you should be quite happy."

"Thank you, sir. I hope my editor accepts it."

"How could he not?" Our wine arrives, and he takes a drink. "You know, though," he says slowly, "there is one thing." My inner hoopla quiets. "There's something missing." His eyes narrow in thought. "Yes, it didn't occur to me until now."

"What?"

"Well, this is a feature, correct? A feature lets you treat the topic more fully, more expansively and thoroughly. Am I right?"

"My piece doesn't do that?"

"Oh, it does a beautiful job—as far as it goes. But remember, all kinds of people will read this. And if the crime rates are as high as you say here, it's likely that some of your readers will have been assaulted themselves."

"So?"

"All you've got here, Nola, is crime and punishment. There's no hope. Especially given what you say about the victims, their disorders, the difficulties they suffer in adulthood—there's no way out for them. At least, not here in your story."

"I'm just reporting the facts."

"Yes, and you do a good job, as far as you go. But there may be other facts, too. The questions we ask shape what we find—and, ultimately, the stories we end up telling. Did you talk with any experts, counselors, therapists, who work with survivors?"

My answer comes out slowly, reluctantly. "No."

"There you go, Nola. That's your last step." He nods firmly. "I'm sure of it." He pats my hand. "All your story needs is a little hope."

When I get back home, I weed through the New Orleans phone book, finding counselors who specialize in sexual trauma and recovery, and leaving a dozen voice mail messages, begging for an interview the next day—which I'll have to squeeze in among a mandatory pedicure and the rehearsal dinner tomorrow. Then on Saturday, I have Marisol and the wedding. On Sunday, there's mass and then lunch with my mother.

The Monday morning deadline looms, and I don't have much time left.

20

When I wake up late on Friday morning, only three of the therapists have called back, and two of them sound more interested in the free PR than in the topic itself. Dr. Shiduri Collins sounds real, so I call her back and she agrees to meet me during the noon hour, between appointments with clients.

Her office is on a quiet residential street, inside a Presbyterian church. "No religious affiliation," she says when she opens the door. "They just give me a good deal on the rent." Smiling, she takes my hand and shakes it firmly. "I like to get that out of the way right up front."

Maybe fifty, maybe older, and at least six feet tall, Shiduri Collins is a linebacker of a woman: broad-shouldered and muscular, her silver hair cropped close to her dark skull. She's attractive, with smooth skin, long lashes, plum lipstick, and a snugly-cut gray suit.

Her office is relentlessly secular, as she's promised: no crosses, no pictures of angels, no annoying little plaques with upbeat spiritual sayings in gold cursive. Dr. Collins settles herself in her chair and gestures toward a small sofa, which is presumably where clients sit. I sink into its squashy cushions. Over her desk hangs one large framed photo of sandstone arches, red and gold. What's that supposed to signify? Endurance? Or is it just a bunch of soothing, rhythmic shapes to focus on while spilling your guts to a stranger?

I lift my Olympus from my bag, hold it up. She nods, and I press it on.

"So can you begin by explaining how you do your work?"

She squares her shoulders and leans back in her chair, settling a look of professional calm over her features.

"Well, I believe strongly in talk therapy as my main mode of therapeutic intervention. But it's often hard to get clients talking when they've been traumatized. For one thing, they may have been warned not to tell." She smiles wryly. "For a lot of the women I see, it's the first time in their lives they've said the details out loud."

"And that's because?"

"There's so much shame," she says. "So much shame, and so much silence. Rape is one of the most stigmatized crimes in the world, so victims often feel dirtied and alone, unable to confide in anyone." She tells me that women are much less likely to report the rape to police if the attacker is someone they know, yet the majority of rapes—eight out of ten—are committed by acquaintances or family members. Many rapes are kept concealed.

"What about children who are raped or molested?"

"Silence is also an issue. With their early trust shattered," Dr. Collins explains, "survivors go on permanent high alert and have difficulty trusting anyone, ever. They conceal their true selves from other people, which leaves them lonely and isolated." She shakes her head and sighs. "It becomes a habit, a way of life, all that hiding. And silence serves only the abusers." Her eyes flash. "So breaking silence is a social and political act, as well as a route to psychological healing."

"But this kind of stuff is on TV now. Why would someone hesitate to speak out?"

"You take an eight-year-old child who's been raped and threatened, and it doesn't matter what people are saying on *Oprah*. Nine times out of ten, that child's going to clam up. So there's fear and there's shame. But another thing that makes talking difficult is that a lot of trauma is stored in the mind and body in ways that language can't access. It gets stored in the brain as a series of flashing images, for example, or it can get lodged in the body as a feeling of tension in the muscles, or the abdomen, or the sexual area. It can be a combination of these and other things." She smooths a hand over her impeccable hair and twists the silver stud in her ear. "My goal is to bring the trauma into language, to get the client to be able to talk through what happened."

"And they do that here with you?"

"That's exactly what we do. Victims of trauma can remain stuck in post-traumatic stress disorder for years if there's no intervention. But we've seen again and again—and I'm talking all over the world now, like after natural disasters and wars—that once a person can form a coherent narrative, her mind begins to heal. 'This happened, then that happened.' Cause and effect. When she can do that, her symptoms immediately begin to decrease. If she can tell her own story, she's on her way back."

"So telling is important."

"It's key." She nods emphatically. Survivors of sexual trauma, she tells me, suffer from high rates of anxiety and depression, which leave them more prone to develop addictions and eating disorders in order to numb out. "And they're coping with other problems. Let's see. Panic attacks, nightmares, exaggerated startle response, flashbacks, and so on—all the symptoms of PTSD." She sighs. "And then, of course, there's the sex."

"What about sex? I mean, do you work with people on their sexual issues? Are you trained to do that?"

"Oh, definitely, and it's very necessary. Survivors of rape usually experience arousal dysfunction, or at least decreased interest in sex. Some develop an outright fear of sex. I help with that. One attack shouldn't rob them of pleasure for the rest of their lives."

I'm scribbling. "Go on."

"Now, survivors of child molestation, as they grow up, tend to respond to sexuality in one of two ways. In the first scenario, some women—or men, of course—shut down entirely, refusing sexual contact of any kind in an effort to protect themselves."

"How do you mean, protect themselves?"

"From the flashbacks and terror that would accompany sex. And let me tell you, that'll mess a person right up: to be in an intimate situation with someone you like, or even love, and all of a sudden you start getting flashes of images, muscle memories, of being molested. This happens to victims raped as adults, too. Some women even have auditory hallucinations—they hear the sound of their attacker's voice."

I try to joke. "There goes that date."

"Exactly. Try explaining all that to the person you're with, when you don't even understand it yourself. It's too scary and confusing, so some people just avoid sex altogether."

"You said there were two ways of coping."

"Yes, and the second one is the complete opposite. Some survivors pursue excessive sexual encounters in an attempt to gain control or mastery over sex. They're trying to control a situation in which they were once helpless and hurt. Unfortunately, this attempt to master sex is condemned by society as promiscuity."

"You mean they get called sluts."

"Yes, when actually they've been violated and need help. This strategy often backfires anyway. Because their sexual boundaries have been damaged, they can choose self-destructive sexual behaviors, even selecting dangerous partners and suffering further damage."

I stare at the undulating sandstone. Red and gold striations ripple through the rock.

"This is a serious soul wound," she continues, "and there's no easy way to recover. These people have been through things no one should ever suffer, and then, when they act out their trauma, they get castigated and isolated. We should be helping them back to a normal life, a life of compassion and trust."

I'm nodding. Everything she says makes sense. "Can you describe what you do to help survivors?"

Dr. Collins smiles. "Happy to." She stands and rotates a dimmer switch until the office softens to a soothing twilight. "If you were a client, this is how the room would be. It helps people talk more freely." She swivels the room back to brightness. "We use this, too," she says, leaning to reach under her desk. She drags a plastic tub full of sand into the center of the floor and sits back down. The sandbox is full of action figures, bright marbles, little plastic animals.

I can't keep from laughing. "For what, exactly?"

She smiles. "Most of my clients aren't used to expressing their feelings verbally. So I have them make patterns with these, and then we talk about it."

Skeptical but intrigued, I uncross my legs and lean forward. "Like on *Law and Order* when they give the kid a doll and say, 'Show where Daddy touched you'?"

"Oh, no, nothing so literal. The arrangements people make are usually fairly symbolic and abstract, like dreams. Then, using what I've learned about the client from our talks together, I interpret the picture. I say out loud what I'm seeing. Sometimes they're immediately shocked—they say, 'Yes, that's true!' or they burst out crying. Sometimes they say, 'No, it means this,' and they correct my interpretation. I sure don't always get it right."

She laughs a comfortable, honest laugh, and I feel myself warming to her.

"Either way," she continues, "they've found some language for things they couldn't say before." She bends from the waist with a soft grunt of exertion and picks up two of the plastic figures. "For example, we've got a Jesus here," she says, "and a Princess Leia." She holds them up. "What a woman does with the Jesus often symbolizes her attitude toward religion, or how she feels about faith and spirituality generally. She might take him out of the sandbox altogether, or build a little mound in the center and put him on top. Or stand him on his head."

"I thought you weren't religiously affiliated."

"I'm not, but we're in the thick of a Judeo-Christian culture, honey, and there's no getting away from that, even if I wanted to. For the women who come here, eighty or ninety percent of them have been exposed to religion in some way. Even if they're not Christians, they've absorbed enough of U.S. culture to use the Jesus that way. So it's relevant."

"And Princess Leia?"

"Well, she's a heroine, right? She's strong. But she needs help. That scene from the first *Star Wars* is iconic, where R2-D2 has the hologram—"

" 'Help me, Obi-Wan Kenobi,' " I quote. " 'You're my only hope.' "

Her brown eyes are warm. "Exactly. That scene is stored in our national image bank—our global image bank, really. I've never worked with a client who hasn't seen that movie. Rich and poor, black and white. And brown," she adds after a moment, as if in courtesy to me. "So the way a client poses Princess Leia might tell me how she's feeling about herself, about her role in her own life in the present day. Does she make Princess Leia central, in charge, standing on her own two feet? Is she isolated, away from the other figures? Is she on her back with animals on top of her, or outside of the tub altogether? Or . . ." Shiduri Collins falls silent.

"What is it?"

Her voice is low. "Or is she buried under the sand?" Her gaze is solid, sad, unflinching. "You can't save everyone." She gazes over my shoulder.

"You really care about your clients."

"Oh, honey, if I could take them all home with me and work with them twenty-four-seven, I would. These women are exiled from their own bodies. And most people don't care." She sighs again, swiveling her chair back and forth, back and forth, in little, impatient arcs.

"You make it sound kind of hopeless."

The chair stops, and her hands open on her lap. "Oh, not at all. Not at all." Her voice is firm. "I'm not the type to bang my head against the wall. If it were hopeless, I would have gotten out of the field a long time ago. No, I've been doing this work for twenty-two years now, and I have seen literally thousands of clients get better. Messed up, hurting women who now are happy, strong people, having healthy sex, living their lives without violence or drugs or fear. They've got self-esteem, confidence, a voice now. They've got their spirit back."

Our time is up, and I thank her. "This is all so helpful, Dr. Collins, and I know my readers will be interested in what you've said. Before I go, I'm just wondering if you'd want to share what drew you to this field in the first place."

She gives me a look like *Don't bullshit me, sweetie.*

"Girl, you know why I got into it." She stares at me for a long minute.

"Are you implying, Dr. Collins, that you were sexually assaulted?"

"Of course I was. And to get to college, I damn near crawled, I had so little faith in myself. But what you learn can change you." She nods and keeps on nodding. "I got help at the free counseling center at Xavier University when I was a sophomore. I went in because I was having trouble concentrating on my homework. Can you believe that? Raped by my uncle for six straight years, and I went in for help because I got a C in calculus. That's the kind of pressure victims put on themselves to keep silent, to push past it all, to succeed on their own." She shakes her head. "Anyway, I got help, and it opened up my life. I realized that I wanted to help other people, other girls."

Ordinarily, I would have been thinking, *Score*. The big reveal.

But I liked Shiduri Collins. I wanted to protect her from public scrutiny.

"Are you sure it's all right for me to include this in the article?"

"Well, it might surprise some folks, but that's okay." She draws a deep breath. "Yes. This is most definitely on the record." She stands, and I follow suit, turning off my Olympus and shouldering my handbag.

When Shiduri Collins opens the door and reaches for my hand, her grip is warm and firm, something good to hold on to. Tough but kind, a person you'd want on your side.

"Like I said," she concludes, "speaking up is a political act. It makes things that much easier for the next person."

I walk down the stairs and out to my car. My silver Olympus is full.

21

At one o'clock sharp on Saturday, I pull up at Marisol's apartment complex in Metairie. She's sitting on the steps, waiting.

"Hey, *chica*!" I call out the car window, forcing a gaiety I don't feel. "What do you want to do today?"

She shrugs and gets in the car.

"So I was thinking, how about the zoo?"

She looks at me, skepticism all over her face.

"Hey, now. The zoo's not just for little kids. If there's one thing New Orleans has got, it's a great zoo."

She stares at me, one eyebrow raised, the rest of her face immobile.

"Seriously. It's so cool, sometimes grown-ups go there on their own."

The eyebrow lifts a millimeter higher, as if in pity.

"Okay, how about this? How about if you go there, not just as a regular kid, but as a zoo judge? A zoo critic? We'll go through the whole thing, and then you can tell me if it's any good as a zoo or not."

She brightens. "Okay." We swing out of the parking lot and onto

Causeway Boulevard. She points a withering finger at the stereo, which is set to news. "Can I change this?"

"Yeah, sure." She taps the tuning button until she finds a hip-hop station.

"You don't like *norteño*? Nothing like that?"

"Pssht. That's my dad's music." From her tone and dismissive little wave, it's clear that no musical form could be more lame. We listen to Wyclef Jean, Rihanna, and Chris Brown all the way down I-10. When Lil Wayne's "Lollipop" comes on, I glance over. She's staring out the window, her expression blank, singing softly along. "Wanna lic-lic-lic-lick me like a lollipop." It's a little weird, seeing those words come out of an eighth-grader's mouth. "C-Call me, s-so I can get it juicy for ya," she sings quietly.

"Hey, wait a minute," I break in. "Do you know what that song's even about?"

She rolls her eyes, like I've suddenly become every teacher, every principal, every boring adult, who ever gave a kid grief.

"Duh," she says.

I try a different tack.

"Did you know he's from here?"

"Static Major? He's dead."

"I know. I mean Lil Wayne."

"For real? New Orleans?"

"Yep. Over at Hollygrove."

"For real? Can we go there sometime?"

Shit. Hollygrove's not the safest, and I'm responsible for her care. "We'll see." With luck, she'll forget about it.

We head downtown on I-10. It's a long, roundabout route, but something in me doesn't want to drive her past Tulane, doesn't want to say, *That's where I went to school.* Something about its massive white stone buildings, its grandeur, the manicured sweep of its lawns, the way young men gather casually for croquet, swinging their mallets, bright sweaters draped around their shoulders like in a J. Crew catalog. So I take the long way to avoid it. On the radio, a lush choir of girls' voices opens a new song, and then Wyclef Jean's sorrowful voice comes on. "Sweetest Girl." *Some live for the bill, some kill for the bill.*

We get off and turn onto Magazine. Traffic is thick, and the Pontiac crawls slowly past the endless little boutiques, the pastel shotgun houses and Creole cottages, the well-to-do New Orleanians and tourists wandering the sidewalks. Marisol stares at the shop windows in naked fascination.

We pass the New Orleans Lawn Tennis Club, where no mere chain link holds the stray balls in. Instead, a high wooden fence, each board set flush against the next, protects the players from gawking hoi polloi as they leap and smack their balls. The other half of the block is occupied by Poydras Home, the peach stucco retirement facility for the über wealthy, with its rolling green lawns and fancy landscaping. Both sides of the block are protected by gates and black security guards; both are cleaned and groomed by black custodians and groundskeepers. Calinda jokes that Poydras Home is where you go when you can no longer swing the racket next door. The rich white people just move over. *Singin' dollar dollar bill, y'all/Dollar dollar bill, y'all.*

"Mira," I say as we turn down the shady drive. Bronze lion statues recline on either side of the entrance to the zoo, and I always feel a little excited when I see them. *She used to be, she used to be the sweetest girl.*

"Huh." Marisol's unimpressed.

It's a Saturday afternoon, and sunny, so the lot is packed, and we have to park far from the entrance gates.

"Come on." I turn the engine off. She rolls her eyes. "Here," I say, handing her the tube of sunblock from the glove box. "Put this on your face." She sighs and smears some on.

But once we've trekked to the entrance, she perks up. The design is cheerful and sophisticated—attractive, bright, elegant—not at all a zoo for babies, and clearly not a depressing place where animals pine in cramped cages. Marisol's standing taller and looking around with interest, and I feel relief. We can see pink flamingoes flocking even before I pay, and Marisol's craning to look. Twelve fifty for me, $7.50 for her—it would cost her family more than sixty dollars to come here, and that's before food and drinks for seven. No wonder they haven't.

We enter, and I hand Marisol my digital camera—well, the *Times-Picayune*'s digital camera—and she grins. "For real?"

"Go crazy."

When we get to the elephant pen, a paunchy, unshaven guy in khaki shirt and shorts, like Steve Irwin with a microphone but without the charm, tells us that "elephants functioned as the original four-wheel drive," and as "the original tanks." We hear about Hannibal crossing the Alps. As whole bunches of bananas are fed to Maggie, a big Indian elephant, I wonder how she would feel about being described in such utilitarian terms. We move on.

The Amur leopard blinks at us from its high crag, then flexes its hind foot and rolls over, bored. Shaggy tan camels lie folded on the dusty earth, belching. A dappled swamp deer wanders by. Although Marisol can't be bothered to read the plaques with their maps and Latin names, she's taking dozens of pictures, holding up the camera to show me the good ones. We stop in front of the Asiatic lions.

"Ooh, he look mean," says a little kid. Two lionesses lie stretched on the warm, grassy earth. "He be smacking you good."

"When I be going to the petting zoo," says his friend, "I be petting a lion."

"No, you ain't."

"I can so."

I share a smile with Marisol. I'm no one to tell them the petting zoo contains only turtles, chickens, goats, and a tired donkey pacing her pen.

The Malayan sun bear can't be seen, and the Asian small-clawed otter sleeps in a dull brown heap. Marisol glances quickly and walks on. I follow.

We both get hypnotized in front of the milky storks. One stork stares askance at us, its long neck folded into its shoulders, hunching, its red-skinned forehead wrinkling each time we shift. Fake cement ruins of Cambodian temples litter the spacious pen, and the sweet scent of Confederate jasmine blows over to us from vines that drape the rock walls.

"He looks like Mr. Elson," says Marisol.

"Who's that?"

"One of my teachers."

"Oh. How come?" I think she's going to say something middle-school rude about the wrinkles. Or the hunch.

"Intelligent," she says, her head cocked to one side. Another milky stork suddenly breaks into gangly, prehistoric flight, its legs dangling immobile below its white body as it glides. "Cautious."

My mouth falls open, and I look at her with new appreciation. She's observant, and her perceptions are generous.

It's a long afternoon, but it goes by quickly. We walk the whole zoo, eat cones of Häagen-Dazs, and ride the safari-jeep simulator, my stomach lurching with each jolt. While Marisol twirls around on the carousel, I stand on the side taking pictures. It's a big, beautiful, old-fashioned merry-go-round with calliope music, and she's picked a big black horse with a carved wooden mane, its legs bent as though leaping—just the kind of horse I would have picked at her age. Something makes me uneasy, though. Maybe it's the calliope.

That cheerful, fake-happy sound of childhood, circuses, and the French Quarter. It sends a quick shiver down my spine.

When she comes down, she immediately frowns. "What's the matter?"

"Nothing." I smile brightly. "Nothing at all." I hand the camera back. "*Mira*. Remember those guys who were talking to you when I picked you up last week?"

She shrugs her slim shoulders.

"Those older guys? Remember?"

"So? We was just kickin' it."

"Well, yeah. Okay. So, but like, has your mom ever talked to you about what's appropriate?" How can I—no mistress of tact—attempt the stranger-danger talk with a girl I barely know, a girl who affects a cool worldliness well beyond her years, who likes guns, who mouths fellatio lyrics without blinking? "I mean, has she ever talked with you about what it's okay for men to say to you? Or how they're allowed to touch you?"

She draws away with a look of sheer adolescent horror, as if I've just initiated a talk about where babies come from. "*Híjole,*" she says. "They're just *guys*."

"Well, look, *lo siento*." I sigh. "But this stuff is serious. Have you seen the story on the news about the missing woman?"

"The one who got took?"

"Yeah."

"Sure." She shrugs again. "Everybody knows about that."

"She went to the bathroom for five minutes, and next thing you know, she winds up dead in the river."

Marisol shakes her head like I'm a pitiful thing. "So what do you want me to do? Quit going to pee?"

"Well, no. Obviously. But you can watch out for guys who seem . . . strange."

She giggles. "All guys are strange."

I laugh, too. "You've maybe got a point there. But that's not what I'm talking about. I mean, *strange.* Creepy strange."

She rolls her eyes. "I can handle it." Moving off toward the wolf pen, she calls, "Can't we just look at the animals?"

I follow her. Two big gray wolves pace the grass. One, scenting us, stops in its tracks. It swings its beautiful, shaggy head our way, and its pale eyes lock on mine for long seconds. Suddenly, I know what to do. I join Marisol at the rail.

"Maybe that's not a real wolf," I say mysteriously. "Maybe it's a *rougarou.*"

She turns to me, skeptical. "A rouga-what?"

Auntie Helene's voice fills my head. *Now the rougarou ain't no pure man, and he ain't no pure beast.* Recycling her crazy old voodoo legend into a cautionary tale, I tell Marisol the story. We lean, watching the wolves, and the legend rivets her like it once held me. I tell her how *rougarous* can't know themselves, how they prey on human flesh, how they never grow old and die, and how, most important, they blend in among regular people during the day. I tell her how to break the curse.

"Let's try it," she says, amused enough to play along, or pretend to. "Let's break the curse." Both wolves have stopped their pacing and are sprawled in the grass, watching us. She leans out over the pen. "Hey, Fur-face!" she calls. "Hey, Fuzzy!"

"You think those are their real names? You've got to call them by their true human names."

"Hey, Lupe! Cesar! Fred! Brittney! I don't know their real names." The wolves stare back, unfazed. "But *oye, mira,* they're looking right at us."

"Yep, that's step two. You have to look into their eyes."

She squints at them as though her dark eyes can shoot laser beams. "And then we gotta kill them?"

The third and last and final. "No. Just spill their blood. You don't have to kill them all the way." I laugh. "But I don't think the zookeepers would appreciate that. And I don't see how you're going to be spilling any blood anyway, young lady."

Too quickly, her eyes gleaming, she says, "If you give me your gun, I could."

"Ah. Well." I shift my handbag to my other shoulder. "And we both know that ain't happening."

"Hmph." She crosses her arms and pretends to pout. One wolf yawns, its rubbery dark lips curling back from its teeth.

"Anyway, my point is, some men, they seem to be one thing— just a nice guy." I think of beige George Anderson. "But they're really something else. Something dangerous. It could even be a teacher or a cop, someone in authority." *An evil mixture most unholy.* "Or just an older boy, someone who seems cool." My neck chills at the thought of Javante Hopkins with his shanks. "You've got to be careful. People aren't always what they seem."

The levee is only a stone's throw away. I think of my recent close call, the man who'd tilted his head like a German shepherd and turned out to carry a knife. But that's not a story I can tell a child.

Marisol's eyes have grown vacant, bored, and she sidles ahead, trying to end the educational part of the tour. I give up and sit down on a stone bench to extract the sharp rocks that have worked their way into the cheap rubber soles of my flip-flops. Marisol runs around, acting more like a kid than I've yet seen her, balancing on the low stone wall that circles the fountain, then running to investigate the bronze statue of a woman whose arm and naked breast are raised to the sky. Bronze cloth swirls strategically around the statue's hips, and a bow is grasped in her hand. A bronze hound leaps at her heels. Marisol skips back over.

"Who's that?" she asks.

"I don't know. What does the plaque say?"

"The what?"

"The sign."

She scampers over to the statue again.

"Diana," she hollers, then runs back to join me. "So who's Diana?"

"Diana," I repeat. "She's a Greek goddess—no, wait. Roman. She's a Roman goddess. A hunter. Yeah, the goddess of the hunt, I think, and of the moon. She's a figure from myth."

"What's myth?" she says.

We drive to Oak Street, where the left-hand shotgun house of Maple Street Book Shop—one of the gems of New Orleans—is devoted to children's books. I ask the woman behind the counter if they have a copy of *D'Aulaires' Book of Greek Myths,* which was one of my favorites at P.S. McDonogh 15. If they're still going to be pushing that classical shit on us in 2008, Marisol may as well know what's up.

"Why, yes, we do," says the woman. She leads us over to the bookcase where it's shelved. She hands it to Marisol but speaks to me. "Isn't this just the most wonderful book?" she says. "Such a classic. Your daughter will love it."

Daughter? I feel like the woman has just drawn a circle around us—a tight, uncomfortable circle. Marisol looks up, too.

"She's my Big Sister," she says.

"Oh, how nice. Your sister. Well, isn't that thoughtful."

Whatever. Now, for a little cultural intervention. "Do you have any books about Mayan or Aztec myths?"

"Hmm. Let me think." She turns to a different case and begins fingering her way through the spines. She turns back to us. "It doesn't look like we have anything ethnic in stock." I refrain from explaining that Greek is ethnic, too. "But we can special-order for you. Would you like to see what's available online?"

"That's okay. Thanks. I'll just get it from Amazon." That's like the worst thing you can say at an independent bookstore, and I see a delicate disappointment fall around her eyes. Well, fuck her. Why should she get my money, if she can't even be bothered to stock the thing? I get out my wallet to pay for the *D'Aulaires'* book.

"Hey, Nola," says Marisol.

"Yeah?"

"Do you think maybe we could spend longer than two hours together next Saturday?"

I stop, surprised, my credit card in midair. "Sure."

"Like, maybe we could do more stuff." The saleswoman plucks the plastic from my fingers and runs it, and Marisol looks suddenly shy. "I mean, if you feel like it."

"I do. Most definitely."

"For real? You promise?"

"I promise. I do."

Rainfall on your wedding day is good luck, or so the superstition goes. As if Rob and Soline need any.

After dropping Marisol off in Metairie, I darted home for a quick shower and got to St. Louis Cathedral in the late afternoon while the sky was still bright and cloudless. We clustered in the little brides' room, primping, laughing, and hugging Soline, who looked like a royal cloud in her short, full dress of white tulle and her necklace of hammered silver.

I kept dashing out to search for Bento, with no success. I called his number, but he didn't pick up.

"So who is this guy, anyway?" my friends kept asking.

"Nobody. Just some guy." But my heart was beating fast.

The very minute everyone's gathered inside the cathedral for the six o'clock ceremony, a torrential downpour begins. What could be better, my mother would say if she were here, than a blessing from Ochún, the orisha of water, moisture, and attraction, the spirit of marriage, love, harmony, and ecstasy?

When it's time, I walk slowly up the black-and-white marble aisle with my hand on the arm of one of Rob's handsome brothers, just as we rehearsed. The mural over the sanctuary features a bunch of men standing around looking noble: ST. LOUIS, ROI DE FRANCE, ANNONCE LA 7EM CROISADE, reads the gold caption, and even I can translate that bit of imperial propaganda. *Geaux,* crusaders!

At the front of the cathedral, I turn and take my place next to Calinda and Fabi. Twenty flags fly over the pews, and the barrel-vaulted ceiling is adorned with portraits of the saints and baby Jesus. There's lots of gold, lots of crimson, lots of cream—Fabi's mom would love it—and it's chandelier heaven: ten brass chandeliers hang over the pews, and a big crystal one dangles front and center. Despite all that light, it's cool and dim inside, and a breeze stirs the flags gently. The main exit doors are flanked by huge action figures of Joan of Arc and King Louis IX.

My fingernails and toenails gleam a buffed and perfect nude, courtesy of the hour and a half it took the staff at Pedicult to make me look naturally flawless. There's not a drop of red lacquer on me. I scan the crowd.

Still no Bento. Maybe he changed his mind. I stare out over the throng of Rob and Soline's friends and relations. It suddenly feels strange to stand before five hundred people, all of whom know Rob, Soline, or both. Family members alone fill up the first four pews on both sides. It's a little painful to contemplate the contrast with my own wedding, should I ever have one. My mother and girlfriends would be there for me, and then whatever friends or family the groom had. It would be so small, we could hold it in a lady chapel somewhere.

Not that I ever will get married. Commitment to anything—except possibly my work—makes my shoulders itch.

Soline looks like a goddess as she walks up the aisle on her father's arm, and the crowd glows beautiful with love. The lovely spring hats the women are wearing, broad discs of lilac and yellow, nod in affirmation as the priest drones interminably about fidelity and trust. To me, it sounds like a commercial for an investment firm. When I yawn, Calinda elbows me, and I almost lose my balance. Stumbling back a little, I try to keep from laughing. Fabi glares, so I stand still, bored and quiet, listening to the roar of the rain, until at last Rob and Soline are kissing and we're all free—free, that is, to stand in a receiving line while five hundred friends and relations shake our hands. The rain keeps pouring, and people crowd around, fanning themselves, looking skyward through the open wooden doors. But once every last hand is squeezed and every last bulb has flashed, the rain eases to a fine mist. We walk down the steps and onto the broad slate pave stones of Chartres Street, their green and gray slicked to a fine sheen.

And there stands Bento.

"Where have you been?" I whack his shoulder with my tiny clutch.

He smiles. "I was in the back. Behind a lady with a very large hat."

Fabi and Calinda materialize instantly at my side. "And who might this be?" asks Fabi, and I introduce everyone.

"Hmm," says Calinda, smiling, shaking his hand. With her free hand, she takes mine. "We've never met one of Nola's beaus before. This is special." She stands there beaming until my fingers can squirm their way loose.

"Don't we need to get going?" I say.

"What's your hurry?" says Fabi. "The bridesmaids' carriage is right here." Two glossy white horses snort. Rob's sister is already seated, and the driver helps Calinda, Fabi, and me up. "You want to ride with us, Bento?" Fabi says.

"No!" I hiss.

"Oh, yes!" says Fabi. "We can squeeze you in."

"This really isn't necessary," I protest through my teeth. Fabi's and Calinda's dates, like everyone else, will be walking the two and a half blocks to the Omni hotel. But Fabi insists, and Bento climbs in, squeezing between her and me.

"So what do you do?" she instantly asks.

I realize I have no idea. I've never even wondered. All I know is that he's a blessed and cursed son, likes to plant marsh grass, and fucks like the devil himself. Now here he is, squeezed under the scrutiny of my friends.

"At UNO, I'm a coastal geomorphologist," he says, his tone formal. The University of New Orleans.

"Oh, that's fascinating," Fabi says. "Tell us about it." Another one of those rich-people strategies. I would have said, *What the hell is a coastal whatsit?*

Bento explains. Coastal geomorphology, it turns out, just means the study of landforms in a coastal region—the impact of natural processes, like erosion, or the accretion from river sediment, but also human actions, and how all those processes shape the land over time. The principle is that if you understand how a complex system works, you can help manage it. I'd thought he was just a weekend do-gooder when it came to the marshes, but it's his full-time job.

His hard thigh presses against mine as we wait for the four carriages to line up and start their nuptial parade. I can feel the bone of his hip and the long muscles of his leg. Which means Fabi can, too.

"Are you from New Orleans originally?" She knows damn well he's not. It's her polite way of saying, *I can't place your accent. Can*

you please categorize yourself so I can drop you in the correct box of my
social classification system?

"I am from Spain."

"Oh, marvelous!" She smiles over at me, widening her eyes mean-
ingfully. What, now he's got European cachet? "Barcelona?" she asks.

"No."

"Madrid?" She's naming the places she's visited. I roll my eyes at
Calinda.

"I am from Lugo, in Galicia."

"Oh, Galicia. How nice." Which means she knows nothing
about it. All I can remember from college Spanish classes is that
Galicia is a green, hilly place, more like Ireland than the tan, hot
rest of Spain.

"Yes, my home has many beauties." The carriage lurches into
motion.

"So what brings you here to us?" Oh, Lord. She's going to inter-
rogate him for the whole ride.

"After Katrina, I was invited by your university to come and
help. My training in Amsterdam was in wetlands, coasts, and water
management systems."

"Amazing! Well, you're just the kind of person we need here."

He thinks for a moment, maybe searching for the right English,
and his hip presses warm against mine as the carriage rumbles over
the pave stones. "When you see a disaster unfolding: to stand aside,
it is not ethical. I had seen New Orleans on TV, and she is very
beautiful." He turns to me and smiles. "French, Spanish, African,
American. There is no city like her." He turns back to Fabi. "You
cannot watch such a beautiful city destroy herself. You are called
to help."

"That's wonderful," Fabi coos.

"America is learning how to treat the environment," he continues. "Learning that everything is not about oil. Many people want

to drill in the wetlands, but America is learning that the marshes themselves are more valuable."

"Oh, please," I break in. "That's just naive. You don't see the city putting up windmills, do you? New Orleans is just as oil-addicted as it ever was. What people want is to get their way of life back."

Bento just smiles. "You can't abandon something because it is damaged. You have to fix it. And you cannot cling to the past. You have to change."

"And have you been meeting some nice people since you got here?" The *right* people, Fabi means.

Luckily, nothing in the Quarter is very far from anything else, so we pull up at the Omni hotel before she can ask for his bank statements.

At dinner in the Grand Salon ballroom, while the string quartet plays Bach, we're served platters of lobster, black-eyed peas, whipped yams, filet mignon, cracklins, and cubed watermelon with a sprig of cilantro toothpicked to each red chunk. Fabi, across the table, resumes her inquisition and finds out that Bento's thirty-five, that he's a good Catholic but doesn't go to church regularly— "Only when I have something to confess," he says, turning to flash me a quick, private smile—and wants children, preferably two or three, but not just yet. It's sweet of her, but a little much. A little much, a little embarrassing, and a little annoying.

Poor Carlo's being left to fend for himself conversationally, and Calinda chose to bring David, the nerdy but sexy one, so the four of us get into a conversation about Mayor Ray Nagin—always a juicy topic for NOLA residents who don't know each other well. The wine's flowing fast, spirits are high, and the opinions are flying when I suddenly overhear Fabi say with breathy admiration, "You're such an *idealist*."

My head pivots, and she doesn't even notice. Her shining eyes are locked on Bento.

Suddenly, I get it. She's not interviewing him on my behalf at all. He's handsome, eligible, and noble. He's saving the wetlands. And as I've told them, he's nothing to me, just a guy. So Bento is not only a man after her own heart, he's fair game.

She asks where he lives, and that clinches it, because when he responds, to my surprise, that he lives off Esplanade, she doesn't say, *Oh, that's where Nola lives.*

"Oh, that's just blocks away from where I teach," she says. "Do you know Cabrini High?"

"By the big cemetery?"

"Yes, that's it. I'm there every day." She blushes. "During the week, I mean."

A waiter leans to offer me red or white wine, and I ask for white. Fabi leans over and points one glossy fingernail at my plate.

"I don't want to cross you, Nola," she says sweetly, "but white doesn't go with steak."

"You're right," I snap. "You *don't* want to cross me." A frown flickers between her brows, but she turns back to him.

"Do you like the teaching?" Bento asks, oblivious.

"Oh, yes. It's my calling."

"This is very good, to find a job that is meaningful. Always I have been caring about water, from when I am a young boy in Lugo. We visited relations once in Ciudad Real, to the south, where the land is dry. It surprised me. I felt sorry for the land and for the people there. But *mis primos* said, 'Keep your sympathy. We like it here.' I began to study water." Bento turns to me and smiles. "But I talk too long. Would you excuse me for a moment?"

"Oh, sure, sure." I nod.

"You have nice friends," he says, and he rises and heads for the corridor.

As soon as he's out of earshot, I turn to Fabi.

"What the fuck was that?" My voice must be louder than I realize, because Calinda suddenly lays her hand on my arm. Carlo turns.

"What was what?" says Fabi.

"Exactly why the fuck are you hitting on my date?"

"Hitting on your—Nola, are you crazy?"

"'Oh, Bento, you're so amazing. You're so heroic,'" I mimic. "'Oh, Bento, I work right down the street from you. We could hook up, easy.'"

Her look is pure shock. "How could you?"

"How could *you*?" I snap back.

"Fabi?" asks Carlo.

She ignores him. "I was just trying to make him feel welcome. Why should you care? You're practically ignoring him."

"Ignoring him?" I'd like to flip the whole fucking table in her face. "I couldn't get a word in edgewise. But don't worry. I'm sure he feels pretty welcome now."

"Girls, stop it." Calinda stands and leans to place a hand on the white tablecloth in front of us. "You can't be doing this. Not today. Not here." I look over, and Soline, though saying something to her mother, is watching us all carefully. I flash her a big no-worries smile. Fabi, turning, smiles, too, and Soline turns back to her mother. "Okay." Calinda sinks back into her chair. "Now cool it."

"Fabi?" Carlo says again, his eyes like a wounded hound's.

She shakes her head. "Nola's seeing things. I've told you how she is."

"What the fuck is that supposed—"

"Drop it," says Calinda, all cold attorney now. "I mean it. Drop it or take it outside."

"You wanna go?" I say, thumbing toward the corridor. "I'm ready."

"Can't you just drop it?" says Fabi, smoothing the back of her updo. "Try to act civilized. For once."

"Enough," Calinda hisses. I've never seen her mad before. Fabi and I both fall silent, staring at our plates. The string quartet springs into Vivaldi, and the clatter of silverware and voices surrounds us. When I look over, David looks puzzled but amused. Calinda just looks pissed.

When Bento comes back and sits down, he gives us all a congenial smile. "What did I miss?"

"Well." I clear my throat. "Funny you should ask. Fabi here was just telling us about this hot guy who rides his bike past the high school every day without a shirt on. She stands on the steps to watch him."

Bento's brow furrows—as does Carlo's—before the gasp is even out of Fabi's lips.

"Nola, what's wrong with you?" Tears glisten in her big, patrician eyes.

I rise to my feet. Bento looks completely baffled.

"I've got to go," I tell him.

"But there will be dancing," he says, catching hold of my hand. "*Cariño,* I wanted to dance." Sweet fool. I lean and kiss his cheek. If he dances half as well as he fucks, then we would have had quite an evening together. But I'm too pissed to stay, and who knows? Maybe Fabi would make a better partner anyway. They can waltz their civilized, idealistic night away.

"I really need to go."

"I will come with you."

"No, no. You stay here. Have a nice time. I just need to go home."

"I will call you?"

"Yes, sure, okay. Call." I glance at Fabi, who's glaring hotly at me while Carlo whispers urgently in her ear. Calinda's shaking her head like we're all a lost cause. "Do whatever you want to do," I say loudly enough for Fabi to hear, and I head over to Soline and Rob.

I kiss their cheeks, wish them all the happiness in the world, and lie that I'm feeling unwell.

Soline rises and we hug. "I love you, girl," she says.

"I love you, too. Call us from Thailand, you hear?" I leave as quickly as I can.

But I make it only to the lobby before I start to cry, furious and hurt in a way that's new to me. I cry hard all the way back to my little apartment.

22

"Nola? Nola!" Hands shake me awake in the dark. Uri. "Wake up! Jesus."

I prop myself up and reach to switch on my lamp. "It's okay. I'm okay."

"You were screaming," he says, sitting down on the edge of the bed. "My God, look at you. You're soaking wet."

I wipe a hand across my forehead, as sweaty as if I'd been running. And my muscles feel just as drained, like I've been struggling in my sleep.

"What's going on?"

"I don't know." Disoriented, I stare at him. All the colors seem too bright, too jagged. "I'm okay. I'm sorry." I grope through my memory, but there's nothing there, like a black tunnel going nowhere.

"You made sounds—these really high, awful sounds."

I shake my head. The shapes and colors of my bedroom start to resolve into their ordinary, familiar selves, and the thick fog in my head starts to clear. "Thanks, Uri. I'm fine. Really." I apologize again.

He looks around my room and sees for the first time all the

shooting targets that I've taped to the walls, a line of dark sentries fluttering with the ceiling fan's breeze.

"Whoa. Isn't this a little morbid?"

Shot, torn silhouettes ring us. "No."

He looks dubiously at the shadowed walls and bullet holes, and rises to leave. "Are you going to be okay?"

"Yeah. I'm fine. Hundred percent." He leaves, shaking his head.

It's Sunday morning. I look at the clock: 5:00 A.M. No point in trying to go back to sleep. I look around, stuck in a strange stupor, trying to decide what to do. My deadline is tomorrow morning, but I'm too groggy to work. Finally, I pull on a robe and pad down to the opposite end of the apartment.

"Will it bother you if I run a bath?" Our pipes are loud.

"Go for it," he calls, his light already off.

I pin up my curls and get the hot water running. When it's full, I sink down into the tub, one steamy inch at a time, and close my eyes, grateful for the soothing effect.

After Katrina, when people were straggling back home and our building's gas was on, the owners of Fair Grinds downstairs let people take hot showers there. The place was always full of shell-shocked, grateful strangers, but they didn't stay strangers for long. When the electricity came back up, Richard and Juliet gave away free coffee and free ice. Everyone had a story of waterline losses, or a stubborn relative who refused to evacuate and was now stuck in Tucson, or an auntie who died in an attic, a grandpa who died at the Superdome, unable to get his meds, or a pet to grieve—or, at the very least, a tale of a terrible fridge. They stood and sat with their paper coffee cups and talked and talked and talked. People couldn't talk enough, it seemed. Since everyone had a story to tell, there was no shame in telling. You could cry in public—people did it all the time. Strangers took each other's hands and held them, or clasped each other in long embraces. It was one long group therapy session all over the city for months as people shared what they'd lost, what they ached for, which scene had shocked them speechless. As Chris Rose wrote for the *Picayune* after the storm, "Everyone here is mentally ill now."

As the city came back, a different feeling came with it, because of people like Richard and Juliet downstairs, people who just opened their doors and gave you a hot shower, hot coffee, the little things that could save your soul.

I soak in the bath until my muscles are loose and rubbery. When I get out, birds are trilling. Gray daylight hangs in the windows. It's still early, and I'm not ready to dress for church, so I pull on sweats and a tank and turn on the news, muting the volume.

The pope is here. Not here in New Orleans, but visiting the United States. Today he'll say mass in Yankee Stadium before flying home on *Shepherd One.* He already made a splash by apologizing for sexual abuse by priests.

Priestly pedophilia was never any shock to me. Invest any bunch of people—priests, Wall Street, presidential administrations—with enough power, and somebody powerless is bound to get fucked.

But what does surprise me is that last month, Pope Benedict added seven new deadly sins to the roster, which had remained the same since the sixth century. I guess he thought it was time for an update. Obscene wealth and environmental pollution, among other things, made the list. And pedophilia is now its very own sin.

I make my buttered toast and café au lait, and sit cross-legged at the kitchen table, dunking my toast, writing up—longhand, from memory—descriptions of my interview with Shiduri Collins. Before I type up the verbatim account my Olympus holds, I want to record my own impressions. A green, leafy, quiet street. A pretty stone church. A kind, capable woman. The promise of healing.

When I'm finished writing by hand, I open up my laptop and begin transcribing the interview. Two hours fly by as I type, rewind, retype, and fast-forward. When I've got the whole interview down, I extract the key points Dr. Collins made and integrate them with my descriptions, distilling everything into one tight, shapely page. Tonight, with fresh eyes, I'll cut it down to a single graph, and then I'll fold that into the story.

I dress for church slowly, absently, my mind on sandboxes and catharsis. I pull my hair back in a long braid, then coil the braid into a bun. My gray skirt, a white blouse, my white granny cardigan— no daughter could be more demure or nunlike.

The clouds look low, dark, fat, and ready to rumble, so I grab my umbrella and head for Mamá's. When I knock, she's ready at the door, so we leave for our weekly dose of official grace.

Mass is dull, as usual. When it's all over, Mamá and I link arms and head back to her apartment. Ordinarily she uses our walk as her own traveling pulpit, delivering her own little mini-sermon on the priest's topic du jour, to make its applications very, very clear in my own life. But today she walks silently beside me, squeezing my fingers.

"Mi niña," she finally murmurs. Her voice is sad. "My most precious pet. You know I would never want to lose you."

"I know, Mamá. I'm fine. You're not going to lose me."

"Ay, don't say that. I would never want to."

"Mamá, nobody's dying here. Cut it out with the gloom."

"Ay, lo siento, lo siento."

"You don't need to apologize. Everything's fine." She shakes her head and keeps squeezing my fingers like we're heading for an execution.

When we walk inside the apartment, I'm astonished. The hot, good smell of roast pork knocks into me. Everything's gleaming, and the table is set for three with sparkling china and silverware.

"Mamá! The place looks beautiful." I'm stunned. For so long, she's taken little interest in homemaking. ("Without you here, *mi'ja*, what's the point?" she would say.)

But now she smiles, shy with pleasure. She lights the candles and turns the oven's dial to PREHEAT. "I need to get out of these *pinche* church shoes," she says and goes off to her room.

I'm tired—from waking so early, from the wine at the wedding, from last night's drama with Fabi—so I open the cabinets, looking for a little hair of the dog.

"Mamá," I call, desperate, "where's your whiskey?"

She doesn't answer, and it takes a full minute before she comes back into the kitchen, buttoning a different blouse.

"I don't keep it anymore," she says.

"What? How come?"

"Ay, haven't you noticed?" She smiles again. "It's been one month and three days." Her eyes are proud. "I go to the AA meetings now."

Unbelievable. A lifetime addiction acknowledged? "No way."

She just smiles.

"Mamá, I'm so proud of you." I hug her. How could I have not noticed for a whole month? "I can't believe it. You're amazing."

"Ay, *mi'ja*, it was time. You know? Time for a change."

"I'm so proud of you, Mamá." I can't stop saying it.

She ties on an apron. "Let me just heat this roast back up," she says, sliding it into the oven.

Unbelievable. My mother's been replaced by Betty Crocker. When I open the fridge, there's only one large plastic container at the front of the top shelf, and the black beans and rice pass my sniff test with ease.

"Those are fresh," she says. "For today. Ledia should be here soon." She flutters around, pouring water into the three glasses, pouring applesauce into a serving dish, fluffing the salad, putting out a plate of sliced guava paste and white cheese.

"Can I help?"

"*Sí, sí*. Put *los moros y cristianos* in the microwave." When the knock comes at the door, I'm busy spooning the black beans and rice into a glass dish.

"*Ay, dios mío*." Mamá crosses herself and slips off her apron.

"I'll be right there," I say, deciding how long to heat the dish.

When I turn, my mother is standing next to a tall, dark woman. Lean, with friendly eyes.

"This is Ledia," Mamá says. The woman smiles. "Ledia, *esto es mi hija Nola*."

My eyes travel down their bodies, and suddenly their interlocked fingers swell to fill my whole field of vision. They're holding hands.

"Holy shit." I collapse backward into a chair. At my words, Mamá crosses herself. "Oh my God," I say. "No way." The room is wobbly. "No fucking way."

My mother comes over to me. "*Mi'ja, mi'ja*, I'm so sorry." Tears swim in her eyes.

"Shit, Mamá, you're a lesbian?" I look from one to the other. "No way. *Imposible*."

"Ay, may God forgive me."

"Forgive you? Mamá, are you kidding?" I'm laughing now. How could I have been so blind? "This is *great*. I'm so happy for you." I clamber to my feet and hug her. I reach to shake Ledia's hand, then figure what the hell, and hug her, too. She hugs back, smiling. "I can't believe it, though. Why didn't you tell me?"

My mother looks shocked. "Ay, Nola, I thought it would upset you. You're so devout."

"Oh, Lord, no, Mamá. I'm not devout." How could she think so? "I love the church. I do. But they've got some things wrong."

She visibly sighs. "*Ay, dios mio*, I'm so relieved. I've been so worried. The way you sit there in church, looking so serious . . ."

Ledia turns to her and smiles. "I told you."

"No more worries, Mamá. I'm glad you have someone nice in your life." I hug her tight. "It's not a sin. It's love. People belong together." Her eyes well up.

Over Sunday dinner, as we tuck into all the delicious food she's made for the occasion, she talks, telling me things I've never heard before.

"How hard it is," she says, "to tell the truth about our desires. In Cuba, I didn't know myself. *Pues sabes,* over there people like me were despised. You could go to prison. I never even let myself think about it. I made myself go out with men. I even loved a few, *como tu papá,* when I got here to the States. And then I was so busy, you know, taking care of you. I went out with men sometimes, you remember? I made myself go. I thought it was the right thing. The moral thing. I hoped I would get married, give you a father. But *en estos días,* I didn't know myself."

Looks like I'm not the only one who's been keeping secrets about my love life. It's strange to think about Cuba that way, to think about my own mother as the target of political condemnation, and to think about the Catholic Church, which she loves, as the source of her shame and fear.

While we eat, she and Ledia steal private, smiling glances at each other, like people who share a delicious secret. Incredible. My mother, in love.

She takes my hand in hers and leans across the table to smooth back a ringlet from my face. Now that the surprise is sinking in, I'm teary with emotion.

"But I'm glad I didn't know myself back then," she says. "*Porque ahora,* I get to know you."

"Oh, Mamá."

"Life is long, *mi'ja.* There is time to make corrections. God gives us that."

There is time to make corrections. That's what I spend all evening doing, in the most literal of ways, alone with my laptop on my bed. I blend the Shiduri Collins interview into the story until the seams are smooth, and then go over the whole thing three more times, reading aloud, polishing. I print out the final version, find two ty- pos, revise and print again, and fasten the pages with a shining silver paper clip. *Nola Soledad Céspedes,* the byline reads. It's the first time in a long time that I've been proud to see it.

My cell phone has been on SILENT all day. When I check it, there's a message from Calinda—"What's going on with you, girl? I'm worried. Call me."—and three more from Fabi, all mingled apology and indignation.

There's another one: "Nola, this is Bento. I call to thank you for a lovely evening *y también* to ask if you would like to go out with me again. Just dinner, no planting of grass." Cute. "I would like to take you out on Friday night, but if you are busy, we can go an- other evening."

I text Bento to say maybe, text Calinda that I'm fine, and plug my phone in to recharge. Fabi can fuck herself.

It's only ten o'clock at night, which feels wildly, pointlessly early. I set the alarm for 6:00 A.M., so I can get to the *Picayune* office in plenty of time to hand Bailey the story, in person, before the deadline at eight. I drink a mug of warm milk and tuck my- self into bed.

But I can't sleep. I lie in the dark, thinking of Patrick Kennedy's stepdaughter. The news has been full of her story since the Su- preme Court decided to put him back on trial. She's in college now. She wants to be a lawyer. But in 1998 she was eight years old, asleep in her bed one morning over in Harvey, across the river. She was just a little girl in her bed, sleeping—her mother had left for work at 5:00 A.M.—when her stepfather came in, put his hand over her eyes, and raped her.

When he couldn't get the bleeding to stop, he called 911, and when the police came, Kennedy lied. He turned over a blood-soaked mattress to hide it from police, and he concocted an elaborate story blaming young black men.

Louisiana sentenced him to death, and on death row he sits to this day, up in Angola.

The issue of race is not incidental. It used to be legal in many states to execute a man for rape, but in 1976, the U.S. Supreme Court finally put a stop to that, because 90 percent of all rapists executed in the United States had been African American. In Louisiana, all fourteen rapists executed in the seventy-five previous years were black. America loved itself a good lynching, and the rape law made it all too easy to get a black man killed. So the Supreme Court changed it.

But nineteen years later, Louisiana changed it back—only in the case of child rape, which the state classified as a particularly heinous crime.

Pedophilia: a deadly sin. Where I live, we believe that men who rape children deserve to die.

But Patrick Kennedy is black. Whether or not he's guilty, to execute him would be to participate in a long, sick history of racial injustice.

There are no easy answers.

"It takes away their innocence, it takes away their childhood, it mutilates their spirit," said the New Orleans assistant DA, commenting on Kennedy's stepdaughter. "It kills their soul. They're never the same after these things happen."

Soul murder. That's what Gwyneth Bigelow called sexual assault. But the corpses don't lie around waiting to be buried. They walk and talk, dead inside. They crawl to college. They pass for normal. They may look lifelike, but that's just technique, like Audubon. They're exiled from their own bodies, their sense of safety in the world permanently stolen, their spirits slashed and scarred.

Kennedy's stepdaughter, which is the only way she's known to the press, is eighteen or nineteen now. Her relatives want Patrick Kennedy dead. Her cousin told CNN that the death penalty is "going to be justice. It's going to be that she can look forwards and not backwards, and not have to look over your shoulders, and one day see him. Or see him coming after her."

The sense of being hunted. Forever. An end to that.

I give up trying to sleep. My brain's spinning, and I turn on the lamp, slip over to the dresser drawer where I'd tucked the joint Soline gave me. *This'll cure what ails you.*

I lie on my back, inhaling the deep sweet smoke, watching the ceiling fan twirl. But it doesn't calm me down. The voices in my head just buzz louder, faster. Panic glues me to the bed. I think, If I just smoke enough.

So I keep sucking it in, until the ceiling twists and buckles above me and I fall into a sleep of clutching, paranoid dreams I won't remember.

23

In the morning, I shower, scrubbing like a fiend to get any traces of pot smoke out of my hair. To look sharp when I see Bailey, I wear a red tank and jacket with my white pants. My nails are still clean and shining from my wedding manicure and pedicure. I look like I'm going on a job interview.

On the car radio, the newscaster announces a summit here in New Orleans today. George W. Bush is hosting Mexico's president and the Canadian prime minister for a meeting to reopen the city's Mexican consulate. Could the status of Latinos here possibly be shifting?

When I get to the office, it's still only seven-thirty. Mary, the first-floor receptionist, startles when she sees me, and when I get up to Lagniappe, Floyd the Droid makes an extravagant show of checking his watch and raising his eyebrows.

I take out my story, put my handbag in my desk drawer, and turn on my computer. I scan my in-box; nothing significant except two assignments from Claire, routine club coverage, which I print out and fold to take with me.

That's it; I can't stall any longer. I pick up the story and take a deep breath. *Oh, please, please, please.* I walk past the art depart-ment, down the long wall of glassed offices, thinking *please* with every step. *Please like it. Please let it be good enough.*

I've been imagining Bailey's face, his pleased surprise, and then—or so my fantasy goes—his dawning realization, as he drops everything else to read my story, that it's excellent, and that I should be moved to the city desk immediately.

So his empty office comes as an anticlimax. His door is open, but he's not there, and Margie's not out front. I walk in and lay the story in the middle of the clear space on his desk. I find a yellow Post-it note and a pen. *Thank you, sir,* I write, and press it to my ar-ticle. Turning, I see several of the reporters in the newsroom watch-ing me like hawks. Chin high, I walk out.

Back at my desk, I get my handbag, tuck the assignments into it, close up shop, and turn for the door. But then I see Claire at her desk, watching me.

I walk over to her, and she visibly braces herself. Several La-gniappe reporters are at their desks, and I speak loudly so they can hear.

"Claire, I've been really out of line lately, and I'm sorry." Her blue eyes open wide. "I've been going through some stuff, but it's no excuse, and I'm sorry." From where I stand, looking down, I can see a thin telltale line of white hair on either side of her part, and I feel a little surge of pity. My own hair grows fast. If it went gray, I'd have to color it every week to keep it a dark and glossy brown. And really, there's no *if* about it. Someday, if I last long enough and I'm lucky, I'll be in her shoes. The realization softens my voice, but I keep it clear and audible. *There is time to make cor-rections.* "Look, Claire, I don't deserve a second chance, and you don't owe me one. But I'd like to try again to get along and work together, if that's okay with you."

Her jaw is hanging slightly open. Pushing her chair back, she stands up, her hand extended, and I shake it. She smiles the faintest, most hesitant of smiles.

"You little shit," she says. "You surprised me." Her smile broadens. "Clean slate, then?" We both know everyone's watching.

"Yes, ma'am. Thank you. Thank you very much."

"Good for you, Nola," she says. "You did the right thing. And Nola?"

"Yeah?"

"Don't call me ma'am."

On the way to my car, it occurs to me that no child, especially no Little Sister of mine, should grow up without tasting Angelo Brocato's Italian fig cookies, a New Orleans staple. I drive to Carrollton, between Iberville and Bienville, and nab a parking spot right in front of the store.

Angelo Brocato's has been a landmark for more than a hundred years, since the great waves of Sicilian immigration came to New Orleans. Inside, big glass cases hold trays of cookies and tubs of gelato. With high ceilings, peach walls, and little chairs and tables, the shop looks and smells like an old-fashioned ice cream parlor— but there's a self-conscious starch of newness about it all, as if the post-Katrina renovations haven't quite sunk in. I grab a bag of fig cookies for Marisol and ask the girl behind the counter to wrap a freshly baked anise biscotti for *mi mamá*.

Getting hungry, I leave my car where it is and walk down the block to Venezia, another old-school Italian place, where the yellow walls daze my eyes and the elderly hostess, her cheeks bright circles of rouge, seats me at a corner table. The middle-aged crowd is busy conversing in low tones. I order the eggplant Vatican, then fiddle with my silverware. I check my cell. Fabi's urgency has dwindled;

there's only a single text message from her: *Call me.* Bento has left another message about Friday night, so I call back, and luckily, he's not there.

"Hey, it's Nola. Listen, yes, okay. I guess so. I mean, I'd like that very much. Dinner with you. On Friday, I mean. Call me back and tell me what time and all that."

Smooth, Nola. Very smooth. I click off and sit there, fooling with my cell, sipping my iced tea, waiting for my eggplant to arrive, piled high with crab, shrimp, and crawfish. I scroll down through the log of recent calls. Shiduri Collins. I push CALL.

"Dr. Collins's office."

It doesn't sound like her, and I hadn't seen a receptionist. "Is this Dr. Collins?"

"No, this is her answering service." She sounds like a girl with a blond ponytail. And kittens. "May I help you?"

"I don't think so." I clear my throat. Take a breath. "I mean, yes."

"Ma'am?"

"Yes. Yes. I'd like to make an appointment."

"Okay." Her voice is cheerful. "What is this in reference to?"

"Excuse me?"

"What kind of issue are you having?"

I look around, but all the diners are absorbed in their conversations. Still, I lower my voice. "I think I'm experiencing symptoms of post-traumatic stress disorder."

"Okay." I can hear her pen scratching. "And would this be due to violence you witnessed, violence you were a target of, or violence you committed yourself?"

"What?"

"Is this disorder—"

"Do I have to answer that to get an appointment?"

"No, not at all," she says brightly. "Dr. Collins just likes to get as much information in advance as possible. And we have to ask that part about committing the violence yourself," she adds confidentially, "now that so many soldiers are coming back from Iraq and Afghanistan. Committing violence can traumatize someone just as much as other kinds of trauma, you know."

"Yeah, I've heard. Are you a psychology student?"

"Yes, I am! How did you know?"

"Just a wild guess."

"I'm in my third year at—"

"Look, can I just get an appointment?"

"Oh, definitely," she chirps. "Can I have your name, please?"

I tell her.

"You know, we had a cancellation for tomorrow."

"Not tomorrow. I've got things to do."

We find a date the following week that works.

When I click off, my heart is pounding, and I have to press my hands on the tablecloth to steady them.

That evening, I vegetate, I deliberate, I walk around my apartment in a stupor. I skip dinner. I run on my treadmill like a good gerbil in its cage. I review my notes for tomorrow's interview. Blake Lanusse. I stare at his photo, his beige face like a face carved in stone. I look into the eyes of the little girls he raped.

My story's already turned in. There's no need to do this, no need to climb the stairs to his weird living room, to hear his obscene chortle, to stare into his pale, disturbing eyes. I could call and cancel right now. But I don't. Another lesson from Tulane: finish what you start.

I check my phone messages; there are three.

Professor Guillory: "You know, Nola, I forgot to mention the other night that full-time journalists don't even need a special license from the Treasury Department to travel to Cuba. If you're interested, you should look into it." For a moment, I imagine seeing the place where my mother grew up, the green mountains, the coast, the blue sea. But also the place that scared her away from her own body's truth. "It might be easier than you think."

Fabi: "Seriously, Nola, call me. Yes, your date was cute, and yes, he was interesting, but I was just being nice to him. Did you know he left right after you did? I mean, maybe I got a little carried away, but I'm not like that, Nola. You know I'm not. We need to talk. I'm sorry. So call me."

And last, there's a voice mail from Bailey, shot through with pride: "Congratulations, Nola. Your piece will run on Tuesday. Below the fold, but front page." He pauses. "This is the kind of work I knew you could do." I squeeze my knees to my chest, hug myself, exhale.

Kneeling next to my bed, my locked fingers pressed to my forehead, I pray. To The Virgen de la Caridad del Cobre, to Ochún, to ancestors I never knew. I pour fresh rum into saucers and slice bananas into a dish, and place them on my little altar.

Carefully, I take down the dark paper targets that have accumulated around me, rolling them up, one nested inside the other. I lay the thick tube of shot things on the floor of the bathtub, and the shower curtain rattles on its metal rings as I scoop it up out of harm's way. When I bend and hold the lit match to the paper tube, it takes a moment to catch, then flares up quickly. Flames run up and down its thick length, all the ragged rips of my bullet holes turning to ash. For good measure, I throw the photographs of Blake Lanusse into the fire, and when everything has burned, I rinse away the blackened pile.

After showering myself clean, I twist up my hair and draw a bath with the recipe my mother taught me long ago, a recipe that, until now, I've ignored. I lace the hot water with honey, incense, and chopped basil, crack two raw and gummy yellow eggs into its depths, and scatter fresh gardenia petals on top. Easing down into the wet, aromatic heat, I lie back, eyes closed, silent, letting the good luck and protection soak into me. If that's all real. If lotions and potions have magical powers, the way my mother believes. I slip down deep into the tub, only my face above water.

In the myth, the legend, the story my mother tells, three slaves went out in a boat. In 1606 (or 1604, 1608, or 1613, depending on which version you hear), off the northern coast of Cuba's Oriente province, a storm blew up in the Bay of Nipe, catching three slaves unaware. The waves were large, and their boat was small. Just as the men were going to drown, the brown Virgin appeared, the gentle Madonna. The waves stilled. The men were saved.

Some say the three men came from the Spanish copper mines. They were there at the coast, the story goes, to collect salt to cure meat. Some say the slaves were two Indians—which is to say, Siboney, Guanajuatabey, or Taíno—with an African boy of ten or so. In some versions, they were fishermen.

Some say the three were caught out on the bay when the wind blew the waves into sharp, killing peaks, and they cried out to the Virgin Mary—and lo, the storm did cease, the waves calmed, and there above them hovered the Lady herself, who said, "I am the Virgin of Charity." Or maybe that's what was written on the tablet she held in her arms. Accounts do not agree.

In another version, the storm blew up and the men and boy made it to shore just fine—but the next day, when the bay was glassy and calm, they saw a radiant light floating toward them, and as it got closer, they could see that it was a statue of the Madonna, riding the waves, borne ceaselessly forward into the future. They plucked her from the sea, and eyewitnesses swore she was not wet: not her dusky face, not her clothes, not the dark baby Jesus in her arm nor the gold globe in his tiny hand.

Once ashore, the little statue was carried from the coast into the mountains, near El Cobre, the copper mines. She supplanted the official patron, Saint James. No matter how many times human hands hauled her back down to the second-rate hut she'd been given, each morning the dark young upstart Virgin would reappear on top of *el Cerro de la Cantera,* the hill of the quarry. Stubborn *mujer,* like a goat. She knew where she belonged. Eventually the people gave up and built her a church on the hill, the only basilica in Cuba, a cream-colored, triple-towered shrine amid the palm trees and agave.

Two hundred and fifty-four stone steps were laid in the side of the hill, so people could climb up from the village to worship, and climb they did, catching their breath at the top, gasping at the green mountains still rising above them. They mopped their brows and crossed themselves and entered the cool blue interior, piling their jewels and votive offerings at the Virgin's gold-cloaked feet, where eventually all manner of tribute and plea came to rest, even my mother's own hand-crocheted baby socks, faded pink, which she dedicated to la Virgen in order that she might herself one day be blessed with a baby girl to love, and that she might do so far away from the cane fields where she'd watched her parents die of lung cancer, overwork, and chronic hunger. Amen. Kneeling, my mother whispered up her prayers to the Virgin of Charity.

Charity. It did not originally mean the narrow thing we think it means today: not merely giving away our leftovers to those in need. *Caridad* is loving kindness. It is love and care for all, for strangers, for three slaves in a boat in a storm.

Who saves us? From where does power come? Did la Virgen rescue the boat from the waves, or did men pull her wooden body from the sea?

I pray to la Virgen de la Caridad. I don't share her grace. Far from it. But I can worship what she stands for. I pull myself dripping from the water.

Wrapped in a towel, I lay out my things for tomorrow. My sober clothes: flat shoes, white pants, a tank the color of charcoal.

My stocked handbag, my clipboard with its thick file.

I flip on the local nightly news. President Bush is planting a tree in Lafayette Square today—Earth Day. That's him: the meaningless gesture, the mission accomplished. Some folks speculate that he's probably shaking hands with someone behind the scenes, because not everyone grieves the effects of Katrina. Since the storm, New Orleans has lowered its food stamp clientele by 51 percent, its welfare rolls by 73 percent. We all remember Barbara Bush touring the Houston Astrodome full of displaced and homeless Katrina evacuees, blithely saying how much better off they were.

A video clip shows President Bush dancing an actual jig, and then he's thanking New Orleans for the good times he had here in his youth, partying. He has no plans to tour the struggling city. I suddenly think of Engels and the carriages of the rich, rolling down clean, shop-lined boulevards. The boutiques on Magazine. George Anderson in his air-conditioned mansion, surrounded by art: *I'm not responsible for every kid in America who got felt up.* I think of the torn-down slave quarters at Moss Manor. Patrick Kennedy's hand over his stepdaughter's eyes.

Justice means taking off the blindfold, taking responsibility. It's about preventing future damage. Getting history right.

Suddenly, breaking news flashes red across the screen. "Another young woman went missing in the French Quarter this morning," says the newscaster. Sixteen-year-old Marisa Nicoletti, a sophomore at Ursulines Convent School, left home on foot at 7:30 A.M. but never arrived at school. Her photograph fills the screen: dark curling hair, dark eyes. A younger Amber Waybridge. When the girl's mother comes onscreen to begin her plea, I mute the sound and pick up my phone.

"Are you watching this?"

"We just got the call," Calinda says. "Believe me, we're watching."

"Same time of day, same area—"

"I know. She even looks like the last vic."

"It hasn't been twenty-four hours yet."

"I know, but under the circumstances—"

"Better safe than sorry," I say.

"Exactly."

A long moment passes as I watch the anguished mother twist her hands on TV.

"Look, I've got to go," I say. "Keep me updated." We click off.

I stand in my silent living room, breathing. Then I press another number on my phone.

"Mr. Lanusse?" I reintroduce myself and remind him of our interview tomorrow. "But something's come up. I wonder if I could come tonight."

24

At ten o'clock at night, Blake Lanusse welcomes me into the red and black cave that is his condominium. There's a bottle of whiskey on the table this time, with two glasses, already filled, and a bowl full of shining fruit. My hands are steady but my pulse is fast.

"So you said you liked the place," he says, gesturing around expansively. All the shutters are closed. In the black chandelier's garish glow, the whites of his eyes look yellow. "My wife did it. Lily." His smile is broad. "I just told her the basic look I wanted, and she did it all."

I take my seat. "Your wife?" I hadn't realized they were married, hadn't glanced for their rings. Now I see his, glinting gold. Had he worn it before? I set the Olympus on the table and press it on. "Is she a decorator?"

"Oh, yeah. Got her own firm. Real successful. She's not here right now, so we can talk. She travels a lot. Consulting." His chair scrapes the wooden floor as he pulls it back and sits down. "Have a drink," he says. "It'll relax you." Neither of us mentions the fact that I kept his secret from his wife. That we're collaborators now. Neither of us mentions the fact that he lied about watching Marisol and me in Jackson Square.

"Thank you, but I'm fine." I cross my legs, bang my knee on the underside of the table, and uncross them again. Straightening his file in front of me, I begin. "Let's talk about your rehabilitation."

"Hoo boy, right down to business, you are."

I look at him pleasantly, waiting.

"Okay, sure. All right. What do you want to know?"

"Thank you, Mr. Lanusse. Can you tell my readers how you knew you were rehabilitated? How did you know you would never sexually assault another child?"

"Assault?" He has the gall to look insulted.

"I'm sorry, Mr. Lanusse. What term would you prefer?"

He looks at me for a long moment. His pale eyes blink.

"Yeah, well, rehabilitation is kind of personal," he finally says. "Kind of embarrassing to discuss." Embarrassed is not how he looks. He looks pissed. "Especially with a young lady like yourself."

"If you would just please try. I'd really like to give our readers a chance to understand."

He takes a drink, looks at me over the edge of his glass. "Yeah, all right. So in jail, they did counseling for a while, but the guy said it wasn't working. So they gave me meds, right? These meds—it was like getting castrated. It just wasn't there anymore, if you know what I mean."

"Are you on these meds now?"

"No, thank Christ." The red light of the Olympus pulses on the table between us.

"Go on."

"So while I was on these meds, they transferred me to this other doctor, right? I saw her every week, and we had to talk about what I did."

"And how was that for you?"

"It was all right. She was an all right lady. She could see I didn't need to be in there for the whole time." He reaches out and grasps an apple from the bowl.

"You convinced her."

"All ladies like a little charm, darling."

"And do you see a therapist now?"

He snorts. "You kidding me? A hundred bucks an hour for someone to ask me how I feel? Please."

Married, unemployed, and doesn't go to counseling. With one hand around the apple, he pulls a jackknife from his pocket and flips it open. It's a big knife, too big for the job, really, with a brown horn handle and a razor-thin edge.

"Mr. Lanusse, studies show that many child molesters were themselves molested as children. Was that the case for you?"

"I'm not sure," he says casually. "Maybe so." His thumb resting easily on the apple's skin, he rotates the fruit with a sure, firm grip, and the peel falls away neatly, even delicately, in a long, smooth spiral of red shine. In my mind's eye, I see the face of Amber Waybridge sliding away from her skull. I see her fingertips sliced deftly, even casually, away. I see—God help me—her nipple, cut off for a souvenir.

My throat is dry. "Mr. Lanusse, did you paddle children as part of your job?"

"As vice principal? Sure. Had to. Spare the rod, spoil the child. James Dobson, all that. If these black kids got beat once in a while instead of running wild, we wouldn't have the kind of crime we've got in this city." The red light on my Olympus flashes steadily.

"And did you have a special room where you would take children to be paddled?"

"Just my office, yeah."

"And then you would close the door. And there was no one else present for these paddlings?"

He looks sharply at me. "Yeah, it was my job, all right? Those kids needed discipline. Somebody had to do it."

"And did these paddlings sometimes lead to the sexual assaults and molestation?"

"Hold on a minute. I signed a paper. I can't talk about the school."

"Okay, Mr. Lanusse." I force a smile. "I forgot that. I apologize."

"Good," he says. His eyes flicker hot and pale. He downs the rest of his whiskey and pours another shot. "You gonna drink that?" he says, gesturing toward mine. "It's not neighborly not to drink."

"Maybe later." I clear my dry throat. "Most sexual predators have committed other offenses before they're finally arrested and convicted. Many, many offenses. An average of—let me see," I glance at my notes, "over three hundred offenses, on over one hundred victims, over an average period of sixteen years before arrest." He glares at me. "Would you care to comment?"

"Not without my lawyer present," he snarls.

"Very well." I unclip the file and open it. "Let's try a different tack, okay?"

"Sure." His rasping voice is hostile. "Whatever."

"Studies have shown that one of the most important signals of rehabilitation is the capacity to empathize with one's victims."

"Oh, right," he says. "Yeah, I empathize with them. I told that to the board."

"Yes, I know. But, Mr. Lanusse, I wonder"—I slide photos of his three victims across the table—"if you could just talk to me about these girls."

He lifts the paper. "What do you want to know?"

"Do you remember these children?" His eyes rove slowly over the images, and he says nothing. I tap the photos. "Mr. Lanusse?"

"Sure," he says. "I remember them."

"Tell me about them."

"They were all students. They were all good girls. Most of the time."

"Can you remember their names?"

He pauses, then pokes one with the finger of his right hand. "That one was Latisha," he says. His finger slides to the next. "Angel." He taps the third one, chewing his lower lip, trying to remember. "Jessica," he says finally. "Sweet Jessica."

My voice is little more than a whisper. "Mr. Lanusse, why did you rape these girls?"

He's quiet for a long moment, draining his glass. When he looks up, his eyes don't focus. "I don't know," he says, pouring more whiskey. "Hell if I can tell you. I just wanted to, and I did it. They were sweet little girls. Pretty. It ain't rocket science." His gaze sharpens. "You going to put that in your paper?"

The air vibrates around us.

"If it would make you feel more comfortable, Mr. Lanusse, I can turn the recorder off."

He nods. "Yeah. Turn it off," he says, holding the girls' photos in both hands. "Can I keep these?" he asks.

My finger hovers above the PAUSE button as we stare at each other for a long minute.

"Guess not," he says finally, and slides them back across the table.

I speak carefully into the Olympus. "I am now turning off the recorder at your request, Mr. Lanusse."

"Yeah. Shut that thing off."

My finger lowers onto the Olympus, and its red light goes dark. I put the girls back inside the file and clip it shut against the board.

"I have another photo I'd like you to look at for me, Mr. Lanusse." I reach into my handbag.

"Yeah. Sure." He pours himself another two fingers of whiskey and tosses them back.

I unfold the flyer of Amber Waybridge and rotate it on the table so he can see her. Her dark eyes lie next to his knife.

"Have you seen this woman?"

There's a long silence as his pale eyes rise slowly to meet mine. When he speaks, his voice is venomous. "Now what kind of a question is that," he says, "to ask a man in his own house?"

"Just a simple question, Mr. Lanusse."

"No, I've never seen that girl before."

"Are you quite sure?"

"I'm telling you, I never saw her."

I exaggerate my surprise. "Not even on these flyers? They're all over the Quarter."

He hesitates. "Well, sure. The flyers, yeah. I've seen those."

"But not the woman herself."

"I told you."

"My mistake." I pull the flyer back across the table. "Another girl has disappeared from the Quarter. Today. A student from the school across the street."

"Is that right?"

"I know you're a concerned citizen, and I thought maybe you could help us with our inquiry."

"Your inquiry." He picks up the knife, turns it over in his hands, opens and closes the blade. "Do they think it's someone around here?"

"Oh, yes. Definitely. The police are getting very close," I lie, "and the forensics experts won't have any problem once they find the kill site."

For just the briefest flash, his eyes dart toward the hallway. When my gaze follows, he clears his throat, shifts in his chair. "Have some of that good whiskey," he says, gesturing at my full glass.

"Her body was mutilated, as I'm sure you know from the news."

"Oh, yeah. Right. I heard that," he says. He waves his fingers vaguely at the left side of his chest. "Too bad."

The room grows very still. Cool air shushes from the vents. Information about Amber Waybridge's cut breast was never released to the media.

"So I'm sorry to bother you about Amber." I fold her away.

"Who?"

"Amber Waybridge. The murdered woman. That's her name," I say, putting my Olympus into my handbag and rising to my feet. I move toward the hallway, the place where his eyes had flicked.

Frowning, he quickly pushes back his chair and steps between me and the hall. He folds his arms across his chest, his knife in his hand.

"There's just one final thing before I go, then."

"Good," he says sullenly. "I'm getting tired of this."

"Oh, I understand, sir," I say, searching in my purse. "I do understand being tired. But we're almost finished."

My left hand is steady as I pull the little photograph out of my wallet and hold it up so he can see. He squints, but I don't hand it to him, don't let him touch it. "*Mi querida Nola,*'" I read on the back. My mother's hand. "8 yrs old. 3rd grade. 1989."

"Mr. Lanusse, do you remember this girl?"

He stares at it for a minute, then begins to nod. And grin.

"Oh, yeah," he says. "Oh, yeah. I can't remember her name, though."

The room swirls red and black around us. Under the whiskey breath and stale cigar smoke, there's the scent of something else. His skin, his sweat, his flesh. Nauseating, familiar. The smell of nightmares.

"She remembers you," I say, and I take out my Beretta and shoot him twice, point-blank, in the chest.

I remember telling Auntie Helene as soon as I got back to Desire.

"Oh, no. Oh, no, no, no. My precious baby girl. No," she said, holding me and rocking us both back and forth as she knelt, but my body stood stiff in her arms. I felt the rocking but couldn't let myself soften into it, couldn't feel the warmth I knew was there. "Who was it?" she said, drawing away and taking my face between her hands. "You tell me which one it was. Auntie will take care of him."

"He don't live round here. He's up to the school. I got in trouble."

She froze and drew back on her heels.

"He a white man?"

I nodded. "I got in trouble," I said again.

She pulled away, her features sliding into a strange stillness I hadn't seen before, and her hands drew away from my cheeks and fell slowly down into her kneeling lap. "A white man." She drew her breath in carefully, closed her eyes as if in prayer, opened them. "You listen here, now. Nobody done touched you. You a fine, clean girl. You perfect. You hear me?"

I nodded. Nodding, she rose stiffly to her feet, her knees cracking.

"That's right. Nothing happened to you. You just stay away from that man. You just stay away, stay away from him, and nothing will happen to you. Stay out of trouble. Behave yourself. Nothing happened to you. You hear?"

I nodded again. My ears felt strange. Hot. Like I was going to fall down, like the earth had gone soft under me. But I was still standing.

"And your mama don't need to hear about this. You understand? You know she gotta lot on her mind with that baby coming and all. She don't need to be hearing about this mess. You hear?"

I nodded again, my teeth thick in my mouth. I hadn't known about any baby. Auntie Helene wiped her hands on her dress, leaving little damp smears of sweat.

"You leave it alone, you be just fine. Just fine." She turned toward the sink, looked out the little window, fussed with a hairpin at the back of her head, muttered a monologue I couldn't hear. She swiveled back to face me. "You a fine big girl, now, ain't you?" I nodded. "A strong girl. What are you now, seven?"

"Eight."

"There you go," she said firmly, nodding. "A big old girl of eight, she can handle just about anything." She tilted her head. "Did he get stuff on you? From his thing?"

I nodded.

"Let's get you cleaned up, then." She ran a bath and washed me like I was four. "Oh, Jesus Lord," she breathed when she saw the blood. "But you not bleeding now," she said. "You okay now. One hundred percent okay."

We didn't speak of it again that afternoon. I watched *My Three Sons* and *The Jetsons* while she undid my hair and brushed and rebraided it, tight and neat, and retied the aqua ribbons in pert bows. She smoothed her hands over my face and arms, murmuring, "You perfect, you beautiful as the day you was born, ain't nothing happened to you," while I stared at the television screen.

When it was time to go, she opened the door of her apartment and made sure I had my satchel and my key, which hung around my neck as always. She leaned down and said, "You a good, clean girl. No doubt about it. You go on home now, and don't give your mama no cause to worry, hear?"

I nodded. "Yes, Auntie." I turned and headed down the sidewalk.

"You take good care, child," she called out behind me, but I didn't turn back.

When I let myself into our apartment, my mother was already

asleep at the desk, her head on her folded arms, her housecleaning shoes kicked off near her limp feet. When I put my hand on her arm, she woke up.

"Mamá," I whispered. "You gonna have a baby?"

At that, her eyes lit up all warm, and she smiled her tired smile. *"Sí, mi'jita, un hermanito o una hermanita para ti.* You want to help name it when it comes?"

"Oh, *sí, sí,*" I said, suddenly excited. I wasn't allowed to have a kitten in the projects. This would be almost as good. For months, I wrote lists of names for a boy or a girl.

But the baby died before it was born. My mother was in the hospital for six days, and she could never get pregnant again.

The bleeding body of Blake Lanusse sprawls on the floor, and quickly I lay the Beretta on the table and slip on my cotton gloves. I crouch and press my fingers to his throat. Looking at his blank eyes, I feel a surge of something like compassion, and into my mind flashes the line from my college professor about Edna P.: *Sometimes even death can be a kind of freedom.*

But his death. Not mine.

I move down the hallway, flinging open doors. But there's no one.

I return to the table, lift his knife, and flick it open. I hold my right arm in front of me, as if barring a blow. Gripping the handle in my left hand, I slash the blade down across my forearm. Pain flashes like a white sear of unimportance, and I toss the knife to the floor at his side.

Bleeding, I peel off the gloves, stuff them into the bottom of my handbag, and call 911 on my cell.

This being New Orleans, it rings twelve times.

When they answer, I stop in front of one of the gold-framed mirrors.

"There's a man down," I say, and the adrenaline in my voice sounds believably like panic. "He attacked me, and I shot him. Come fast. He's dying." It's a lie. He's already dead.

I give the address, and when the dispatcher asks for my name, I stare into my own dark eyes. Bright red blood slides thick down my arm. *The third and last and final.*

"Nola," I say. "Nola Soledad Céspedes."

25

On Tuesday morning, my feature story runs. In the large, gorgeous photograph on the lower half of the *Times-Picayune*'s front page, Mike Veltri walks up Lake Avenue toward Deanie's, the gold light of evening glowing ahead of him. A last-minute addendum to the story, phoned in from the ER while a doctor stitched up my arm, explains that the story's reporter was attacked while interviewing a released offender—an offender who's now the prime suspect in the Amber Waybridge case—and that she killed him in self-defense.

When the police had arrived, they'd found sixteen-year-old Marisa Nicoletti, bound and gagged, in a room concealed at the back of the hall closet. It was a safe room, soundproofed, that Lanusse had installed after he'd bought the place and before he'd married Lily. The girl had been stripped and fondled, but not yet raped. Not cut. Her dark eyes swung to me as the EMTs carried her out.

By the time I make it into the *Times-Picayune* office that afternoon, my arm swathed in white bandages, the newsroom is abuzz. The newspaper's in-box is already crammed with more than a thousand emails to the editor, calling for a crackdown on the violent offenders—as well as for reforms of the registry laws, making them

more lenient for nonpredatory offenders. The stream of public opinion isn't letting up, and the boys over at the city desk are eyeing me
with an entirely new kind of interest. Something like respect.

Bailey comes over and smacks the issue down on my desk.

"Well, honey, you did it," he says. "Crimestoppers called. They
got with the NOPD, and they're going to run a full-page ad with
photos of fifteen of the worst of these guys. They're going to track
them down."

"That's great." I grin up at him. He can call me "honey" all he
wants. "So can I move my things?"

He grins back. "Don't miss a beat, do you? Give me a day or two,
but yeah. We're adding you to the city desk. Crime. That okay with
you?"

My new niche. I nod and rise to shake his hand. "Thank you,
sir."

"You did it, kid," he says. "You're the one who did it."

Bento calls, his voice proud and excited. He'd seen my name, read
the story, and shown his colleagues at UNO. He's full of questions
about how it all happened. *"Felicidades,"* he keeps saying. *"Felicidades."*

It's a sweet new glow, having a man who's proud of my work. He
invites me again for dinner on Friday night.

"I found a place," he says, "where we can dance merengue." I
imagine our bodies: warm, close, moving.

A success is one thing. But there's something strange and pleasant about having someone to share it with.

I have one phone call left to make. Outside the *Times-Picayune*
building, the sun's glare is bright, the heat pulverizing. Sitting alone

on a cement bench, I stare at the rows of parked delivery trucks and the city's skyline. Thumbing through the numbers on my cell, I find the one I want.

Once I saw an accident in the Quarter. A car crunched into the wheel of one of those carriages that tourists pay fifty bucks to ride around in. It was only a minor collision at slow speeds, but the horse panicked, hurling all of her heavy brown muscle against the harness and kicking at the wooden traces until they splintered. The horse broke free, trotting through the halted traffic, breathing heavily. The shattered traces lay in the street.

Getting free of Desire, I didn't care what I broke or left behind.

I take a deep breath while Evie Wilson's number rings.

"Yeah?" she says.

"Evie, hey. It's Nola Céspedes, from the paper."

"Hey, Nola." Her voice is easy and warm. "What's up? You need some more quotes?"

"No, no. I'm good. The story's out. Listen, I was wondering—"

"It came out already? In what issue?"

"Today's. Listen, I was—"

"Am I in there? Did you use my name?"

"Yes. You were great." I smile. "Thank you. Thank you so much."

"I'ma need to get me a copy of that."

"Would you like one mailed to you? I can do that."

"Oh, yeah. Sure, that'd be nice. My kids are not gonna believe this."

"Listen, Evie, would you like to go to lunch sometime? Some day while your kids are at school?"

"Lunch?"

It's an impossibly bourgie thing to suggest. Ladies who lunch: Does that even compute in the Upper Ninth? But I can't very well invite myself over to Evie's kitchen table for macaroni and Lipton's.

She's taking her time deciding, and I feel guilty, like the judged.

I stretch my legs out in front of me nervously, rub my finger across a satiny scar on my shin. Heat radiates up from the cement, bathing my calves.

When she finally speaks, her voice is soft and honest. "I don't want to front you, Nola. Truth is, I don't think you and me got a lot to say."

"I hear you." Why would a mother struggling in poverty want to spend time with someone like me—someone who got away, someone who couldn't even remember her name? I stare up at the blue sky, the scattered wisps of clouds. I have no persuasive argument to offer, no logical appeal. Just my hope. "But Evie, could we try?"

And Evie Wilson, who has no reason to be generous with the likes of me, says yes.

Thursday evening, my Pontiac slides through the early dusk toward the Quarter. On WWOZ, the Blind Boys of Alabama sing about how free they are at last, and I hum along. *I can't speak for you,* growls the singer. *I speak for me.*

Storm clouds are moving in over the city as I park on Chartres and head inside K-Paul's. Out on the second-story balcony with its iron railing, Fabi and Calinda are waiting at a table, and the front section of the *Times-Picayune* is propped against a bottle of champagne. I run my finger along the bumpy yellow stucco of the wall, feeling suddenly shy. When they rise to hug me, I press a dozen pink roses, her favorites, into Fabi's hands.

"I have trust issues," I say, kissing her cheek. "I'm going to work on it."

"Hush, now, *hermana,*" she replies, kissing me back. "We're all good."

Chartres Street rolls flat and straight in both directions, so we all have views of the eighteenth- and nineteenth-century buildings with their low, uneven roofs and little dormer windows, like the skyline in photographs of Paris.

The champagne is crisp and perfect. Overhead, ceiling fans stir the breeze. Cane-syrup muffins, dark, hot, and sweet, arrive at the table, and we tear them open, smearing them with fresh butter. What Fabi and Calinda want to talk about, of course, are my feature story, my gashed arm, and Blake Lanusse's death.

"So that's why you were all interested in the Waybridge case," says Calinda, "and what those files were for."

"Hey, I've got those for you, by the way. You can put them back."

"Like anyone's missed them." She laughs. "But I just can't believe you never told us. All this time, you were working on this major story—a story that was going to rock this town, and get you a *promotion*—not to mention finding that girl's killer."

"And saving that other girl," adds Fabi.

"And you never told us." Calinda's hands fly up in disbelief. "We're your best friends!"

"You've always been like that," chides Fabi. "So private about everything."

"I'm sorry. I know."

"If you had just *told* us—"

"I know. A lot of things would have been different. I'm sorry."

"No wonder you've been so weird lately. This shit would stress anyone out," Calinda says.

Her phone suddenly rings. It's Soline, calling from Lampang. Calinda talks with her for a moment and then lays the phone down on the table as the waiter arrives with our food.

"Am I on speaker?" comes Soline's long-distance voice. "Girls, I've got news. I didn't want to tell y'all before the wedding, because I didn't want to steal any thunder from the big day, but—"

"You're pregnant!" Fabi shrieks.

Soline's warm laughter travels around the world. "God, no, girl," she says. "What's wrong with you? I just barely tied the knot. No, I signed the papers to open another Sinegal. In Miami!"

"Woo, girl!" cries Calinda, lifting her glass.

"Damn straight," says Soline. "Makes sense, right? Same heat, same humidity. My dresses are going to *rule*."

We laugh, congratulate her, and pepper her with excited questions, which she answers, her voice delighted.

"Listen, ladies," she finally says, "I've got to get back to the marital bed. It's the middle of the night here. I just didn't want to miss our weekly."

We say our good-byes and hang up, excited for Soline. Even when the sky blackens and the waiter comes over to help us drag our table next to the sheltering wall, I don't mind. Rain spatters our ankles and thunder rolls above us, but we laugh and talk and eat our alligator sausage, our duck boudin, our shrimp and corn maque choux.

The storm moves east as live zydeco pumps up loudly from the sidewalk below, and the sky melts to a swath of pink pearl. When dessert comes, we take turns carving slivers of the hot bread pudding with our spoons, scraping up the Courvoisier sauce from the plate.

Our conversation circles back to my recent escapades. "You just barely escaped death," says Fabi, *todo* dramatic. "We could have been at your funeral right now."

"I don't think he intended to kill me," I say slowly, feeling the doubled truth in the words. "I don't think he really knew what he was doing."

"Yeah, well, whatever," says Calinda. "Let's see that cut."

"Oh, come on."

"You come on. Take that tape off." When I peel it back and pull the dressing away, a long, garish line of black stitches circles my arm like a dark bracelet. Calinda whistles.

"Oh, my God," says Fabi, tilting my arm this way and that with her light fingertips. "Just imagine if that had been your throat."

"Yeah." In fact, I had imagined it: the long, slow slice, and then the silence. "But I really don't think he intended to kill me," I repeat.

"But you had to make sure," says Fabi. Gusts of cool wind freshen our faces. Down below, the rain-rinsed asphalt and sidewalks shimmer, slicked with light.

"Yeah," I say. "I had to make sure."

And if I had been planning his execution for weeks, ever since I first requested his file and saw my chance, saw his perp shot leering up at me—his face like stone, his pale eyes familiar as nightmares—who's to say? No one knows I tracked Blake Lanusse through his own hunting grounds. I deleted the photos from my camera and computer, and burned the only hard copies. Auntie Helene, the only person I ever confided in, is long dead.

If there's one thing I've learned how to keep, it's a secret.

Scribes, historians, journalists—we record events in the sloppy medium of language, struggling to grasp a moving reality that's slippery like clay spinning under our hands. We try to create a usable shape out of mud in motion. We pledge fidelity to the facts.

But sometimes we tweak it a little. The one who survives tells the tale. And the tale that survives is the one people like, the one that brings magic and hope.

I don't show my friends my other fresh wound, a tattoo on my left shoulder blade, a small blue fleur-de-lis like the kind the French branded on the shoulders of the women they sent here long ago. Corrections girls.

After Katrina, searchers spray-painted an *X* on every flooded house in New Orleans. They sprayed the date it had been searched and the number of dead bodies found. Since then, a lot of houses have been repainted, blotting out the *X*s. But a few homeowners, when they repainted, deliberately skirted the *X*s and numbers, leaving those markers as a record for all to see, a memorial to honor what had been survived. Pride. *We're still here, damn it.*

Maybe it isn't such a bad thing to be marked for life, to wear your history on your skin.

When the waiter finally brings our check, a sudden breeze catches the small paper curl, lifting it into the air above us and twirling it out over the street. We laugh, and the waiters and other diners laugh, too.

I'm no child; I know the waiter will just go back inside and print out another copy. I know the bill will always come due. But for this single, lovely moment, we all watch it blow away, a small white swirl, spinning into the rose-colored dusk.

It wasn't the city that hurt me. It wasn't New Orleans I hated. *There is time to make corrections,* my mother said. And now I have made them, and I can let it all go.

I can forgive the city for having been a victim, ravaged by storms and then neglected. I can forgive myself. *Rethink, Renew, Revive,* as the post-Katrina T-shirts say. I can love the city, love myself.

"Listen," I begin, taking my friends' hands in mine. "I never told y'all where I grew up."

Gratitude

For reading
Sandra Scofield, Bryn Chancellor, Edie Simms, Barbara Brandt,
Emily Levine, Monica Rentfrow, and Belinda Acosta

For loving and improving this book—and for your patience
Mitchell Waters, Karyn Marcus, and Edward Allen

For a generous education in noir
Katherine Bergstrom at A Novel Idea

For your advice, encouragement, y amistad
Sandra Cisneros, Lorraine López, Stephanie Elizondo Griest,
and Amelia María de la Luz Montes

For your kind interest and support
All my colleagues at the University of Nebraska–Lincoln
and the University of Nebraska Press

For being a touchstone
Kim Coleman, Kate Janulewicz, and all the folks
at Indigo Bridge Books

For your fascinating, meticulous, and beautifully written research
Ned Sublette, author of *The World That Made New Orleans:*
From Spanish Silver to Congo Square, to which this
novel is indebted

For sharing your stories
Dave Stout and Angelle Goudeau MacDougall

For photographing Nola's city
Charles Gullung

For being the best Little Sister anyone could dream up
Amara Castellanos

And for everything, always
My family